What people are saying about One Woman Falling ...

"Melanie Campbell brings an authenticity to her story and an empathy for the struggles her characters face that will tug on the heart of every reader. This is an author to watch."
Author Patricia Lee, Mended Hearts series

"This is a powerful, memorable story of a woman struggling to retain her sanity and survival while protecting the welfare of a pre-school daughter when marriage turns toxic. Waterfalls serve as metaphors that mark her physical and spiritual journeys filled with danger, beauty and love."
Dean Rea, author and retired journalism professor

"Melanie Campbell bravely speaks to a sensitive topic with authenticity and grace in her debut novel *One Woman Falling*. Her combination of well-developed characters, setting, and suspense create a powerful narrative that takes the reader on a transformative and emotional journey."
Elisheba Haxby, Author, *The Ninety-Nine Series*

One Woman Falling

One Woman Falling

Whispers of Grace Series

Melanie Campbell

MBI

One Woman Falling
Published by Mountain Brook Ink
White Salmon, WA U.S.A.

The website addresses shown in this book are not intended in any way to be or imply an endorsement on the part of Mountain Brook Ink, nor do we vouch for their content.

This story is a work of fiction. All characters and events are the product of the author's imagination. Any resemblance to any person, living or dead, is coincidental.

Scripture quotations from *THE MESSAGE*. Copyright © by Eugene H. Peterson 1993, 1994, 1995, 1996, 2000, 2001, 2002. Used by permission of NavPress Publishing Group.

Scripture quotations marked "NKJV" are taken from the New King James Version. Copyright © 1982 by Thomas Nelson, Inc. Used by permission. All rights reserved.

The Team: Miralee Ferrell, Nikki Wright, Cindy Jackson
Cover Design: Indie Cover Design, Lynnette Bonner, Designer

Mountain Brook Ink is an inspirational publisher offering fiction you can believe in.
Printed in the United States of America

Acknowledgments

Writing One Woman Falling was a journey. I couldn't have completed it without the love and support of special people God put in my life.

My husband encouraged me to pursue my writing dreams. When money was tight, he still found a way for me to attend my first Oregon Christian Writers Summer Conference. That was the beginning of the sacrifices he has made to give me the tools and time to write. When the journey got tough, he didn't let me quit.

My children's love has fueled me through some of the toughest challenges of my life, including the writing of this novel. They believed I was better at this writing thing than I actually am, and I couldn't let them down. There is nothing quite like having your children excited to see you realize your dream. I hope I make them proud.

My parents always believed in me and in my writing ambitions, even when I couldn't believe in myself. I am forever grateful for them.

My husband's sweet grandma, Opal Robbins—known to her family as Nannie—introduced me to Kathleen Ruckman. Kathleen told me about Oregon Christian Writers and encouraged my writing goals. Kathleen was a guiding light in my writing journey.

Kail Harbick, Elisheba Haxby, and Jesse Rivas were my first writing critique partners. I couldn't have made it through the first (and second) draft of this novel without them. Elisheba and Jesse have seen the writing of this book to the end. Their encouragement, brainstorming, and critiquing were priceless. As an added bonus, they are just plain fun to hang out with.

Kori Cheek was one of the first people to read this story

from beginning to end and has always been an encourager.

I am grateful for my current critique group, The Fictitious Five: Patricia Lee, Dean Rea, Amanda Bird and Dorcas Smucker. I am honored to be part of a talented and highly qualified group. They have made me a better writer. I'm excited to continue to share in this writing journey with them. Also, I owe a special thank you to a previous member, Jeanette Mirich, for her support and guidance.

My talented and sweet friend, Sara Nicholas, provided the song lyrics in this book.

Miralee Ferrell at Mountain Brook Ink has been a wonderful editor through the process of bringing this novel to print. I'm so thankful God had her sit by me in Cynthia Ruchti's coaching class. I look forward to continuing to work with Miralee and the amazing people at Mountain Brook Ink.

Above all else, I am grateful for Jesus. He never gave up on me, no matter how far off the path I wandered.

Dedication

For Grandpa and Grandma, in loving memory

The voice of the LORD is over the waters;
the God of glory thunders,
the LORD thunders over the mighty waters.

PART ONE: THE RAPIDS

Chapter One

BEFORE THE WATERFALLS, THE DREAM WAS all I had.

I stood near the base of high-desert mountains similar to the ones where I'd lived as a child. Sharp peaks of gray against a cloudless sky stretched before me as far as I could see. Grandpa was in front of me, wearing his old brown cowboy hat. He was fit, strong and determined—untouched by the cancer that took his life.

A path behind Grandpa curved into one of the mountains and disappeared around a distant corner. The only sound was a faraway roar, as ominous as the doom and uncertainty that fell over me. Choking back tears, I pleaded with Grandpa. "I can't do this alone."

Grandpa shook his head. "Cassie, you have to go."

"Can't you go with me?" I felt like a little girl, certain my plea would spur Grandpa into action. The darkness that lurked around the corner of the trail ahead couldn't harm me if Grandpa was at my side.

"I'll always be with you." Grandpa's soft blue eyes penetrated my soul with love.

How could he leave me alone in this desolate place with nothing but a narrow path to guide me? I was too weak, too naïve, and too afraid of being alone.

As if hearing my thoughts, Grandpa reassured, "Cassie, I've given you everything you need. Remember what I taught you."

Then he vanished. There was no place to go but forward. And I would go alone.

I didn't realize a dream could alter the course of a life. Sometimes change begins when we least expect it, in quiet whispers on the darkest nights.

A damp chill from the thick fog outside seeped through the front door as Derrick left. I shivered. Right before dawn, I dreamt about Grandpa again. The familiar heartache of the dream rested on me like the fog clung to the manicured lawn outside, a barrier between the hope of spring and the potential warmth of the early morning sun.

I made my way through my morning routine with my four-year-old daughter, Renee. By late morning the fog lifted, revealing a pale blue sky and warm sunshine—a rare treat for the Willamette Valley in mid-March. "Renee, honey, put on your shoes and we'll go outside for a bit." I helped Renee tie the laces on her sneakers, then swung her around over my head, making her squeal in delight. My chest ached with the realization she'd soon be too big for me to pick up. Next year she'd be in kindergarten and my days would feel empty without her contagious smile.

Before following Renee to the back yard, I grabbed my kitchen shears. The daffodils were in full bloom, and some of the tulips were starting to open. A flower arrangement would look nice on our mahogany dining table.

Renee blinked in the sunlight, her cheeks dimpling into a huge smile. She ran to the small wooden play structure her dad had built for her and climbed up the bars. My heart warmed at the sight, thinking of Renee enjoying countless hours this summer engulfed in the simple pleasures she'd find right outside her door. Picking strawberries, running through sprinklers, counting the apples on the young trees, spending time in the garden with her dad. I had a beautiful home, a successful husband, and a precious young daughter. It was everything I always wanted ... almost everything.

Cassie, you have to go.

Grandpa's voice echoed in my head, and my skin prickled. I cut enough flowers for a simple bouquet and called Renee to come in.

After lunch, I put my daughter in her room for a nap and sat down. The morning newspaper lay on the coffee table, untouched. I almost never looked at the paper anymore but today, reading sounded better than the drama of daytime talk shows.

I fingered through the pages. When I came to the outdoors section, a picture of a large waterfall covered the top half of the page. The water was pure white as it cascaded down a sheer rock cliff. Tall fir trees lined the small portion of the river that was visible before the fall, and green moss covered the grey rock above the pool where the fall ended. Spray obscured most of the pool in a white mist. It was dangerous, beautiful, wild. Altogether different than the picturesque view from the window of my living room. Something stirred inside me.

Cassie, you have to go.

For some reason, I missed my grandpa more now than I had three years ago when the sting of death pierced my heart. Perhaps that was why I couldn't get the dream out of my head. I stared at the picture of the waterfall, searching. I could almost see him behind the veil of water, beckoning me to join him. Maybe I was losing my mind. Derrick often told me I was crazy. "Just like your mother," he would say, slurring the "m" when he had too much to drink.

Was Derrick more perceptive than I realized? I wasn't sure what was true anymore. I took my kitchen shears and cut out the picture of the waterfall. Only I needed to know why. It was a nice picture. That was all.

The phone rang while Renee was still resting in her room. I checked the caller ID and picked up the phone.

"Is it a good time?" Nannie didn't waste time with formalities.

"Yes, he's not home yet. How are you?"

"I'm doing fine, sweetie. When are you coming to visit? Renee's probably grown a foot since I last saw her." Nannie's voice was tender, not accusing, yet pangs of guilt stabbed at my chest. In the past year, I'd only visited my grandma three times. With her living in a retirement home an hour and a half away, the drive and visiting took more time from my day than Derrick would allow. My mind searched for an excuse for not visiting Nannie that didn't give away my true reasons, though she had probably guessed long ago what kept me away. Nannie had never approved of Derrick and warned me seven years ago I was making a terrible mistake by marrying an atheist. I thought I could change him, make him believe.

Instead, he changed me.

"Nannie, I'd love to come see you, but Renee is such a handful, it's hard to make the drive over without any help. Derrick's been working long hours lately, so he can't come with me." No lies there, only omissions.

The line was quiet, and I imagined Nannie sitting in her padded rocking chair, her short hair dyed the ash brown of her youth, fluffed and sprayed with Aqua Net.

"Well, I can give you money to stay in a motel when you come. That way you're not driving so much in one day."

"That'd be nice, but Derrick ... wouldn't like me to be gone overnight." I pulled at the hem of my shirt. I couldn't even imagine telling Derrick I would be gone for a whole night.

"Are you two still seeing the marriage counselor?"

I closed my eyes, not ready to admit how the counseling had failed. In desperation and loneliness, I had confided in

Nannie about Derrick's increasing use of alcohol and his growing temper. She'd encouraged me to seek marriage counseling. Derrick had gone along at my request, but by the third appointment, he was done. He didn't like what the counselor had to say. "Derrick didn't really see eye-to-eye with the counselor." My face turned hot at the admission. "I tried to go without him, but he insisted I stop." To put it mildly. I leaned against the dining table. Why did I suddenly feel so weak?

"Cassie, Derrick is your husband. He's not God. At some point, you need to realize what's best for you and Renee, then do it." Nannie's soft voice was full of conviction. I felt like a teenager again, sneaking in through the backdoor of my grandparents' house past my curfew, thinking they were too old and oblivious to notice.

"You don't understand." Tears stung my eyes. I bit my lip, my hold on the lie slipping away. "He'll divorce me if I do anything like that, Nannie. He would even take Renee from me."

"Honey, if you allow him to keep mistreating you, what does that show Renee about how she should be treated? He might decide to divorce you rather than change, but there isn't a judge in this country who will give him custody. He's an alcoholic." The word made me nauseous.

I wanted to believe Nannie. It was logical. But I could see Derrick's face during our late-night fights. The coldness in his eyes, the threats believable and real. He hadn't always been like that. Even this morning he had been charming and playful, making funny faces at Renee while he ate his breakfast, and complimenting me on the eggs I had cooked. If I hung on a little longer, maybe we could make it.

"When his business settles down a bit, he'll drink less and things will be better. He almost never loses his temper in front of Renee. He's a good dad." I stood in the living room and looked out the sliding glass door. Renee's play structure sat grounded in the yard, its primary colors vivid in the sun. Three large, raised garden beds flanked the west edge of the yard. Soon, Derrick would be spending his evenings there, tending seedlings. At those times, he reminded me of the soft-spoken, nature-loving boy who had won my heart years ago.

"Nothing is going to change until Derrick admits he has an addiction and gets help. Do you really want Renee to grow up with alcohol as a part of her day-to-day life?"

Goose bumps covered the back of my arms as dozens of childhood memories flooded my vision. I saw my mom and smelled the sweet and acrid mixture of perfume and hard liquor. I felt the coldness of the car and pangs of hunger as she left me alone while she went in the bar and didn't come back for hours.

"If he leaves me, I won't have anything. How will I raise Renee?"

"What will you be losing?" Nannie's voice escalated. It wasn't like her to lose her temper, but there was a new desperation in her tone. "Cassie, what is the house worth? Is it worth your sanity? Your life?"

"No." The tears I'd been holding back fell down my cheeks. "I don't know what to do. I'm ... trapped. I don't even have a job." *And I've never lived on my own.*

"So this is what you do while I bust my rear to make a living?"

Impossible. It was too early in the day. I spun around.

Derrick stood in the entryway, his briefcase in hand. The look on his face said he was standing there long enough to hear things not meant for his ears.

"Nannie, I have to go. 'Bye." I set the phone down on the dining table.

"Did I interrupt your husband bashing?" Pain flickered

6

in Derrick's eyes, but his voice was low and heavy with his typical sarcasm.

Heat rose in my neck while my mind raced through what I had said, trying to think of a way to spin it so it didn't sound bad. But there was no covering up the truth.

"Honey," I murmured, trying to appeal to him. "Nannie wants us to come visit her and ... she doesn't understand why we don't."

Derrick threw down his briefcase and walked toward me with measured steps, his head cocked to one side. The intensity of his stare, the light perspiration on his forehead, the loosened tie around his neck ... he'd had a drink before coming home. Probably more than one. I stepped back against the glass door.

"You know why you can't see your precious little Nannie? Because she's white trash, exactly like you. I don't want that rubbing off on our daughter."

I cringed at the familiar words—*white trash*. I had my mother to blame for the title. Here I was, caught talking about my husband behind his back. That's not what good wives from respectable families did. Maybe I was no better than my mom. I focused on the ground and hunched my shoulders, trying to make myself disappear.

Cassie, you have to go now.

Derrick scowled, then turned and headed toward the kitchen. I heard the refrigerator door open, then slam shut. I forgot to stock his beer. I headed toward the pantry closet, but when I got there, Derrick had already grabbed a beer off the shelf. He popped the cap off, put it to his lips, and gulped it down. My stomach turned.

"I guess that's what I get for coming home early." Derrick laughed sardonically, and his eyes turned the calculating green I'd become all too familiar with. He brushed past me and strolled into the living room.

I was speechless. It was only 3:30. If he drank at his usual rate, he would be drunk long before Renee was in bed. If I woke Renee from her nap now, I could put her to bed a little earlier. I'd make dinner early too. The food would help counteract the effects of the alcohol, and a well-prepared meal might help appease Derrick for the evening.

By the time dinner was ready, Derrick had downed a six-pack. He ignored me, and took intermittent breaks from the basketball game blaring from the television to play with Renee. She laughed as her dad tickled her or chased her around the room, pretending to be a bear while she was a rabbit. She was too young to care about the yeasty smell of beer on his breath, his slowed speech, or the ruddiness of his cheeks. To her, he was simply Daddy. The weight in my stomach grew.

Dinner went well. Derrick devoured the steak and potatoes but pushed his salad aside. I had no appetite. I glanced at the clock. 6:00 p.m. In one more hour I could tuck Renee in bed and steady myself for the imminent fight with Derrick. Maybe he would fall asleep too. For a moment I let myself imagine a quiet evening alone, curled up on the couch, watching an old episode of *Friends*. Then the phone rang. I looked at the caller ID and almost didn't answer, but I couldn't do that to my precious Nannie.

"Cassie, is everything okay? You hung up with such abruptness earlier. I couldn't stop worrying about you and Renee. With Derrick's temper ..." Nannie's voice was weary. She must have been overcome with concern to call when she knew Derrick might be home.

"Yes," I lied, trying to keep my voice neutral. "Everything's great."

Derrick looked at me with narrowed eyes. "Who are you talking to?"

Derrick would see right through a lie, and even if he

didn't, he would check the caller ID as soon as I hung up.

"It's ... Nannie."

Derrick's cold glare was more effective than any words.

"Nannie, I need to go. Can I call you tomorrow?" The words rushed out of my mouth.

"What's going on?" Nannie wouldn't let the issue die. I shouldn't have opened up to her. Someday I would learn to keep my mouth shut.

"Nothing. I just have my hands full." I kept my eyes on Derrick. His jaw was clenched, and his glare had turned into a scowl. I needed to hang up. "Nannie, I ..."

It was too late. Derrick darted over and grabbed the phone out of my hand before I could touch the "end" button. With his other hand he grabbed my wrist and yanked my arm behind my back. Sharp pain seared through my shoulder. I screamed and fell to my knees. Derrick's voice was vehement as he spoke to Nannie. "If you really care about your granddaughter, then you should stop calling. Because every time you do, she's going to pay for it." Derrick slammed the phone down, ending the call.

My heart pinched at the vision of Nannie sitting alone in her room, worried about Renee and me. Ignoring the pain in my shoulder and my awkward position, I looked up at Renee, still sitting at the table with what was left of her dinner. She darted a leery glance at her dad.

Derrick leaned over me, pointing an accusing finger. "You need to tell your precious little Nannie to stop calling. If she doesn't, I'm pretty sure I can make that feeble heart of hers stop beating for good."

A chill bit deep into my bones. Renee wailed. She was old enough now to understand Derrick's harsh words.

Derrick released my arm and placed his hand on the back of my neck, under my hair. He pulled on the layers of hair closest to my neck. I winced as my head was yanked back, now eye to eye with my husband.

"I won't have my wife talk about me behind my back. You *are* replaceable."

Renee cried louder. "Mommy! Daddy!"

Derrick let go of me and straightened. I fell on my hands, grateful for the release of the pain. Derrick turned to Renee, and spoke softly. "Quiet down, Pumpkin, everything's okay."

Renee shook her head and cried louder. Derrick's fists clenched and his jaw tightened. I scrambled to my feet, ready to run to my daughter. Derrick was quicker. He reached for Renee and picked her up. Bile rose in my throat and my knees turned to water. "It's okay, Sugar Bug." I spoke as evenly as possible, though my voice was shaky, desperate to calm Renee.

My gaze was locked on Derrick's clenched jaw, and I fought the urge to pull Renee from his arms. Any action from me would only make things worse. After a couple of moments, her crying ceased. Derrick's face was once again soft, and his fists were no longer clenched. Renee was okay and Derrick was calm, but every nerve in my body still screamed danger.

"Let's find a cartoon for you to watch while Mommy cleans up." He spoke soothingly to Renee and gently brushed her tears away with his fingers. As the adrenaline subsided, my shoulder throbbed, and my head spun.

Derrick had never used such physical force with me. He'd held me against a wall and lifted his hand as if he would hit me, but he'd always stopped, and he'd never done such a thing in front of Renee. It wasn't that long ago that he would have an outburst but regain his composure quickly, reassuring me with a hug or soothing words, as he had just done with our daughter.

After setting Renee on the couch and turning on a cartoon, Derrick marched over to me and leaned in close. I flinched instinctively. His eyes narrowed, and he motioned toward Renee. "See what you've done?" he whispered. "Some mother you are." He continued down the hall, grumbling obscenities. I ran to Renee and put her on my lap, rocking her side to side.

Renee looked at me with solemn eyes. "Mommy, you shouldn't make Daddy so mad."

Her words stung. I remembered Nannie's warning only hours ago. What was Renee learning from what she witnessed? How would it affect who she became? How long until Derrick's anger with me boiled over and hurt our daughter?

Cassie, you have to go now.

A chill ran down my neck. I had nowhere to go.

I wanted to call Nannie back so she wouldn't worry, but if Derrick caught me, it would only make things worse. I headed to the kitchen to clean up. When I was down to the last couple of dishes in the sink, I heard footsteps down the hall. Derrick had showered and changed into jeans and a t-shirt. His eyes were clearer, and his cheeks were freshly shaven, I turned my focus back to my task and ignored the pounding in my chest. Derrick entered the kitchen and stood behind me as I rinsed the skillet. I didn't turn to face him. His breath was warm on my back, and I smelled the mint of mouth wash.

"Renee deserves better. You'll probably leave her, like your whore of a mother left you." Derrick's mouth was so close to me, his lips grazed my ear as he spoke. I kept on task, ignoring the oft-used insult. My pulse beat in my neck, and a sharp, needle-like pain flared in my temples.

Derrick sneered. "That Nannie of yours is a piece of work. Your grandpa must've been one whipped little man."

A growing, wild animal chained up inside me for too long was unleashed. I spun toward Derrick and screamed. The sounds that came out of me were guttural, full of rage. I slapped Derrick across the face with the wet dish cloth in my hand once, then again, before pushing him backward with all my strength.

"Enough!"

Derrick didn't fight back. He laughed, looking past me and out the kitchen window. I raised my hand to slap him again and froze with my arm in mid-air. A flashing blue and red light reflected off the glass cupboard behind my husband.

The doorbell rang.

Chapter Two

I SWUNG AROUND TO FACE THE window, the wet dishcloth still in my hand. The spinning blue and red lights of the police car illuminated the dark street in front of our house. It made no sound. The doorbell rang a second time, followed by a loud knock.

Derrick's voice, low and mocking, came from behind me. "That's quite a show you put on for the officers outside. Do you want to get the door, or should I?"

A cold tremor went through my body. The bright overhead florescent lights of our kitchen made the garden window over the sink a virtual camera lens into our home. I tossed the limp rag in my shaking hand into the sink, where it landed on the last dirty dish.

Derrick sauntered to the door and answered it with a solemn look on his face. I studied his clean-shaven profile. His dark eyelashes, wide jaw and generous upper lip gave him an innocent, boyish expression. Derrick used his salesman voice—the same easy-going, charming cadence that attracted me to him when I was seventeen-years-old and hungry for romance.

Renee ran to the kitchen, her face contorted in confusion, a crease in her brow. I swooped her up and held her tightly, finding as much comfort from her as she did from me. The next thing I knew, Derrick pried Renee from my arms, and two officers stepped into the entryway. A short, young officer asked me to step outside and answer a few questions. I walked out onto the entryway, and he closed the door behind us. His navy-blue uniform, along with the holster he wore, made him seem especially stocky. He looked at me with calculating eyes, holding a notepad and pen in his hand.

"Would you mind telling me, ma'am, what is going on here this evening?"

I spoke around the lump in my throat. "My husband and I were having a small argument."

The officer nodded and scribbled something on his notepad. "When you say argument, are you referring to a verbal dispute, or did it get physical?"

"Uh... verbal... mostly. Nothing serious." I cringed, hearing the waver in my voice, ignoring the throbbing in my shoulder.

The officer looked directly at me. Even under the mediocre porch light, the contempt was clear on his face. "Do you understand, ma'am, if there was any physical attack by your husband or you this evening, we will need to take one of you into custody?"

"No. I didn't know. But everything is fine." I looked down at the cement walkway.

"Did you know your grandmother called the police department tonight? Why do you suppose she did?"

The officer's eyes were hard, emotionless—the judgmental stare of someone who's made up their mind about who you are and how little you matter. Memories of my mom, with a blackened eye and bloody nose surfaced. It was a darkness in me I couldn't escape.

"I have no idea why my grandmother called. I guess she heard us arguing earlier when I was on the phone with her and overreacted." I gazed past the officer, careful not to look him in the eye.

He nodded and jotted more notes. Behind me, the front door opened, and the other officer came out on the walkway, nodding at his stout partner. I waited for the worst to happen. I could see it now, a carefully orchestrated nightmare, compliments of Derrick and my lifelong ability to be in the wrong place at the wrong time. The cops were going to cuff me and take me to jail. Me, not Derrick. It would be me who was charged with a crime, not the man whose anger permeated our home and made me feel like I was constantly walking on eggshells.

The stout officer slammed his notebook shut. "If everything is fine here, we won't be taking up anymore of your time." His eyes met mine, and the look on his face softened. "I highly suggest you talk with your grandmother about *why* she dialed 9-1-1." He glanced at his partner, then back to me and spoke barely above a whisper. "Do you understand?"

I nodded in agreement, blinking back tears. I knew why Nannie had called the police. She feared the worse. The only thing to be gained by talking to her about it was to hear all the reasons why she felt that way. Was that why the officer wanted me to call her?

The rest of the night was a blur. I bathed Renee and dressed her for bed, as if nothing had interrupted our nightly routine. Derrick didn't speak to me, but I heard his sardonic laugh intermittently, mixed with the familiar whoosh of a beer cap being popped off. He undoubtedly saw the police incident as a victory and was celebrating.

I tucked Renee in after her usual bedtime routine, but each time I turned the light off, she begged for one more story. By the third attempt to leave her room I was irritated, weary from holding back tears and faking smiles. I briskly grabbed yet another book off her shelf, and plunked myself onto her bed. Renee looked at me with her immense emerald eyes, her bottom lip sucked in tight.

Her chin quivered for a moment. "Do you still love me, Mommy?"

A sharp pain pierced through my chest. "Of course I do. Mommy would never, ever stop loving you." I wrapped my arms around her tiny four-year-old body and hugged her close. How could she equate the events of tonight into the sum of a lack of love for her? All I wanted her to know was love and security. I would do anything for her. Instead of reading another book, I held her close to me, stroking her soft brown hair and quietly humming a song. Finally, I felt her relax, and her head rolled onto my arm. I carefully tucked her into her pink and white princess bed and tiptoed out of the room.

I crawled into my own bed, physically and emotionally exhausted. The television blared from the living room, where Derrick would undoubtedly stay until he was near the point of passing out. I pulled the pillow over my head, determined to fall asleep and leave the horrible day behind. My mind had other plans. Every time I closed my eyes, an image from the last twenty-four hours popped into my head. I saw Grandpa's face from my dream, sad yet stern. Derrick's mocking expression when the police showed up. The officer's jaded gaze as he listened to my story. Renee's eyes filled with fear when I tucked her into bed.

Then there were the voices.

You have to go now.

Is it worth your sanity?

You'll probably leave her.

We will need to take someone into custody.

I thought about my options. I could stay and play my part in the charade. But if I did, I was certain I would either lose my mind or my life, leaving Renee with her alcoholic father, and no one to protect her. Or, I could get up while Derrick was in a drunken sleep and sneak out with Renee. I'd be able to pack enough clothes for a couple of days and get some money from the ATM before Derrick could close our bank accounts. But where would I go? Derrick would follow me, and I would end up back where I started, with an angrier husband. Memories of sleeping in the back of my mom's car, her in tears and driving away from another relationship gone wrong, snuck into my thoughts. No. If I was going to leave, I needed a rock-solid plan. I needed to be the epitome of the responsible, caring parent.

I needed a job. Once I had one, I could secretly start looking for a place to live. Meanwhile, if I was shrewd with the household budget, I could stash away enough money for a deposit on an apartment. I could make it work. Maybe. A familiar saying of Grandpa's popped into my swirling thoughts, "Anything is possible." Was it really? Maybe for other people, but I doubted such an optimistic outcome for myself. I had to believe, though, for Renee, the promise held true. She deserved a better future. She deserved a home that wasn't full of anger and fear. She deserved a childhood better than mine. The dream of happily-ever-after was my goal all along. It seemed I had failed. Miserably failed. Now it was time to make it right.

By the time I was done strategizing my escape, the pillow under my head was soaked with tears. I sat up, turned the pillow over, and wiped my eyes. The pillow was cool and comforting against my cheek.

You have to go now.

"Yes, Grandpa, you're right." I whispered. Then I drifted into a dreamless sleep.

Chapter Three

I PUSHED THROUGH THE ROTATING DOORS of the Park Place Professional Building, feigning confidence. The heels of my new black pumps sank into the plush maroon carpet as I made a beeline to the elevator. One of the security guards for the Park Place Business Bank, which occupied the first floor of the building, smiled and nodded at me, his weathered and kind face providing small comfort to my anxious heart.

The Sunday morning following the police incident I woke up with hope and determination. While Renee watched cartoons and Derrick perused the commentary section of the Sunday paper, I discreetly looked through the help-wanted ads. Monday morning, I went to Walmart and bought a prepaid cell phone. Derrick wouldn't allow me to have a cell phone, claiming that a stay-at-home mom had no use for one. I couldn't risk a potential employer calling the home phone. Hiding the cell phone wouldn't be easy, but it was my only option.

Monday afternoon I emailed my resume to the law office of Wardwood, Rosen, et al., replying to their ad for a legal secretary. Wednesday morning, someone at the firm called to see if I was available for an interview the following day. I'd run a mental marathon in the last twenty-four hours, figuring out what to wear and a way to sneak out of the house without Derrick getting suspicious of my whereabouts.

I joined a small group of men in business suits waiting for the next elevator. When the doors opened with a soft chime, they looked at me and waited in gentlemen-like manner for me to step in before them. I smiled and moved forward, conscious of their eyes on me as I pushed the button marked eight, then stood against the wall. I stared at my shoes and focused on my breathing, hoping my heart would slow down before we got to the eighth floor. Why couldn't I shake the feeling I was a little girl secretly playing dress up in her mother's closet, hoping to not get caught?

The entrance for Wardwood, Rosen et al. was immediately visible when I exited the elevator. Two grand double doors, framed by windows on each side, greeted me. Listed in gold on the door was a total of nine attorney's names. The receptionist who called and scheduled the interview didn't tell me which attorney needed a secretary.

A mousy looking receptionist greeted me with a smile and told me to take a seat. Large leather chairs lined the reception area, surrounding a small coffee table with magazines such as Forbes fanned perfectly across the top. I was completely unprepared for the interview. My outfit was from my old work wardrobe, outdated. The attorneys I had worked for before I had Renee specialized in worker's compensation and disability cases, and they had small, humble offices that smelled of mildew and stale cigarette smoke. The law office I sat in now practiced business and real estate law and was in the most prestigious office building in town. I told myself this was one of many interviews, simply a practice run. It wasn't like anyone ever got the first job they interviewed for when beginning a job search. Especially when they'd been out of the workforce for over four years. I straightened in my chair, pulled shoulders back, and forced a fake smile.

A tall man in a black business suit entered the reception area. "Ms. Peterson?"

He was not what I was expecting. My previous bosses were elderly, overweight, and looked like they spent too much time under fluorescent lighting. The man standing in front of me was probably at least ten years my senior, but the only signs of age on his face were a crease between his thick eyebrows, and faint lines around his eyes. His six-foot-tall, wide-shouldered frame didn't look soft at all. This was someone who made it to the gym regularly.

Flustered, I jolted up and extended my hand.

The man had a firm handshake. "My name's Brian Sutton. Let's go chat in the conference room." His eyes scanned me head to toe, then he turned on his heel and walked toward a door across the reception area. I followed him, feeling even more girlish as I scurried to keep up with his long strides.

A large table with elegant padded chairs filled the conference room. Brian motioned at a chair. "Have a seat."

I sat as gracefully as I could, willing myself to relax. *This is simply practice.*

Brian thumbed through papers sitting in front of him. I stared at his thick, dark hair, speckled with a hint of gray. It was wavy but heavily gelled. Brian picked up a paper that looked like my resume and sat back in his chair. His dark brown eyes studied me for a moment before he spoke.

"So, it looks like you worked as a legal secretary for about four years?"

I cleared my throat. "Yes."

"Working on disability cases?"

I nodded, then remembered it was an interview taboo. "Yes." I hated the small, childish sound of my voice.

Brian put my resume down. "You haven't worked in over four years—why now?"

I fidgeted in my seat. "Well, I had a baby and wanted to stay home with her while she was young."

"And now you're ready to go back to work?" His question was quick, emotionless.

"Yes."

Brian looked me in the eye, and I felt myself shrinking

into the big chair. "What's your typing speed?"

"Fifty words per minute." I answered without thinking. That *had* been my typing speed four years ago when I typed every day. I doubted I was that fast now.

Brian nodded, the crease in his brow deepening. He tapped his left hand rhythmically against the table, and I noticed the glint of a gold wedding band on his finger. He stilled his hand and looked directly at me, his eyes penetrating. What was he seeing when he looked at me? No doubt my full cheeks, framed by the ringlets of my long reddish-brown hair, made me look younger than almost twenty-nine years old. It didn't help I'd cut my bangs myself that morning, and they were too short, sitting above my eyebrows.

"Why do you want to work in a law office, Ms. Peterson?"

In my nervousness, I fought back an anxious laugh. Who really wanted to work in a law office? I couldn't tell him the truth—it was the only thing I knew how to do, and it paid well. Or I needed to leave my alcoholic husband and had no one to turn to for help.

I straightened in my chair and forced a small smile. "From my previous experience, working for attorneys is very rewarding. There's never a dull moment, and I enjoy being part of a team and meeting deadlines." I focused on Brian's nose. It was too large for his face, and that imperfection helped me relax. "Plus, there's usually room for advancement, and now that my daughter is older, I'm ready to continue in my career goals."

I forced my hands to lay still on my lap, ignored the perspiration on my back, and hoped he believed my spiel.

Brian nodded, picked up a pen, and wrote something on my resume.

He continued to write as he spoke. "You'd be working for Cynthia Steelborne, our newest associate. She recently returned from maternity leave and isn't planning on going on any more leaves any time in the foreseeable future."

His writing stopped, and Brian looked up at me. "What plans do you have for the future, Ms. Peterson?"

My heart throbbed in my throat. "What do you mean?"

Brian chuckled and his steely eyes lit up. Were my motives transparent?

"Let me put it this way—are you looking for a long-term commitment, or something to get you by for now?"

I exhaled. I could answer honestly. "I'm definitely planning on working full time on a long-term basis."

Brian asked more questions about my previous job, all in quick succession while he tapped a pen on the table. I got the impression my answers didn't matter, he'd already made up his mind. He leaned forward, his elbows on the table. "Tell me more about you. What are your hobbies?"

I never understood those types of questions in an interview. What did it matter what I did in my spare time, if I got the job done?

"Oh ... well ..." I paused, heat rising in my neck. What *did* I like doing in my spare time? I was a mom and a housewife who had to give an account to her husband for every excursion from home. I didn't have spare time. I didn't have hobbies. All I really had was Renee. But that would not be a good answer. The man sitting across from me was career-minded, looked athletic, and was married to a woman who was probably also successful. My mind searched frantically for an answer. I saw myself in the yard, cutting flowers, then coming in to look at the outdoor section of the newspaper. I remembered childhood days when Grandpa had taken me fishing, and my later teen years when Derrick and I spent Saturdays down by the river, seeking its cool in the heat of summer.

"I love the outdoors." I said, a hint of honest enthusiasm

in my voice.

Brian raised his eyebrows and smiled. "Really? What's your favorite outdoor activity?"

My heart raced. Cutting flowers didn't sound very outdoorsy or interesting. I hadn't fished in years and wouldn't even know how to go about it without help.

I shrugged my shoulders and smiled, glancing around the room for inspiration. My eyes landed on a portrait of the sun setting behind a mountain, and I heard Grandpa's voice from my dream. *I've already given you everything you need.*

With eerily calm assurance I finally replied. "I love going for hikes, especially to see waterfalls."

Brian's eyes gleamed, and his mouth twitched. "Interesting." He straightened in his chair. "I'm going to see if Cynthia is available to come meet you, if you don't mind?" He picked up the phone sitting on the table before I could answer. I was surprised. Maybe he was going through all the motions of the interview to be fair, but something about him didn't strike me as that type of person.

A few moments later the conference room door opened and a woman breezed in. I stood for the introductions. Cynthia was about my age, with dark brown hair pulled back in a tight bun. She wore a skirt, plain beige blouse, and almost no make-up. The stark contrast between her simple and plain dress and Brian's polished look was startling and gave me hope. Cynthia looked like someone I could relate to, someone who wouldn't make me uncomfortable.

Brian introduced us, then asked Cynthia to take a seat next to me. She gave him a quizzical look but did as he said.

Brian summarized my work experience, told Cynthia I was also a mom, and let her know my typing speed.

Cynthia's brow creased. "Her experience sounds good, but being out of the work force four years, and only having a typing speed of fifty, raises some concern."

My cheeks turned red. I wasn't sure if it was because she talked about me like I wasn't there or because she obviously didn't think I was good enough for the job.

Brian shrugged. "Fifty words per minute isn't bad. She wasn't spending all day doing transcription at her previous job. There aren't many firms left that do things that way. She did in-depth, independent work, which I'm sure will come in handy in the future. I don't see any reason why she can't keep up with your *limited* workload." Brian's eyes were daggers as he spoke to Cynthia, and it made me realize when he looked at me earlier, he had been comparatively warm and kind.

Cynthia opened her mouth to speak, then bit down on her bottom lip. "You're the boss."

Brian laughed, picked up the pen, and made more notes on my resume. I watched his hand move, hoping I could decipher what he was writing. I willed myself to relax. Obviously, I wasn't going to be hired for this job. Cynthia didn't think I was good enough, and despite Brian's arguments, her opinion had to carry weight.

Brian ended the interview by dismissing Cynthia and asking me if he could call and check my references. I agreed and rushed out of the building. I wasn't good enough for this firm, but the interview had been helpful practice.

Once in my car, I allowed the tears to fall. I mourned the life Renee would never have—a steady, loving dad; the companionship of a sibling; a mom who was there when she got home from school. All the things I never had would also never be hers. It was my fault. Would she suffer through poverty too, because I couldn't get a decent job? Maybe I was "a piece of white-trash," like Derrick said.

The next afternoon, the cell phone vibrated in my shirt

pocket. It was Brian. His voice caught me off guard. In my nervousness at the interview, I somehow hadn't noticed how smoothly he talked.

"We'd like to offer you the legal secretary job."

I was shocked. And scared. "I'm sorry, I can't take the job," I blurted, my heart stabbing my ribs.

"Why don't you want the job?" he asked, obviously irritated.

"It's not that I don't want it." I hesitated, biting my lip. "I don't think I *can* do it. It's been a long time since I've done much typing. I would be slow."

Brian was quiet on the other end of the line, and I felt like the word "LOSER" was stamped in bright, red letters across my forehead. I couldn't understand why Brian was offering me the job. Cynthia didn't like me. I didn't type fast enough and had been out of the workforce too long. I was a mom, a housewife, a maker of dinner and beds.

"You have excellent references, Cassie." Brian's reply was gentle, but firm. "I'm willing to bet the typing will come back to you quickly. We don't expect you to be burning up the keyboard on your first day."

He said "we." Did he mean Cynthia consented to him hiring me?

I fidgeted on the other end of the line. "I don't want to be a disappointment." Failure wasn't an option. Renee's future depended on me succeeding.

Brian chuckled. "Why don't you give it a try. You might surprise yourself."

I agreed to start in two weeks.

Chapter Four

FINDING DAYCARE PROVED TO BE MORE difficult than finding a job. Taking Renee with me to look at daycares was out of the question. She was curious and talkative, and likely to say something that might raise her father's suspicions. When I finally narrowed my search down to a home daycare that had an opening and sounded decent, I left Renee with our next-door neighbor, Serena, and lied about my destination, as I had for my interview. I had another doctor's appointment. My lack of ingenuity was going to make Serena think I was seriously ill.

The daycare was in a cul-de-sac of older homes. Nothing about it set it apart. There was no sign, no toys in the front yard, and I didn't hear any commotion when I knocked on the door. I double checked the address. Unless I'd written it down incorrectly, I was in the right place.

The woman who answered the door took me by surprise. She was an average-looking, middle-aged woman, except for having unusually long black hair, with wide grey streaks. She had one of the warmest smiles I'd ever seen. It wasn't the lets-put-on-a-good-show kind that I saw when I looked in the mirror. It was genuine, warm, and lit up her face and brown eyes.

"You must be Cassie." Her voice had a slight southern drawl.

I nodded, holding back hope.

"Come on in." She glanced behind me as she stepped out of the doorway. "Did you bring your daughter?"

"No. I left her with a friend." I didn't offer any more explanation. I stepped into the living room, which was littered with toys. Small children sat at a table coloring, a baby slept in a swing, and a blue heeler stood in the middle of it all, seeming to guard the group. It tilted its head and woofed at me once, then lay down. A wonderful aroma from the kitchen cut through the smells of dog hair and baby formula.

The woman offered her hand. "My name is Bonnie Sampson, but you can call me Bonnie."

I smiled. I'd been so discouraged by the time I reached the last number on my list, I didn't even bother asking for the name of the person I was going to meet. All I'd asked about was price and availability.

We exchanged small talk, then I asked one of the questions that weighed on me. "Do you watch the kids by yourself, or does your husband help you?" I tried to sound casual, but the truth was I didn't feel safe with a man watching my daughter. A childhood filled with the revolving door of my mother's boyfriends had taught me to be cautious about strange men with children.

Bonnie tilted her head, a slight twinkle in her eye, almost like she understood what I didn't want to say. "Mr. Sampson passed away seven years ago."

"Oh, I'm so sorry." I stammered.

Bonnie nodded, smiling. "He was a good man."

It struck me that she had introduced herself as "Mrs." though she was seven years a widow. Is that what true love was like? Devotion unstoppable, even in death?

Bonnie answered my questions patiently, even though she was interrupted several times by children's voices, asking questions or pleading for a new game to play. She asked me questions too, about Renee—what she liked to eat, what her favorite activities were, if she'd been in daycare before. The longer I talked to her, the more I felt the tension easing from my shoulders.

"Do you live nearby?" Bonnie asked.

How did I respond? My home with Derrick was only five minutes away, but if I continued down this path, I wasn't sure where I'd be living. There were a couple of affordable apartments I was looking at in the next couple of days. Neither one of them was near Bonnie's house, but they were reasonably close to my job. I hadn't thought about logistics.

"Not really," I twirled a strand of hair around my finger. "But I'll be working downtown, so, you know, there aren't really any home daycares close to that." I didn't tell her I couldn't afford to put Renee in one of the child care centers downtown.

Bonnie nodded. "You won't be alone. I have kids here who live nearby and ones whose parents live on the outskirts of town."

Bonnie's questioning turned to a different subject. She asked about the job I was starting, and about my husband's occupation. Knots multiplied in my stomach when I talked about Derrick. Then a question caught me completely off guard.

"What's your passion?" she asked, as if she was wanting to know something as simple as whether I liked cream and sugar with my coffee.

"My passion?" I shrugged. "What do you mean?"

Bonnie's head tilted again, a knowing look in her eyes. "The one thing you love to do the most."

I shrugged my shoulders, feeling a sense of déjà-vu. Brian had asked about hobbies, and I'd come up with hiking to waterfalls. It sounded good, but it wasn't true. I couldn't remember the last time I hiked anywhere further than down the street.

Instead of lying, I quickly turned the tables to get the spotlight off me. "What about you?" I asked. "Do you have a passion?"

Bonnie laughed. "Oh, I have many. I love kids,

obviously." She gestured to the room full of children. "But I also love gardening and treasure hunting."

Treasure hunting? That sounded interesting, but looking at my watch I realized I was running late. I shook Bonnie's hand again and thanked her for her time. I hurried out the door before she had a chance to ask any more questions.

Peace, unfamiliar and comforting, settled over me on the way home. I had found a place for Renee. I would check Bonnie's references, of course. But from what I saw, I knew I could feel safe leaving Renee with Bonnie Sampson while I worked, regardless of how far I had to drive to get her there. Bonnie was warm, friendly and nurturing. And she had a passion.

The sun was beginning its evening descent when I pulled into my driveway. *What's your passion?* The question nagged at me. I couldn't remember the last time I was passionate in a good way about anything.

I looked at the clock on the dashboard. I had forty-five minutes to retrieve Renee from Serena's, then get dinner on the table before Derrick walked through the front door. What was my passion? The answer was simple. My passion was survival.

The Friday before I was scheduled to start at the law firm, everything was ready and in place. I'd paid for the first month at an apartment near downtown. It was small but clean. I had even hired a moving truck. They were scheduled to show up Monday morning, right after Derrick left for work. I had prepared everything … except myself.

Derrick's behavior over the previous two weeks had gone from snarky to stand-offish to bordering on civility. I worried that he knew what I had planned. Had he found the bags of toys and clothes I had hid in Renee's closet? Had he noticed that I didn't pay the utilities yet this month, so I would have more money put aside for my first month away? Or maybe I was doing all this work for nothing. Derrick had not called me a name, made a threat, or even glared at me for days. Was he starting to see the error of his ways? If I tried hard enough, I could almost forget all the times we had fought. I could shrug off the threats, forget the physical pain he cunningly inflicted without leaving marks. What if Derrick's change in behavior was a sign that I should stay?

I thought about how I would explain my change of heart to Brian Sutton. No doubt I would never get a job with that law firm in the future, but there were other jobs out there. The apartment, the daycare … it could all be stopped with a phone call. I could take it all back, step away, and continue life as usual. Not a perfect life, but not so bad either.

If only I could talk to Nannie. I had called her the day after the police incident, telling her that everything was fine and there was no need to worry. Not being truthful with her made me feel awful, but I couldn't risk her continued interference. I also couldn't take the chance of her knowing my plans. If I did leave, she might be the first one Derrick called, looking for me. The less she knew, the better. At least until Renee and I were safe in our new home, and Derrick had a chance to calm down. Not having anyone to talk to made my body feel heavy. Loneliness sank its talons into me, raking at my heart.

That night, after putting Renee to bed, I approached Derrick. He'd only drank a few beers so far. He had been cordial, almost pleasant. I sat next to him on the couch, where he was engrossed in a car magazine. One of *his* passions was automobiles. Derrick had apparently been doing a lot of reading that evening, and the coffee table was littered with various hot rod magazines. The story about the waterfall that I had clipped from the newspaper was also on the coffee table. I'd left it out by accident earlier in the day, when I'd been gazing at it, searching for answers. It now sat with a water ring on it, left from Derrick's bottle of beer. The words in the water ring were blurred. Lost forever. A coaster sat next to the newspaper clipping, dry as dust.

My heart clenched in my chest. I took a deep breath, willing myself to not become angry. It was, after all, simply a clipping, not an irreplaceable, historic document or photograph.

It didn't matter.

I nudged Derrick's arm, and he looked at me quizzically, a small gleam in his beautiful green eyes. I put my head gently on his shoulder, like I used to do, not so long ago— back in the days when he would caress my cheek, or run his fingers through my hair. How long had it been since he had shown me any sign of affection? Nine months? A year? All I wanted was for him to put his arm around me and say, "I love you and I'm sorry." Those six words could save us.

Derrick pulled back from me, a tight smile on his face, the gleam in his eyes more intense. I waited. Expectant. Hopeful.

"Why don't you make yourself useful and fetch me another beer?"

I slowly rose to my feet, the weight of a thousand rocks in my stomach. I brought him a fresh beer and set it on the coaster. He kept reading his magazine while I set the empty bottle aside, and carefully picked up the waterfall story. I'd take it away where the water ring could dry. Eventually, the words it blurred might reappear, and it would be whole again. If I was careful and kept it safe.

Because it was important.

Monday evening Derrick would be coming home to an empty house.

Chapter Five

MY NEW APARTMENT WAS BLUE. THE carpet, the countertops, even the mini-blinds were varying shades of blue, like someone couldn't quite make up their mind which version they liked best. Thankfully, the walls were plain and white. I was completely unpacked in one day. Of course, I didn't have much. The only furnishings I'd brought were the things I knew Derrick wouldn't miss, mainly the faded green couch and outdated TV we kept in the rarely used den. I'd brought the TV trays and Renee's bed, dresser, and toys. I'd convinced myself if I didn't take anything too valuable, Derrick's anger would be subdued. Renee's reaction to moving had been surprisingly simple. She watched the movers pack our meager belongings into the truck, a solemn expression on her face. She ran to me when they took apart her bed. "Mommy! Don't let them take my bed. Where will I sleep?"

"Don't worry, Sugar Bug. We're going with your bed. You're going to have a new, beautiful room."

Renee's brow furrowed, then her eyes lit up. "Like a princess?"

I smiled, feeling pleased with my secret. "Yes, like a princess."

Renee giggled, and I could see the gears moving in her little mind. I was thankful I had already decorated her new room with princess curtains and wall decals before our move. Knowing I'd been smart enough to think of that detail amidst the stressful and hectic week, boosted my confidence on an otherwise nerve-wracking morning.

I left Derrick a note.

Derrick,

I can't live with you anymore. Your drinking has changed you. I know you will be angry. I will contact you in a few weeks and we can talk about things. This isn't how I want it to end. I believe marriage counseling can help us, if you're willing to give it another try. I'll always love you.

Cassie

My heart ached too much to walk away without a word. Despite all of Derrick's brutal words and drunken anger, he was still Renee's father, and my first love. Part of me hoped if we did end up divorced, we could still be friends. Without me around to incite his fury, maybe Derrick would be a better person.

The first night in our new apartment, I didn't sleep at all. I laid awake on the couch, my ears tuned into every little sound; the creak of the floorboards in the apartment above me, the sound of a faucet being turned on nearby, and worst of all, the sound of footsteps on the sidewalk outside. How long would it take Derrick to find me?

I spent the next day preparing for my new job. My first stop was the cell phone store, where I exchanged my prepaid phone for a regular one with the same number. Then I took Renee to meet her new babysitter, Bonnie. Even though I thought Bonnie was wonderful, my heart sank when I pulled into her driveway. I didn't like the idea of leaving my only child for over eight hours a day. I knew there were countless moms who did so, either by choice or necessity, but trying to explain it to Renee was tricky.

"Where are we?" she asked, her head craned to look out the window.

"We are at your daycare. It's where you'll stay while I work."

"I want to go with you, Mommy. Not here."

I unbuckled Renee from her car seat. She clung to me with her arms and legs. I couldn't put her down.

"You'll love it here. There's other kids to play with, and lots of toys, and a really nice lady named Bonnie."

Renee buried her face in my neck. It wasn't like her to be this clingy and shy, but I supposed it was expected with the changes we were going through.

Bonnie opened her front door and didn't seem at all perplexed by Renee's shyness.

I followed Bonnie through the house as she gave us a tour. Renee raised her head off my shoulder when she heard the voices of other children. She didn't smile at any of them but looked curiously around.

I shuffled out the door with Renee clinging to me like a frightened monkey. Renee's meet and greet with her new daycare hadn't gone as smoothly as I hoped.

Bonnie smiled. "Tomorrow won't be as bad as you think. Trust me."

That night for dinner I made macaroni and cheese with hot dogs. I couldn't remember the last time I'd made something simple for dinner. Renee was thrilled, but I barely touched my food. The stress and exhaustion of the last two weeks was catching up with me. I'd been going on adrenaline. All my secret planning had taken a lot of time out of each day, leaving me going non-stop and at a hurried pace to make it look like I was home all day. The entire time I worried I'd be caught. It amazed me, really, that I'd gotten away with it. But it had taken its toll. Dark circles surrounded my blue eyes, and my fair skin was overly dry and starting to flake. I'd worn my hair in a ponytail almost every day and rarely washed it. I'd skipped so many meals, I had to start wearing a belt to keep my jeans on. I heard Derrick's voice in my head. "You're such a scrawny twig, I could snap you in two."

I bathed Renee right after dinner, knowing we both had an early morning ahead of us. While I was rinsing the soap out of her hair, she asked the question I'd been dreading.

"When is Daddy coming? I want to show him my room."

My heart ached as I studied her freshly washed face, her eyes closed so no water could get in. Such innocence—trusting, full of hope. I had rehearsed the answer in my mind, chosen the words days ago. Yet I still felt unprepared to answer her question.

"Mommy and Daddy want you to be happy. We love you more than anything in the whole world."

I poured the last cup of water on her hair, then wiped the water away from her face. Renee opened her eyes. I could see a hint of fear in them, but more so, I saw love.

"Renee, do you remember how, sometimes, Mommy and Daddy would argue?"

"You argue a lot." Renee replied, her mouth turned into a frown.

I wanted to tell her I had tried to hide it from her, tried to give her a good life. Now wasn't the time for explanations. She was far too young to understand.

"Yes, we did. It doesn't make for a happy home. That's why Mommy got her own home, and you're going to live with me. Daddy's staying at our old house."

Renee titled her head. "So ... we can all be happy?"

"Yes." I nodded, fighting back tears. "We can all be happy."

"But will I get to see Daddy in our old house?"

I had to choose my words carefully. I was still hoping for a resolution with a happily-ever-after, but I didn't want to make a promise I couldn't keep. I didn't want broken promises to be my legacy.

"I believe so. But it might be a while."

Renee looked down, and seemed to study the few

remaining bubbles in the bathtub.

"I might miss him, if it's too long."

I kissed her on the forehead. "Daddy will miss you too."

I couldn't hold back the tears. I rested my face on top of Renee's wet head. There were no words to comfort her. No words could describe the pain in my heart.

I pulled back, quickly grabbed a towel, and wiped my tears before Renee saw them. Then I picked Renee up out of the tub and wrapped the towel around her, carrying her to her room like a baby. We did our usual stuff, as if it was a normal day. A bedtime story, a song, kisses good-night.

But before I walked out the door, Renee called to me.

"Yes?" I replied, turning around.

With eyes wise beyond her years, Renee solemnly answered, "I don't miss Daddy, yet."

Settling in on the couch, there was one last thing I needed to do before starting my new job the next day. As far as Nannie knew, I was still with Derrick. She never really approved of Derrick, and had basically told me to leave him … or had I misunderstood? I couldn't exactly see Nannie telling people at church, "Praise the Lord, my granddaughter left her husband." Wasn't divorce a sin? I wasn't divorced yet, but I was pretty sure the whole "submit to your husband" thing didn't mean leaving him and not telling him where you went.

Poor Nannie had already gone through the disgrace of how my mother turned out. It seemed cruel she would have to suffer my shame on top of it.

I dialed her number. She had a phone in her room at the retirement home. Hopefully she was still awake.

"Hello?" Nannie's voice was soft, groggy.

"Did I wake you?" My guilt multiplied.

"Cassie? Is everything okay?"

"Yes, everything's fine. Don't worry."

"You don't usually call this late. Is Derrick not home?"

I took a deep breath. *Here goes.*

"That's one of the reasons why I called. Renee and I moved out. We moved into an apartment. I have a cell phone and I want to give you my new number in case ..."

"You left him?" Disbelief was evident in Nannie's tone, and something else, but I couldn't quite figure it out.

"Yes. I couldn't do it anymore. It got too bad." I didn't know what else to say without saying too much. I pulled on the hem of my shirt, twirling the end around my finger.

"You did the right thing, Cassie. You know what's best for you and Renee."

There was so much reassurance in Nannie's tone. More than I ever expected. Relief flowed over me, tears sprung from my eyes and words tumbled from my mouth.

"I left while Derrick was at work ... before that, I was getting everything ready and trying to keep it hidden, which is why I didn't call you sooner ..."

There was only a moment of silence. "Don't you worry about not calling me sooner. Now is what's important. How are you holding up?"

I evaded the question by telling Nannie about my apartment, then about the job I would be starting the next day. Talking about my new job made my stomach do flip-flops.

"Honey, that's a lot to take on. But I know you can do it. You've always been smart. Your new boss will adore you."

All I could see was Cynthia's disapproving face, but I shook the thought away.

"What about Renee? Who's going to watch her while you're at work?"

"I found a nice at-home daycare. I took Renee there today to introduce her to everyone. She was really shy."

Nannie sighed. "I wish I could be there to help you,

sweetie. If only I was ten years younger!"

I smiled. Nannie had been saying, "if only I was ten years younger" since I was nine-years-old and went to live with her and Grandpa.

"I wish you were ten years younger too." I thought of the younger Nannie who raised me when my mom wasn't around. She was so full of energy, and always taking on one project or another. "Maybe this weekend Renee and I can come see you?"

"Only if you're feeling up to it. I would love to see you both, but you need to rest. You've been through a lot and this is a whirlwind of change for both of you."

"Yes, it is. But I miss you. You and Renee are all I have." As soon as the words left my mouth I wanted to reach in the air and snatch them back. Nannie still held out hope for Sharon—her only child and my mom. I'd given up on her long ago. I couldn't understand why Nannie didn't do the same.

"You have more on your side than you know, Cassie." Nannie's reply was soft yet heavy with love.

I wasn't sure what she meant, and I didn't want to know. I couldn't afford to count on anybody for anything. Making a good life for Renee and keeping her safe was up to me, and me alone. My grandparents had been my saving grace when I was young, but now Grandpa was gone and Nannie was more helpless than me. If anything, I needed to be taking care of *her*. The weight of it settled on me, a dark cloud ready for a storm.

I alone would be the one to keep my daughter safe and blaze a path for our lives that was full of the things every child should have—security, love, happiness, and the opportunity to follow your dreams.

"I do know, Nannie." I lied. "I have everything I need." The words echoed in my mind, and I saw the Grandpa from my dreams, a cowboy silhouette against a dark mountain. I shivered as chills ran down my arms. I shook the goosebumps off, willing the image out of my mind. Grandpa was gone, like my childhood dreams of happily-ever-after. I longed for my Grandpa's strength, his optimism, his wisdom.

But all I had was myself. That would have to be enough.

Chapter Six

I SHOOK A COUPLE OF TYLENOLS out of the bottle on my desk and glanced at the clock: Three p.m. Today was my third day at the firm, and I had yet to take a real break other than quick lunches, too afraid of falling behind on my work. Cynthia had kept me busy and checked on me frequently. She'd had one of the other secretaries show me how to use the different office systems and where to find things in the library and copy room.

Thankfully, the amount of pure transcription she'd given me had been light, but whenever she handed me a tape, I detected a hint of a challenge in her eyes. I pretended I was unfazed by the workload, but I kept up because I came into the office at least fifteen minutes early and stayed about twenty minutes late each day, working non-stop. But now it was Friday afternoon, I was caught up, and needed something to wash down the Tylenol.

One of the perks of working at Wardwood & Rosen was a refrigerator full of free beverages. The breakroom was empty when I entered. I opened the fridge door and surveyed the contents.

"Hey girlie, if you're looking for the bottled water, I brought in a couple of cases." I turned around to see Missy Langdon, the office runner, standing behind me and setting a case of bottled water on the table.

During my previous, and brief, conversations with Missy I had learned she was twenty-two-years-old and the youngest employee at the firm. She did all the errands, copying, and supply ordering. I'd heard from another secretary that Missy worked as a lingerie model on the side. I could see why. She was tall, lean, tan, and beautiful. Her long brunette hair was streaked with golden highlights, and her brown eyes always seemed to sparkle. But despite all this, she didn't give me the impression she relied on her looks to get by. She had a confidence in her step and an aura of strength.

"Oh, thanks, exactly what I'm looking for." I closed the refrigerator door and walked toward the table.

Missy tore apart the plastic covering on the case of water bottles and tossed me one, then grabbed another and opened it. "So, what do you think of Wardens with Roses so far?" Missy asked, an extra spark in her eyes.

"What?" Was that the name of a rock band? I was completely out of touch with popular music.

Missy chortled. She glanced over her shoulder, then spoke in a low voice. "It's a little nickname a lot of us have given this place. You know, instead of Wardwood, Rosen et al." Missy shrugged her shoulders. "Trust me, it's fitting."

I smiled, thankful to be let in on the inside joke, but also more uneasy about my job. "Is it really bad? I mean, so far everyone seems … nice."

Missy cleared her throat and studied me for a moment, like she was seeing me for the first time. "Hey, don't worry, I'm sure you'll be fine. But … remember you're swimming with sharks." She opened the fridge and started loading water bottles onto the shelves. I wanted to ask her more questions, but I needed to get back to my desk. I felt now more than ever the urgency to keep up on my workload.

By a quarter after five, my desk was cleared, and I was on my way home. The afternoon was warm. I thought about the weekend ahead—the first weekend without Derrick in over seven years. A wisp of loneliness encircled my heart, but I willed it away with thoughts of taking Renee to see Nannie. It would be a good weekend.

When I walked into Bonnie's house, Renee came running

headlong at me, nearly knocking me over. She grabbed my leg and looked at me with adoring eyes. Bonnie smiled and shook her head. "I think she's happy to see her mama."

It was good to see Renee happy. Dropping her off in the mornings was not easy. She would cry and cling to my leg until Bonnie gently pulled her away. I lifted Renee up into my arms for a bear hug. The tenseness in my shoulders eased, and my heart felt like it would burst with love. There was much to be happy about. For a couple of days, I could let the stress of a new job go, enjoy a peaceful weekend with my daughter, and see my loveable Nannie too.

As I drove home, I glanced in my rearview mirror at Renee. She had a small smile on her face and contentedly tapped her feet together, keeping rhythm to the country song playing on the radio.

"Mommy, when we get home, can I play outside?"

I thought about the options of outdoor play at the apartment complex. There was one swing set with a teeter-totter, faded, worn, and sitting on a patch of grey bark mulch. It was not an inviting place, especially compared to the outside playing Renee had always known. It had been a tough week for her. Though she'd been a bit insecure and occasionally tearful, she had been a trooper and deserved a reward. One of her favorite spots to play was a big park off of River Road, not too far from where we'd lived. Thankfully, Derrick had never accompanied us there. It had an array of playground equipment, lots of room to run, and plenty of benches for moms to sit and watch their kids.

"How about if we stop by the park before we go home?" I asked, glancing at Renee again.

A smile spread across her face, and her eyes grew wide. "To the one we always go to? With the big slide?"

"Yes." I turned the Explorer in that direction.

"Will you go down the slide with me?" Renee looked out

the window, probably expecting us to be pulling into the park at that moment.

"Of course, I will." I chuckled at her enthusiasm. It felt good to laugh with genuine happiness, instead of faking it. I took the side-streets as far as I could before turning onto River Road to get to the park. Fitful butterflies invaded my stomach. This was close to "home." What if Derrick saw my car and followed me? He could be driving home from work right now. I shook the thought away. He usually took a back-route to avoid traffic. I couldn't let my paranoia steal the joy of this moment with Renee.

The parking lot for the park was full, so I had to find a spot on the street. The air was full of the sound of children laughing and squealing. A ring of tall fir trees surrounded the play area, so more than half of it was shaded, but it also felt protected and separate from the wide-open expanse of the rest of the park. I was thankful it was crowded. Something about it made me feel safer. Renee tugged at my hand, urging me to run instead of walk to the playground. She was soon off climbing a play structure. The benches were full. I had no place to sit, but I didn't mind. I'd been sitting most of the day. I stood in a patch of sun and watched Renee play. The way she crossed the bridge on the play structure made me smile. She was so cautious and serious about it.

A few minutes later, Renee ran up to me. "Will you go down the big slide with me now?"

I looked around, self-conscious. Most of the other parents were dressed in jeans, and some brave souls wore shorts. I was wearing a pair of slacks, black pumps and a floral long-sleeved blouse. I shrugged. At least it was machine-washable. I took Renee's hand and we made our way to the slide. Getting up the ladder in pumps was difficult, but I managed. When we got to the top platform, we stood for a moment looking at the view. Through the branches of the tall trees, much of the park was visible, as were the nearby streets. The sky was crystal blue and deepening in color with the descending sun, not a cloud in sight. I breathed deeply of the early spring air, lightly scented with the blossoms of the cherry trees that lined the road to the park.

I saw something red in the corner of my eye. I turned toward the main road parallel to the park. A shiny, red Ford truck crept down it. My heart quickened. Was it Derrick's truck? It was hard to tell through the tree branches.

"Come on Mommy, let's go down the slide!" Renee urged, obviously done admiring the scenery.

I patted her on the hand. "Hold on a second, Sugar Bug, Mommy's looking at something." I peered toward the road. The truck was getting closer. An unmistakable silver stripe lined the side of it. My heart skipped a beat. It *was* Derrick's truck. Had he spotted us on the main road and followed us here?

I plopped down at the top of the slide and tried to smile on the way down it with Renee. What would Derrick do if he found us? Renee was ready to run to the swings when we got to the bottom of the slide, but I grasped her hand.

"Come on Mommy, I want to go to the swings!" She squealed, trying to pull away from me.

"We need to go home now. There's a swing set there." I pulled her toward the car, my eyes scanning the street.

"No! I don't want to go! I want to play here." Renee screamed, resisting my grip on her hand.

Other parents smiled and turned away. I picked Renee up, and carried her kicking and crying across the park and toward my car, hoping Derrick didn't drive down the side-street where I'd parked.

My heels sunk in the grass as I took a short-cut toward

the road. Between Renee's squirming and my lack of traction, I was out of breath by the time I reached my Explorer. Luckily, it was at the end of a cul-de-sac, behind a large Suburban, making it hard to see from the main street. I fumbled with the straps of Renee's car seat, my hands shaking. After what seemed like a Herculean feat of buckling Renee in, I turned to walk around to the driver's side.

I almost made it to my door when I felt my arm grabbed. I was yanked backward. Renee looked at me through the car window with wide eyes, her mouth gaping.

I could hear her small voice through the half open door. "Daddy?"

Derrick's fingers sank deeply into my arm, making me wince. I turned to face him. This was the moment I'd been dreading for days. At least we were in a public place, which I hoped would restrain his actions. A quick survey of our surroundings confirmed there were no people on the sidewalk in the cul-de-sac, and shades were drawn in the nearby homes. Just my luck.

"You think you can up and walk away? Did you think I wouldn't find you?" Derrick's voice was low and deadly.

"I was going to tell you where we were … after you had time to think about things." My voice shook. I reached for the driver door, pulling it wide open. Derrick closed the short distance between us, pinning me against the inside of the door. Renee stared at me and her father, fear contorting her delicate features.

Derrick's breath was hot on my forehead. "Oh, I've had time to think all right. I've thought about what a low-life I married, and how much she's going to pay for thinking she can take my kid and leave without a word."

"Mommy!" Renee cried out. Her bottom-lip quivered. I instinctively reached my free arm toward the backseat, squirming against Derrick's weight.

"You're upsetting Renee," I said, my throat tight.

"I'm upsetting Renee? I think the bad parent award goes to the one who ran off. You've probably already had a man or two in your bed. Following in your good ole' mom's footsteps." Derrick's eyes were hard. I wanted to slap him. Instead, I let my body go limp, hoping he would let me go if I didn't resist.

"Leave us alone, Derrick." I forced myself to speak evenly. "When you're ready to talk in a calm and civilized manner, you can let me know."

Derrick's grip on me loosened, and I slid into the driver's seat. I reached for the handle, hoping to shut the door and push the all lock button, but Derrick's hand was firmly against the window, holding the door open. Like a deer in headlights I stared at him. What was he going to do? I couldn't imagine him seriously hurting me in front of Renee. What I could imagine was him forcing us into his truck and taking us home. I didn't even try to guess what would happen afterward. But I wasn't going back. And neither was Renee.

"You need to leave." I tried to add authority to my voice, but I felt pathetically small.

Derrick shook his head. His eyes settled on me, cold as ice, and his mouth formed a small, twisted smile. "Who's going to make me leave, Cassie?"

I cleared my throat, and took a deep breath. "I need to get Renee home and feed her dinner." Calm and logic. Isn't that what police used in hostage situations?

For a moment, Derrick looked confused. Then he removed his hand from the door. But before I could sigh with relief, he opened the back door. "Come on Renee, you're going with me."

She immediately started to cry. "Mommy?" I twisted around in my seat, reaching for my daughter in the back.

Seeing her face had turned ashen, my own fear turned to fury.

"If you don't turn around and walk away, I am calling the police." As I spoke I reached in my purse and pulled out my new cell phone. I quickly unlocked the phone and hit the number 9.

"Fine." Derrick said before I could hit the one. He stepped back, and was again at the driver's side, leaning in toward me. "I'll leave. But you're not getting away with this. I could call the police right now and turn you in for kidnapping." Derrick glanced at Renee, who was still sobbing. His eyes softened for a brief moment.

I'd already considered the possibility of Derrick calling the police. But I couldn't see them arresting me without proof of wrongdoing. I was another woman who'd left her husband with a child in tow. It happened all the time. Still, the memory of the last time the police showed up bit at me, like an annoying horse fly.

"We need to talk when Renee's not with us, and when we are both calm." I spoke softly, a peace offering.

"You'll be hearing from me again, dearie. And you're not going to like what I have to say. I promise you." Derrick stepped back and slammed my door. I jerked my hand inside to keep from having my fingers squashed. Derrick opened the back door. "I'll see you later, Pumpkin." He spoke softly to Renee. Then he closed her door and turned to me and smirked before he turned on his heel and sauntered away.

Once he was out of sight, I got out of my seat and pulled Renee from her car seat. I held her, gently swaying back and forth, the way I did when she was a baby.

"I miss Daddy." She choked out the words like each syllable hurt.

My heart constricted. How confusing this must be to her. Her entire life was ripped in two. I knew she loved her dad. But I could tell she also feared him. He scared *me*. Loving someone and being afraid of them ... the two emotions didn't belong together ... or at least they shouldn't exist together. But the truth was, for me, and now for Renee, love and fear were inseparable.

I dried Renee's cheeks with the back of my hand. "I'm sorry, baby girl." I spoke barely above a whisper. "You'll see him again. Daddy's upset right now."

Renee nodded, an ancient wisdom in her innocent eyes.

Chapter Seven

IT FELT GOOD TO DRIVE AND not be in a hurry. The air was cool but the sun was bright, promising a warmer day ahead. I'd packed a bag of toys for Renee, and she started playing on her tablet as soon as we hit the interstate. I scanned through the stations on the radio, settling on the country station that was playing an upbeat song. The music filled the car and I sang along.

I turned off the interstate shortly after Albany, heading into the trees. It'd been nearly six months since the last time I'd made the trek to Nannie's home. On one hand, I could understand why she chose a retirement home in a small, remote town. Woodhaven Assisted Living was quiet and peaceful, and Nannie loved nature. But how much could she enjoy the world from the view of her bedroom window, or in the small courtyard of the facility? Undoubtedly my practical Nannie had taken the price into consideration. I was willing to bet Woodhaven was less expensive than the retirement homes that were in the city and closer to hospitals.

We wound through the country road. State park signs marked the road to Silver Falls Park. I'd heard of Silver Falls, but never been there. It boasted ten waterfalls, all on one hiking trail. I never paid much attention to the signs before, but now they beckoned me. Maybe on the way back, Renee and I could find one of the shorter hikes to the falls.

Woodhaven looked more like a large, rambling ranch house than a care facility. The long rectangular building was set back from the quiet street. A circular driveway led to a Porte-a-chalet, which didn't flow with the rest of the building's design. Birch trees lined the manicured front lawn. I pulled into the small, mostly empty parking area at the side of the building.

Inside the building, we were greeted by a small, gray-haired woman who looked like she should be a resident and not an employee. She sat behind a dark wooden desk, the only light coming from a pale fluorescent overhead and an antique-looking desk lamp.

"We're here to see Eula Jean Bradford." Saying Nannie's full name felt odd.

The lady lifted her eyebrows and looked me up and down in quick assessment. "Oh, Eula so rarely gets visitors." As if I didn't feel guilty enough, the steady stare-down from the lady's pale blue eyes made me squirm.

I didn't like this place.

We made it to Nannie's room. I knocked on her door, then opened it and stuck my head in. "Nannie?"

"Come in." Nannie's voice was soft and welcoming.

A plaque sat on a table in the entry. It showed a cross against a sunset. Written on it were the words, "How much do you love me, I asked Jesus. This much, He said. Then He stretched out his arms and died." The familiar item from my childhood made my stomach hurt with homesickness, but I pushed past it, leading Renee into the room.

Nannie hadn't aged since the last time I saw her. The gentle curls of her dyed hair were perfectly in place. Nannie's makeup was fully done, right down to a light eyeliner, and she wore beige slacks and a pale green blouse. The light scent of Estee Lauder's *Beautiful* filled the room. Nannie was pulling herself up from a rocking chair, leaning on a cane. Seeing her broken and fragile was unsettling. I sped across the tiny room and reached out my hand to help her finish getting up. Nannie's long, cool fingers, with perfectly manicured nails, wrapped gently but firmly around my hand. Renee stood a few feet back, her lips sucked in. I knew she was longing to run to her great-grandma, but the expanse of time between visits was making her shy.

Nannie smoothed out her blouse and beamed. I wrapped her in a hug. "I've missed you so much, Nannie." My throat ached from the lump I swallowed.

She squeezed me gently. "I've missed you too. It's been too long." She patted the back of my head, something she'd done whenever I was upset for as long as I could remember. "And who is this you've brought with you? Could this be my favorite great-granddaughter?"

I turned to Renee and saw the grin on her face, but her eyes remained uncertain.

"I think Nannie wants a big hug."

Renee ran to Nannie and wrapped her arms around the leg opposite of the cane. Nannie bent to give her a hug. I flinched, ready to catch her if she fell, but she didn't. Nannie slowly pulled herself back up, and Renee beamed, eyes bright.

We settled into the cozy room. Nannie sat in the padded rocking chair. Renee sat on her lap and munched on graham crackers, crumbs falling everywhere.

Nannie asked about my job and the new apartment. When I told her about both and confessed my unease with my new boss, Nannie laughed and waved her hand at the air. "Women make the worse bosses. Keep your nose to the grindstone and you'll be fine."

"I hope so."

"It sounds like Brian likes you, and he has more weight than Cynthia."

My face burned. I knew Nannie didn't mean Brian was attracted to me, that he liked me as an employee. Even the slightest allusion to attraction and Brian made my heart race. Even *if* we were both single, he would have been out of my league.

For a moment the only sound was the crunching of

graham crackers.

"I have a new room!" Renee chirped in.

"I heard about that." Nannie's voice was cheerful. "I heard you have Cinderella on your walls."

Renee nodded, beaming proudly.

Nannie and I exchanged a look of understanding. I knew she probably had many more questions about all the changes in our lives, but now was not the time to discuss them.

"And I go to daycare and there are a lot of kids there. Even big ones." Renee bugged her eyes and puckered her mouth.

I smiled at Renee's animated storytelling. Grandpa would be proud.

Nannie's jaw dropped in feigned surprise. "Oh my! That must be fun, and a bit scary."

Renee shook her head. "I'm not scared. Mommy says I'm very brave."

Nannie pulled Renee to her chest and gave her a big hug. I bit my lip, commanding the tears starting to form in the corners of my eyes to go away. I was fiercely proud of my little girl.

We went to the dining room at Woodhaven to have lunch with Nannie, who insisted we stay and wouldn't let me pay for our lunch. The stale smell of age mixed with the antiseptic air of an institution stifled my appetite. After my turkey sandwich arrived, I realized not having an appetite was a good thing. The sandwich was bland and dry. I looked around the room of elderly people, most of whom were older looking and in worse shape than Nannie. She didn't belong here—there was too much life left in her. In my heart I collected another debt against Derrick. If he had been a different kind of husband—loving, supportive, unselfish — Nannie could have lived with us after she broke her hip. But

I knew better than to even ask. Now, I was in a tiny two-bedroom apartment and barely making enough to pay my bills. After everything Nannie had done for me, it seemed I should be able to give something back. But all I had to offer her was heartache.

Like mother, like daughter.

"Did I tell you I received a phone call from your mother a few weeks ago?" Goosebumps popped out on the back of my arms. *Speak of the devil.*

"Nope." I took another bite of my cardboard-like sandwich.

Nannie nodded, picking at her salad with a fork. "It sounded like she's doing okay. She's living with a friend in Florence."

I could see mom living in a coastal town. She loved the ocean. "Which friend?"

"Not a male one, believe it or not." Nannie piped, untethered hope in her voice.

I knew better than to get my hopes up on my mom's transformation.

"Interesting. Is she working?"

"Odd jobs, here and there. But she said she's been working really hard to stay sober. The friend she lives with has been taking her to AA meetings."

I looked at Nannie, who smiled wistfully. I knew she would never give up on her daughter. I glanced at Renee, dutifully eating her peanut-butter and jelly sandwich, sitting upright and lady-like in her favorite pink dress. I couldn't imagine being in Nannie's shoes and having a child who was an alcoholic. I refused to even entertain the thought.

"I haven't talked to her in quite a while."

"She asked how you were doing. But it was before ..."

I nodded. It was before I left Derrick. What would Mom think? I always sensed she really didn't approve of Derrick, but her opinion held little weight with me.

After lunch, Nannie suggested we go out into the courtyard to admire the landscaping and take advantage of the unseasonably warm spring afternoon. I agreed, but a familiar anxiety was building in me, an urgency to return home.

"Are you okay, sweetie?" Nannie asked.

"Yes. I keep feeling like ... I'm out past my curfew or something." I laughed, realizing how ridiculous it sounded.

Nannie lovingly squeezed my arm. "You're the captain of your own ship now."

I nodded. I wanted to say, "And what if I sink it?" but I held my tongue.

We followed the sidewalk to a bench in a small courtyard. Nannie walked slowly, relying on her cane, determination in her eyes. When we got to the bench, I held Nannie's arm to help her sit.

The courtyard was full of rhododendrons, azaleas, and other plants I didn't recognize. They were beautiful, but to me, they didn't compare to the big magnolia tree Grandpa and Nannie had at their old home, or the rose bushes which Nannie once cared for so tenderly. Renee found a small stick on the ground and dug at the soft dirt.

"Are you happy here, Nannie?"

Nannie sighed. "All things considered, yes."

"All things?" I asked.

Nannie nodded. "Part of me wants my own home, surrounded by the things your grandpa and I spent our lives acquiring. And," Nannie lifted her eyebrows. "to be left alone. Not be checked on by a nurse, not have someone else decide when and what I eat." Nannie shook her head. "And you had the pleasure of trying the food here. I want to push those cooks out of the kitchen and make some fried chicken or bake a lemon meringue pie."

I couldn't help but laugh at the image ... and I could almost see Nannie doing it.

"But I know I can't live on my own anymore. It's hard for me to walk, or do anything really, with this darn hip." Nannie patted the side of her leg, a light scowl momentarily flashing across her brow. "But you know," Nannie chirped, her face brightening, "I have everything I need here." Nannie patted my knee, a genuine smile on her face.

Another family joined us in the courtyard. A middle-aged man with dark hair pushed a wheelchair containing a frail, grey-haired woman down the walkway. An attractive woman followed, holding the hand of a little boy. They stopped at one of the benches. The three adults sat, and the boy climbed onto the man's lap. The man tickled the boy, and both women laughed as the boy jumped up, laughing, and hid behind a tree, ready to play a game of hide-and-seek.

Nannie and I smiled at the scene. I looked over to Renee, who had stopped digging. She broke the stick, a frown etched deeply on her face.

"Renee, come here." Renee got up slowly, keeping her eyes on the ground.

As soon as she reached me, she blurted out, "I want Daddy!"

I held out my arms, but she pulled away, tears falling down her pudgy cheeks.

"Why didn't Daddy come too?" Renee cried, staring at me angrily.

"He couldn't ..." I stammered, not knowing what to say. I could feel the stares of the family on the bench, and my face reddened.

"Maybe we should go inside and get ice cream," Nannie offered with the gentle, faked enthusiasm of an experienced parent. She held her hand out to Renee, who recoiled and defiantly crossed her arms.

"I don't want ice cream. I want Daddy!"

"Renee, come here now!" I hissed. This wasn't like her. If she ever misbehaved, it was at home, not in a public place—until recently, anyway.

She kicked at the dirt, messing up her sequined pink shoes and creating a cloud of dust.

I turned to Nannie. "We better go. I'm sorry."

Nannie nodded, the sparkle gone from her grey eyes.

I helped Nannie up, then grabbed Renee, who squirmed against me. I carried her into the building, trying to help Nannie at the same time, but being of little use. Renee fought against my grip, and her soft crying turned into howls of "I want Daddy!"

"Renee, stop!" I whispered, on the verge of tears myself. I patted her back and held her close. Her body relaxed a little, and her screaming turned into a soft sob.

With the help of a disapproving orderly, we made it back to Nannie's room, my arms like lead, Renee still sobbing.

"I think we should go." I wasn't sure if I was sad or angry, or both.

Nannie stood near me and rubbed Renee's back, "She may need a nap. It's been quite a week for her. For her mom too."

I looked into Nannie's eyes and saw the love there. I didn't know what I'd do without that love. We said our goodbyes and I promised to return soon. "Maybe next time we can go on a field trip." Nannie smiled and shook her head, but I saw the glimmer in her eyes.

Renee cried for the first fifteen minutes of the drive home. When I finally tuned it out, the sobbing stopped. I looked in the rearview mirror, and saw her fast asleep, mouth gaping wide. Her shoulders shuddered, and she drew in her breath, but didn't wake up. The poor thing had cried herself to sleep. Doubt made my stomach knot up. Was I doing the right thing? Would I ever know for sure?

The brown state park signs appeared on the road. Silver Falls.

I glanced back at Renee's peaceful, sleeping face. There would be no waterfalls for us today.

Chapter Eight

HALFWAY THROUGH THE SECOND WEEK OF my new job, the feeling of a routine had taken hold. After putting my packed lunch in the break room fridge, I made a beeline for my cubicle, smiling or nodding at the other secretaries I passed. The attorneys rarely appeared before nine a.m., creating a more relaxed atmosphere in the early morning.

Only one tape in my inbox. Cynthia was still dictating when I left the office the day before, so the tape was new. Keeping up with Cynthia grew easier each day. After settling in, I took a small, framed picture out of my purse. I'd bought a frame during a trip to Walmart the evening before and inserted a recent snapshot of Renee. My heart ached looking at the image, the feeling of separation tugging at my heart.

I positioned the photograph on a clear corner of my desk. Renee smiled in the picture, with dimpled cheeks and large emerald eyes full of love. She had been doing better this week. After our visit with Nannie, I worried outbursts over missing her dad would become a regular occurrence, but there had been no more tears.

I hadn't heard anything else from Derrick. When I drove, I constantly checked my rearview mirror, looking for a red truck. I didn't get out of my car anymore without glancing at parked cars. But maybe I was being paranoid. How nice it would be to not walk around fearing the worse. Soon I would have to get the courage to contact him and give him my new address and phone number. After all, he was still Renee's dad.

"Hey, sexy mama. Happy hump day." The top of Missy's face peeked over my cubicle.

Even though Missy was several years younger than me

and didn't have kids, she was the one I found myself talking to most often. Missy sauntered around the corner of the cubicle. I checked the clock on my computer screen: 7:59. Cynthia never came in before 8:05. I was safe to chat for a few minutes.

"I can't believe it's already Wednesday," I said. "This week is going fast."

"And that is a good thing, as my friend Martha Stewart would say."

I shook my head and smiled at the prospect of Missy and Martha Stewart being friends, even in theory. Then again, Missy and I were becoming friends, and we were as different as night and day.

"How are you adjusting to doing things old-school style?" Missy motioned toward the transcription machine on my desk.

I shrugged. "Not what I'm used to, but I'm starting to get the hang of it." The law office where I was employed before Renee was born had been small, and in my role as a legal assistant I felt more like a coworker of the three attorneys than a subordinate. This office definitely had a different atmosphere.

We talked about the current office gossip. The topic was Josephine, a secretary at the firm. Josephine's boyfriend, rumored to be a married man, was flying in to visit. The idea made my stomach turn, but I tried not to let it show. I was no longer a wife. These things shouldn't bother me.

"Who would want to date a married man?" Missy whispered, leaning into my desk. "I haven't dated anyone in a year, but I'm not that desperate."

I couldn't imagine Missy being desperate nor fathom the idea of why someone so beautiful and spunky would go a year without dating. Men hit on her every day. Josephine was a different story. She was average-looking and approaching middle-age. I heard she'd never married and didn't have any kids. She exuded loneliness.

Suddenly Missy straightened up. "Yes, the copier has been fixed." She said a little too loudly. "Thanks for catching the jam before it got crazy around here."

I tilted my head, uncertain what Missy was talking about, then heard Cynthia's voice, "Good morning!" She smiled warmly at Missy, then turned to me. The smile was quickly replaced by a furrowed brow.

"Cassie, did you finish the tape I left last night? I need to send it to the client ASAP."

"Oh, not yet ..." I glanced at the clock. It was 8:05. She expected me to have it finished five minutes after my start time? Even if it was a short letter—which I doubted by the pile of documents it was attached to—no one could have transcribed it in five minutes.

"I'll let you get to work," Missy said. She backed out of my cubicle, mouthing something as soon as she was behind Cynthia. I couldn't quite make it out, but it was three words and the last one seemed to start with a "B".

"I'll get right on it." I tried to sound confident and forced a smile.

Cynthia smiled back, fake as an early morning newscaster, minus the makeup and well-kept hair, and turned on her heel. I saw an apple in her hand. Based on previous tapes, I knew the next one I transcribed would include loud chomps of her eating the morning snack while she talked into the Dictaphone. Nice.

By a quarter to noon, my brain was numb and my wrists were tired. Lunch was soon, but instead of hunger, a gnawing unease grew in me. I paused, uncertain where it was coming from. I was keeping up with my work and nearing my mid-day reprieve. My mind raced to Renee, but I knew if something had happened to her, Bonnie would call right away. An image of Derrick's face, a twisted grin and cold eyes, surfaced in my mind. My cubicle seemed darker, and my heart skipped a beat. I willed myself to push through my negative thoughts and finish my work.

Lana, the firm's receptionist, appeared in my cubicle, an exaggerated expression of concern on her face. "There's a guy here asking for you," she whispered.

"What does he look like?" Blood rushed to my head, and my heart kicked into double-time.

"Tall, kind-of husky, dark-haired."

My heart slowed. Definitely not Derrick. "Okay. I'll be right up,"

"Cassie, I think it's a process server."

"A what?"

"I think you're getting served." Lana's voice sounded urgent.

I followed Lana to the reception area, unable to wrap my mind around what she had said. A man stood, tapping his foot, a thick stack of papers in his hands.

"Cassandra Peterson?"

I nodded, unable to find my voice.

"I'm personally serving you these papers on behalf of Derrick Peterson." He handed me the papers.

"Thank you," I mumbled, looking down at the papers in my shaking hands. It was a legal proceeding, that much was obvious. *Derrick Peterson, Petitioner vs. Cassandra Peterson, Defendant, Motion for Dissolution of Marriage.* I couldn't breathe.

I felt an arm around me. "Come sit down, honey, I'll get you a cup of water." Lana led me back toward my cubicle. Several pairs of eyes watched me as I walked like a zombie to my desk. I plopped down in my chair. I was geared up for angry phone calls, a loud pounding on my door late at night, maybe even having my tires slashed. But not this. The papers in my hand felt heavy, full of death.

Lana returned with a cup of water. "Take a few minutes and breathe." Her brown eyes were full of sympathy. "You don't have to read it right now. I bet Cynthia will let you go home early if you need to."

I shook my head. "I'm going to take my lunch a few minutes early." As if I could eat with this hanging over my head.

Lana crossed her arms and sighed. "You're tough, girl." I watched her walk away and knew the gossip train was about to take off.

I stared at the paper, forcing myself to concentrate. I needed to know what it said. The first page indicated Derrick had an attorney, Rachael Carmichael. I broke out in a cold sweat. He could afford an attorney. I could barely pay my rent. I breezed through the section titled "Division of Property." He wasn't offering me much, but it didn't matter. I had nothing when I married him, and I left with the only thing I'd really gained—my daughter. The next section of the document was about custody. My stomach flip-flopped. I moaned, unable to hold in my emotion. The words on the page blurred and my hands trembled. How could he?

Derrick Peterson shall have sole legal custody of Renee. The black words stood out, searing my heart. He wanted to be the caretaker of a child he had never bathed, rarely fed, and seldom put to bed? The man who worked sixty or more hours per week so he could buy his next toy wanted to be solely responsible for the needs of a child? How would he care for Renee when she was sick? He would never hear her call for him at night, as he lay in bed, passed out, drunk, and snoring.

My heart beat so loudly, I was sure the entire office could hear it. Part of me wanted to run ... to Bonnie's and pick up Renee, throw a suitcase of clothes in the back of my

SUV and take off to … somewhere. I shuddered. Add a few shots of tequila to the picture in my head and I was Mom. Was that Derrick's plan? To prove I was exactly like my mother, his prophecy of my ineptitude fulfilled?

"Knock-knock."

Brian towered over me. I sat up straight, willing myself to smile, but my expression felt more like a grimace.

The corner of Brian's mouth twitched, but his eyes showed concern. "Is everything all right, Cassie?"

"Everything except for this." I waved the divorce papers in front of me. Tears rose to my eyes. What was I doing?

"Let's chat in my office."

This couldn't be good. Did Derrick serve me at work to jeopardize my job? I envisioned his face, eyes hard as rocks, and heard his mocking laughter.

I followed Brian to his office, my head down, avoiding the eyes I felt watching me.

Once in Brian's spacious office, he closed the door behind me. The far wall was lined with windows, a view of downtown Eugene spread across them; buildings against a backdrop of low hills covered with trees. The sky was overcast and growing darker. A spring rain storm was on the way.

"Let me take a look." Brian held out his hand. I paused for a second, processing what he said, then timidly handed him the legal document.

"Have a seat." Brian nodded toward the chair across from his desk.

He eased behind his desk and began reading the divorce papers. I sat down and tried to calm my racing heart. I expected a reprimand for my personal life interfering with work, not concern or help with my situation. It felt surreal.

I tried not to watch him as he read, but my eyes kept falling on him. His brow furrowed, and he shook his head slowly. A moment later, he mumbled something under his breath I couldn't make out and flipped over the page. I played with the hem of my shirt, twisting it into a knot.

After what felt like an eternity, Brian reached the last page of the document and sat back in his chair. He rubbed his chin and stared at me for a moment. I shriveled in his scrutiny, wishing I could disappear.

"Catch me up a little, Cassie."

"What do you mean?"

Brian smiled. "I need a bit of a background to put this," he patted the paper in front of him, "into perspective."

I couldn't believe we were having this conversation. I was here to work, not to share my problems with the world like one of those reality TV shows. But I really did need help ... I had nowhere else to turn.

"We were married seven years."

Brian nodded encouragingly.

I gave him the briefest synopsis I could, leaving out the worst parts. We married young after Derrick finished college and bought a house shortly afterward. I had worked full-time until Renee was born. I explained the last couple of years had been rough. I didn't elaborate on why.

"Any infidelity, addiction, or abuse from either of you?"

My face burned. "Derrick drinks a lot," I whispered.

Brian's eyebrows lifted, accentuating the faint lines on his forehead.

"Does Derrick have any DUIs, or arrests related to drinking?"

I shook my head. Wouldn't that make things easier if he did? My world would go from varying shades of grey to black and white.

"Anything else? Did he ever hit you?" His voice was gentle.

I shifted in my seat. Was what Derrick did considered

abuse by the law? I never had bruises to hide. Not visible ones.

"No, he never hit me." Not exactly, anyway.

"Were you planning on hiring an attorney?"

"I can't afford it." I slumped in my seat.

Brian picked a pen up off his desk and grabbed a yellow legal pad. He quickly flipped through the pages again, making notes on the legal pad.

I sat without a word while Brian took notes. After a few moments, he set the pen down and put his hands behind his head, leaning back in the chair. He looked relaxed, not at all fazed by the drama of my life. "I'll see what I can do for you, free of charge."

"Are you sure?" If I had been working for the firm for a year, it wouldn't surprise me, but I'd been there less than two weeks. His offer felt overly generous, especially considering how much he charged per hour.

"Piece of cake," Brian winked. "I know his attorney. I'll give her a call. She knows full well you're entitled to half of the house. It would be ridiculous for you to agree to this. Not to mention he should be paying alimony."

"What about custody?" I asked. The money part was important, but paled in comparison to Renee's well-being.

"Custody matters get tricky. Most judges favor the mother, but there's a couple out there who don't always go that direction." Brian paused and looked away, shrugging his shoulders. "These days, it's most common to find parents sharing custody and parenting time. Fifty-fifty."

I bit down on my trembling lip. Share custody with Derrick? I might as well have stayed with him. Actually, it was even worse, because I wouldn't be there to keep my daughter safe.

"And"—Brian raised his eyebrows—"he's attached a Status Quo Order for parenting time. Has he seen your daughter at all since you left?"

I thought of the confrontation at the park. "Not really. He doesn't even know where we live. I'm not sure where he got my work address."

Brian's gaze was on me again, a mixture of compassion and calculation. "People are easy to find with a little help, especially if he knows your license number. You need to let him see your daughter when he requests it, as long as his requests are reasonable. Otherwise, you'll end up on the wrong side of this through the court's eyes."

Tears welled as I tried not to panic. "What's considered reasonable?"

Brian shrugged. "This isn't my area of expertise, but from what I understand, it's kind of an arbitrary thing. Your safest bet is to let him see his daughter as often as he wishes. At the very minimum he should be allowed to see her the amount recommended by the state for a child her age."

My mind spun with a thousand different scenarios, tumbling down a slippery slope to hell.

"Let me see what I can work out with his attorney," Brian rested his arms on the desk, leaning toward me. "But I can't represent you, technically. Think of this as a favor from a friend."

A friend? I barely knew Brian. Being referred to as his friend made me uneasy, yet honored. "Thank you," I said, but it didn't seem like enough.

Brian glanced at his watch. Before he could say another word, I got up to leave, my weak knees barely holding me.

Chapter Nine

"YOU HAVE TO TAKE RENEE THERE tonight?" Missy sat on the edge of my desk, talking between bites of a Subway sandwich. Cynthia was at a continuing education seminar, removing one stressor from my day.

I nodded and sipped my tea. Missy had brought me a sandwich, but I was too nauseous to eat. Brian had contacted Derrick's attorney the same afternoon I was served and let her know he would be filing the response in the divorce case. During the days that followed, a flurry of information was exchanged, including my address and phone number. Derrick's attorney requested a settlement conference to "negotiate matters that cannot wait for court." Brian agreed, assuring me after the fact that it was for the best, and we might be able to avoid court altogether.

"Brian said I need to take the 'highest of high roads,' which means letting Renee see her dad. Since Derrick called and asked to have her this weekend, I have to let her go. Especially since we have the settlement conference scheduled for the week after next. I have no room for objection."

"Maybe she could come down with the ... stomach flu." Missy made quotation marks with her fingers.

I shook my head. "From what Brian told me, I'd still have to let her go."

Missy rolled her eyes. "Stupid attorneys."

I nodded. "And expensive. I'm glad Brian is helping me for now, until I can find an attorney I can afford."

"I have to help my dad with some fencing on Saturday, and Sunday morning I have a photo shoot, but maybe after that we could hang out." Missy wadded up the paper wrapper of her sandwich and threw it in the wastebasket by my desk.

"I'll need to do *something* to keep my mind occupied." I hadn't allowed myself to dwell on the weekend ahead. Now it was here.

After Missy left, I kept having to rewind the tape I was transcribing because I couldn't focus on the words. The last time I had such a heavy feeling of foreboding was the night before Grandpa died. It was the first time I had the recurring dream of us at the base of the mountains, him directing me to the path curving into darkness. I woke up in tears the next morning, an ache in my heart. Renee was a year old at the time, and even her two-toothed smile didn't lighten the weight on my chest. Nannie called before I'd finished my first cup of coffee. In the wee hours of the morning, Grandpa had succumbed to the cancer he'd battled for seven months. Though I wasn't surprised, the news brought me to my knees. It was like something was ripped from me and dragged through a hole in the atmosphere, to a place I couldn't see and would never reach.

Knowing I had to let Renee go with Derrick for an entire weekend was an eerily similar feeling. I pushed my foot on the dictation pedal. This was not death I was facing. It was Derrick. He probably wouldn't be able to handle taking care of Renee for the entire weekend. In the past I couldn't even get him to watch her while I went to the grocery store. He would probably have me pick Renee up before Sunday night. I was sure of it. Almost.

Brian appeared at my desk halfway through the afternoon. I bit my lip, waiting for bad news. Was my premonition of doom being fulfilled in the form of an unexpected turn of events in the divorce case? Brian held his hands behind his back in a business-like pose, but the corner of his mouth twitched, and his eyebrows rose slightly.

My shoulders lurched, and heat ran up my neck.

"I noticed you don't have a calendar." His voice was smooth, concerned. He brought his hands forward and put something on my desk. It was a wall calendar, the twelve-month kind, with pictures. On the front cover was a picture of a massive waterfall with white walls of water crashing against a rocky bottom.

"Working here hasn't changed your love for chasing waterfalls, has it?" Brian's tone was light, but his deep brown eyes held a warmth that touched my heart. He remembered the response I had pulled out of nowhere during my interview — that my favorite pastime was hiking, especially to waterfalls. I opened my mouth, searching for a thoughtful response.

"Oh ... thank you." Who was I to think I could come up with an intelligent response? I could hear Derrick in my head, an echo that I couldn't silence. *You're a dimwit Cass. Face the facts.*

Brian's gaze flicked to the calendar. "I hope it inspires you to enjoy life a little ... despite everything else." He put his hand on my shoulder, giving me a quick, gentle squeeze.

I nodded, fighting back the tears wanting to creep into my eyes. "I'm sure it will."

After an uncomfortable three seconds of silence, Brian excused himself and left my cubicle. I flipped the calendar over and saw miniatures of the waterfall pictures it contained. Flipping it back to the front, I read the title: "Waterfalls of Oregon." These weren't random photographs of waterfalls. They were all ones I could see for myself. My skin tingled, and for a moment it was as if Grandpa were standing behind me, looking over my shoulder.

I'll always be with you.

For a moment, the darkness inside me was washed away by a wave of peace.

By the time I pulled into Bonnie's driveway to pick up Renee and take her to Derrick's, I was almost convinced everything would be okay.

Bonnie's living room was full of kids, and her blue-heeler, oddly named Red, was asleep in the middle of the room. He raised his head when I walked in, then went back to sleep.

Renee ran to me. "Mommy!" She nearly knocked me over with her embrace. "Guess what? Today I found a caterpillar!" Her face was full of the innocent delight that belongs only to children. I squeezed her tight, soaking it in.

Renee's hair was a mess, there were dirt stains on her shirt, and red goo crusted in the corners of her mouth — probably ketchup. Bonnie didn't keep things neat and tidy, and she let the kids be kids. I would need to clean Renee up before going to Derrick's. He wouldn't look favorably upon Renee's appearance. Hopefully I never had to have him pick her up at daycare. He would demand she be put in a place more sterile and structured, like the environment where he'd grown up.

"Renee is very excited about seeing her dad tonight." Bonnie walked across the room.

"Yeah." I didn't know what else to say.

Bonnie studied me for a moment, a hint of concern in her eyes. "You should do something for yourself this weekend. Try to enjoy it."

My heart softened at Bonnie's motherly concern. I didn't know how to tell her what my fears were. Even if I had words, I wouldn't say them in front of Renee.

"She'll be okay." Bonnie said softly.

"I hope so." Soon enough I'd know if Bonnie was right.

Around the corner from Bonnie's I pulled over, grabbed

baby wipes and a brush, and cleaned Renee up. She complied with a smile on her face, feet tapping against the seat.

Renee's backpack sat beside her, filled to the brim with clothes and her snuggly. Derrick had requested I send half of her clothes with her. "You left nothing here," he had said during our tense telephone conversation, "like you planned on never bringing her back. I'm sure the judge will like to hear about that."

I had wanted to respond, "I wonder what the judge would think of your drinking?" But I knew better than to poke at that hornet's nest. Derrick hid his drinking, and his temper, as well as I'd hidden my scheming to leave him. Of course, I had no proof. Now I had to let Renee spend a weekend with him. Would it be better if I went back to him? I shuddered at the thought, like stepping over a rotting, dead animal.

No, I wouldn't go back.

After Renee looked presentable, we continued to Derrick's house. I parked on the street, not in the driveway. My heart pounded in my chest. I wasn't sure what I was more afraid of, leaving Renee or facing Derrick. I couldn't let him see my fear. He was like an animal who sensed weakness, and weakness fed his fury.

Renee was bouncing in her seat. "We're home!"

My stomach clenched. It never occurred to me that for Renee, this house was still home.

I got Renee out and grabbed her bag. In a flash she was gone, running for the front door. "Renee, wait!"

I ran after her, leaving the car door ajar. I caught up with her and grabbed her arm as she reached the house and turned the door handle. "Wait for Mommy."

Renee pulled and squirmed against my hold. "I want to see Daddy."

The door swung open. Derrick stood in the entryway, chin high, his full lips in a tight smile. Renee broke from my grasp and threw herself at his leg, hugging him tight. I swallowed the lump in my throat.

"Hey, kiddo." Derrick ruffled Renee's hair. He hadn't seen her in over two weeks, and this was the depth of his affection, a pat on the head. What was she, a dog?

I handed him Renee's Disney princess backpack. Derrick took it and waved it in my face, within a quarter-inch of my nose. "Doesn't look like half of her clothes are in there." The condescending tone in his voice made me feel right at home and sick to my stomach at the same time. No one talked to me in such a way at work, not even Cynthia. It struck me that until now, I didn't realize how demeaning Derrick's tone was. Now I realized how small and insignificant I felt, and I couldn't wait to be out of his presence. What I couldn't shake, what froze my feet and squeezed my chest, was the fear. I was leaving Renee with this jerk for an entire weekend. I didn't want to set him off.

"You don't have to return any of the clothes in the bag, just her stuffed bunny. She can't sleep without it. I'll bring more clothes when I pick her up."

Renee looked at me with questioning, wide eyes. "You're leaving?"

Derrick set the backpack behind him, keeping a death glare on me the entire time. He didn't need to say a word. I had never explained to Renee that she would go alone to her dad's this weekend. How could I have assumed her innocent four-year-old mind would understand I couldn't stay too? Now, her proclamation of, *we're* home took on an entirely different meaning. I was so wrapped up in myself and my own pain, I didn't see her misunderstanding.

I kneeled down, eye-to-eye with my daughter. "Sugar Bug, it's going to be you and Daddy this weekend. Mommy can't stay."

Tears welled up in Renee's eyes. "But I want you to stay home with me."

A piece of my heart broke off, piercing my chest.

"I can't." I choked out the words and squeezed Renee's hands. She pulled away and dropped her chin to her chest. Two large tears dropped to the polished wooden floor.

"Nice job, *Mommy*." Derrick's voice from above fell on my head like acid rain. I reached out for Renee to give her a reassuring hug, but in one fell swoop Derrick picked her up. I jolted to my feet, desperate to hold my daughter.

"Say 'bye to Mommy." Derrick's voice took on a chilling, child-like tone. Renee buried her head in his shoulder. He smirked, a gleam in his eyes, and continued in the child-talk. "You'll see Mommy on Monday. 'Bye-bye Mommy. Have fun."

The door closed in my face, followed by the soft clink of the deadbolt latching.

A simple wooden door separated me from my child, but it may as well have been an ocean. One fragment of hope claimed its place inside me. I would see Renee again. She would forget about being angry at me. Someday she would understand. I told myself these things as I walked to my car.

Climbing into the driver's seat, Derrick's last remark hit me. "You'll see Mommy on Monday." We never discussed exactly when Renee would be returned to me. We had agreed that I was dropping her off and picking her up. Derrick hadn't asked where her daycare was, so I assumed I would pick her up at his house Sunday night. Wasn't that the end of the weekend? My knuckles turned white as I gripped the steering wheel and stared at the house I used to call home. Was Renee snuggled in her daddy's arms? Had she stopped crying? Up until a few weeks ago, she had never been away from me longer than a couple of hours. Now I was facing the possibility of her being gone three nights in a row.

I rested my head on the steering wheel, my eyes too blurred to drive. "God, please keep my daughter safe." I said the words out loud, surprising myself. With baited breath, I waited for an answer, but the only sounds were the hum of a passing car and the chirping of birds in the nearby plum tree. I imagined Renee in her old room, waking with a fever and calling for a glass of water, and Derrick passed out, oblivious to her cry. I imagined Derrick, with no one to coax him into responsible behavior, driving drunk with Renee in his truck, and running a red light. Without me there to take his anger out on, I imagined Derrick calling Renee unspeakable names, wounding her soul.

I squeezed the steering wheel tighter. "Please, God, she deserves better. I beg you."

As a child, I had pleaded with God for help. Alone, late at night, my mom at a bar. I was eight-years-old, hungry and scared of the dark. I had called out to God then, and a peace had settled over me, a calming reassurance all would be well. Morning came and my mom had come home. But it was months later, after many more nights alone and missed meals, before Grandpa and Nannie brought me to live with them. I never understood why God let me suffer so long. Loneliness became a part of who I was, as concrete to me as my blue eyes and the unruly waves of my auburn hair.

With everything in me, I wanted to protect Renee from that pain, but the law left me with no choice. If I didn't let her go with Derrick this weekend, I risked the chance of losing the custody battle. A short period of pain to prevent a long period of pain. What kind of God forced a mother to choose the lesser of two evils?

How could I put my hope in a God like that?

I wiped my eyes and turned the ignition. A week and a half from now, Brian would represent me in the settlement conference. He would stand up to Derrick. I remembered Brian's brown eyes, the sincerity in his voice when he reassured me he could handle Derrick's attorney. Tall with broad shoulders, confident in himself. He could keep my daughter and me safe, and fight for us in a maze of paperwork and legal landmines.

Driving away from Renee and the home that had been ours for over seven years, I remembered Brian's hand on my shoulder, squeezing me gently.

I would put my hope in Brian.

Chapter Ten

WHEN I WALKED INTO MY APARTMENT, the silence gave me chills. No squeals, no cries, no questions. The drapes were drawn, making the living room dark and tomb-like. In Renee's room down the hall, the setting sun shone through the thin drape on her single window, infusing the bedroom with a soft light. My chest tightened. I darted across the living room and shut the door.

I wanted answers from Derrick. Maybe I had misheard him. Maybe he didn't say Monday. Regardless, once we had a parenting plan ironed out, this would not happen again. Unless he got custody. I shook away the thought. I'd wait until right before Renee's bedtime and call to say goodnight.

Twenty minutes later I sat on the couch in yoga pants and a t-shirt, eating a Lean Cuisine and watching the news. The food settled my stomach and the multiple catastrophes and scandals the newscaster reported helped me forget my own troubles. The weather forecast for the weekend was scattered showers, perfect weather for the wasteland of a weekend ahead of me.

At 7:40 p.m. I dialed Derrick's number. The line rang four times, then it went to voicemail. I heard my voice, instructing the caller to leave a message. He hadn't bothered to change the greeting since I left? I didn't leave a message and a few minutes later I called again. No answer.

Why didn't he answer? All the made-for-TV movies I'd seen flashed through my mind. Derrick had packed up Renee in a car that wasn't registered in his name, and he was on his way to Mexico. No, he wouldn't go to such an extreme. Derrick loved his possessions too much to leave them behind. I tried his cell number and was greeted by

Derrick's business voicemail.

I re-dialed Derrick's cell again at 9:00 p.m. He never answered. *He's trying to upset you. Renee is fine.* The voice in my head—one that sounded like a calmer, saner version of my own—reassured me. I would have to try again in the morning.

I couldn't sleep past six a.m. but forced myself to wait until eight before trying again. This time, Derrick answered.

"I want to talk to Renee." My heart was racing. Not enough sleep, two cups of coffee, and anxiety didn't go well together.

"She's still in bed." Derrick spoke in a muffled voice, his version of a whisper.

"I tried calling last night. Several times. You never answered."

"I didn't want you to upset her. You did enough when you dropped her off."

My heart ached, remembering Renee's look of betrayal when I told her I wasn't staying. "One of the reasons I tried calling was to explain to her why I didn't stay and to tell her I was sorry." Tears fell down my cheeks, and I brushed them away with the back of my hand.

"I explained it all to her. Don't worry, I'll always make sure she knows the truth."

The truth? Derrick wouldn't know the truth if it strutted in front of him adorned in bright neon lights. I squeezed the phone in my hand, wanting to throw it across the room.

"When Renee gets up, have her call me." I gritted my teeth.

Derrick snorted. "I'll let her know you called, but I can't make her talk to you if she's still upset."

My stomach clenched. I wanted to head right to Derrick's house and bring Renee home. "Then I'll call later when she's up. If you don't answer, I'll come over and talk to her in person."

"Okay." I could hear Derrick moving on the other end of the line, then a sound in the background like a door opening. "You go ahead and try." His voice was louder now, and I realized he must have walked outside. "But let me tell you something. I kept a record last night of how many times you called, and let's just say it was excessive. Not to mention you dropped Renee off here in an upset state because you were too self-centered to explain to her that you left our home because you wanted to be single again. If you show up, I'm going to call the police and have you arrested for harassment." I envisioned the small, menacing smile on Derrick's face

I stood and gulped for air, forcing myself to stay calm. It was as if Derrick was in the room instead of across town, his accusing gaze burning me down into a pile of ashes on the floor. Was he right? Could he have me arrested for harassment if I went to his house and demanded to talk to Renee?

Paralyzing doubt swirled through my mind. If I went to Derrick's, Renee would be subjected to the confusing and scary drama of the police knocking on the door, even if they didn't arrest me.

"I'm not putting Renee through that." My voice was shaking, but I pushed through. "I will pick her up tomorrow at five p.m."

"Who says you're picking her up tomorrow? You can pick her up Monday morning at eight. That's the end of the weekend in my book."

Derrick was going to make sure this weekend was as hard on me as possible, and there was nothing I could do about it without a written parenting plan in place. He knew as much. I could hear it in his voice.

I closed my eyes and breathed in. It wouldn't be this way

forever. The sun would set and rise twice, and I would see Renee again. "I need to pick her up earlier than that. I have to be at work at eight."

"Not my problem," Derrick retorted. "You either pick her up at eight Monday morning or pick her up from daycare after work. Which, by the way, is information you need to give me. I don't even know who you're leaving my child with during the day."

I sat on the couch again, an elephant of defeat on my shoulders. "Fine. I'll pick her up at eight." I pushed end before Derrick could respond. Explaining to Cynthia my reason for being late on Monday was preferable to dealing with Derrick. Right now, I didn't care if I lost my job, my apartment, anything. All I wanted was to hold my daughter and tell her I loved her. The ache inside my chest was more than I could bear.

By the time evening rolled around, all the laundry was done, I'd shopped for food and stocked the cupboards, and even taken a brisk walk. From my apartment, I could hear people coming and going in the parking lot. Laughter and light-hearted conversation wafted in through the living room windows I'd opened for fresh air. The days were getting longer and warmer despite the drizzle outside, and the promise of spring was strong. The excitement of it tugged at me, beckoning me to be part of the buzz, to see what lay beyond the walls of my apartment.

I needed to get out of here. But to where?

I picked up my cell phone. No missed calls. It was seven o'clock. If Renee was home with me, she'd be in the bath, playing with her Little Mermaid doll and singing to herself. I glanced at her bedroom door again. Loneliness encircled me, a murky ocean intent on swallowing me into extinction. I stared at my phone, desperate for light.

I would try calling Renee one last time, despite the

consequences. Before I could hit the green button, my phone buzzed with a call. I looked at the caller ID. It wasn't Renee, or Derrick. My heart sank, but I answered the unfamiliar number anyway.

"Hey, what's up?"

I struggled to recognize the female voice on the other end of the line. "Um ... not much. What about you?"

"You know, same old thing. Fighting off the men, taming the horses."

I laughed as much in relief as I did at Missy's joke. "Sounds like you're busy!"

"Yeah, but the good news is my modeling gig for tomorrow got cancelled."

My heart lightened with hope. "What are your new plans?"

"I'm glad you asked. I was thinking about our conversation the other day. You know, about auto maintenance. How about if I come over for coffee in the morning and show you how to change the oil in your Explorer?"

I chuckled at the idea, imagining us under my SUV in the parking lot of my apartment complex.

"Seriously!" Missy chortled. "You'll have every single guy worth knowing wanting your phone number if they see you working on your own car. It's a sign of independence."

I wasn't convinced of the sex appeal of changing my own oil, but I was honored Missy was willing to take her time to help me. Plus, it would use at least a few hours of the never-ending weekend, not to mention save money on auto maintenance.

"I think that sounds great!" I hoped my voice held more enthusiasm than doubt.

Missy showed up Sunday morning in attire quite different than what she wore to the office—faded jeans, a

George Strait t-shirt, and laced brown work boots. Her hair was pulled into a tight pony, and she wore little make-up. She came with all the tools, including the oil and filter, and a bag of maple bars.

"Do you want a cup of coffee?" I offered, motioning Missy to come inside my apartment.

"Sure." Missy grinned.

We sat at my small kitchen table, sipping coffee and nibbling on our pastries. "How are you doing?" Missy asked.

I shrugged. "Getting up on a Saturday morning and having nothing to do kind of reminds me of when I was a teenager."

"So, like, a couple of years ago?" Missy smirked.

"It seems like a hundred years ago. I can't even remember who I was back then." I shook my head. "But I was obviously very stupid."

"Don't be so hard on yourself. You ended up with a great kid, and you're still young and smart." Missy gulped down the rest of her coffee. "Just don't remarry too soon. Take time to remember who you were and figure out who you are now."

Missy was right. A fresh wave of loneliness swept over me. "You are wise beyond your years, Missy Langdon."

Missy shrugged. "I'd say I'm a quick learner. Speaking of which, are you ready to take another step on the Ms. Independent path and get that oil changed?"

Changing the oil was not as easy as Missy suggested it would be. Though she guided me through the process, I struggled to remove the oil drain plug from the pan and didn't enjoy the feel of laying on hard blacktop. When we wiggled our way out from under the hood, a light rain was drizzling over the edges of the carport covering. Missy admitted changing the oil in my Explorer was more difficult than changing the oil in her Dodge truck. "But on the bright side, now you know how. You'll never have to pay for an oil change again."

I nodded in agreement as I rubbed the spot on my back where the towel I had laid on failed to protect me from the black pavement.

"So, what's your plan for the rest of the day?" Missy gathered up her tools.

"I don't have any." The rest of the day stretched before me, as unremarkable as the last.

Missy put her tools in her truck, then leaned against the hood, her arms crossed, staring at the walkway. "What you need is a hobby."

"Yeah, I know. Though Lana says what I need is a boyfriend."

Missy looked me straight in the eye. "That's the last thing you need."

I nodded my agreement, not wanting to admit part of me longed for romance—my life with Derrick had been barren of any real caring for so long.

"You need to find something you can do when Renee's not here. Maybe then you can kind of look forward to the times she's gone and something that takes your mind off all you're going through."

I shook my head. This is where Missy could never understand me. I wasn't the mom who looked forward to her kid being gone for an entire weekend, especially with someone like Derrick. Nevertheless, I pondered out loud, "Something I can do when Renee's not here ... oh, I know, I'll take up napping and deep cleaning." I smiled at my own joke. Missy didn't look amused.

"I noticed the calendar you put up at your desk ... the one with the waterfall pictures. You like the outdoors, right?"

I nodded, remembering the epiphany I had when Brian gave me the calendar. "I would love to see all the waterfalls in the calendar. Maybe that sounds stupid."

"No. It's an awesome goal!"

Raindrops splattered on the walkway. "I will, this summer."

Missy rolled her eyes. "Don't be such a tourist. You're an Oregonian, a strong and free woman. Rain can't stop you."

"I suppose. Maybe next weekend." Hiking alone in the rain sounded more desolate than adventurous.

"Have you ever been to Trestle Falls?"

"Nope." Though I'd spent most of my life in a state with abundant rivers and falls, I had been to only a handful.

Missy unfolded her arms. "All right then, let's go."

PART TWO: THE FALL

Deep calls to deep
In the roar of your waterfalls;
All your waves and breakers
Have swept over me.

Chapter Eleven

MISSY INSISTED ON DRIVING HER TRUCK to the waterfall. She said Trestle Falls wasn't too far south, about twenty-five miles east of Cottage Grove. "It's pretty remote and not on the way to anywhere—definitely not a Mommy-I-need-to-pee tourist destination."

I chuckled at her description. "You really don't like tourists, do you?"

"Nah, I don't mind tourists, unless they're from California."

"Oh, well I can totally understand that." I decided now was not the time to tell her I'd spent a few years of my early childhood in northern California.

The low rumble of the diesel engine filled the cab, mixed with a pre-recorded country music show blaring from the radio. It wasn't long before we found ourselves on a narrow two-lane road. The houses were farther apart, and what constituted a dwelling changed. Brick and mortar homes gave way to manufactured homes, then to faded, mildew covered trailers encircled by rusty cars. One trailer we passed was missing an entire wall, revealing its contents for the world to see. It wasn't long after passing it Missy had to swerve to miss two tires sitting in the middle of the road.

"Hard to believe people live like this, isn't it?" Missy jerked her head toward the debris littering the landscape.

"Yeah." We drove by a row of tiny dilapidated houses on the creek's edge. Any of the places we passed could've been a place my mom and I called home when things were at their worst. Soon we were past the trailers and in the forest, seeing campgrounds instead of piles of junk.

Finally, we reached a pullout before a bridge. When I got out of the truck, I was thankful I had brought a warm hoodie; the air was much cooler up here in the shade of tall pines. The rain had let up, and the only water falling was intermittent drops from the rain-soaked trees overhead. We crossed a bridge that went over a creek. Trestle Creek, according to the sign next to it.

"Have you come here a lot?" I asked. Missy had been unusually quiet on our drive.

"I've been a couple of times. It's been a while."

"It's beautiful." I took in my surroundings—the hum of the creek, the sigh of the breeze moving through the top limbs of the trees. No cars or people in sight. Before we were married, Derrick and I often spent early Saturday mornings fishing, allowing us to be alone, away from the vigilant watch of my grandparents. Something about those mornings and the fresh scent of the river captivated me like a kid on Christmas morning. The thrill of a fish taking the bait, the adrenaline of hooking them and reeling them in. It seemed like a million years ago.

Missy stopped. "Here's the trailhead. Are you ready for this?"

A faded sign read, "Upper Trestle Creek Falls 2.1 Miles," The trail cut into the steep hill, zig-zagging its way up, but I couldn't see too far because of the density of the forest.

"Let's do this."

Missy led the way, and though she didn't move fast, I had to push myself to keep up with her on the steep trail. I had hoped to absorb the tranquility of nature, but instead I focused on breathing and ignoring the burning muscles in my legs. If I was going to start hiking, I needed to get in better shape.

Missy looked over her shoulder, then came to a halt. "Let's stop for a few minutes." She grabbed the phone out of her back pocket and took pictures of the trees towering over us. I inhaled the life-rich air. Time outdoors was one of the things I missed from my younger years. Everything changed when Derrick started the car dealership, eager to make a name for himself and support our family. It did support our family. But it also seemed to be the precipice that came between us.

He's an alcoholic. Nannie's voice echoed in my head. He was. But he hadn't always been one.

We continued up the hill. With every step I took, the world and its problems faded farther away. The trail was narrow, steep, and dotted with roots and rocks. Keeping myself from stumbling and falling down the hill, breathing and forcing my legs to keep going—these became my sole purpose.

We came to an indent in the path marked by a narrow fall of water making its way down the moss and fern covered hill. I stopped to take my first picture.

"And there you have it, the infamous Trestle Falls." Missy boomed, her arms spread out in a showman-like style.

"Seriously?" I'd expected something a little bigger.

Missy grinned. "You think I'd bring you all the way here for that?"

We continued along the path. Moments later, I heard the soft roar of rushing water. The trail had leveled out, so I was able to breathe easier. I picked up my pace, keeping in time to my quickened heart rate. We came upon a bend in the trail, and I saw the real waterfall through the trees. Missy smiled, seeming to share my excitement. We hurried ahead until we had a better view. The trail became muddy and we maneuvered around several rocks. We found a little alcove with water dripping off its edge and stood in its shelter to watch the falls.

Mesmerized by its raw beauty, the fall held me. For a moment, nothing but the sound of rushing water filled my head. No echoes of Derrick's voice. No worries about paying bills. Not even concern for Renee or Nannie or what my future held. Was this what peace felt like? I stepped closer, letting the water from the alcove drip on my face, hopeful the drips would conceal my tears.

Missy put her hand on my shoulder. "Ready to head back?"

I smiled, and the sensation tingled my cheeks. "I'm going to take a few pictures first." Like a mother with a newborn baby, I snapped pictures with my phone from every angle I could, hoping to capture the beauty I saw with not only my eyes, but with my heart, my soul.

Renewed, we made our way back to Missy's truck. "That's one down." Missy quipped when we reached the bottom of the trail. "You should get a scrap book or something and keep track of the falls you see."

"Good idea." I was short of breath even though the trek back had been all downhill.

"You only have to go to one a month to see every fall on the calendar in a year." Missy talked with ease, not at all winded by our adventure.

I stopped to take a deep breath. Sweat beaded at my brow, and my shirt was starting to stick to my back. I removed my hoodie, tying it around my waist. Goosebumps rose on my arms, but I wasn't cold. "I want to see them all, not only the ones in the calendar."

"All of them? Like every waterfall in the world?" Missy teased.

Waterfalls had never been a part of my and Derrick's outdoor adventures. Our time always centered around fishing or hunting—the things Derrick enjoyed most. This seeking of waterfalls, this was new. It was *mine*. Was this what Bonnie meant when she talked about having a passion? Something that called to me and I would pursue, even if it didn't make sense to everyone else?

"I'm going to see every waterfall in the state of Oregon." The confidence in my voice surprised me.

Missy raised her hand for a high-five. "Now that's a strong, independent woman talking."

Chapter Twelve

YOU'RE A PIECE OF WHITE TRASH, like your good ole' mom. Derrick's voice in my head was louder than the Lady Antebellum song blasting on the country station. I bit down on my bottom lip and focused on the road. The clock on the radio read 7:55, too early on a Monday morning for most of the attorneys to have shown up, but late enough for Lana to be answering the phone. I pulled over around the corner from my former home.

"Wardwood, Rosen, et al." Lana's sultry voice held an edge.

"Lana, it's Cassie."

"Hey, girl, what's going on?"

I paused, debating what to tell Lana. "I'm going to be late getting in this morning because—"

"Monday morning flu, huh?" Lana sounded amused.

I shook my head. Such simple problems were not a part of my life. "No. I'm fine. But my daughter isn't. I need to figure out daycare before coming in. Please tell Cynthia I *will* be there, but a little late."

"Oh, honey, I'm sorry to hear that." Lana's voice turned syrupy.

"I've got to go. I'll see you soon." I hung up before Lana could squeeze in another question.

I inched my Explorer up to Derrick's. Was it possible to drive on eggshells? If I showed up even one minute early, he may get angry and do God-knew-what. On the flip-side, it was morning and he should be sober.

My stomach hurt when I rang the doorbell, either from lack of food or anxiety. Maybe both. Derrick opened the door. He was clean-shaven and wearing a light blue dress shirt that added a grey tint to his birch-leaf green eyes. It seemed incomprehensible those eyes could hurt me. The light, bitter-sweet scent of Giorgio Armani wafted on the air, the same cologne he'd worn when we met twelve years ago. My voice caught in my throat. No wonder Derrick had swept me off my feet when I was barely seventeen. He was handsome in a boyish, innocent way—in a movie he would've played the boy next door, not the evil villain.

"Renee's almost ready. Hang on a minute." Derrick disappeared down the hall, leaving the front door wide open. I hesitated on the front step. Should I step inside?

Cartoons played on the TV in the living room, and the smell of eggs and toasted bread filled the air. The aching in my stomach increased. The house drew me in, like Goldilocks when she came upon the house in the woods. Before I could take a step in, Derrick reappeared with Renee. If hearts sang, mine was belting a love ballad. Renee's hair was combed back into a crooked ponytail, and her backpack was attached to her back, matching the pink outfit she wore. Her face was clean and she was neatly dressed.

"Hi, Sugar Bug." I held out my hand, inviting Renee to join me outside. Instead of rushing to me the way she did when I picked her up after work, Renee furrowed her brow and grabbed Derrick's dark grey trousers.

"I don't want to go to daycare." Her bottom lip puffed out defiantly.

Derrick patted her on the head. "It's time for Daddy to go to work. You need to go with your mother."

"Renee, honey, you love going to Bonnie's. It's fun there." I squatted down to Renee's eye level and tried to ignore the creepy feeling I was kneeling before Derrick.

"I want to stay here! I don't want to go." Renee's quivering lip gave way to a sob.

I pulled Renee into my arms, breaking her grip on

Derrick's pants, and stood. She was a resistant weight in my arms.

"Daddy will see you soon. Very soon." Derrick spoke to Renee but stared straight at me. "Have fun dropping her off this morning." There was a glimmer of a secret in his eyes and I didn't know what to make of it. I didn't have time to play Derrick's games. I turned away without a word and walked to my car. When I glanced back at the house, Derrick was still standing in the doorway, a smirk on his face.

I carried a tearful Renee into Bonnie's. The living room was full of sleepy kids watching Sesame Street, or quietly playing with Legos at the play table in the dining room.

"Looks like she had quite a weekend." Bonnie greeted me with a sympathetic smile.

I tried to return the smile, but my facial muscles seemed to be overtaken by the heaviness in my chest. "I guess she did."

"It's pretty typical for weekend dads not to enforce a bedtime."

"So this is something I need to get used to?" I couldn't hide the bitterness in my voice.

"It'll get better." Bonnie's reply was gentle. "I've been doing this long enough to see families go through this in several different ways. Most of the time, as long as Mom and Dad remember to keep their focus on the best interest of the child, it works out fine. The kids adjust."

I remembered Derrick and the smirk on his face when I left. He didn't seem concerned about Renee at all.

"And what if he …. they … don't keep their focus on the child?"

Renee shifted in my arms, and Bonnie put her hand on Renee's back and rubbed softly.

"Then you have a problem." Bonnie met my gaze. She held out her arms. "Here, I can put Renee down for a nap. You're running late."

I reluctantly handed Renee over. I trusted Bonnie, but I didn't want to go.

"Oh, wait. She'll want her bunny. I'll be right back."

I ran out to the car and grabbed Renee's backpack out of the backseat of my car, noticing how light it was. I unzipped it. No clothes in sight, only a few empty candy wrappers. I unzipped the front pocket, hoping Peesh, Renee's beloved snuggly, was in it. But he wasn't there. Anger flared in me, hot as fire. Didn't Derrick know Renee needed her snuggly, especially now? I hurried into the house. Bonnie was returning from the bedroom, her arms empty.

"He didn't return Renee's snuggly," I blurted out.

Bonnie nodded, unfazed. "That's too bad. But Renee will be okay."

I nodded, but my shoulders tightened. How would I get Renee's bunny from Derrick? I didn't see her falling asleep tonight without it.

"Sometimes it's best to have two comfort objects, one for each home. There's less stress in going back and forth that way." Bonnie spoke softly.

"I guess Renee and I will be going to Walmart after work today." I pushed the thought of my checking account balance out of my mind.

Psst! I turned toward the whisper. Missy was standing on the other side of the fax machine by my cubicle. I took a fax cover sheet and a few stray papers off my desk and met her at the machine.

"How'd it go this morning?" Missy whispered.

I shook my head. "I survived." I shuffled the papers in

my hands.

"Glad to hear. I didn't want to use my 45 and a shovel this week." Missy took the tray out of the fax machine and filled it with new paper.

The weight on my shoulders was too great to laugh at Missy's joke. "I should get to work. I have plenty of it."

Missy looked over at my desk and shook her head. "Yeah, Cynthia looks ready to pounce on someone already this morning."

Great. "We'll have to catch up at lunch, but probably not today."

"Sure thing. I'm holding you to it." Missy pointed her finger at me in mock reprimand.

I spent the morning pounding away at the keyboard. In my peripheral vision I caught glimpses of Lana walking by a couple of times, but I ignored her. I wanted to track down Brian and get his input on the situation with Derrick, and find out what to do if he demanded to have Renee again this coming weekend. My stomach turned at the idea of going through two weekends in a row without my daughter.

I took off my headphones and sent the document I was working on to the copy room printer. Brian's office was in between my cubicle and the copy room—if I took the long way around. I ambled down the hall. Brian's door was open. My heart pounded against my chest with such force my ribs ached. I stopped three feet away. No, I would simply walk by Brian's door and hope he saw me. If he didn't, then I could try to catch him later, or get Missy to throw a hint at him to come talk to me.

I kept my head high and stared straight ahead to breeze by Brian's office. I held my breath as I walked by the open door—and suddenly found myself stepping on a foot and ramming into a chest. He had emerged unexpectedly from his office.

I stepped back quickly, tripping over my own feet. Brian caught me by my elbow, saving me from falling. Speechless, I looked up. Brian's eyes sparkled.

"I'm … sorry … so clumsy." I fumbled for words.

"It's a good thing you're petite." Brian let go of my arm. The faint scent of him, a woodsy smell with a hint of leather, radiated from the warmth of his body, inches from me. Part of me wanted to fall into him again, to feel his strong but smooth hands against my skin.

"I was heading to the copy room. It's been a busy morning."

Brian raised a brow, and the corner of his mouth twitched. Had I said something wrong? Or was he amused I literally ran into him?

"How was your weekend?" he asked.

"Actually, kind of rough. Derrick had Renee, and I didn't get her until this morning."

The look in Brian's eyes shifted from amusement to concern. I held my breath, hoping to hear him say, "Don't worry, I'll take care of this," even though I knew it was ridiculous and impossible. The way he stood there, towering over me in a non-threatening, protective way made me feel like a little girl playing the part of the damsel in distress.

Brian looked at his watch. *Probably a gift from his wife.* The sobering thought severed the magnetic pull, and I stepped away, creating a more appropriate distance between us.

"I have a meeting in five minutes. Let's talk after lunch."

"Thank you." My throat hurt, probably from swallowing my pride. I turned on my heel to head to my desk.

"Cassie."

I stopped and looked over my shoulder at Brian, whose amused smile had returned.

"Yes?"

"The copy room is that way." Brian motioned to the hallway behind him.

"Oh … yeah." I tittered, attempting to make light of my mistake. "I guess I need to dye my hair blonde."

I avoided eye contact as I marched by, but sensed Brian's gaze on me. Once I was a few steps past him, I glanced over my shoulder. Brian was still standing in front of his office, arms crossed, watching me. I met his gaze for a second. The amusement they'd shown moments ago was gone, replaced by a dark somberness.

Brian sat behind his mahogany desk, the top of which was barely visible beneath file folders and yellow legal pads. I stood inside the doorway, hesitant to sit down, not wanting to assume we were going to engage in a long conversation.

"Please close the door and have a seat." Brian motioned to the chair across from this desk.

I did as he asked, my pulse racing. Once I was seated, Brian leaned forward, resting his elbows on the desk.

"What did your soon-to-be ex-husband do this weekend that is causing you concern?"

I inhaled deeply. Desperate to not appear hysterical or immature, I tried to remain emotionless and factual as I relayed the events of the weekend, the things Derrick had said.

Brian listened intently, and when I was done, sat back in his chair. He looked at the wall to his left, tapping his fingers on his desk. I followed his gaze to a framed print he had on the wall of a man rock-climbing, with the caption, "The question isn't who is going to let me, the question is who is going to stop me."

Brian turned his focus to me. "He's playing you, Cassie."

"What do you mean?"

Brian leaned forward again. The lines in his brow betrayed his age. I wondered exactly how old he was. Maybe Missy knew.

"It sounds to me like Derrick is trying to get you to react in such a way that he can use your actions against you in court. He's hitting you where it hurts the most—by using your daughter as bait."

My blood turned to hot lava. Part of me had feared this, had known it, but didn't want to believe. Derrick loved Renee, didn't he?

"It's quite common," Brian said. "He probably doesn't even realize he's doing it, exactly."

"Then what can I do? I mean, can he get Renee again this weekend?" I clenched my hands in my lap.

Brian's eyes darkened. He was looking at me the same way he did during my interview. It was almost like he was assessing my abilities. "Like I've said, this isn't my area of expertise. I can only tell you my view from dealing with other legal matters, what I've seen my divorce clients do, and ..." Brian spread his hands in front of him, "my viewpoint as a man."

My shoulders slumped. I knew what I was going through was not his area of expertise, but he was all I had.

"So, what is your opinion, then?"

Brian pushed away from his desk and stood up. "I have two theories." He walked over to the window and stared at the skyline, his hands in his pockets. "I'm not sure you'll like either one."

I bit my bottom lip. The serious tone in Brian's voice was not making me feel any better.

Brian turned from the window and his eyes had changed again, playful and confident once more. The furrow in his brow was gone, and he returned to his desk and plopped down in the chair. I was on the edge of a cliff with an unyielding wind at my back.

"You can play a version of the 'let them eat cake' game. Let Derrick have Renee all he wants. When he sees it's not getting to you, and when he experiences how much work it is to take care of a young child on a regular basis, he'll voluntarily take less parenting time."

I shook my head. "I can't. I don't trust him."

Brian shrugged. "Like I said, you're not going to like either option."

"What's plan B?" It had to be better than plan A.

"Frustrate his every move." There was a deadly seriousness to Brian's voice, sending a chill down my arms.

"How?"

"Stay within the boundaries of the law, but don't give in for even one second where you don't have to. He had Renee last weekend, so it's perfectly logical for you to have Renee this coming weekend."

"I don't have to let her go?" I practically jumped out of my chair. I liked this plan better already.

Brian held up his hand. "There's more to it."

I slumped. Of course there was.

"Call him tomorrow and ask him if he wants to pick Renee up for a midweek visit on Wednesday or Thursday."

"But—"

"And if he doesn't agree to either of those days, then he doesn't get to see her at all. Period. If he calls later and says he wants to see her this weekend, you tell him he missed his chance for a mid-week visit and the coming weekend is yours."

Should I try to explain to Brian that Derrick would do more than say a few disparaging remarks if I told him no to anything? "What if … he's really mad … and shows up at my apartment? He found me at the park one time and—"

"Did he threaten you? Did he hit you?" Brian sat straight

up, his brow furrowed.

"Well, no." Derrick hadn't hit me, he'd squeezed my arm and pinned me against the car door. But it didn't leave a mark and it only hurt for a few moments. I knew that wouldn't count. Part of me wished he would punch me, leave a bruise. Then the pain he caused would make sense to everyone else.

"Then if he shows up uninvited again, tell him to leave."

"What if he doesn't?" I met Brian's eyes, hoping he could understand, for a moment, the fear that enveloped me when Derrick was angry. We looked at each other in silence, his brown eyes comforting me and yet causing butterflies to stir within me at the same time.

"Then you call the police." The soft finality in Brian's voice silenced the questions I still wanted to ask.

Chapter Thirteen

NANNIE WAITED FOR US ON A bench under the Porte-a-chalet in front of the retirement home. Renee ran and wrapped her arms around Nannie's pastel blue skirt. "There's my favorite little girl." Nannie beamed, her grey eyes sparkling. I held my arm out to Nannie, helping her to the car. She patted my hand. "And there's my favorite big girl."

I smiled and kissed Nannie on the cheek, breathing in the scent of her bath powder. The delicate fragrance reminded me of being Renee's age and playing dress up with Nannie's clothing and jewelry. Those were the comforting type of memories I wanted Renee to gather, not ones of drunken fights or being afraid.

My heart swelled with thankfulness for the day. Monday night I had done as Brian suggested and called Derrick to offer a mid-week visit with Renee. Derrick had not answered so I left a voicemail. He never returned my call. Picking Renee up from daycare on Friday afternoon was like hearing the sound of hundreds of coins dropping out of a slot machine.

We arrived at Nannie's church in time for the ten a.m. service. I expected the church Nannie attended to be the classic small-town white church with a steeple. To my surprise "The Hope of Stayton" met in the cafeteria of the local grade school. Folding chairs were set up in rows, and a small band consisting of a keyboardist, a guitarist, and a drummer were playing when we arrived.

Nannie, Renee, and I found a set of three seats near the back. Renee reached for me, crawling on my lap. She surveyed the cafeteria with curiosity. No more than seventy people filled the room, and they ranged in age from newborn to Nannie's age. A table with coffee and cookies lined one wall. Another table with coloring books and markers sat in the back, and a couple of kids not much older than Renee were coloring. The relaxed mood was welcome, a different atmosphere than I remembered from the church I attended with Nannie and Grandpa when I was growing up.

The music soaked through my will to simply go through the motions. The lyrics described someone who was struggling, not someone who had it all figured out. I set Renee in her chair, stood up and attempted to sing along with the words on the screen, but emotions welled up inside me and made my voice crack. When the music ended, I settled with a thud in my seat.

"Can I go color at the table?" Renee whispered in my ear. I glanced toward the back. A girl about Renee's age had joined the boys.

"Yes," I said. "But be quiet when the preacher is talking."

Renee ran over to the table, and I cringed as the clacking of her little heels echoed in the small cafeteria. Nannie smiled, her eyes bright, and patted my knee.

"Good morning!" The preacher greeted the church, and everyone greeted him in return, a few with an "Amen!" Nannie wasn't exaggerating when she said her pastor was young and handsome. He couldn't have been over thirty-five years old and dressed semi-casually in slacks and a polo-style shirt. He had short blond hair, spiked on top. Dark, thick eyebrows accented his soft blue eyes. He sat on a stool as he spoke into a microphone, like he was talking to a group of friends.

After the initial announcements, the pastor began his sermon. "Imagine you're travelling west, you hit Salem, then keep going until you get to the coast, hop on a boat and sail all the way to Japan," A few giggles sounded from the audience. "You keep going around the globe by car or plane or mule. Whatever's available." A light wave of laughter rippled through the room. "You keep going and next thing you know you're in New York, and after you stop for a Corned Beef and Pastrami sandwich you hitch a ride and finally end up here in Stayton." The preacher scanned the congregation. "At what point did you stop going west?"

A middle-aged man in the audience shouted out, "You didn't!"

The preacher smiled. "That's right. No matter how far west you go or for how long you keep trucking along, you're still going west." The preacher paused, a wistful smile on his face. "West never meets the east. They are always opposites."

I concentrated on the story, grasping at the preacher's point.

The pastor stood and paced the front of the room. "That is how far God removes our sins from us, no matter what those sins may be. He casts our sins so far away, He doesn't even remember them."

Several in the room nodded agreement.

He continued. "And the amazing thing with God is, He doesn't stop pursuing us, no matter where we go. In His great love, He longs to find us and bring us home, to forgive and forget our sins."

His gaze fell on me, and goose bumps rose on my arms. I glanced over at Nannie and saw tears formed in the corners of her eyes. She reached into her purse and pulled out a Kleenex.

Soon the musicians were up front again, playing a soothing song while the preacher offered those seeking God or forgiveness to come forward for prayer. Several made their way up to the front, where others greeted them and then prayed.

Nannie turned to me, her eyes now dried by the tissue she had slipped back into her purse. "We should stay a bit so you can meet Pastor Matt."

"Umm ... don't you want to go out to lunch? I'm sure Renee is starving." A tinge of guilt poked at me for using my daughter as an excuse to leave. Did the members of Nannie's church know I was separated? Or would their first question to me be, "where's your husband?"

Nannie turned in her seat, looking at the table of children. Renee had a crayon in her hand and a smile on her face as she colored a page. "It doesn't look like she's starving to me. Besides, there's plenty of cookies left on the hospitality table."

There's no getting out of this. One person after another came up to Nannie and greeted us. Nannie introduced me with pride and motioned toward Renee as an introduction to her great-granddaughter. Nannie had made a home for herself at this church. My apartment—my life—was desolate in comparison. I pulled out my phone to check for missed calls or text messages. Nothing.

"Mrs. Bradford, who are these lovely ladies sitting with you?" This voice I recognized. I looked up from my phone to see the preacher, Pastor Matt, as he took a seat by Nannie. Renee ran up to us at the same time and climbed onto Nannie's lap.

"This little princess right here is Renee, my great-granddaughter." Renee made eye contact with Pastor Matt and giggled at the charismatic man.

"And the beautiful young lady sitting next to me is my grand-daughter, Cassie." Nannie beamed. Her happiness gave me courage to hold out my hand.

"It's nice to meet both of you." Pastor Matt smiled and shook my hand.

"Likewise. That was a great sermon, Pastor." It seemed like the appropriate thing to say.

Nannie nodded agreement.

Pastor Matt chuckled. "Well, I'm glad you liked it. But please, call me Matt."

A woman came up and beckoned Matt's attention. He rose and excused himself. "I hope you'll come visit us again, Cassie."

I smiled and nodded. Who knew? Maybe I would.

We drove to the retirement home for lunch. "So, did you like the church?" Nannie asked.

"It was nice." It had been nice, despite my discomfort with being in church.

"Pastor Matt is a wonderful man. My heart breaks for him, though. He lost his wife six-months ago. She had an aggressive form of cancer."

"That's terrible." Thinking back, I had seen a note of sadness in his otherwise peaceful, easy-going countenance.

Nannie nodded. "I'm not sure how much longer he'll stay in Stayton. I pray for him every day."

My jaw tightened. Why would God let such a horrible thing happen to a man who devoted his life to Him?

"I'm surprised he even wants to keep pastoring." Bitterness oozed from my words.

I felt Nannie's gaze. "Cassie, honey, the bad things that happen to believers isn't because God's punishing them. It breaks God's heart more than we can imagine. But He always finds a way to work all things for our good."

I sighed, not ready for a religious conversation with Nannie. "Well, I hope He can turn the sandwiches at the retirement home into something good, because I'm starving."

"Mommy, can we stay longer?" Renee looked up at me with hope-filled eyes. I turned to Nannie.

"Let's sit and visit a bit, but then it's naptime for Nannie." Nannie smiled at Renee and patted her shoulder.

"And I bet this young lady will be taking a nap in the car on the way home."

Back in Nannie's room, I checked my cell phone. Two missed calls from Derrick. My heart quickened. What would he badger me with now? I set the thought aside to visit with Nannie. We chatted about safe things—my job, the other residents at the retirement home. We steered clear of talk about Derrick, or my mom. Part of me wanted to know if she'd heard from my mom, but then, why should I care? Mom obviously didn't care about me.

Nannie's perspective of her peers made me laugh. In her mind, she would never be one of those "old-timers." Renee entertained herself by exploring the tiny living space, looking at old photographs and memorabilia.

The sound of clanging metal stopped me in mid-sentence. Renee stood on a chair below a shelf that held a few mementos. A music box, now playing a broken melody, lay on the floor beneath her.

"Renee!" Nannie reprimanded.

I jolted up and took Renee off the chair. The music box had opened and spilled its contents, which consisted of a heart shaped piece of wood. I set Renee on the bed and picked up both the box and the piece of wood. The lid to the music box sat ajar. I attempted to close it but the loosened hinge kept the box from closing all the way. The erratic melody slowed, then ceased. The box was made of metal, with an intricate design of roses along the sides, and an engraved blue bird in a cage on the top. I had vague memories of the box from my childhood. It had been kept in a glass curio shelf in the dining room, along with delicate wine glasses which were used on special occasions. I had never seen the wood heart. The wood was smooth, almost glass-like. Someone had spent a lot of time sanding it to perfection.

What a strange thing to put inside a music box.

"I'm sorry, Nannie!" Renee's tearful apology came from behind me.

Nannie sat motionless in her chair, tears welled up in the corners of her eyes. "Is it broken?" she whispered.

I returned the music box to its shelf. Renee's eyes were wide and her face ashen, tears on the verge of falling. A reprimand could wait until we were on our way home. I sat on the bed and pulled Renee onto my lap. "The hinge is loose, but I bet it's fixable ... I'm sorry, Nannie. I can have it repaired."

Nannie shook her head, "No. It's okay. I never listen to it anymore." She smiled, but I could tell it was forced. Nannie reached out to Renee. "Don't worry, sweetie. Accidents happen. Come give Nannie a big hug." Renee jumped off my lap and ran to her great-grandma. Nannie embraced her, but kept her eyes closed.

"That music box has been around as long as I can remember. I don't think you ever told me where it came from." I didn't want to pry, but Nannie's response had my curiosity piqued.

"Oh my goodness, let's see. I've had it since before your mother was born, Cassie. A good friend gave it to me."

"What about the wooden heart? It's quite unusual."

Nannie looked different, guarded—an expression I didn't associate with her.

"The wooden heart ..." Nannie looked away, a touch of a smile in her eyes. "One of my best childhood friends gave that to me."

Before I could ask another question, Nannie spoke to Renee. "I think its naptime, sweetie. All this fun has worn Nannie out."

Renee made an exaggerated frown-face, and Nannie kissed her forehead. Before saying our good-byes, I took the mysterious box off the shelf. "I can't let this stay broken. I'm going to see about getting it fixed."

Nannie's brow furrowed and her hands fluttered. "Well, I suppose. But not if it's too much money. Like I said, I don't listen to it anymore. It sits on the shelf, unused."

Clearly Nannie didn't want to share any more about what it meant to her. Maybe when I came up to visit without Renee, she would be more forthcoming. After getting Renee situated in her car seat with snacks and her tablet ready, I checked my cell phone again. Now I had six missed calls, and one voice message. They were all from Derrick.

Time to head back to reality. The sobering thought mixed with the image of the broken music box and the wooden heart, creating a weight in my stomach. I wasn't ready for another week of my new reality, but whether I liked it or not, it waited for me.

Chapter Fourteen

"TODAY'S THE BIG DAY." MISSY HANDED me a Snapple iced tea. I'd taken advantage of Cynthia's long telephone conference with a client to have an early lunch. Other than the two of us, the breakroom was empty.

"I don't think I'm ready for this." Butterflies did acrobatics in my stomach. In only a couple of hours Derrick would arrive with his attorney. Brian and I had met once since I nearly ran him over in the hall, and we discussed the details of the conference. Brian had assured me the conference was an informal meeting to establish a temporary parenting plan until we went to court. Telling me not to worry about facing Derrick and discussing the future of my only child was like telling a guard dog not to bark at the mailman.

"Well, I can't wait to meet Mr. Wonderful." Missy's eyes twinkled mischievously. "What's his favorite beverage? I can put a little something extra in it, make sure the meeting's cut short by him running to the little boy's room."

"I think *I* need something to calm my nerves."

"Charlie keeps a fifth of Brandy in his desk. Maybe I could sneak you a shot."

Charlie was one of the founding partners of the firm. I wondered if he had a drinking problem. Crazy what some people could accomplish despite an addiction, while others were made homeless by their choices. What a hazy line, and one that had woven its way into my entire life; one I didn't want in the fabric of my daughter's life.

"No brandy for me. I'll stick with my tea."

"Knock-knock." Brian stood at my cubicle, dressed in a crisp navy-blue suit. "Let's chat in the conference room while we're waiting for Mr. Peterson and his attorney." Without waiting for my reply, Brian turned and walked toward the main conference room.

I followed him, willing myself to be strong. Today needed to be victory, a blanket to wrap around my fears of keeping my daughter safe.

"I think we've gone over your position on this case pretty well, but I want to make sure we're on the same page and play this out right for the meeting." Brian handed me a yellow legal pad and pen. "Have a seat."

I sat at the conference table and wondered if I was supposed to take notes. I wrote the date down on the paper, an old habit from my days at the previous firm I worked for.

"Don't write down what I tell you, simply listen." The sternness in Brian's voice almost made me drop my pen.

"Cassie …" Brian lowered his voice and leaned in close. "The notepad is for you to jot down notes for me during the conference. Sit up straight and don't let anything he says affect you."

I blinked away the tears that erupted in the corner of my eyes. The tenderness radiating from Brian was a stream of water to my dried-up heart.

"That being said," Brian straightened in his chair, "I want to treat today as practice for court. From what I've heard about Mr. Peterson, he's not going to agree to anything reasonable unless his attorney talks him into it."

"But today he has to agree to something, right?" I couldn't continue with the wishy-washy parenting time until the hearing.

Brian laughed. "He doesn't *have* to agree to anything, but if he doesn't at least make some concessions today, it's going to look bad for him in court."

"What do I need to do?"

"First of all, no matter how much Mr. Peterson may misrepresent the truth or taunt you, don't say anything in return. When you're asked a question, say only enough to answer the question. Nothing more."

I nodded. Keeping my mouth shut wasn't new to me.

"If I have an issue with the question being asked, I'll ask for clarification. If you don't understand the question or are not sure how to answer, I want you to paraphrase the question back to the person asking."

I nodded again, but my hands were shaking.

"If you have a question for me during the conference, jot it down on the legal pad, and push it toward me." Brian set his hand on mine. The intensity in his gaze stopped the breath in my throat.

"Do you have any questions?"

I had a million questions, but none Brian could answer. I cleared my throat. "No."

Lana appeared in the doorway. "Ms. Carmichael and her client are here."

Brian stood. "I'll show them in. Go ahead and bring in coffee."

My heart pounded against my chest as I waited for Brian to return to the room with Derrick. I stared at the picture of the mountains on the wall, the same one that had inspired my off-the-cuff reply to Brian's question about my hobbies. Hiking and waterfalls—an answer inspired by a recurring dream of my grandpa. If only Grandpa were with me now. Derrick never mistreated me in front of Grandpa and was never so vile to me before Grandpa died. But more than that, I had never felt as certain of anyone's love as I did of my grandparents'.

"Right this way." Brian's baritone voice interrupted my thoughts. I turned toward the doorway as Derrick entered. He was wearing a grey V-neck sweater over a white dress shirt, the collar neatly tucked down, and crisply pressed black slacks. His hair, which was thick and unruly when it got long, was freshly cut close to his scalp, and his green eyes were crystal clear.

Brian motioned for Derrick and his attorney to sit across from me, and I fumbled through the formality of introductions. Ms. Carmichael was middle-aged and slightly overweight, with dark hair and black glasses. When I shook her hand, she looked me directly in the eye and did not smile. I wondered what Derrick had told her about me.

Brian took a seat next to me. "As we discussed on the phone, the goal for today is to address the status quo order regarding custody and parenting time." Brian opened the file folder in front of him and picked up a pen.

"Yes, our position is your client does not have the right to remove Renee from her home. Yet she did so without even giving my client the courtesy of a phone call." The frown lines on Ms. Carmichael's face deepened.

"My client had her reasons for doing so, which I'm sure we will discuss in detail at the hearing."

Derrick snorted, and his attorney patted his arm, hushing him like a mother with a child. "Whatever her *reasons* were, it was no excuse for her to abandon her husband and their home, and it is reprehensible, under the circumstances, that she denied my client time with his child." Ms. Carmichael lowered her chin and looked at me over the rim of her glasses. "And that is also something we will discuss at the hearing."

All the blood in my body seemed to rush to my stomach. Derrick smiled at me tightly, a cat playing with a half-dead mouse.

Brian waved his hand and rolled his eyes. "The 'he said she said' reasons for the divorce aren't relevant to our purpose for today. The focus today is on their four-year-old daughter and what is best for her until this issue is in front of a judge." Brian tapped his pen on the folder in front of him. "And this would also be a good time to discuss alimony. My client is prepared to file her own pro se motion. But I think it would be cost-effective for both our clients if we come to a temporary agreement on these issues today."

I held my breath, ready for Derrick to explode, but he only glared at me. I found it interesting how he wouldn't look directly at Brian. Was he intimidated by him?

Ms. Carmichael shifted in her seat and scribbled on the notepad in front of her. She pushed it in front of Derrick. He started to speak, then narrowed his eyes and looked away. A moment later he scribbled on the legal pad with such force I could hear the pen's marks on the paper.

Ms. Carmichael cleared her throat, then spoke to Brian. "We didn't come prepared to discuss alimony—"

"This is an informal conference." Brian shrugged. "We could spend the next half hour discussing how we think the Oregon Ducks are going to do this year."

I sucked in my cheeks, stifling a smile.

"I'm sure my lovely soon-to-be-ex-wife would love to waste our time since she's probably paying you in favors instead of with money, but some of us have to actually earn a living."

The room fell silent and my face burned. Ms. Carmichael's mouth gaped open, but she recovered quickly and leaned over to whisper in Derrick's ear. I stared at the table, mortified and unable to even venture a glance at Brian.

Ms. Carmichael straightened in her chair. "We can discuss alimony after we discuss Renee's living situation and parenting time."

Brian nodded. "Fair enough. The parenting time should be pretty straight forward."

Ms. Carmichael pushed a document across the table toward Brian. I tried to read it as it passed by me. It looked like a parenting time schedule. "Renee should be living at the only home she has ever known during this time. The consistency would be best for the child. Ms. Peterson can have parenting time every weekend."

Brian tapped his pen on the table, a crease in his forehead. "I would like to ask Mr. Peterson a few questions."

Ms. Carmichael nodded. "Of course. I will have follow-up questions for your client as well."

Brian leaned forward slightly toward Derrick. "Mr. Peterson, how much have you been involved in the daily care of your child?"

"I've been very involved." Derrick met Brian's eyes briefly, then turned his focus on me. He was self-assured again, and there was something in his expression I couldn't read.

"Oh? So how many times have you given Renee a bath? Or stayed up with her when she was sick?"

Derrick shrugged. "I don't really keep count."

"Can you give me an estimate? Less than five? More than 100?"

"Look, I work for a living. Cassie was a stay-at-home mom. She did that stuff ... except when she had her breakdowns. Then, if I hadn't been there, who knows what would have happened to Renee."

"What the—" I started to rise. Brian put his hand on my shoulder. I wasn't supposed to say a word. I had to sit and listen to Derrick make up incredible lies. I grabbed the hem of my shirt and pulled on it.

"Let me get this straight—you're asserting Ms. Peterson has emotional breakdowns?"

Derrick nodded. "Yeah. I tried over and over to get her to go see a psychologist. I even went to marriage counseling with her a few times, hoping she'd figure out she needs help. She probably hasn't told you, but mental illness runs in her family."

With a shaking hand, I scribbled a note for Brian, who was making his own notes on the document Ms. Carmichael had given him. I pushed the notepad toward him. "HE IS LYING!"

Brian nodded, but kept his gaze on Derrick and leaned back in his chair, looking slightly amused.

"So ... you're telling me Ms. Peterson has a mental illness severe enough to cause breakdowns, yet you were fine with leaving Renee with her all day?"

Derrick snarled, finally looking Brian in the eye. "What was I supposed to do? And she never physically harmed Renee, but she did neglect her. I'd come home and the house would be a mess, and Renee would be dirty and still in her pajamas. She'd come running to me and say she was hungry. Then I'd find Cassie staring at the T.V., or locked in our bedroom, all the lights out. When I'd confront her about it, she'd scream and throw stuff at me."

It was getting increasingly hard to hold my tongue. How could Derrick tell outright lies without even flinching?

"That's an interesting story, Mr. Peterson. Do you have any evidence to back it up?"

Derrick looked right at me, a glint in his green eyes. "There is record of the police visiting our house. Of course, I didn't want my daughter to see her mom dragged off to jail, so I covered for her. But I'm pretty sure the police knew what was going on and could probably testify to as much."

My boiling blood turned to ice. Something slipped in me, a feeling I recognized from previous fights with Derrick. I held onto the edge of the table, afraid I'd fall off my chair from the swirling thoughts in my mind.

Brian's gaze was locked on Derrick. Everything Derrick

said didn't seem to even cause him to flinch. "Mr. Peterson, this isn't a courtroom. Your assertions are not being recorded, and there is no judge or jury to impress." Brian shot a judgmental glance at Ms. Carmichael. "I'm sure your attorney has informed you of such."

Ms. Carmichael leaned forward, the table cutting into her arms. "Mr. Peterson is simply stating his concerns, which is the reason he filed the status quo order. He is deeply concerned about the safety of his daughter."

"You mean *their* daughter, don't you Ms. Carmichael?" Brian nonchalantly crossed his arms. "You know as well as I do, there are no compelling factors at this time to give temporary custody to either party."

I came out of my freeze and turned to Brian, about to ask him what he was doing, but a quick dart from his eyes silenced me. I slumped in my seat, defeated.

Derrick leaned over and whispered something in Ms. Carmichael's ear. She nodded, and Derrick sat back in his seat, his face unreadable as stone. I focused on the table. I couldn't look him in the eye. If I did, I wouldn't be able to hold myself together another moment.

"My client is willing, albeit with great hesitation, to agree to a temporary order recognizing joint custody with Ms. Peterson and implementing the standard parenting plan for a four-year-old."

Brian didn't flinch. "There's more than one 'standard' parenting plan for a four-year-old Ms. Carmichael. We're meeting here to clear the waters, not add more mud to them."

Ms. Carmichael sighed, opened the manila folder in front of her, and flipped through the pages of a document. She creased the corner of a page, then handed the packet to Brian. "I know this isn't your area of expertise, Brian, but there are three basic options. We are proposing a variation of option B, which is designed for parents who have both been actively involved in the child's day-to-day care."

I scribbled on the legal pad, engraving the paper with my pen, and pushed the pad toward Brian. *He's never been "actively" involved!*

Brian nodded at my note but didn't respond. He studied the packet Ms. Carmichael handed him, then flipped through a few pages and handed it back. "We'll concede to your proposed plan for the interim." Brian turned his focus to Derrick—he was like a pit bull staring at a chihuahua through a wire fence. "But please advise your client this is a legally binding plan, and Ms. Peterson will not hesitate to have it enforced to the full extent of the law."

Derrick turned to me, his eyes like lasers. "Goes both ways. You're not going to get away with the stunts you've pulled in the past."

"I've never—" Brian grabbed my arm. I was going to explode from held-back defenses before this meeting was over.

Ms. Carmichael frowned and opened her small briefcase. "I'm assuming you will accept service on behalf of your client?" She handed a document to Brian. Derrick made a noise, half laugh, half grunt. His tight smile made my stomach turn.

The fine lines between Brian's brows deepened as he scanned the papers. What did the papers say?

"I see we've moved on to the immediate financial issues of this case." Brian smoothly pulled a document from under the folder in front of him and pushed it across the table. Ms. Carmichael scanned it, then pushed it toward Derrick, along with the legal pad she was taking notes on. Derrick's ears and the muscle in his jaw twitched.

Ms. Carmichael cleared her throat. "My client and I will need time to look over this document before we agree to anything."

Brian shrugged. "As long as you have it to me by the end of tomorrow, I won't file a motion and order to show cause."

"This is ridiculous." Derrick swiped the paper away with his hand and turned toward me. "You're not getting away with this."

What had Brian presented to Derrick's attorney? Now Derrick was about to explode.

Ms. Carmichael pushed herself up from her seat and motioned for Derrick to do the same. "Please advise your client she needs to provide Mr. Peterson with the name and address of Renee's child care provider before any order will be filed."

"We will get that to you by tomorrow." Brian stood, towering over the rest of us, "Go ahead and draft a proposed custody and parenting order, and send it to me for review. I'd like to get it filed before the end of the week. I'll be watching for the signed agreement tomorrow."

The meeting was over, and I wasn't sure who had won.

Nannie was waiting to hear how the settlement conference went, but I waited until after I put Renee in bed to call her. Partly because I didn't want Renee to hear the conversation, partly because I was trying to make sense out of it myself, and, I dreaded telling her things she wouldn't want to hear.

"What is Plan B?" Nannie's voice was higher than normal.

"It basically gives Derrick visitation every other weekend from Friday night to Sunday evening, and every Wednesday night."

"That's ridiculous. What about his drinking?"

"I know, Nannie. But I don't have proof that he drinks excessively, and the state is really big on equal parenting rights for mothers and fathers. But this is a good-enough-for-now plan to get us through until the hearing, which should be within the next few months."

Nannie was silent for a moment, then sighed. "This isn't what I prayed for, but we need to trust God. He has a plan."

Tears burned my cheeks. How could God's plan involve putting my daughter at risk? Nannie's faith was beyond my comprehension.

"The good news is Brian is seeking temporary alimony and child support and is certain I will get it." It was the one silver lining in the day that I could offer.

"Good! What comes next? Is Brian preparing for the hearing?"

I stared at my lap. There was no more good news to convey. "Brian can't represent me at the hearing. He said I need to find an attorney who specializes in divorce and custody."

"Oh ... but don't you need quite a bit of money to hire an attorney?"

Quite a bit. That was putting it mildly. "Yes, but I may be able to find one who will wait to be paid until the divorce settles." It was theoretically true. No need to burden Nannie with a problem she had no ability to remedy. I didn't tell her about the financial restraining order that prevented Derrick and me from accessing our joint accounts.

After brief small talk, I wished Nannie a good night. I needed my sleep to be at my best for work the next day.

Now more than ever, I needed my job.

Chapter Fifteen

I SPREAD MY WATERFALL WALL CALENDAR out on my desk and pulled off a sheet of notebook paper to write down the names of the falls I might be able to visit over the weekend. I would need something to distract me. The signed temporary orders had been exchanged. The parenting plan was legally in effect. Renee would be going to her first required weekend stay with Derrick. I was due to receive my first alimony and child support check, for a whopping $800, on the first of the following month. Derrick always had tricks for making it look like he made less than he truly did when he filed our taxes, and now he was using that skill to pay me less than I was actually due.

Brian said when it came time for the hearing, things would be looked at with more scrutiny. I barely survived on my salary, and the modest addition to my income still left me unable to hire an attorney, especially after the costs of daycare. So far, all of the calls to attorneys had been fruitless. I couldn't find any who would take my case without a significant retainer. The knots in my stomach multiplied at the rate of rabbits. May 5th was circled in red on my calendar. I had a mere five more business days to find an attorney.

"Good morning, Cassie." I jumped at the sound of Cynthia's voice. I looked at her non-smiling face and furrowed brow, then glanced at the clock: 7:57 a.m. I still had three minutes until I was officially on the clock.

"Good morning." I pushed the calendar aside and smiled with all the warmth I could muster.

"I wanted to stop by and let you know the deadline for filing the Draker Response is today, so we need to make it top priority this morning."

I nodded. "No problem."

Cynthia glanced at the calendar, then turned her focus back to me. "I won't have a lot of time for revisions, so you should have one of the other secretaries look over the pleading before you bring it back to me."

My heart skipped a beat and blood rushed to my cheeks. Was she saying my work was inadequate? "Um ... I will."

Cynthia inhaled, threw her shoulders back, and put on the most fake smile I had ever seen. "Well, time to get to work. Have a great morning!" She turned and left.

Maybe you should have one of the other secretaries look at it. Cynthia was basically saying my work was inadequate. If my work was not up to par, then how long would I have my job?

Halfway through the afternoon, I paused the tape I was working on and slid the headphones down to rest on my shoulders. The cool office air soothed my tired ears. I'd skipped lunch and ignored Missy's attempts at small talk. I needed a quick break. I reached under my desk and fumbled inside my purse for my cell phone, the cord of the headphones stretched to their limit.

Knock-knock. I jumped, hitting the edge of the desk. I clutched the back of my head and squinted against the sudden pain.

"Didn't mean to surprise you. Are you okay?" Brian's hand was on my shoulder, his voice low and soft.

"It's not your fault. I was trying to reach my phone without taking my headphones completely off." I forced a smiled, remembering the last time Brian had surprised me and I had stumbled into him. He probably thought I was the clumsiest person on the face of the planet.

"You know, you are allowed to take breaks around here. It's actually the law." Brian slowly removed his hand. My skin tingled, and I sucked in my breath. I couldn't let my mind go there. "Attorneys don't like to break the law." Brian winked at me.

I gazed at Brian's face, trying to read his intentions. Deciding he was playful, I smiled and forced a little laugh. "I think I'll plead the fifth on my break-taking habits."

Brian shook his head but was still smiling. "The reason I stopped by was to see if you've had any luck finding an attorney."

The familiar sense of dread washed over me. "No. I haven't."

Brian frowned. "Have you checked with family and friends about getting a loan?"

I nodded, not wanting to explain that my family basically consisted of one grandma in a retirement home and an alcoholic, destitute mother. My only friends were my current coworkers. My heart pinched, and I fought off the urge to feel sorry for myself. I rubbed the tension in the back of my neck.

"Let's have a meeting in my office in five minutes. I'll buzz Cynthia and let her know I need to steal you for a moment for an assignment."

"I'm working on a deadline right now. I don't think she'd be too happy."

The playful look left Brian's eyes, and he crossed his arms. He stared at the multi-colored industrial carpet for a moment, seemingly irritated. "All right, I don't want to step on Cynthia's toes."

I nodded in agreement.

Brian tilted his head. "It'd probably be better if we meet after work. Are you free this evening?"

My heart skipped two beats and I tried not to look surprised. "Well, no ... I mean no, I'm not busy. I'm free. Renee will be going to her dad's so ..."

"Perfect. Let's meet at The Good Old Days Grill at 6:30."

I stumbled for words. "So, um, are you going to tell me how to file the response or ..."

Brian looked over both of his shoulders, then leaned over and whispered, "Cassie, don't say anything to anyone about this, but yes, I'm going to help you." His dark brown eyes met mine. They held a confidence foreign to me, and something else I couldn't identify.

Don't say anything to anyone. Why did that one statement keep re-playing through my head? I desperately wanted to talk to Missy about it, but it was impossible at work without taking the chance of others hearing. Besides, Brian had said not to tell anyone. I was certain he'd explain when we met, then I could call Missy afterward and talk to her about it.

The restaurant Brian suggested surprised me. The Good Old Days Grill was an old burger and fry dive way on the eastern side of Springfield. I would've pinned Brian as a customer of one of the trendy downtown Eugene restaurants. I barely had time to go home and freshen up before heading out.

When I pulled into the parking lot of the restaurant, I searched for Brian's Lexus. It was nowhere in sight. It was hard to see inside the restaurant because the windows were painted with swirly, red and white lettering and a checkered pattern that covered the lower half of them. I tapped on my steering wheel, uncertain if I should go in or sit in my car and wait.

The roar of an engine made me jump. A motorcycle had pulled into the parking space next to me. The rider, tall and well built, loosened the straps of his helmet. I tried not to stare, but my curiosity was stronger than my sense of etiquette. When he pulled the helmet off, it took a moment for the black hair, chiseled face, and long nose to register in my mind. Brian? I didn't know he rode a ... I searched for an insignia and saw what I suspected. Harley-Davidson. Brian rode a Harley? A small bubble of laughter erupted from me as Brian turned my direction. I waved a hello and opened my car door.

"I didn't recognize you at first." I blurted.

Brian smiled and grabbed a small leather carry-all from the bike. "I wish I could take a picture of you right now."

"A picture of me? Why?" My face flushed.

"You remind me of a little kid who sees their teacher at the grocery store. It's a look of confusion and surprise ... mixed with a bit of adoration." Brian gestured toward the restaurant entrance.

"Yeah, I was surprised." I laughed heartily, trying to make light of the last part of his comment. A bit of adoration. Nannie always said I was an open book. How I wished I could slam the cover shut.

The restaurant was the seat-yourself kind. Brian led me to a small booth at the end, near the restrooms. "This looks like a quiet spot, don't you think?" He waited for me to take a seat. I nodded and slid into the red vinyl seat. Menus stood in a holder against the wall, right by the salt, pepper, and ketchup. The place had the typical fried food smell of a burger joint, and songs from the 1960s played on low quality speakers. Like the motorcycle, it was hard to see this place as part of Brian's life.

I opened the menu and tried to focus on the selections. "So, what's good here?"

Brian chuckled. "Well, their burgers of course." Brian tapped on a picture at the top of the menu with the tagline *Lane County's Favorite Burger.* "And the milkshakes. You can't go wrong with the peanut butter milkshake."

A hamburger did sound good and given the fact I'd lost

about ten pounds in the last two months, my figure, at least, could afford it. I wasn't sure how Brian kept in such good shape if this was his typical choice of food.

"Sounds delicious. A little fattening, maybe, but delicious."

"Sometimes you need to let yourself live a little, and not worry about tomorrow." Brian's voice was smooth, almost melodic.

Goosebumps prickled my arms. What was that look in Brian's eyes? I shifted in my seat. "That kind of thinking doesn't usually work out too well for me."

Brian raised his eyebrows. "Well when it comes to food, at least, I hope you'll try."

I smiled, but the awkward feeling clung to me. Part of me said he was flirting, but that didn't make sense. He was married, he was my boss, and he was nearly fifteen years older than me, even if he didn't look like it. Listening to him talk about Derrick and my case, I was convinced he had the highest moral standards. A person like Brian wouldn't stoop to an office affair. He was simply being playful. He had a far better sense of humor than Derrick, and I wasn't used to this kind of playfulness.

After we placed our orders with a young waitress, Brian pulled out his leather binder and opened it. I saw the divorce pleading, with several scribbled notes in the margins. I wondered what Brian's advice for me was going to be this time. He flipped through the pages of the pleading for what seemed like an eternity, then shook his head and leaned back in his seat.

"Here's the thing, Cassie. I have no perfect solution for you."

My heart sank, and I nodded my head. Perfect solutions were beyond my hope.

"First of all, divorce and custody are not my area of

expertise; secondly, you work for the firm where I'm a partner. It could raise questions if I were to represent you."

Derrick's words from the informal settlement conference echoed in my head. *I'm sure she's paying you in favors.* My ears burned. Of course Brian wouldn't want to put himself in a position that would start such rumors.

Brian leaned in, resting his elbows on the table. "But let me tell you what I can do, then you tell me if you're game."

I warily met Brian's gaze. Serious but tender eyes met mine.

"I already filed my motion to withdraw from your case when I returned the acceptance of the alimony and child support. You are officially pro se at the moment."

"Yes, I know. I'm on my own."

Brian nodded. "Technically, yes. Often a judge gives a certain leniency and even special consideration to defendants who don't have an attorney in these types of cases. It happens all too frequently."

"The judge will feel sorry for me?" I couldn't hide the bitterness in my voice. Sympathy wasn't what I wanted.

Brian shrugged. "Perhaps. But the point is, you don't have to have a perfectly presented case. You do, however, need to be prepared."

My already overworked head hurt trying to figure out where Brian was going with his line of thinking. "I really appreciate how you're willing to help me, but if you can't represent me, then—"

"I'm going to basically tell you what to put in your response, then I'll help you prepare for the court date. You'll file everything pro se because, for all intents and purposes, you are representing yourself. You have a big resource most people don't." Brian shrugged. "Think of it as your own personal app for winning your divorce case."

Despite my aching head and heart, I couldn't help but

smile at Brian's humor. "You're an app now?"

"Only for you." Brian winked.

Much to my relief, the waitress arrived with our food. My growling stomach helped push the questions out of my mind. Brian picked up a French fry and popped it in his mouth. From the size of the burger in the red basket in front of me, I was glad I didn't order a double.

"Like I said earlier, you need to keep this between us. I'm not sure some of the other partners in the firm would approve. Not to mention at least one of the associates."

I knew by associates he meant Cynthia. Even he could probably tell she did not like me. "Yes, you told me." I picked at my fries, waiting for Brian to start eating his burger before I started mine. "I won't tell anyone."

Brian bit into his burger and nodded. I noticed his left hand was ring-less. Strange. I couldn't remember seeing him with his ring off before.

"I can't thank you enough for your help ... meeting me in off hours and everything. I'm sure your wife would prefer to have you home eating dinner with her." Hopefully my question seemed sincere and casual enough to bely my curiosity.

Brian frowned and looked away for a moment. "My wife and I are going through a trial separation."

My heart dropped. "I'm so sorry." I should have kept my questions to myself.

Brian shook his head. "It's been a long time in coming. A select few at the office know. I don't really want it to be the focal point of conversation in the break room."

"I completely understand. Trust me."

Brian chuckled. "I'm sure you do. You and I may not be in the same boat, but I think we're floating down the same river, so to speak."

A bit of the weight on my shoulders fell away as we

continued eating and talking. Why Brian had ever decided to do so much for me was beyond my comprehension, but at least now he felt more like a friend to me than a boss. His separation explained why he was helping. The pain of a lost and dead relationship was as fresh to him as it was to me. Sharing a meal, sharing our stories. It was enough to take my mind off what Renee was doing in this moment, at home with Derrick.

"What are your plans for the weekend?" Brian asked between bites.

I swallowed and wiped my mouth. To my surprise, I had almost finished the burger. "I was actually hoping to go for a hike, see a waterfall or two." I didn't mention searching for a music box repair shop. It would undoubtedly sound boring.

Brian's eyes lit up. "Very good. Which ones?"

I shrugged. "I haven't had time to look at where they are yet, but there's a few on my list."

"What are the names? I might know where they are."

I dug through my purse for the piece of paper where I'd scribbled the names of the falls. My heart fluttered when I looked at the list, but I couldn't tell if it was from the excitement of my plans or from the interest radiating from Brian.

"The first one I wrote down is Latourell Falls."

Brian's eyebrows lifted. "That's up in the Columbia River Gorge. Unless you're planning on an overnight trip, I'd save that one for when you can devote at least one whole weekend to hiking the Gorge. What's next on your list?"

"Spirit Falls."

Brian dipped a French fry in ketchup. "Spirit Falls is east of Cottage Grove. Not hard to find and a pleasant short hike."

It sounded like a good place for a beginner to go, though my heart needed something more along the breathtaking category.

"I also have Proxy Falls, Abiqua Falls, and South Falls."

I laid the list on the table. Reading it made me remember why I needed the distraction. What was Renee doing right now? Was Derrick feeding her dinner? Was he drinking? I knew the answer to the last question, and my stomach turned. Maybe a big burger for dinner wasn't such a great idea.

"Are you okay?" Brian's voice was edged with concern.

"I'm fine. Just wondering how my daughter is doing."

Brian shoved his dinner basket aside and leaned forward. "Cassie," his voice was soothing. "I can't say I know what you're going through, but I *can* say I honestly believe your daughter will be fine. If you let your fear weigh you down, you'll never really live your life. You might as well lock yourself up and throw away the key."

Tears stung my eyes. I couldn't let myself cry. I blinked and shoved the list back in my purse. "I know. It hits me hard at times. It's not an easy adjustment."

Brian touched my hand lightly. "Tough adjustments are something I do understand." He pulled his hand away and sat straight again, his fingertips drumming the table edge. Why was my heart fluttering?

Brian cleared his throat. "Back to your list. South Falls is part of the Trail of Ten Falls, about an hour east of Salem. Are you sure you are an Oregonian? Silver Falls State Park is called the 'crown jewel' of the Oregon parks system."

I laughed. "Well, I did live in northern California for a few years, so maybe I lost my Oregonian status. I've heard of Silver Falls but have never been."

Brian mouthed a "wow" and shook his head again, but his eyes smiled. "Abiqua Falls I have heard of but never explored. Seems like it's a bit of a drive if I remember correctly. Proxy Falls is up on the Old McKenzie Highway.

I'm not sure if the road is open for the season yet."

My heart sank. It sounded like the two viable options on the list were Spirit Falls or Silver Falls State Park. One didn't sound like enough and the other sounded like too much. "I guess I'm going to have to think about it a bit." I hoped my disappointment didn't show.

"One of these weekends, if you want a hiking partner to explore Silver Falls, let me know." Brian was still sitting up straight, his hands on the edge of the table. He was looking away, out the window. Did he really want to go with me to Silver Falls, or was he simply being nice? And why not this weekend?

"No crown jewel of Oregon for you this weekend?" I teased, hoping to draw out his intentions.

Brian laughed. "The Trail of Ten Falls is a full day venture. A project landed in my lap and is going to keep me busy most of the weekend."

It took a moment for me to realize what he meant about a project landing in his lap. Brian was using his weekend to help me. My shoulders tightened. The last thing I wanted to be was a burden, yet I desperately needed help.

"I can't tell you how much I appreciate this. If there's any way I can pay you, I will." It was the truth. Maybe after the divorce was over and I received my share of the house, I could pay Brian.

"You don't need to worry about that right now. Focus on you and your daughter. And get out there and live a little." Brian's eyes met mine for a moment with an intensity that sent a warm wave through my body.

Chapter Sixteen

THE WEATHER FORECAST FOR THE WEEKEND appeared to be inaccurate when I woke up Saturday morning. I heard the steady rhythm of rain and my heart sank. Maybe Sunday would prove better for waterfalls. My focus today would be on taking Nannie's music box to the repair shop. Hopefully the fix would be affordable. I checked my phone for text messages and missed calls, only to find that I had no notifications. Ready or not, I was utterly alone for two whole days, but I was determined to make the best of it.

The clock shop was on the edge of an older residential Eugene neighborhood, in a Victorian style house that was painted purple, yellow, and green. I circled the block a couple of times looking for the closest possible parking space, not wanting to get drenched in the rain, but the nearest spot was still almost a block away. I clutched the paper bag holding the music box to my chest and sprinted through the downpour. The steady rhythm of tick-tocking and the musty odor of old things greeted me when I walked in the door of the shop. Various clocks lined the walls, many with pendulums. Grandfather clocks were arranged in no particular order throughout the room, and mantel clocks covered antique wooden display cases.

Cuckoo! Cuckoo! I jumped when a bird sprung out of one of the clocks that lined the walls.

"Can I help you?" A tall, elderly man stood behind a counter, a strange pair of glasses pushed onto his forehead.

I stepped closer and cleared my throat. No music boxes in sight. Maybe Google misunderstood my search terms. "Yes. I'm looking for someone who can repair an antique music box."

The man nodded and removed the binocular-like glasses from his head. He motioned toward the bag in my hand. "You have it with you?"

I took the box out of the bag and gingerly set it on the counter. "It belongs to my grandmother. She's had it for as long as I can remember."

The clock man gently lifted the lid. The duo of birds moved slowly, the broken melody almost gone. "Hmm. This is unique. Looks like it's from the late '30s, maybe early '40s." He picked up the box and turned it over, holding the lid shut, and ran his fingers along the bottom. "Hmm." His bushy grey eyebrows pinched together, and he set the box down. Holding my breath, I waited for his verdict.

"I don't get many music boxes in here. People today with their digital do-dads, hurrying here and there and downloading music on their iPhones ... music boxes are rarer than a cuckoo clock these days." The man's pale blue eyes settled on me.

I nodded. "Like I said, this is my grandma's. But my daughter is the one set on hearing it play again." I felt like I was baiting a hook. If I didn't say the right thing, this man would send me away and the box would never get fixed.

"Hmm ..." He looked down at the box for a moment, as if contemplating his answer. Then he stood up straight, his eyes misty. "The hinge will be an easy fix. I'll take a look at the inner mechanism and see what I can do for the melody."

A spark of hope flared in my chest. "Thank you. How long do you think it will take?" The cost was on my mind, but I didn't pose that question, anticipating he would throw me a number with the completion date.

"Give me a week. It shouldn't take more than two or three hours to repair, but I have a few projects ahead of it."

I sighed with relief. Surely clock repair men charged less than attorneys, and a few hours couldn't add up to much more than a hundred dollars. He handed me a form to fill out with my contact information and tied a tag with my name to the leg of the music box. If he could get it fixed by next Saturday, I could take it to Nannie when Renee and I visited her.

The rain was on break when I walked to my car, adding to my sense of victory. Now if I could find out why the music box was so important to Nannie. She wasn't the kind of person to put a lot of value on material things, so there had to be a sentimental reason. I wondered if it had to do with my mom, but it didn't quite add up. The box was too old. The only thing that made sense was it reminded her of grandpa, yet she said it was a gift from a *friend*. Then there was the wooden heart she kept inside it. The wooden heart was now tucked safely in a drawer in my nightstand. I would need to make sure I put it in the box before I returned it to Nannie. Maybe then she could tell me the story of its origins.

Driving back to my apartment, I thought of the day I'd gone to live with my grandparents. The safety and warmth of their home welcomed me, offering a promise I could be a little girl again. But the uncertainty of life with my mom's out-of-control drinking had left me afraid and jaded. I didn't see things the way other nine-year-olds did. Months passed before I lost my fear of nightfall. Routine, schedule, and gentle love slowly chipped away at the wall I had built up to keep myself safe. My grandparents never left me alone at night. Dinner was always on the table by 6:00 p.m. The electricity was never shut off, and the house was always warm.

Despite the goodness that surrounded me, I never did feel like a little girl again. Making friends was hard. The girls who might've understood me were also the ones who got in trouble. The last thing I wanted to do was disappoint my grandparents, so I stayed away from that crowd. I didn't have a best friend until I was seventeen, when I met Derrick. For the first time in my life someone understood me and accepted me for who I was. His soft green eyes lit up every time he saw me, and his boyish grin gave me butterflies.

Now instead of butterflies, I had unending nausea. I didn't want to be a scared little girl who had to fend for herself, again. Yet, here I was.

I bought a cheap paperback at Walmart, hoping to lose myself in the story of another life, but I couldn't focus. If I wasn't worrying about Renee, then I was reliving the past, trying to make sense out of what life had become. It was a puzzle with too many missing pieces to put back together. By Saturday night I was determined to never spend another weekend alone, no matter what. Maybe I would get a second part-time job. I checked the weather app on my phone for the Sunday forecast. It called for only periods of rain, and a high in the mid-60s. I looked up the directions to Spirit Falls. If I left first thing in the morning, I could easily get back before it was time to pick up Renee. The trail didn't sound difficult, though it would undoubtedly be muddy after today's downpour. Muddy or not, going there would beat staying home alone.

The trail sank beneath my feet, dampened by the rain. I walked at a leisurely pace, not really admiring the scenery but instead concentrating on the moist earth smells, with the promise of spring in the air. The air was cool but there had been no rain today so far, only patchy clouds and soggy ground.

I tried to quiet my mind, taking in the soothing sounds of the forest–the gentle breeze through the boughs of the moss-covered trees, the steady hum of the waterfall as I got closer. In only a few hours I would have my daughter back in my arms. Maybe then the tension in my shoulders would cease, and the anxiousness in my heart relent.

A hiker coming up the trail caught me off guard, pulling me out of my thoughts. He was an older man wearing a cowboy hat. As he passed, something from the pocket of his vest caught a beam of weak sunlight and sparkled. Though he did not carry a fishing pole, he reminded me of my grandpa when he went fishing. I imagined a baited hook, sailing through the air, landing on water. An ache, a longing, spread in my heart. A memory. Not of grandpa, but of Derrick.

Fishing was one date my over-protective grandparents approved of when I was a teenager. I'd met Derrick in March and spent most of the spring and summer on the river. Fishing, talking, laughing. Sitting on blankets in the shade of a tree, sneaking kisses. Derrick, tying on my hook for me. He didn't seem to mind at all, his mouth curved into a slight smile as he made the knot perfect. Me, proudly baiting my own hook and casting my line into the river, but not quite far enough to avoid the snagging dangers of the shoreline. Derrick, standing behind me, helping me to cast it out further, over and over, until I could do it alone. His face close to mine, blond hair gleaming in the sun. His birch-leaf colored eyes watching me like he couldn't get enough. The feeling when his lips touched mine, the warmth of coming home mixed with the power of electricity.

Where had that Derrick gone? What had I done to make those soft silvery-green eyes change to fire-hardened glass? To make those lips turn from kisses to cruelty, twisting fragments of truth into vengeful lies? Why had his boyish grin turned into sadistic, mocking laughter?

I picked up my pace. The falls was near, and I needed to get there, to put abundant space between me and the man in the fishing vest. My brisk walk soon turned into a jog. My chest ached, eyes stung. I pushed harder, sliding at times down the sloping, muddy trail. Small drops of rain landed on my head. Looking up through the green boughs of the trees, I saw a grey, darkening sky.

Now wasn't a time for thinking. The rain was coming, and I needed to get to the falls and back or risk getting drenched. I continued on, nothing but muscle and breath and desperation.

I saw the falls through the trees ahead. It was not a massive fall, but big enough to send a mist up into the air for several feet. I walked to the end of the trail and watched the water, letting its steady roar fill me, my aching chest breathing in the mist.

It wasn't enough. I touched the wooden guard rail. It was damp, but not too slippery. I swung one leg over it, straddling it like a horse, then heaved my other leg over, almost slipping when both feet landed on mud and slime covered rock. The mist was strong here, trying to penetrate my clothing, soaking into my shoes.

Finally, I was at the base, water from the falls nearly within reach, threatening to crush me. I looked up at the wall of water, its power undeniable.

The memories of the younger Derrick swirled in my head, and the saltiness of my tears mixed with the fresh, cold droplets covering my face. I wanted to reach into the past and bring him here, have him tell his present self to get his act together, make him see what he was doing to our daughter. Make him love me again. Have my best friend back.

I remembered the plaque hanging on the wall in Nannie's room. "Love never fails." I knew it was from the Bible, the supposed book of truth. But if love never failed, why was there divorce? If love never failed, why had Derrick changed? I waited for the water to answer, but no answer came. The steady roar continued, soaking me, washing me, and the bitter pain eased. When the tears were gone, I made my way back up to the trail, feeling accomplished and soothed. My pain was gone, for now, but the feeling of emptiness had grown. I couldn't fill it with any more memories of the man I had loved.

I arrived at Derrick's at 4:55 p.m. to pick up Renee. Parked at the curb, I waited until exactly 5:00 p.m. before walking up to the door and knocking. A walking on eggshells moment, the type I was used to from the last several years of being married to Derrick. If I did everything right, then hopefully he wouldn't be angry. I rang the doorbell, the strangeness of doing so still new to me. No answer. I rang it again then knocked. The door creaked open. Derrick's scowling face greeted me.

"Is Renee ready?"

"No." Derrick glowered, holding the door open enough for me to see his face, but not into the house. "Renee's sick. She probably got it from the filthy daycare you have her in."

Renee was sick? He should've called me. I stood on tiptoes, trying without success to see over his shoulders into the darkened living room. The only sound was the television. "Where's Renee?"

"She doesn't want to go back to your place tonight. She wants to stay home with me."

My stomach flip-flopped. He couldn't do this. "Our parenting plan clearly says Renee is supposed to be with me starting at 5:00 tonight. If she's sick, she needs me." My voice wavered at the end of my sentence.

"So you want to force our sick four-year-old daughter to go stay with you tonight in a place that doesn't even feel like home to her, then pass her off to your unsanitary daycare tomorrow, instead of letting her stay here with me until she feels better? Wow. You're a really caring mother."

Derrick's face was ruddy, his eyes hazy. He'd been drinking. More than a few beers.

"She's supposed to be with me tonight, Derrick. If she's too sick to go to daycare tomorrow, I'll stay home with her."

"I guess you can afford to stay home since your little attorney friend filed your stupid motion for child support and alimony." The haziness in Derrick's eyes was replaced by the heat of unchecked disgust.

Now my face was red. I took a deep breath, willing my heart to slow. Staying calm and focused was the only way I'd have any chance of getting Renee back.

"It's time for Renee to come with me."

"You need to get off my property, you piece of trash." Derrick snarled, his fists clenched. My heart stung, a fresh wound delivered by the intensity of my memories earlier in the day.

The soft green eyes of the boy I'd loved were forever gone.

"I will leave as soon as I have Renee." I felt myself shrinking, but my feet remained firmly planted on the front entry.

"If you don't leave right now, I'm calling the police and having you arrested for trespassing."

Could he do that? I had a reason to be here—my daughter. Unless Renee was with me, I wasn't leaving. I pulled my phone from my back pocket and noted the time. I forced my voice to be even. "It's 5:05 on the second Sunday of the month. Our current parenting plan clearly states that Renee is supposed to be with me right now. If the police show up, that's what I'll tell them."

Derrick snickered, and took a step closer, bringing his face within inches of mine. "Oh really, so who do you think they're going to believe? You ..." Derrick poked sharply at my chest with his index finger, "or me? Because I can tell you right now, the last time they were here the only reason they didn't take you to jail was because I asked them not to, for Renee's sake."

Blood pounded in my ears, and my vision grew blurry. Was that true? I didn't know, and I couldn't think. I replayed the events of the night in my mind. All I really remembered was how small I felt—as I did now. But this time Renee was on the other side of the door and I needed to get her *home*. "Call the police. I'll show them the parenting time order in my glove box. It'll make it pretty clear why I'm here." I didn't really have the order in my car, but Derrick didn't know that.

Derrick sneered and stared at me a moment, unmoving. I held my place, and my breath. Would he believe my bluff?

Finally, he stepped back. "Fine, Cass. Take Renee to your little hovel of a home. But you need to find a new daycare. If you keep taking Renee to that filthy daycare I'm going to waltz right in and take her out. Then I *will* find another place for her to go, even if it's out of the state." He turned and walked back in the house, slamming the door behind him.

I froze, Derrick's words circling in my head. What did he mean by 'out of the state'? He couldn't move with Renee without court permission ... unless he was going to flee like a criminal. Taking Renee would be kidnapping. Who in their right mind would risk that over a stupid daycare? There was no logic to it at all.

The door opened again, and Renee came out. All of Derrick's stupid threats washed away as I took her into my arms. Her hair was messy, and her eyes half open, like she had woken from a deep sleep. It was awfully late for a nap, but I didn't let it get to me. I had her in my arms now. Her backpack wasn't attached to her. No matter. It was replaceable. Derrick stood in the doorway, the scowl still etched into his face.

"I meant what I said, Cass. Every word. If things go bad, you only have yourself to blame."

I turned and walked away in silence, ignoring the dark cold that settled inside me with his words. *You only have yourself to blame.* I was nine-years-old again but this time there was no safe haven. My knight-in-shining armor, my best friend, was my enemy—and my precious daughter's future relied on every decision I made.

Chapter Seventeen

I HELD RENEE IN MY LAP, snuggling her close. The somber blueness of my apartment walls in the fading light of the day fit my mood. The moment I had put Renee in my car, her demeanor had changed from sad and sleepy to angry and tearful. She kicked the back of my seat all the way home. Each kick was accented by a shrill scream and her refrain, "I want to go back! I don't want to go to daycare!"

I calmly explained, over and over, "I'm not taking you to daycare. We are going home." But my words were lost in the depths of Renee's temper tantrum.

She finally quit fighting against me once we arrived at our apartment, and her cries turned into soft sobs when I carried her in and sat down on the couch. My entire body ached—legs from hiking, arms from carrying a protesting child, and my heart from seeing Renee's outburst. Darkness pressed down on me, squeezing out any remnant of peace this morning's hike had brought.

"I'm sorry, Renee. I'm so sorry you don't feel good." I squeezed my daughter closer, kissing the top of her head.

"I threw up four times." Renee spoke in a tiny, hoarse voice.

"Throwing up is the worst, isn't it?" I brushed the hair away from Renee's face and looked at her eyes. They were glassy, the skin around them dark.

Renee nodded, tears falling down her cheeks. "I wanted you, Mommy, but Daddy said you didn't answer." Her bottom lip quivered.

My temples pounded. When had Derrick tried calling me? I was out of cell phone range less than four hours. Four hours in the middle of the day. Did Derrick try calling me during that window of time? I didn't have any missed voicemails. No text messages.

"Did you start throwing up around lunch time?"

Renee shook her head. "I threw up in my bed. It was still dark. Daddy wouldn't wake up." Haunted emerald eyes looked up at me. "Daddy had to clean up and he said bad words."

I bit my bottom lip to keep from screaming. My baby had been sick and alone. As if that wasn't bad enough, Derrick had made it sound like I couldn't be reached. I had tried to pretend everything would be okay.

I was wrong.

"I'm sorry you were sick. It's not at all your fault if you didn't make it to the bathroom. I wish ..." my voice cracked. "I wish I could have been there."

Renee nodded and hugged me, her tiny arms wrapped around my neck. "Mommy, I don't like daycare anymore. Daddy said it's why I got sick. Because of daycare. He said if I stay with him, I won't get sick."

I squeezed Renee in a tight hug, then pushed her back so I could see her face. "Sugar Bug, the daycare didn't make you throw up. Sometimes people get sick. Even before you went to daycare you would get colds or tummy bugs."

Renee's brow furrowed. "But daddy said it was daycare."

I inhaled and exhaled, searching for words a four-year-old could understand, pushing my anger toward Derrick away so it didn't come through in my voice. "People get sick bugs from other people. There are other kids in daycare, so you could get sick from one of them. But you could also get bugs from going to the grocery store or the park."

Renee twisted her hands, her brow still knitted together. "Do I go to daycare tomorrow?"

"If you are sick, then no, we will stay home."

Renee laid her head against my arm, her hand on my

shoulder. "I think I'm still going to be sick."

Renee slept through the night without any sign of illness but had a low-grade fever when I checked on her at six that morning. I didn't try waking her up. She would need a good day of rest to recover. What to do? On top of missing work, I would also miss staying *after* work and typing up Brian's dictated response in my divorce case. It was due Tuesday. The timing couldn't be worse. Maybe I could go in early tomorrow and get it done, *if* Renee was better by then.

After calling Lana and leaving a message for Cynthia about my reasons for not being at work, I sent a short text to Brian explaining what happened and asking if Tuesday morning would be too late to get the response typed up. I sipped coffee and watched my phone, desperate for a response.

Finally, one came through. *Meet here 7 am tomorrow. No worries.*

I breathed a sigh of relief. No worries. I wish. Next, I called Bonnie for the second time that morning.

"Well hello again, is Miss Renee feeling better already?" Bonnie's sunny voice made me smile.

"No, not yet … but I'm betting she will be fine tomorrow. Which brings me to the huge favor I need to ask of you." I pulled on the end of my oversized t-shirt.

"What do you need?" Bonnie's warmth gave me courage.

"Is there any way I could drop Renee off at 6:30 tomorrow morning? I need to get caught up at work for missing today."

The line was silent for a moment. "Well, sure you can. I get up before the roosters anyway. Renee is such an easy kid. I'd love to have her."

Relief washed over me. Crisis averted, for now. "Thank

you so much."

Renee and I spent a lazy day at home, wearing our pajamas, snuggling and watching TV, eating chicken noodle soup and crackers for lunch. We both needed the time together. But worry made me restless and kept me from fully enjoying the day. The response was due tomorrow. I still needed to type it, Brian needed to review it, and it had to be filed and prepared for service. How would all that happen during one day, when my desk would undoubtedly be buried in work?

I texted Brian again, but an hour went by and he didn't respond. Probably with a client. Maybe I was being a nuisance. *You're so needy, Cass. One of these days you have to grow up.* Derrick's voice, from when the honeymoon was over, but before things went from bad to worse.

Renee fell asleep on the couch, and I lay down beside her. Sleep curled around me, welcoming me in. My phone buzzed.

"How's Renee feeling?" Brian's business-like tone greeted me.

I sat up, a surge of adrenaline running through me. Now I could talk to someone and figure things out.

"She seems better. I think she'll be ready for daycare tomorrow. I arranged to take her in early so I can be at work at seven. Will that be enough time to do everything though? I could try to come in even earlier, but I don't—"

"Cassie ... breathe. We'll get it done."

I sighed. "Sorry for rambling."

Brian chuckled. "I understand. You are under a lot of stress. It's going to be okay."

Should I tell him what Renee had said? There had to be something we could add to my response to get things expedited and limit Renee's time with Derrick.

Summoning my courage, I began. "Renee was a mess

last night." I told Brian all the details of what she said happened and Derrick's words to her.

Brian made a low growling noise on the other end of the line. It reassured me. If it made him angry, then as Renee's mother I had every right to be livid.

"He's quite a piece of work. I'm sorry you had to go through that."

"Can we put something in the response about it?"

Brian took a moment to respond. "Cassie, I understand why you're upset, but it isn't enough to make a request for an expedited hearing. For one thing, Derrick could have a believable counter-argument for every assertion you make. For another thing, Renee wasn't physically harmed."

"She was mentally harmed!" Renee stirred on the couch. I lowered my voice. "What am I supposed to do?"

"You write it down. The date, the times, what happened. Every detail. You keep track of everything he does and when you get to the hearing, you tell the judge your story." Brian's voice remained level, but the iron hands of fear and frustration squeezed my chest.

Tears welled in my eyes. "The hearing may not be for months. How much worse will things get by then? I'm afraid of what Derrick will do."

"What you do is you don't let him see you sweat. Guys like him are motivated by the misery of others." Brian's response didn't lighten the weight on my shoulders.

Months of playing a game. Is that what I had to look forward to? Because I *was* sweating. Maybe I could fake my way through and put on an act when I talked to Derrick, but a piece of me died each time Renee spent a weekend with her dad. Would there be any of my heart left by the time of the hearing?

I pressed on the office door, but it didn't budge. It was locked, and the frosted floor to ceiling windows on each side of the massive door were dark. What if Brian forgot about me coming in early? I tapped on the dark wood. A tall, lean shape moved through the reception area and the door swung open.

"Missy? What are you doing here?"

"A friend in need is a friend indeed." Missy winked as I walked into the dark room. "I heard you might need a little help this morning."

We walked to my desk. The files and papers stacked on it were not as deep as I expected.

"I've been filing away the stuff Lana worked on yesterday, and I went through the stack of tapes still sitting on your desk." Missy motioned to my full inbox. "I can go ahead and tackle the short ones. Brian's tape and the exhibits are in your chair. He thinks you can have the rough draft done by the time he comes in this morning."

Overwhelmed by the kindness, I couldn't find words of thanks. Tears welled in my eyes. "Missy … this is amazing. I didn't even know Brian talked to you about it." I wanted to hug her, but she didn't seem like the hugging type.

Missy waved her hand at me. "I'm glad to help. Brian talked to me yesterday about what was going on …" Missy's brow lifted. "I'm glad he did, since you kind of left me in the dark."

Warmth spread through my cheeks. "I'm sorry. It all happened so fast, and I figured I'd talk to you Monday. Then, Renee was sick." I left out the part about being worried about Missy's questions.

Missy nodded, her eyes studying me. "It's a good thing Brian's helping you, but be careful."

"What do you mean?"

"What I mean is, he's a man, he's married, I've seen the

way he looks at you ... and I've heard rumors about other conquests."

Other conquests? The way he looks at me? My mind swirled trying to take it all in. One thing Missy was wrong about—Brian wasn't really married, he was separated. But I couldn't betray his secret. "Brian and I have a work relationship, and he's helping me with this as a friend. I don't think I'm a 'conquest.'" I forced a laugh, making light of the remark.

Missy shrugged. "I'm saying having one jerk to deal with is enough. You don't need two."

I nodded. "Thanks, Missy."

I got right to work on Brian's tape, and soon found myself smiling. He regularly inserted little sarcastic remarks for my benefit. "Mr. Peterson is the owner of a small auto sales company, even though he is both an imbecile and has short-man's syndrome. Cassie—scratch that last part. New paragraph." What would have been an emotional and depressing project ended up making me laugh. Brian was right about how long it would take. I had the first draft typed, printed, and on his desk by 7:55 a.m.

When Cynthia made her appearance at my desk at 8:05 a.m. sharp, I was already transcribing a landlord-tenant agreement. Missy walked by my cubicle and in her cheeriest voice said, "Good morning, ladies!" Behind Cynthia's back, she winked at me with a mischievous smile. I fought to keep a straight face while Cynthia droned on about everything that had to be done ASAP.

Shortly before noon Brian brought me the redlined corrections for the response. He looked over his shoulder before whispering. "Try to take care of this when Cynthia is having lunch. The less she knows, the better."

I nodded. To my relief, not many corrections were needed. I could take care of them while Cynthia did her lunch time routine of eating a large salad then going to the restroom to brush her teeth. I had the corrections done and the printer waiting for it to spew out my papers when Cynthia passed by, on her way to the bathroom. Her brow furrowed. "Cassie, shouldn't you be having lunch?"

"I'm already done." I smiled, hoping Cynthia's curiosity wouldn't draw her to look at what was coming out of the printer.

"Well, I hope you are refreshed. We have quite a busy afternoon ahead."

I nodded and smiled. Great. I still needed to look over everything one more time, then sign the response and the certificate of mailing. I had maybe two minutes before Cynthia returned from brushing her teeth. I ran to Missy's station and found her browsing the internet for shoes. "Cynthia's cutting her lunch short, and I'm not done. I don't know what to do."

Missy closed her browser and turned toward me. "Where is she?'

"In the bathroom." My heart hammered in my chest.

Missy grabbed the bottle of tea off her desk and made her way toward the restrooms. "I can give you an extra five."

I scanned the pleading and signed and dated in the appropriate places, then put everything in a brown envelope in Missy's inbox.

"I am so sorry, Cynthia. I'm a bit jumpy today. Too much tea I guess. I hope I didn't ruin your shirt." Missy's voice carried over the cubicles.

Cynthia's fake laugh trailed behind Missy's voice. "I think I got it washed out soon enough. Lucky for me I was right by the bathroom sink."

Oh, Missy! I sucked in my cheeks to keep from bursting into laughter. Had she really walked into the bathroom and purposely spilled her drink on Cynthia? Her bravado left me speechless.

By four p.m., the response was ready for Missy to take to the courthouse. Brian gave her another pleading to file at the same time. The other pleading wasn't due until the following week, but Brian had it ready early in order to have a valid excuse to send Missy on a run to the courthouse. I was packing up my stuff for the day when Missy stopped by my cubicle and handed me a large manila envelope.

"Here's your date-stamped copy. The Petitioner's copy has been mailed."

Staring at the blank brown envelope, the last of the adrenaline from the day drained from my nerves and was replaced by an overwhelming sense of gratitude. I had done it. Or, actually, *we* had done it. Because of my new friends and coworkers, a well-crafted and legally sound defense had been filed on my behalf. I was one step closer to being free from Derrick, one step closer to keeping my daughter safe.

"Thank you." I couldn't keep my voice from cracking.

Missy grinned, her arms folded across her chest. "It's been fun. I like to see people get what they deserve, and your ex deserves a swift boot in the buttocks." Missy lowered her voice, and leaned closer. "And I might have enjoyed spilling my tea on Cynthia a little too much. Really, I should be thanking you."

We both laughed. What a difference a day and good friends could make. Bonnie may only consider herself my daughter's babysitter, but her willingness to take Renee in early had saved the day. Missy showed up to work an hour before her start time—and off the clock no doubt—because she knew I would need help. How many twenty-two-year olds were that caring and wise? Then there was Brian … although his actions often perplexed me, and my heart's response to his kindness may not be appropriate at times, there was no denying he had gone above and beyond to help me. Two months ago, none of these people were in my life. Now, in a strange but wonderful way, they were my family.

Chapter Eighteen

I CLUNG TO THE WALL OF a mountain, refusing to look over the edge of the narrow trail. The wind howled, whipping my hair across my face. I brushed it aside and caught a glimpse of Grandpa slightly ahead, walking the trail with ease. I called out to him, but my voice was silent against the powerful wind. With both hands against the rocky wall for support, I ventured a glance down. A never-ending abyss was only inches from my feet. One wrong step and I would fall. I lifted my chin and squinted against the relentless wind. Grandpa was now far ahead, about to walk around a bend in the trail, out of my sight.

"Grandpa!" My throat burned from the effort to be heard. Grandpa stopped and looked back. His mouth moved. I couldn't hear a word over the moaning of the wind, but his loving blue eyes were vivid, despite the distance between us.

I leaned forward, desperate to hear his words. Grandpa lifted a hand to each side of his mouth. "Cassie, hold tight and keep your eyes ahead of you."

I took a step forward, hopeful, not looking and not holding on to the rock wall. My right foot landed on air. The skin of my fingers scraped against the rocks, struggling to find a grip.

I woke up with arms flailing, close to the edge of my bed. Renee had crawled in my bed during the middle of the night. Though she was tiny, with her feet facing me and her head facing the other edge, she had taken up more than half of the bed. I turned her toward me and held her close, hoping to ease the fear and racing heart left from the dream. Losing my footing had been as real as the softness of Renee's cheek on my arm. I ached to talk to Grandpa. Why had I lost my footing in the dream, when Grandpa was right there calling me to him? I shuddered. The dream was simply a remnant from my hike last weekend, memories of the past combined with the stress I was under. Nothing more.

The first light of dawn was peeking through the sides of the cheap white window blinds in my bedroom. So much for sleeping in on Sunday. I had called Nannie on Friday night to make plans to visit this weekend. Her voice sounded weak, barely audible. A summer cold had her down. The music box repair shop had not yet called. As much as I hated to, I would put off the visit to Nannie. In another two weeks I would again have Renee for the weekend, the music box repaired, and Nannie hopefully feeling up to having company.

My phone rang. Derrick's name showed on the caller ID. What a way to wake up. I had not heard a word from him all week. At least it was early morning, and he would be sober, maybe even the nicer version of himself.

"I want to talk to Renee."

That was not Derrick's "nice" voice. I pulled the phone from my ear and looked at the time: 6:45 a.m.

"She's still asleep." I forced my voice to sound upbeat, unafraid.

"Taking after you now, is she?"

I looked at the ceiling. "I can have her call you when she gets up."

"Whatever." Derrick cleared his throat. "By the way, nice job on serving the response." Bitterness punctuated each syllable. "I didn't get it until yesterday. I'm not sure what kind of game you are playing, but you can bet my attorney will be checking with the court to see if it was filed on time."

My heart thrummed like a racehorse. Why hadn't Derrick received the response until yesterday? Did the envelope get wrongly addressed? Would it affect the validity of the response? Unless, of course, Derrick was lying.

"It was filed *and* mailed on time." The steadiness in my reply belied the shaking of my hands.

"Pretty impressive for uneducated white trash. In fact, I'm pretty sure you must've had a little help. Maybe in trade for—"

"I don't have an attorney. I filed it on my own." I was lying by omission, but it didn't matter. How I filed the response was none of Derrick's business.

Derrick laughed. "Nice one, Cass. But keep in mind I *know* you and what you can and can't handle. Judges aren't stupid. The judge will see right through your little lies. He'll see what you *really* are. When he does, you won't stand a snowball's chance in hell of getting custody of Renee."

A deep chill sliced through me, and everything in the room slanted left then right. The way Derrick spun things made me dizzy. I took a deep breath and closed my eyes.

Hold tight and keep your eyes ahead of you. Grandpa's voice, rising above the wind.

"Do you want me to have Renee call you or not?"

"I'm working today. Now that I have to pay your stupid alimony, I'm back on the sales floor to make the extra money. It's okay, though, my attorney and I have a plan."

I bit my lip to keep from asking what his plan entailed.

"Since I haven't heard from you, I'm assuming you haven't found another daycare. So, I will. It's my right to do so, in case your little friend didn't tell you."

Heat seared through me. I was like an insect on a hot day, caught under a magnifying glass held by a sadistic child. "The daycare issue can be decided at the hearing."

"You go ahead and keep telling yourself that, dearie. But I'm going to be at the daycare Monday morning, and if you drop Renee off, I'm waltzing right in there and taking her out. Even if I have to take her to another state."

My pulse pounded in my ears. It was the same threat he

had made before. Was it only to ruin my weekend with Renee, or did he mean it this time?

After Renee was up and watching a Smurf movie, I locked myself in my room and garnered the courage to call Brian.

"He'd have to file something, and he would need a legitimate basis for filing it. Unless he has a valid reason to demand a different child care, he would basically be throwing money out the window on his way to nowhere simply to harass you." Brian's no-nonsense answer was meant to put me at ease. Instead, it only heightened my concern.

"He says he'll find a new daycare if I don't. What if he does? What if I go to pick her up from Bonnie's Monday afternoon and she's not there because he put her in another daycare?" I pulled at the hem of my pajama shirt.

"Hmm." The line went silent. Did Brian understand my fear? If he were a woman, or a parent, he'd understand. This was my daughter's wellbeing we were discussing.

"He might do that, Cassie. The guy's a jerk and finds great joy in tormenting you. But how well do you think that's going to go over with a new daycare, assuming he finds one? How will his making such a rash and arrogant move look to the judge when you get to court?"

I hadn't thought about either repercussion, but it made sense. Derrick might pull a stupid trick, but in the end, it would hurt him in court. Not to mention the time and expense he would go through to find a daycare. But it was unfair to Renee, who would be the one to suffer from his vindictiveness. It had taken her all week to get over the fear Derrick had instilled in her of Bonnie's and the daycare making her sick. How much more damage would he do?

"So, you're saying I shouldn't do anything? Not find

another daycare, or even worry about it?"

"Deal with his actions as they arise but ignore his childish threats." Brian's voice was silky, confident.

"It's hard to listen and ruminate and not be able to actually do anything." My voice cracked. At least Brian couldn't see the tears streaming down my face.

"I'm sorry I can't make it all go away for you. But I believe you are strong enough to get through these next couple of months and win this battle." His voice held conviction and tenderness. If he were here and I could fall into his arms, lay my head against his chest ... I willed the image away. Why did my mind leap to more than friendship when all Brian showed me was kindness?

"Thank you. You're right. I need to keep the end in mind." Nannie always said a girl needs to keep her chin up when she's feeling down. I wondered if she'd ever been as down as I was right now, knowing the long road ahead of me. A pang of guilt hit me when I realized Nannie had been through her own hell, watching her daughter spiral down into the depths of alcoholism.

Hold tight and keep your eyes ahead of you.

I'm trying, Grandpa. I'm trying.

My only choice was to warn Bonnie what she might be facing with Derrick. I put it off until Monday morning when I took Renee to daycare.

I scrutinized Bonnie's house, trying to see it through Derrick's eyes. It had its familiar scent of oven-baked meals, baby powder, and Goldfish crackers. Not something you'd find in a scented candle, but homey. Toys littered the floor, but the carpet was only mildly stained and appeared recently vacuumed. The sofa end tables showed a light layer of dust, but there was no old food lying around or any evidence of ill-health. Family pictures covered the walls. It was a look I loved, but Derrick hated. He preferred walls that only displayed a few pieces of well-placed art. Other than personal preference for decorum and housekeeping, I couldn't see one single thing Derrick could legitimately call out as a danger to Renee.

I helped Renee pull off her new backpack. Hopefully this one would make it back from her next visit with Derrick. I looked at Bonnie. "Can I talk to you for a minute?"

Bonnie tilted her head. "Sure, let me put this little guy in the play pen." A toddler with messy blond hair was on Bonnie's hip, his tiny fist tightly holding a teething ring.

I stood by the front door, away from the children. It seemed as private a place as any without going into another room and shutting the door. Renee was already playing with Legos at a child's table on the other end of the room. I had rehearsed the words to say to Bonnie, a way to give her enough information so she wouldn't be taken off guard if Derrick showed up, but not so much that she would be worried. Selfish fear nagged at me. What if she decided the drama in our lives was more than she wanted to deal with, and said she could no longer watch Renee?

Bonnie came up to me, a small smile on her face but concern in her eyes. "What's going on? Is Renee okay?"

I nodded. "Renee's fine. But I need to talk to you about her dad. We might have a problem." I looked away for a moment, drawing in a deep breath.

Bonnie touched my arm. "I've been doing this for thirty-five years, Cassie, I've heard about everything there is to hear. Just tell me."

Exhaling, I looked into Bonnie's caring eyes. Telling her my ex-husband thought her daycare was subpar felt cruel.

"Derrick has different ideas about child care than I do. He likes things to be more formal and structured, like one of those daycare centers downtown. He told me if I didn't find another daycare, he would."

Bonnie frowned. "Are you giving me notice that Renee is leaving?"

I shook my head. "No. Renee loves it here. I believe this is a great place for her. I'm not pulling her out. But Derrick told me *he* would. Until final custody is decided, the decisions are fifty-fifty. I mean, he technically can't pull her out of here, but that doesn't mean he won't."

"Ah … one of those." Bonnie raised her eyebrows and smiled. I was relieved she wasn't upset but perplexed by her response. Had she really encountered this type of thing before?

"I wanted to warn you because Derrick told me he was coming here this morning to take Renee. He can be …" How could I describe Derrick's threatening, controlling nature?

"A big bully?" Bonnie asked, knowing in her eyes.

I nodded. Bully was a good word for him, though it didn't seem strong enough.

"I've dealt with my share of bullies. About half of them simply need someone to listen, to hear their side of a story. Another good percentage need someone to stand up to them and not back down."

Could it really be that simple? My gut told me Derrick was an exception to any rule. I had spent years listening, and it hadn't made a difference. Standing up to him seemed to anger him more, yet it was what everyone said I should do. Would his anger reach a boiling point, then fizzle out before a life-changing explosion?

"I think Derrick is the second type. Hopefully, though, he doesn't show that side to you. He's usually pretty good about putting on a nice front." I left out the details of his degrading attitude toward certain types of people, especially women.

Bonnie frowned. "Do you happen to have a copy of your parenting plan?"

I nodded and patted my purse. "I have it right here."

"Can I make a copy of it before you leave? If he does show up—which I doubt he will—I will point out the parenting time to him."

The toddler in the playpen whimpered. Bonnie looked over her shoulder to check on him. The well-behaved blue heeler, Red, got up from his dog bed by the back door and went to the playpen, ears turned up.

"That sounds like a good idea, but what if he doesn't listen?"

"Well, then, I'll call the police." Bonnie nodded toward the dog. "And while I wait for them I guarantee you Red will be by my side. Renee won't be leaving this house if I have anything to say about it."

As if on cue, Red trotted over to Bonnie and sat by her side. Bonnie chuckled and patted him on the head, then turned to me. "With Jesus watching over us and Red by my side, no harm will come to anyone in this house."

Bonnie looked at me with light and peace in her eyes. She wasn't afraid of Derrick. She wouldn't allow herself to be bullied. She had a guard dog who ran to the protection of the children or Bonnie if anyone here was threatened. And she had Jesus. I wasn't willing to bank on that one, but Bonnie's faith was still reassuring. The tension in my back eased, and I exhaled. Time to get to work.

Chapter Nineteen

"YOU LOOK LIKE A FORCE TO be reckoned with this fine morning." Brian's voice caught me off guard, stopping me short. He stood by the reception desk. Lana wasn't at her station.

I smiled. "I'm not sure if that's an insult or a compliment, so I'll choose the latter."

Brian chuckled. "Trust me, it's a compliment. How'd it go this morning?"

He remembered our conversation. My heart warmed at the look of concern in his eyes. "It went well. Drama-free."

Brian winked. "Some people are a bunch of hot air. You see that a lot in short-man's syndrome."

I bit my cheek, holding back laughter. Compared to Brian, Derrick's stature was a bit lacking. "So, Derrick has short-man's syndrome?"

Brian shrugged, a twinkle in his eyes. "From what I've seen, he meets all the criteria."

I couldn't help but grin on the way to my desk. Between the satisfaction of handling this morning on my own and Brian's comments and humor, this week was off to a good start. I didn't know if Derrick would show up at Bonnie's or not, but I had dealt with the threat and not freaked out. With Bonnie's wisdom to guide me, I left her house in confidence, not tears.

Worry nipped at my self-assurance, "What if ..." but I shook the uneasiness away. I needed my job, my income. I couldn't let my fear of what Derrick might do keep me from working and supporting my daughter. My landlord didn't care about my fears, only my rent check.

As I was putting on my headphones, my phone vibrated.

Bonnie's number flashed across the screen. Cold swept over me.

"Cassie ... Derrick showed up right after you left." Bonnie's voice was calm but concerned.

My heart skipped so many beats the room spun. "Is everything okay? Is Renee still there?"

"Yes, Renee's still here. All is well. But Derrick was fit to be tied. He demanded Renee come with him, but I told him no way, and let him know I had a copy of the parenting plan and would not hesitate to call the cops."

"Did he leave then? I'm so sorry about this, Bonnie. I hope no other parents were around."

"Luckily, no one came in during our little ... conversation. He threatened to turn me in to the state for a health violation." Bonnie chuckled. "I'm not sure which one he thinks I'm breaking."

I shook my head, jaw clenched. "He's such a jerk."

Bonnie exhaled. "I might agree with you on that. But, Cassie, I need to warn you." She paused, and I held my breath. "He said he was going to set things straight with you. Which doesn't sound like a threat, exactly. Except—"

All I could hear on the other end were the sounds of kids playing. Why had Bonnie stopped mid-sentence? "Except what?"

"I don't know. It was his eyes, I guess. The look in them. I've never seen someone that angry."

I nodded, understanding what Bonnie meant. I hated that she was subjected to the Jekyll part of Derrick's personality, yet it was validating. Those wrathful eyes weren't simply my imagination. But if Derrick was showing this side of himself to others, what would he do next?

"Thank you, Bonnie. I'll keep my guard up. Let me know if you hear anything more from him."

"Don't worry about Renee. She's safe here with Red and

me." Bonnie's smile came through in her reassuring voice.

I wanted to ask more questions. How did Renee respond when Derrick arrived? Was she upset? Those questions would wait until after work. My daughter was safe and that was all that mattered.

I felt it before I saw anything. A creepy, tingling feeling down my spine. A sense the clouds in the sky had darkened. I tried to brush the warning off. Five more minutes and Renee and I would be home. Renee was chatting non-stop in the backseat about her day. I listened the best I could, my ears tuned in for the word "Daddy," anxious to know if the morning's events had scared her.

I glanced at her through the rearview mirror, and that's when I saw it. Derrick's truck behind me, about three car lengths back. My grip on the steering wheel tightened. I kept my speed at 55, watching for the exit that would take me to my apartment. Without using a signal or slowing down, I turned off onto the exit, then glanced in the mirror. The red truck had followed. Coming to the stop sign, I glanced in the rearview mirror again. The truck came to a stop. Derrick was behind the wheel, a scowl on his face.

My cell phone was in the cup holder next to me. I picked it up as I turned left. Who did I call? What did I say? I didn't have an answer to either question. I put my phone down. It was still daylight. People would be out and about at the apartment complex. Derrick wouldn't act out in front of strangers. He always put on his charming salesman persona for the rest of the world.

Except for today with Bonnie.

As I pulled into the apartment complex, a quick peek in my rearview mirror confirmed Derrick was still behind me. With shaking hands, I maneuvered into my designated parking spot. Derrick stopped his truck behind my SUV, blocking me in. I turned off my engine and sat for a moment, unsure of what to do. I didn't see anyone around. Derrick didn't get out of his truck. My best option was to jump out of my vehicle and make a beeline to my apartment door.

"Renee, go ahead and unbuckle your seatbelt, okay?"

Renee looked confused but did as I asked. I threw my purse over my shoulder, grabbed my keys and opened my door. Without looking in Derrick's direction, I opened Renee's door and pulled her out of her car seat, then slammed her door. I reached into my still open driver's side door, grazing the top of Renee's head on the roof as I grabbed my phone out of the cup holder. Why hadn't I put it in my purse?

"Daddy?" Renee's tiny voice sent shivers down my spine.

Derrick marched toward me. The look in his eyes was one I'd seen before—fury. Except this time it was like gasoline had been thrown on it, creating an inferno.

An inferno focused on me and closing in.

I punched numbers on my phone. Calling 9-1-1 didn't come naturally, but Nannie's number did. Three digits in and the phone was ripped from my hands and thrown back into my car. I backed up, standing between Derrick and my car door.

"Calling your lover-boy?" Derrick growled. Renee buried her face in my neck.

"No. I was calling Nannie." Confession came too easily for me.

Derrick's laughter was cold but deep. "Your Nannie? What's she going to do for you dearie, knit you a blanket so you can hide from the truth?"

There it was again. The truth. I reached into my Explorer for the phone Derrick had thrown and slipped it in my purse. To my surprise, he didn't stop me. I shut the door and turned toward my apartment.

"Where do you think you're going?"

"Leave me alone, Derrick." I kept walking, my shoulders tight, sensing Derrick behind me and expecting to feel his hand on my hair any moment.

Looking right, then left, I noticed a couple of people on the sidewalk further down. They had stopped and were staring in our direction. I made it to my door.

"You might want to move your truck. People are staring," I said without turning around. The footsteps behind me stopped. A sigh of relief escaped my lips as I pushed my apartment door open. Derrick moving his truck would give me plenty of time to get inside, double lock the door, and check the windows. But as soon as I walked into my apartment, steps rushed behind me, and the door slammed shut. A loud click told me the deadbolt was latched.

Icy dread surged through me. I turned around.

"Let's get a couple of matters straight." Derrick stood by the closed door, his finger pointing at me.

I stepped backward toward the kitchen area with its sliding door. If I made it there, I could escape. Then I remembered the board I kept at the bottom of the door for extra security. There was no way I could bend down to remove the board and unlock it fast enough, especially with Renee in my arms.

Derrick took slow steps toward me, closing the distance. "Divorce or no divorce, you are the mother of *my* child, and you *will* do what I say when it comes to that child."

I cringed at the way he referred to Renee. She buried her head deeper into my neck. My shoulder was wet with her silent tears.

"Second, if you are going to insist on getting alimony from me, then that means I own a part of you. Nobody in this world gets something for free, Cass. Payment time is coming." Derrick half-smiled. Danger flickered in his eyes.

It was a look I'd seen before— the times when I had resisted Derrick's advances because he had been drinking and I couldn't tolerate his touch. A wave of nausea gripped my stomach. I fought the urge to double over. I scanned my apartment. The window blinds were closed. No one would know what was going on inside.

While making a show out of shuffling Renee around on my hip, I pulled my phone out of my purse. "I'm going to call the police if you don't leave right now." I forced the words out of my constricted throat, barely above a whisper, and pushed the nine with my thumb. Before I could touch the one, Derrick closed the short distance between us and grabbed my wrist, twisting it. I lost my hold on the phone and it fell to the floor. Derrick hovered over me, not letting go of his grasp on my upheld arm. Renee was between us, wrapped around me in a death grip.

Renee's fingers digging into my shoulders spurred me to action. I couldn't let her witness any more. Ignoring the pain in my wrist, I stepped backward. "Help! Someone help me!"

Derrick lunged toward me, grabbing the back of my head with one hand and covering my mouth with the other. He pushed me back into the dining table. Its edge cut into my legs, steadying me. I used the extra support to kick. I couldn't reach high enough to cause any real damage, but battered Derrick's shins enough to loosen his hold on my head. I twisted my chin from under his hand and screamed.

"Shut up!" Derrick hissed. His eyes blazed as he covered my mouth once more. This time turning his wrist up to cover my nose. I couldn't breathe. Renee's body quivered with silent sobs, but she didn't lose her hold on me. *No! Please God, not with Renee in my arms!*

A loud knocking at the door pierced the quiet. Derrick froze, his eyes boring into mine. The knocking continued, and a muffled voice came from the other side. "Is everything okay in there?"

Derrick backed away. I sucked in air, my body weak. In a blink Derrick's demeanor changed to relaxed composure. He took brisk steps toward the door and opened it. I couldn't see who stood on the other side but heard a man's voice. "What's going on in there?"

Derrick shook his head. "Hey, man, sorry to cause a ruckus. My wife and I ..." Panic ripped through me. He was going to try and get rid of the guy with a lame story. The sliding door was maybe three feet from me. In one swift move, I swooped down, took out the security stick, and unlocked the door. Before Derrick realized what was happening, I opened the sliding door and stumbled onto the patio. I saw a gray-haired man at the front door. A woman stood behind him, her phone in hand. She turned to me, and for a moment our gazes met. I crumbled to the ground, still holding Renee in an iron grip. The woman walked toward me, a cell phone held to her ear. Her voice sounded like it was at the end of a long tunnel, echoing in my ear. "We need an officer right away. It's a domestic dispute."

Derrick was gone by the time the police arrived. He had sauntered to his truck, climbed in, and drove off. The man who knocked on the door had helped me up and into my apartment.

I rested on my couch, and the man sat next to me. He was talking, but I couldn't focus on his words. Renee's shaking body stilled, and she peeled herself away from me. Swollen, wide eyes stared up at me with an uncertainty that stung my heart. Her innocence was slipping further and further away, down a river filled with my regret.

Someone knocked on the door. I jumped. The man put

his hand on my shoulder. "That's probably the police. Let me get the door."

A young police officer entered the living room. He was of average height but slender with lengthy legs and a long neck, reminding me of a giraffe. I wrapped my arms around Renee, pulling her close.

The officer knelt by me. His eyes were a soft blue, reassuring. He spoke to Renee. "Hey, there. I'm Officer Meyer, but you can call me Alex. What's your name?"

Renee looked at me, uncertainty all over her face. I nodded at her. "You can tell him your name."

"R-r-renee." Her voice quivered, barely audible. My throat burned from holding back my tears.

"Renee is a pretty name." Alex reached into his pocket, pulled out a sticker. "Renee, I need to talk to your mommy. I have a sticker here for you. Would you like it?" The sticker was a large star and looked like a badge. Renee sucked in her lips, but nodded.

Alex smiled and glanced around the room. "I have coloring pages and crayons in my car. If I have my partner get them for you, do you think you could go sit at your table and color while I talk to your mom?"

Renee nodded again, this time with a bit more enthusiasm. Alex got up and opened the door. Another officer and the lady who had called the police stood on the sidewalk. Alex spoke to them, then turned to the man who had helped. One day, I would find out his name.

"Sir, would you mind speaking to my partner outside? I'm afraid we're going to need your statement."

The man stood up and nodded, relief evident on his face. Within moments, the coloring pages had arrived and Renee was coloring at the table. Alex pulled a chair out of the kitchen and set it across from me in the living room.

"Miss, I know it's hard to talk right now. Can I get you a

glass of water or anything?" His voice was soft.

I shook my head. Time for me to pull myself together.

He nodded and sat in the chair. "I need to ask you a few questions about what happened tonight." He held a clipboard with papers on it, a pen ready.

I exhaled and nodded. *Here we go.*

Alex asked all the basic questions. Were Derrick and I still married? Had he done this before?

"He's never been like he was tonight." Beginning with seeing him in my rearview mirror, I recounted the events of the evening.

"You were calling 9-1-1 when he grabbed the phone from you?"

"The second time, yes. The first time I was calling my grandma."

His sandy eyebrows knit together. "Why your grandma?"

I shrugged my shoulders. "I didn't know who else to call."

Alex made notes on his clipboard. "But your second call, you were dialing 9-1-1, correct?"

I nodded again, confused as to why it mattered. Alex continued the questions—how did Derrick stop me? Did he physically harm me? I answered the questions the best I could. Alex studied my face and asked me to lift my hair off my shoulders so he could check for bruising on my neck. Next, he looked at my wrist. "Are you in pain anywhere? Do you feel like you need to see a doctor?"

"No." I didn't have any signs of physical harm. The realization made my heart sink. My word against Derrick, once again.

Alex nodded and made more notes. He looked up and watched Renee coloring, then scanned the room. His eyes landed on a portrait of Renee from the year before. In it she wore a full smile, dimples showing. Her eyes were bright and full of innocent joy. Now Renee sat at our tiny dining table, her brow furrowed as she pressed hard on the crayons, filling the spaces with deliberate, focused strokes. Her cheeks were red and spotty from crying.

Alex turned to me, his face determined. "This is what you're going to do. Tomorrow morning, be at the courthouse by eight a.m. and ask for Victim Services. They will assist you in filing a restraining order."

My mouth dropped. A restraining order? Derrick would be infuriated. "I … I can't do that."

"Cassandra, I'm submitting this report, and criminal charges will be filed against your husband. Taking your phone away from you while you're attempting to call 9-1-1 is a crime, not to mention trespassing and harassment. You *need* a restraining order." Alex looked in my eyes, genuine concern in his expression.

I ran my hands through my hair. Adrenaline shot through my veins and I stood up. "What will happen once the report is filed?"

"We will be visiting him tonight to get his statement. My advice for you is to stay somewhere else tonight, if possible, but I'll let him know I'm on duty all night and plan on patrolling this area." He paused, drawing in a breath. "A court date will be set. You'll have to testify. Your neighbors who showed up tonight might be called to testify … it's all in the DA's hands."

I paced back and forth. If charges were filed, Derrick would … I couldn't even imagine. My main concern was Renee. If Derrick could turn this against me in a custody battle, he would do so, and with a vengeance.

"I can't do this. He'll—"

"Filing a protective order is the only thing you can do that *will* stop him. Trust me. Guys like him aren't stopped by a simple no. If you file a restraining order, it tells him you're done putting up with his treatment." Alex stood and nodded toward Renee. "You have more than yourself to think about, as I'm sure you're aware."

I stopped pacing and looked at Renee. She had filled in every white area of the coloring page and remained quiet this entire time. Did she understand what we were talking about?

"Cassandra, look at me." I looked Alex in the face. He was young, probably under thirty, yet he held a wisdom in his eyes I hadn't seen in many men twice his age. "Say it. Say you are going to the courthouse first thing in the morning and filing a restraining order."

My mind whirled. Daycare. Work. Cynthia. My paycheck. Renee.

I nodded, my throat too tight to speak. Fear and hope swirled around me, each staking its claim in my spine.

"I want to hear you say it."

I looked at the portrait of Renee on the wall, and the tears that pride had held back reached the corners of my eyes. I swallowed against the noose around my throat, and my gaze settled on Alex's concerned face. "I will file a restraining order tomorrow."

Chapter Twenty

THE GRAY CONCRETE OF THE COURTHOUSE matched the color of the sky. A line of people waited to go inside. Some talked and laughed, but the majority kept to themselves, with eyes that reflected either desperation or hopelessness. Shivering in the morning fog, I took my place in the back of the line. Around my neck was a necklace Nannie had given me many years ago, a tiny gold cross on a delicate chain. I wasn't sure what prompted me to wear it today. Maybe I needed a part of Nannie with me. I hadn't told her what happened. Not yet. If I wasn't granted the restraining order, knowing what Derrick had done would only make her worry more.

At exactly eight a.m., a man in a dark suit opened and held the glass doors and the line moved forward. He wore an earpiece, and when he lifted his arm a holstered gun showed.

My heart pitter-pattered in my chest. An urge to turn and walk away tugged at my feet. Then I thought of Renee. Her safety was more important than my fear of entering the unknown.

When I got to the door the dark suited man asked, "Do you have a court appearance today, ma'am?"

I shook my head. "I need to go to Victim Services." Shame rushed up my neck, coloring my face.

He nodded. "You'll need to pass through security, then take the elevator up to the fourth floor."

I swallowed. Passing through security didn't look like fun. People were removing their belts, and one man was requested to take off his boots. The women submitted their purses for a pass through the metal detection machine. A young woman with a baby sent her diaper bag through. The baby wailed from her carrier, and the sound echoed in the concrete room. "She needs her pacifier," the woman explained to the stone-faced security guards.

Several men wearing suits and carrying briefcases went through a separate line, avoiding the security check. Guards nodded and greeted them as friends. It took a moment for me to realize the men in suits were attorneys on their way to court.

After making it through security, I found the elevators. Other women accompanied me, and several looked more tired and scared than I felt—all except for one with a nose ring and blue hair. The scowl on her face and fierce anger in her eyes said she was ready to punch the first person who crossed her. I stared at the lighted numbers above the door. The elevator stopped at each floor. It was only 8:15, but the courthouse was abuzz with activity.

The bell chimed for the fourth floor and I exited with the other women. The blue haired lady pushed herself to the front. She marched directly to the sign that read, "Victim Services" and swung open the wooden door. The other women, including myself, shuffled along, following her footsteps. A sense of oppression encircled me. The only comfort was the welcoming aroma of coffee.

The Victim Services office had a waiting area lined with chairs, tables, and assorted magazines. A child's play area was set up in one corner. There were no windows, and even the door to the hallway held only a small rectangle of an opening.

"Have you filed for a protective order before?" an elderly woman at the counter asked. I shook my head, unable to find my voice.

The woman nodded and handed me a clipboard with what looked like one-hundred pages of paper attached to the top of it, along with a ticket with the number five. "Go ahead and look this over while you wait for one of our specialists. She can help you fill out the paperwork properly."

I took the stack of papers to a nearby seat and leafed through them, reading the requirements for a restraining order. I easily met the relationship and age ones, but when I came to the "abuse" section, my stomach flip-flopped. The form read:

In the last 180 days the person who abused you must have:

- physically injured you or
- tried to physically injure you or
- made you afraid that he or she was about to physically injure you or
- made you have sexual relations against your wishes by using force or threats of force.

Derrick had definitely made me afraid, but the physical injuries were so minor there was no proof. I did have a small bruise on my leg where I had hit the table when backing away from Derrick, but there was no mark on my wrists to show where he had forced me to drop the phone. He'd twisted my arm on the night Nannie called the police, but I didn't tell the officer who interviewed me what happened. If Derrick saw I listed the arm twisting as an incident, he would note that fact to the judge. He would make me look like a liar. I scanned the women near me. One had a bruised cheek and a cut lip. Another woman's hands shook and dark circles lined her eyes like she hadn't slept in days. The blue-haired lady was writing intensely, the flower at the top of her pen shaking under the vigor.

I didn't belong here. Things weren't that bad with Derrick, and I was most definitely not one of these women. I stood to take the packet back to the receptionist.

Keep your eyes ahead of you. Grandpa's voice, from my last dream of him. I looked straight ahead. A poster of an impressive waterfall hung on the opposite wall, above one of the vacant seats in the room. It looked exactly like the one I had clipped from the newspaper months ago. Goosebumps covered my arms.

Hold tight. My fingers grasped the cross necklace around my neck. Like a hug from Nannie, calm wrapped around me, and any doubts about being in the Victim Services office drifted away. I settled into my seat.

"Number five?" A woman's husky voice called out.

A nicely dressed, middle-aged woman with dark skin surveyed the room. Bouncing out of my seat, I held up my ticket like an overly eager contestant on The Price Is Right. A small smile flashed across the woman's face. "Good morning. My name is Joanne." She held out her hand.

"My name's Cassandra, but you can call me Cassie." I shook her hand, hoping mine wasn't too damp.

I followed Joanne through a doorway and into a small room containing only a desk and three chairs. "Go ahead and have a seat." She motioned to a minimally padded chair on one side of the desk.

Joanne sat across from me and folded her hands on the desk. "Did you look over the petition?"

"Yes, I looked over the questions. There was an incident last night with my husband. The police officer said charges were being filed and I should get a restraining order right away."

"Well, let's fill this out and get you in front of the judge this morning." Joanne gently pulled the packet from my hand.

I answered the questions Joanne asked without hesitation, until we came to the part about the incidents. "In the last 180 days—that's about six months—has your husband caused you bodily harm?" Joanne asked the question without looking at the paper. She had obviously filled out this form many times.

I squirmed in my seat. "Not exactly."

Joanne tilted her head toward me and raised her dark eyebrows. Deep brown eyes peered into mine. "What do you mean by 'not exactly'?"

Looking away, I focused on the flat gray carpet. "I guess I mean no, he hasn't really caused any physical damage. Just some pain."

"And what did he do to cause pain?"

I shrugged. It all seemed so minor compared to the bruises on the lady in the lobby. Or compared to stories on the nightly news. "He grabbed my wrist and twisted my arm. Pulled my hair. Put his hand over my mouth to keep me from screaming."

"I would say that falls under the category of bodily harm, wouldn't you?" Joanne's voice was full of conviction, but not harsh.

I nodded in agreement. "Yes, but it could be a lot worse."

"Honey, if you don't do something to stop him, it will get worse. That's why the police told you to file the FAPA."

"The what?"

Joanne smiled. "That's short for Family Abuse Prevention Act. It's the restraining order."

Of course. I worked for lawyers. I should know nothing in the legal world had the same name as it did on the street.

Joanne continued with the questions. "Did you have any bruises or cuts after these incidents with your husband?"

I shook my head. The bruise on my leg didn't seem worth mentioning. What Derrick could do if he discovered I made him out to be a woman-beater would be far worse.

"Now I need you to briefly describe each incident that has happened in the last 180 days, starting with what happened last night. We don't need the entire back story, only a description of the threats he made and the physical things he did to cause you harm."

Reigning in my emotions, I reiterated the events of the night before. Joanne nodded encouragingly while I talked, easing my discomfort. "Now I'm assuming this isn't the first time something like this has happened?"

"No … shortly after I left, there was another time when he was waiting at my car when I took my daughter to the park." I went on to provide the details, making sure to note how Derrick grabbed my arm. Joanne glanced at a large clock on the wall. "It's almost time to head in. I think we have enough to get the FAPA granted. But is there anything else you feel needs to be recorded?"

I swallowed. "I don't think my daughter is safe with Derrick. Can the restraining order include her?"

"Has he caused your daughter any physical harm, or threatened to harm her?"

Derrick's threats played out in my head. When it came to Renee, he didn't threaten to hurt her, not physically anyway. "No, but he has threatened to not bring her home. He's threatened to put her in a different daycare. He lies to her and upsets her. She's always tired when she gets back from visiting him." The words spilled out as I pulled on the hem of my shirt.

Joanne leaned toward me. "I know those things hurt a mother's heart. But the judge won't grant a FAPA order for a child for threats to take her away, or for being rude. Not even for what might be called verbal abuse. Unfortunately, you can't even get an expedited custody hearing for those things."

Brian was right. There was nothing to be done, even after the events of last night. My shoulders sank with defeat.

Joanne pushed the papers toward me and handed me a pen. "Here, honey, you need to sign. Let me tell you something I've told a lot of other women in your situation.

Even though the order is only for your protection, and not your child's, in reality it does help protect your child. Because seeing or hearing what he does to you, hurts your little girl too."

I nodded my agreement, but my stomach turned. If Derrick couldn't take his anger out on me, that didn't mean it would simply go away. Who would be the new recipient of his rage? Holding the pen, I paused before signing. Was this really the best way to protect Renee? I looked at Joanne, who was watching me.

"Trust me. This is a step in the right direction."

The judge was an older man with thinning dark hair, heavy jowls, and black-rimmed glasses. He read through my petition quickly, without emotion. "Are there any other matters before the court regarding you and the defendant, or your child?"

"No ... well, yes. We filed for divorce."

The judge looked at me over the rim of his dark glasses, then turned to a computer at his desk. He fiddled with the keyboard and stared at the screen.

"It looks like there've been some criminal charges entered into the system."

I didn't say anything. Officer Alex had followed through on his word.

The judge's eyes did not waver. "Ms. Peterson, I am granting a temporary protective order. Victim Services will assist you in getting the defendant served. Please be aware the order is not punishable until served. The defendant will have thirty days to request a hearing. If he doesn't request a hearing, the order is valid for one year. Do you have any questions for the court?"

I shook my head, then remembered that wasn't

acceptable. "No, Your Honor."

In five minutes, I was back in the Victim Services office and given directions to the sheriff's office, who would serve the restraining order. By ten a.m., I was back in my SUV and completely drained. I read the restraining order in my trembling hands. Derrick couldn't be within two hundred feet of my apartment or my work. He couldn't come anywhere near me, and he could only call or email about parenting time and other issues regarding Renee. This was a victory. Or was it? The nagging fear of how he would respond to the criminal charges and the restraining order tempered any sense of victory I felt.

If I knew Derrick, it wouldn't be long before I found out exactly what he thought about what I had done.

Chapter Twenty-One

"THIS IS MAX FROM THE TICK-TOCK SHOP. Your music box is ready for you to pick up."

Music box. With everything going on, the music box repair completely slipped my mind. "Great! How much do I owe you?"

"It took a bit longer than expected. It's an interesting piece. Any-who, the charge is seventy-five dollars."

Seventy-five dollars? I swallowed. It wouldn't kill me. Creative budgeting at the supermarket was my new hobby. Plus, one unexpected benefit of my trip to the courthouse was the pamphlet from the Victim Services office about a food supplement program, and it looked like I would qualify. What was it Nannie always said? *He giveth and taketh away.* Maybe for once God was balancing the scales.

"Will you be open this Saturday?"

"Yes, Ma'am. I open at ten a.m. By the way, I don't take checks. Only cards and cash."

"Okay, I'll see you Saturday." I exhaled with relief.

I turned toward my waterfall calendar, soaking in the picture of Latourell Falls. For once my desk was clear, Cynthia was on a conference call, and I could focus on something other than what was right in front of me. This weekend was mine with Renee. I would pick up the music box Saturday, and we would visit Nannie on Sunday.

Hopefully the music box and our accompanying her to church would brighten Nannie's day. Worry had tinged her voice each time I had spoken to her since the last incident with Derrick. Hearing that the restraining order was granted and in full effect, and a criminal court date was set, seemed to ease her anxiety—not to mention my own—yet I could tell something was still eating at her.

Any day now the District Attorney would be calling about the criminal trial. I was holding my breath, ready for Derrick's retribution. He texted me the previous Wednesday afternoon, stating he couldn't pick Renee up for her midweek visit due to a work commitment. It may or may not have been true, but it gave me welcome relief. Dread crept over me at the thought of Renee going back to Derrick's. I had done all I could, for now.

The same grey-haired woman sat at the reception desk of the retirement home. "Please sign in, dear," she purred when Renee and I entered the building.

Nannie had nixed my plans for a Sunday visit and requested Renee and I come up Saturday instead. It was downright out of character for her not to jump at the prospect of our accompanying her to church. When I asked if she was okay, she had responded, "Oh yes, everything is good. Very good in fact." There was even a note of a smile in her voice.

"Mommy, come on, come on!" Renee pulled on my free hand. She was excited to give Nannie the repaired music box. At Renee's insistence, we had put it in a gift bag, covered in layers of tissue paper.

The receptionist smiled at Renee and waved her hand at me. "I can put your name down, go on ahead."

Renee tugged on my hand again. We made our way down the halls to Nannie's door. In her excitement, Renee didn't bother knocking. She forged ahead, turning the handle, releasing my hand and rushing into the room.

"Nannie! Nan—"

My heart leapt into my throat and I rushed into the room. At first everything looked the same. Nannie was sitting in her favorite chair, her makeup and hair done as usual. Then my eyes rested on the seat next to her, and I understood why Renee had suddenly gone quiet. A stranger sat there. At least to Renee, the woman was a stranger. But it was a face I knew well.

My mom smiled at me, lines accentuating her light brown eyes. "Hi, baby girl. It's been a long time."

Renee ran to me, confusion in her eyes. "Who is that?" she whispered, tugging on my jeans. I put my hand on her head, unable to find words.

"I'm your grandma, Renee. Don't you remember me?" Mom stood and took a step toward us.

I shook my head and narrowed my eyes at my mom. "What are you doing here?"

"Cassie ..."

I turned toward Nannie's gentle voice. Now I realized why she had wanted me to come today instead of tomorrow. Heat flared in my chest. Why would Nannie do this to me, especially with everything else I was going through?

"Cassie, please. Would you sit down and listen?" Nannie begged. I looked her in the eyes—so full of hope, of love. It was beyond my understanding. My mom had caused Nannie so much pain. How could Nannie forgive and forget so much?

Renee's eyes darted between me, my mom, and Nannie. I took Renee's hand and made our way to Nannie's bed, which was the only other place to sit in the room. I sat on the bed, putting the gift bag at my feet. Renee sat beside me without a word, staring at my mom in bewilderment. No one anything for a good thirty seconds.

"I've missed you so much, Cassie." My mom's voice, which had varied between hoarse and scratchy for most of my childhood, was now high pitched, strained with emotion.

Forcing myself to look at her, I blinked away tears. She

definitely looked healthier. The last time I had seen her, three years ago, her skin had been dry and she had dark bags under her bloodshot eyes. Her hair had been limp and slightly greasy. Now her skin, though more wrinkled than most other fifty-three-year-old women, was clear, and she even wore a light dusting of eye shadow and a smattering of mascara. Her dishwater blonde hair was full and healthy, with lightly feathered bangs that showed wisps of grey. The little girl in me wanted to run into her arms, but I knew better than to let my guard down.

"Why now?" My words were strained. "Why do you show up now, when I'm already going through hell?"

Mom looked to Nannie, who nodded at her encouragingly. "I've been sober for a year. I've been afraid to come see you, or anyone. Afraid I would be hit by a trigger from the past and fall off the wagon. Then ..." Mom crossed the short distance between us and took a seat on the bed, next to Renee. She smiled at her granddaughter. Mom's smile hadn't changed. Big and genuine, unashamed of her nicotine stained teeth. She sighed and glanced at Nannie again, then returned her gaze to me. I didn't want to look her in the eyes, yet like a fish on the end of a hook, I was lured in. "When I called to check on Nannie, she told me what was going on."

Tears streamed down Nannie's cheeks, etching lines in her rouge. How could I be mad at her? She was only trying to help. She didn't understand I couldn't forgive the way she did. My mom's alcoholism had stolen my childhood, and despite my best attempts, I had been a textbook example of an alcoholic's child. Not by becoming one myself, but by marrying someone who was. Then again, Derrick wasn't a heavy drinker when I met him. Maybe I was cursed. I stared at my worn-out sneakers. The soles were separating from the upper part of the thinning shoe. Pretty soon there would be a hole in them, exposing my big toe.

That's what's happening to your heart right now. Was that Grandpa's voice, or my own? It didn't sound like either.

Bitterness sprang from my chest and to my tongue. "I'm not really sure how you showing up is going to make anything better."

"Cassie, please." Nannie reached for me.

"No, Mom, she's right." My mom's voice was level. I felt her eyes on me. I couldn't look up. Renee scooted closer to me, and snuggled into my arm. I patted her knee reassuringly. The last thing she needed was more drama in her life.

"I know I've made mistakes. Lots of mistakes. I can't take any of them back. What I can do is be here for you, *now*. Whether you realize it or not, you and Renee need family. I don't have any money. I don't have anything to offer you except my love and my support." Mom's voice cracked. "I'm proud of you, baby girl. It took a lot of courage to get away from that ... situation. I want to help you and Renee get through this any way I can."

Tears ran down my cheeks. I couldn't afford to be vulnerable. Derrick would use any sight or sound of my mom against me. Mom had an undeniably shady past. Yet, to not carry this burden alone. To have family. Whether I wanted to admit it or not, I hated being alone. Should I give my mom a chance, and put mine and Renee's already broken hearts on the line?

Renee reached her hand up to my face, wiping away a tear. "It's okay, Mommy. I get sad sometimes too." Her wise emerald eyes looked into mine.

I reached for her tiny, soft hand and brushed it with a gentle kiss. I would want forgiveness someday, for all the hurt I wasn't able to protect her from.

There had been too many dark days, too many empty

years. For Nannie's sake, I would try. I looked at my mom. Her eyes held a thousand burdens, ones I may never understand.

"It's worth at least talking about," I whispered.

An hour passed before I knew it. At first, we stumbled in our attempts at conversation. Nannie kept steering things in the right direction, picking up where Mom or I would leave off, filling in blank spaces. Renee warmed up quickly. Though Mom was a stranger to her, the idea of having another grandma seemed to fill her with awe. She listened intently to every word Mom said. When she offered to play hide and seek, Renee jumped at the opportunity. My mom's attempts to hide in Nannie's small room made us laugh. She hid under a blanket at first, then tried to squeeze herself into Nannie's small closet. I'd forgotten this side of my mom. Her ability to be a big kid, to live in the moment. It was a trait she'd gotten from Grandpa, and one I admired.

Mom plopped down beside me on the bed, out of breath from playing with Renee, but smiling. Renee peeked her head from under the bed, her hair full of static, pointing in all directions. "Mommy! We need to give Nannie the present!"

In all of the unexpectedness, I'd forgotten about the gift bag at my feet. "You're right. Do you want to hand it to her?" I winked at Nannie, who looked confused.

Renee scurried out from under the bed and with a proud smile handed the bag to Nannie.

"My goodness, what is the occasion?"

"Mommy fixed it, Nannie. Look!" Renee stood on her tiptoes and ripped out the tissue paper she had so gingerly put in the pink bag.

Nannie reached in the bag and pulled out the music box. Sadness deepened the lines on her face, and her eyes glistened.

"Open it!" Renee clapped her hands excitedly, unaware

of the awkward silence in the room. I reached for Renee to pull her toward me and give Nannie space.

Nannie hesitantly lifted the lid, and the melody of the box filled the room. My mom shot up from the bed. "I need a smoke." She grabbed her purse and headed toward the door.

"Where you going?" Renee's attention was now on Mom.

"I'll be back, Sweet Pea." Mom answered without turning and sped out the door.

"What got into her?" I asked Nannie. She was watching the birds in the box do their dance. Tears formed in the corners of her eyes. "Nannie, what's wrong?"

Nannie closed the box and set it down on the end table by her chair. "It's been a long time since I've heard that melody. As for your mom ..." Nannie looked at the door Mom had walked out, as if she could still see her there. "She has her own way of dealing with things."

Nannie was keeping something from me. I studied her face, looking for answers, waiting for her to say more. Instead she put on what I knew to be her smile-like-everything-is-great face and drew in a deep breath. "Are we ready for lunch?"

Mom found us in the cafeteria, sitting at a table for four. The scent of cigarette smoke followed her, and without thinking I scrunched my nose. Nannie shot me a warning look, and I forced my face into what I hoped was a neutral expression. I knew what Nannie was thinking. Mom had only been sober one year. Now wasn't the time to make her feel bad about another vice.

"When do you have to head home?" I smoothed the napkin on my lap. Whether I wanted to admit it or not, I was enjoying our unexpected family reunion and didn't want it to end. Who knew when Mom would come visit again.

Mom and Nannie exchanged glances. Mom looked back down at her bowl of soup, stirring it with her spoon. "I was going to talk to you about that."

"Your mom and I came up with a plan." Nannie piped up, her eyes bright.

An uneasiness came over me, the feeling of being kept out of a secret "Okay ... what's the plan?"

"Look, don't feel like you have to agree to this, because I completely understand if you don't." My mom put down her spoon and looked at me with uncertain eyes. "We were thinking ... what if I came and stayed with you for a while? You'd have someone there if certain people show up when they shouldn't, and I could help with Renee." Mom glanced at her granddaughter, who had already finished her peanut butter and jelly sandwich and was now playing a game on my phone. The love in Mom's eyes was evident, as was her uneasiness in suggesting she come stay with us.

Derrick's voice echoed in my head, *your white trash mother isn't welcome in my home.* Derrick had never liked my mom but treated her with common decency on the few occasions when we saw her. After Grandpa died, it was like the tether that kept Derrick in check broke, and he made demands—what he called house rules—when it came to my family. The number one rule was my mom was not allowed in our home. I was only allowed to let Renee see her if she happened to be at Nannie's when we were there. Mom made Derrick's rules pretty easy to follow, because I hadn't seen her at all since Nannie went to live in a retirement home. Now she was here, and she was sober. Now, I didn't share a home with Derrick, and he couldn't tell me who I could and could not have in it. Why, then, did the idea of having my mom live with me fill me with terror? I felt like Derrick was behind me, waiting for me to give the wrong answer. If he was upset about my daycare choice, what would he do when he found out my mom was living with me?

"It's a great idea, but ..." I searched for the right words, not wanting to hurt Mom's feelings. "I think I should talk about it with the attorney who's been helping me. I don't want to do anything that might hurt the custody battle."

"You're afraid of what Derrick will say." Mom's voice was bitter. She knew me too well.

"Sharon, Cassie has a point. She wants to do everything right for Renee's sake." Some things never changed—Mom and I disagreeing, Nannie trying to make peace.

Renee perked up at her name and looked around the table. No one said anything, and Nannie and I pasted on fake smiles. Renee returned to her game. Mom leaned back in her chair, the soup forgotten, and watched Renee. Her eyes had gone hard. My mom's way of avoiding tears.

What would Grandpa do? He was the wisest man I had ever known, and he loved all of us. I thought of him sitting at the table, watching our conversation. While Nannie made peace, he'd speak his mind, even if his words made one of us mad.

Remember what I taught you.

The last time we were all together was Grandpa's last Christmas. Mom showed up late for dinner, but sober. Nannie, who worked hard all day on the meal and had a pet peeve about timeliness, complained the food was getting cold. Grandpa hadn't said a word about Mom being late. Instead he wrapped her in a bear hug. "It's good to have my girl home," he'd said, his voice full of love and acceptance. Derrick had been silent at the table, the ice in his eyes enough to put a chill in any meal.

"I'll text Brian this weekend and get his opinion. Either way, I don't see why it would hurt to have you come stay with us a couple of days."

Nannie's eyes glistened, and a smile filled her face. "An excellent idea."

My mom nodded at me, thankfulness and sorrow mixed in her expression. She turned her focus to Renee. "What do you think about Grammy coming to stay with you for a few days, Sweet Pea?"

Renee looked up, an expression of awe on her face. "Fun!"

We worked out the details after lunch, sitting in the courtyard under the shade of a cottonwood tree. The temperature was more summer like, and even in the shade the afternoon was warm. By mid-afternoon Nannie looked drained. Her eyelids drooped, and the heat had dampened the edges of her hair. "I think it's time for my afternoon siesta," she said, a tepid smile on her face. We walked Nannie to her room.

The music box was still sitting on the table next to Nannie's chair. Renee ran to it, then stopped. She turned to Nannie, and asked in her most polite voice, "Nannie, can we listen to the song one more time? Please?"

Mom and Nannie exchanged a look, part tenderness, part pain. Nannie put her hand on Mom's back, patting it like she did mine when I was upset. Why would Mom be upset about the music box? Tired and a bit irritated with being kept out of the secret, I had to ask. "Okay, so what's up with this music box? You both look like we dug up a corpse or something."

Mom smiled. "It's nothing, Cassie. We haven't heard it in a long time, that's all." She nodded toward Renee. "Go ahead, Sweet Pea."

Renee beamed, opening the lid. The haunting melody played again, the sound filling the room. My mom's face went blank, devoid of emotion. Renee twirled in a circle, her hands reaching in an arc over her head like a ballerina. Nannie smiled faintly as she gazed at Renee, seeming to see more than her great-granddaughter. "Memories ..." she murmured.

Memories, indeed. What were they not telling me? Maybe over the next couple of nights, mom would open-up and tell me the mystery of the music box.

Chapter Twenty-Two

"Why in the world would your mother staying with you hurt your custody case?" Brian's voice held more than a trace of amusement.

I had mustered the courage to call Brian late Sunday morning. My questions were too involved for a simple text message. There also might have been a small part of me that wanted to hear his voice. An image of his face kept invading my mind. In fact, he was the first thing I thought about when I woke up Sunday morning. I told myself it was only because I needed to talk to him about my case.

He was out on a run along the river when I called. "My mom isn't exactly Mrs. Brady, if you know what I mean." I could hear the sounds of passers-by on the other end of the line.

Brian sighed. "Does she have a criminal record?"

I had to think for a moment. "Not that I know of."

"Has she ever hurt Renee?"

"No! Of course not."

"Has she ever hurt you?"

Not physically. A thousand images from my childhood cascaded through my mind. Abandoned? In a way, yes. Broke my heart? Definitely. No physical damage was ever done. Still, if Brian didn't know more of the story, he couldn't adequately answer my question. "My mom had a hard time after my dad died. She started drinking quite a bit. We moved a lot, she had too many boyfriends and more than one was physically abusive to her. I went to live with my grandparents when I was nine." I rushed on before Brian could interrupt or misunderstand. "She straightened out a bit afterward. She still drank, but she would come and visit me and be normal, for the most part."

There was silence on the other end of the line, the only sound the faint rushing noise of the river. "I'm sorry, Cassie. I had no idea your childhood was anything like that." Brian cleared his throat. "Does your mom still drink?"

"No, she quit … about a year ago." I cringed at my confession. One year sober suddenly didn't sound too impressive.

"Good for her! And for you. I don't see any threat to your custody case by having your mom around. Of course, I would proceed cautiously, not only for legal reasons, but for the well-being of you and Renee."

Relief washed over me. "I was hoping you would say that. All I can hear sometimes is Derrick's voice. He hates my mom."

Brian chuckled. "I'm shocked. Imagine an abuser hating his victim's family."

An abuser. The label didn't feel right, like a new shirt that hadn't been washed yet and made you itch. "So, it's normal for someone like him?"

"It's classic. Was there anyone you cared about, other than Renee, you can honestly say Derrick liked?"

I went over the short list in my mind. Derrick seemed to like my grandparents and even my mom at first. As time went on, though, he collected a list of grievances against them and eventually each member of my family earned his contempt. He made sure not to show it around Grandpa. As soon as Grandpa passed away, the full depth of Derrick's disdain for Nannie and Mom became vividly real. My friend list was short when Derrick and I met, and over time he found flaws in each one and discouraged me from seeing them. Eventually they all stopped calling.

"I guess not." My heart dropped. I'd never realized how much I had lost over the years.

"Well, there you go." Brian paused. "It's a beautiful day. You should get out and enjoy it. Take your mom and daughter to the park, have a picnic."

I smiled. Sober or not, my mom wasn't exactly the picnic in the park type. Maybe we could go for a drive down to the river and get our feet wet. "Thank you, Brian. For everything."

"Of course. Another thing … the weather next weekend is supposed to be gorgeous. Renee goes to Derrick's next weekend, right?"

I didn't want to think about it. "Yeah."

"If you're up to chasing more waterfalls, I'd love to go with you." Brian's voice was soft, inviting, luring me out of the darkness of my fear of leaving Renee with Derrick.

"I would love to." Tears welled up in my eyes.

"Are you sure you don't want to leave Renee with me? It'd save you money on daycare, wouldn't it?"

Mom stood on the sidewalk, still in her pajama pants and an oversized T-shirt. I loaded Renee into the backseat of my SUV before she piped up and agreed with her grandma. I carefully shut the door, insulating her from our conversation. "It wouldn't actually save me money. I have to give a two-week notice to my daycare lady before taking Renee out, and I pay for each month in advance."

Mom's eyebrows knit together. "Well that's a rip-off. Give your notice today."

I sighed. "I appreciate you wanting to watch her. I really do. I should talk to an attorney at work about it though. Derrick has made a big issue out of daycare, and with joint custody he will have a say in where Renee goes."

Mom rolled her eyes. "He doesn't give a rat's behind about where Renee goes for daycare, he wants to control you."

Her words stung. I was afraid to leave Renee with Derrick because I didn't trust him, but the idea that he didn't care at all made me feel hollow.

"I'll see you tonight." I waved at my mom as I backed out of my parking space.

It had been odd having my mom around all weekend. On one hand it was comforting having someone there, not being alone. It was nice to ramble on about my job and my new waterfall goal. Yet it was also nerve-wracking. Renee took to Mom right away. It was like she had been there on a regular basis her entire life. Watching them, I worried. What if Mom decided to leave, and we didn't hear from her in months? What if she started drinking again? I knew that hurt all too well, and it was one I couldn't stand putting my daughter through. Regardless of what Brian may advise, the real reason why I didn't take Renee out of daycare and have Mom start watching her was because I didn't know if she'd stay. A white lie, yes, but a necessary one. This new leaf she'd turned over was still pretty green. It needed more time under the sun before I knew it could withstand the heat.

"Can you believe you're halfway through your probationary period?" Cynthia's eyebrows raised in what I knew was mock surprise. She had been at my desk before I came in, unusually early for a Monday.

"Wow, time flies. It seems like I started working here last week." I returned her fake smile, even though my heart hammered in my chest.

Cynthia nodded. "Exactly what I was thinking. It definitely doesn't feel like you've been working here three months. You still seem so ... fresh."

What did she mean by fresh? "Oh, well, thanks. It's

definitely been an adjustment from being home full-time, but this is such a great place to work. The time really has flown by."

Cynthia smiled tightly, and her eyes glimmered. "Good to hear." She turned and walked away, leaving a stack of files on my desk and unanswered questions in my mind.

Missy popped in as soon as Cynthia was gone. She leaned in, putting her hands on my desk. "I've heard certain poisons don't come up on blood screens," she whispered, the familiar sparkle in her hazel eyes.

I laughed, but only half-heartedly. "Then I need to get a batch of something good. Maybe there's a two-for-one deal?"

"Uh-oh, did Mr. Wonderful ruin your weekend?"

I shook my head. "Actually, believe it or not, I didn't hear from him once. It was a good weekend." Which either meant he was taking the restraining order to heart, or he was conniving a plan for retaliation. Based on previous experience, the latter was most likely. Instead of filling Missy in on my never-ending fears, I gave her the details of my visit to Nannie, and my mom's surprise re-appearance.

"Whoa ...that had to send you for a loop." Missy's eyes widened.

"Yeah, it did at first. But having my mom around has been nice, so far. I feel safer. Renee seems happier. I hope she stays the course, know what I mean?"

Missy nodded sympathetically. "Any word on the restraining order hearing?"

I sighed. "No, not yet. I think I might run it by Brian and see what he thinks about the lack of a response. I don't see Derrick not fighting it."

"Maybe his attorney knows he has a losing case?" Missy looked over her shoulder, then leaned close and her voice dropped. "Have you heard the latest gossip about Brian?"

Heat ran up my neck. "I didn't know Brian led a gossip-worthy life." I smiled, trying to downplay my nervousness about her remark. Had the news of his separation made its way through the office circuit?

"Oh, Brian has been the focus of gossip more than once, trust me. But the latest rumor is him and his wife are having a bit of marital difficulties."

I tried to look surprised. "That stinks."

Missy shrugged. "He probably deserves it. He's been known to be a little too friendly with certain women, if you know what I mean."

My heart hammered in my chest. There was no way I could tell Missy anything about my and Brian's plans to see a waterfall. She'd think I had something to do with his marital problems, even though Brian and I were only friends.

"I hope he keeps helping me with my divorce case," I replied, my mouth suddenly dry.

Missy whispered. "And I hope he doesn't try to help you with *more* than your divorce case."

I brushed off the remark. "He wouldn't. Besides, my life is a hot mess. Who would want any part of that?"

Missy moved in closer, her face inches from mine. I could smell her spearmint gum. "That's exactly the problem. Certain types of men are known to take advantage of women in your situation. I know Brian has been really helpful so far, but if he's having problems with his wife, he might try to soothe his wounds the best way he knows how. Here you are … beautiful, vulnerable, needing his help."

The seriousness in Missy's expression was something I hadn't seen before. I returned her gaze, hoping she couldn't see the guilt gnawing at me.

"I'll be careful. I promise." I felt terrible keeping a secret from the woman who had become my best friend. If I did see Brian outside of work, I would have to come clean and let her know. Besides, it wasn't like hiking was a real date.

"Will Grammy be at our home when we get there?" Renee screamed over the Toby Keith song I had blasting on the radio.

"I think so." I smiled at her in the rearview mirror. I wasn't able to call and check on Mom during work because she didn't have a cell phone. Part of me worried she would be gone by the time Renee and I got home.

Renee smiled and kicked her feet together, the sunlight coming in through the window bringing out the depth of green in her emerald eyes. I swallowed the lump in my throat, trying not to think about Renee's upcoming overnight visit with her dad. The idea of anything tarnishing the light in her eyes was more than I could bear. My mother's words from the morning rang in my head—*he doesn't give a rat's behind about where Renee goes for daycare, he wants to control you.* His love for Renee had to be bigger than his need to torture me. If it wasn't, he wouldn't even bother with seeing her, would he?

The smell of ground beef and onions cooking on the stove filled the small apartment. Renee dropped her backpack and ran into the kitchen. "Grammy! I'm home!" she squealed. A wave went through me, part nausea, part heartfelt warmth. Was this really my mom, cooking us dinner and being greeted by her granddaughter? Mom had never been much of a cook, at least not from what I remembered. Nannie did most of the cooking whenever we had family gatherings. Mom washed dishes. This changing of roles felt surreal.

Mom turned the corner into the living room, holding Renee in her arms. Renee beamed, and looked at her grandma with pure adoration—probably the way I had looked at Nannie when I was little. "How was the office?"

I shrugged. "Typical Monday."

"Did you talk to your attorney?"

Guilt washed over me, but I shrugged it off. "Yeah," I lied. "I'll tell you about it later."

Mom nodded. "All right." She looked at Renee and smiled. "Grammy's making spaghetti for dinner. Do you like spaghetti?"

Renee excitedly bounced in Mom's arms. "Yay! Scetti!"

Mom laughed. "Okay, Sweet Pea, why don't you go put your stuff away in your room, and Mommy and I can finish dinner."

Renee obediently grabbed her backpack and headed toward her room. I hated lying, but trying to explain the truth was worse. Besides, if I *had* talked to Brian, his advice may have aligned with my gut instinct. "Brian said I should definitely leave Renee in daycare for now because it shows more stability. He recommended I wait until after the custody hearing to make any changes."

I waited for mom to scowl, to curse, to tell me how ridiculous it all was. Instead she nodded thoughtfully. "I guess that makes sense. How long until your hearing?"

My chest ached. This was the mom I had seen on and off as a child, the one I longed for all these years. "Hopefully before the summer is over. We should be receiving a date from the court any day."

"That's not so long, in the big scheme of things." Mom turned back to the stove, where steam was rising from boiling water.

"I keep telling myself the same thing."

Chapter Twenty-Three

WEDNESDAY CAME ALL TOO SOON. I sprayed a tiny bit of my perfume on one of Renee's stuffed animals and tucked it in the bottom of her bag. I had read in a parenting magazine a stuffed animal or blanket with a mother's scent would soothe an upset baby. Renee wasn't a baby, and she might never pull out the stuffed animal, but I found a small measure of comfort in knowing a part of me would be with her. When I told Renee it was her dad's night she didn't say a word, only nodded solemnly, her eyes emotionless.

"Will Grammy still be here when I get back?" Renee asked as she hugged me goodbye in Bonnie's living room.

"Of course." I said, though I hated to make promises I wasn't certain I could keep.

Renee grinned. "Goodie!" She paused a moment, still clinging to me. "Mommy, don't forget my lipstick kiss."

I laughed. "I could never forget." I kissed Renee in the middle of the forehead, leaving a kiss mark in my favorite dusty rose color. "How's that?"

Renee reached up and gently touched her forehead. "Okay, you can go now, Mommy."

I forced myself to smile, but it hurt. I never wanted to let her go, but today was worse. "Thank you, Sugar Bug. I'll see you tomorrow!" I turned away before Renee saw my tears.

After work I stopped at the row of mailboxes near the entry of the apartment parking lot. More often than not my mailbox was empty so I hadn't even bothered checking it in a few days. Today, the box was full. Most of it was junk mail and flyers, but one envelope caught my eye with its professional typescript and familiar name—Rachael

Carmichael. Derrick's attorney. I glanced in my rearview mirror. Another car was behind me. Reading whatever the envelope contained could wait until I was in my apartment.

I scanned the parking lot as I pulled into my assigned space. Mom's car wasn't in the guest parking. My heart stung, and I swallowed the lump that formed in my throat. Of course. Shouldn't I have known better? Renee's question at daycare echoed in my thoughts. Why had I told her yes? *Thanks, Mom. Now I've lied to my daughter.*

I marched into my apartment, which smelled faintly of cigarette smoke, not because mom had been smoking in it but because everything she owned carried the scent. There was a note on the table. The infamous notes. At least mom never left without saying goodbye. I plopped down on the couch and picked up the ripped sheet of notebook paper covered in swirling cursive writing.

"Hey Kiddo - Ran to store to get popcorn and corn syrup. Thought we could make some popcorn balls. XOXO Mom."

After picking my jaw up off the floor, I laughed out loud, the sound echoing in the quiet apartment. Mom and I hadn't made popcorn balls since I was a preteen. Mom hadn't left. She even had something planned to distract me from my distress about Renee's visit with Derrick. For the first time all day, hope bubbled in my chest. We'd have to save a popcorn ball for Renee. She would love it. And, now that I knew I wouldn't face the evening alone, I would wait until Mom returned to open the envelope from Derrick's attorney.

Right after I changed into yoga pants and a t-shirt, Mom arrived with a Safeway bag in her arms. Part of me wanted to run up and hug her, but not only did I feel too old for that, it seemed awkward. This was the first time it had been just mom and me since before Derrick and I married.

"Are you good with having leftovers for dinner?" Mom carried the bag into the kitchen and set it on the dining table.

I followed her into the kitchen. "Definitely. Earlier today I was thinking we could watch old movies tonight."

Mom grinned, pulling out the bag of popcorn kernels. "I already looked through your collection. What are you more in the mood for? *When Harry Met Sally*, or *Romy and Michelle's High School Reunion*?"

"I'm more in the mood for comedy."

"Then Romy and Michelle it is." Mom searched my face with the all-knowing look of a mother. "How are you holding up?"

I shrugged. "As best as I can. Tomorrow can't come soon enough. But then there's the weekend to get through." I couldn't look in Mom's eyes, the empathy in them was too overwhelming. "I don't know how I can keep doing this."

"It makes me sick, Cassie. That man shouldn't be able to get away with all he has done. If he hurts that baby girl in any way, shape, or form, it'll be the last thing he does." Mom's voice had an all-too-familiar edge to it. I shuddered.

"I'm not sure if that makes me feel better or worse," I mumbled, my eyes focused on the checkered vinyl floor. Mom definitely didn't have Nanny's soothing ways. "I wish Grandpa was still around. Derrick wouldn't have ever pulled this stuff when Grandpa was alive."

Mom nodded, and a wistful smile lit up her face. "Dad was the kind of man who commanded respect without saying a word. I think Derrick was always a bit afraid of him." Mom unpacked the groceries, folding the empty paper bag and setting it aside.

"Renee would have had Grandpa wrapped around her finger." My heart ached at the thought. The only male influence in my daughter's life was her alcoholic father. How would that shape her relationship with men in the future?

Mom was unusually quiet. No grunts, no laughs.

Glancing up at her, she looked lost in thought "I think someday you'll meet a man who'll be a good dad to Renee, and a good husband to you. Don't let your heart get hard, like mine did. And don't … you know." Mom's sorrowful brown eyes settled on me.

"I won't," I whispered. I shook away the heaviness of the conversation, remembering the still unopened envelope from Derrick's attorney. "It looks like I have something from Derrick's attorney in the mail."

"What do you think it is?"

"I'm kind of scared to find out." My knees suddenly weak, I pulled a chair out from the table, sat down, and tore open the envelope. It contained a letter and a two-page legal brief. I scanned the short letter twice, making sure I was reading it correctly. My breath caught in my throat. "Wow."

"You're killing me here."

"Sorry. I'm just shocked. If I'm reading this right, Derrick no longer has an attorney." I set the paper down and rubbed my temples.

"Cool. Makes it easier to beat him in court, right?" Mom opened the cupboard and pulled out a big pot. She had really made herself at home.

"I guess. I don't know, Mom. I mean, maybe he's hiring a better attorney, which leaves me in an even worse place than before."

Mom shook her head. "Isn't the attorney you work for helping you?"

I nodded. "Yes. Maybe I'll give him a call. I think I heard he's out for meetings all day tomorrow, and I don't want to wait too long for answers."

I stepped out the front door and called Brian's cell.

"You miss work already?" Brian's tone was playful.

"Too funny. I take it you're still at the office?"

"Actually, I just ended a call and was getting ready to

leave. Your timing is enigmatic but perfect."

Enigmatic? I tried to laugh, but the sound came out like a dying horse's last breath. "I'm glad to hear that?"

Brian chuckled. "I was on the phone with Ms. Carmichael. She gave me an unofficial and slightly unethical courtesy call to let me know she no longer represents your ex."

Brian's choice of words now made sense. "I got the notice in the mail this afternoon, which is why I'm calling. I don't know what to make of it. Is he hiring another attorney?"

The line was silent. Brian cleared his throat. "He might. But he didn't fire Ms. Carmichael. She fired him."

My heart did a triple beat. "What do you mean?"

"That's really all I know. Ms. Carmichael called to warn me he had verbalized his wish to harm me and said she had removed herself as his attorney. She said his temper was, I quote, 'unsettling.'"

A cold wave rushed through my body. Derrick was usually charming with women—until they found themselves on his "people who are against me" list. There was no gray for Derrick. You were either all for him, or all against. First, he'd shown his true colors to Bonnie. Now it sounded like he'd lost his temper with his own attorney.

He was getting worse.

"What should I do?"

Brian sighed. "I wish I could tell you. For now, sit tight. He's digging his own grave. Having a restraining order against him and a pending case in criminal court isn't going to make him the prize client for any reputable attorney. Not to mention he'll have to come up with a new retainer."

It was a small consolation, but only enough to turn my anxiety level down from panic attack mode to my normal constant unease. "That's good to know. Maybe he won't be able to hire a new attorney."

"Exactly. And I truly don't see him representing himself well."

"But what about the threat he made toward you … did she say what it was?"

"Nope. And I'm not too worried. From what I've seen of him, I'm confident I could take him down in my sleep, with one arm tied behind my back."

I smiled at the thought. "I'm sure you could." I paused, staring at a crack in the sidewalk where a tiny weed, barely noticeable, was pushing itself through. "Thank you, Brian. I'm sure when you hired me you didn't realize what a mess of a situation you were getting yourself into."

"Hmm." Brian's voice went low, almost sultry. "True. But it's a beautiful mess."

Butterflies erupted in my chest. How should I respond? Before I could utter a word, Brian ended the conversation. "Have a good night, Cassie. I'll see you Friday." Then the line went silent.

A beautiful mess. I didn't really know what Brian meant. What I did know was that I liked the sound of Brian's voice when he said it.

My hands were covered in butter and stickiness when I heard my phone buzzing in the living room. I grabbed a paper towel and hurried to it. Derrick's name flashed across the screen. My heart jumped. Hopefully it was only Renee calling to say goodnight. With the restraining order in effect, Derrick wasn't supposed to call me for any reason outside of parenting.

"Have you lost your freaking mind, Cass?" Derrick yelled into the phone, and my paper-towel clad hand almost dropped it.

"Wh-what are you talking about?" I already knew the answer.

"You have your drunken whore of a mother living with you now? If you think I'm letting Renee go back to you with that vagrant living there, you've got another think coming."

I plopped down on the couch, my knees too weak to hold me up. "First of all, my mom isn't living with me, she's visiting. Second, you can't do that." Despite my best efforts, there was a slight tremor in my voice.

"You know, Cass, your little games are getting old. Like the restraining order you filed. Do you have any idea how much trouble you're going to be in when I go to court on the bogus criminal charges, and I'm found not guilty? I could sue you."

He could sue me? For what? I shook the thought out of my head, refusing to get dragged down the rabbit hole of his reasoning. "The restraining order is in effect, which means you can't contact me unless it has to do with parenting matters."

Derrick snorted. "That's why I'm calling, genius. I just told you. I won't have my daughter near your mother. As far as I'm concerned, she's in imminent danger if your mother is around. So I'm not bringing her back tomorrow. In fact, I'm taking this as my opportunity to find another daycare."

The tightening in my chest was unbearable. I curled my knees in, hugging them close with my free hand. Mom was standing near me now, but I couldn't look at her. "You have no authority to do that, Derrick."

"Try to stop me, Cass. It'll be the last thing you do." The phone beeped, the call over.

I set the phone down and dropped my head in my hands. "I can't win. I can't win."

Mom touched my shoulder and gently sat down next to me. "What did he say?"

"He said he's not bringing Renee back, because you're here." I didn't want to hurt my mom's feelings, but part of me was angry with her. If she had been a better mother, if she hadn't been an alcoholic, Derrick wouldn't be able to use her against me.

My mom's body stiffened, but she didn't get up. Her hand rubbed my back reassuringly. "I'm sorry, baby girl. Maybe it would be best if I left."

Would it matter? If I called Derrick back and told him my mom was leaving, would he take Renee to Bonnie's tomorrow? "I'm not sure it'll make a difference at this point. He won't believe me." I sat up, wiping the tears off my face. "We have a temporary parenting plan. He has to follow it, or he'll get in trouble. If he doesn't bring Renee back tomorrow, I'll call the police. Then, we'll go from there."

"It makes me sick, that he can do this to you." Mom got up and slowly paced back and forth in front of the couch. I didn't have the energy to move and had lost all interest in making popcorn balls. I picked up the sticky paper towel I had put down on the couch at some point during Derrick's phone call.

Mom's pacing came to a halt. Her eyes were filled with tears. "I swear, Cassie, if he harms one hair on that baby's head, I'll—"

"I don't see him hurting her, Mom. At least not on purpose. He's never laid a hand on Renee. What worries me is how he'll mess with her head. Or he'll run off to Mexico or something and take her with him."

Mom looked away. "It's my fault."

I shook my head, "Mom . . ."

"I need a smoke." Mom swooped her purse off the floor and bolted to the door.

"It's not your fault." I offered, my voice weak.

Without turning around, Mom answered. "You don't even know, Cassie. You don't even know." Then she walked out the door.

Chapter Twenty-Four

RENEE DIDN'T RUN TO ME WHEN I picked her up from daycare. When I called her name, she ignored me and continued building a Lego house, oblivious to her surroundings.

"She's been like that since she got here." Bonnie whispered behind me.

"But she's only been here for about an hour, right?" These were the details I needed to know for my journal, especially since the police had proven themselves unhelpful when I contacted them. Bonnie had called me midmorning and asked if Renee was ill when she didn't show up at daycare. My calls to Derrick had gone unanswered. I feared he had made good on his threats from the evening before.

Bonnie nodded. "She snarled at me and went straight to the Legos. Derrick signed her in without saying a word, then turned and left."

Anger bit at my already tight shoulders. "Did he put down the time, like he's supposed to?"

Bonnie smiled. "He signed but didn't put a time ... but I added a note by his signature with the check in time: 4:08 p.m."

I walked to Renee and reached down to pick her up, but she turned away from me. "Renee, honey, it's time to go home."

Renee shook her head, tears bursting from her racoon eyes. "No! I don't want to go back there! You're a bad mommy!"

I stepped back, shock rippling through my body. Kneeling down, I tried to make eye contact with Renee. She stared at the wall. "Sugar Bug," I whispered. "It's time to go home. Grammy's waiting. I bet she's making dinner right now."

Renee turned to me, her brow furrowed. "Grammy is bad too. Don't let her hurt me, Mommy." Tears welled in Renee's eyes.

"Renee, what do you mean? Grammy would never hurt you." My voice went up an octave, though I tried to keep it steady. Renee's fear and anger were so strong, it was hard to control my own emotions.

"Daddy told me. Grammy is bad, and she hurt you when you were little. Now she's going to hurt me, and you let her because you ... you ... d-d-don't ... love me!" Renee hit me with curled hands, over and over, as tears poured from her bloodshot eyes.

I picked Renee up, though she pummeled me with her fists and kicked my thighs with her feet. The physical pain was nothing compared to the breaking inside my chest. Bonnie's soothing voice rose above Renee's tears, and I saw her put a hand on Renee's shoulder. "Renee, your mommy loves you and she would never, ever hurt you."

Renee pulled away from Bonnie, almost hurtling herself out of my arms. I bit on my bottom lip and shook my head. "I don't know what to do."

"Take her home and love her. It's all you can do right now." I nodded and turned toward the door, my crying, kicking daughter in my arms. Bonnie followed and handed me Renee's backpack. It was always lighter coming back than when it left. Bonnie caught hold of my arm, giving me a reassuring look. "It's going to be okay. I'll be praying for you both."

I blinked back tears. "Thank you." I wasn't sure how much more I could take.

Renee kicked the back of my seat and screamed for the first ten minutes of the drive home. I gritted my teeth, weighing my options. Any parenting book would surely say

Renee needed to be disciplined for her behavior, but how could I punish her for her entire world being in turmoil? When I had looked in her eyes, I saw heartache and fear mingled with anger, not rebellion or stubbornness. A few turns away from the apartment, Renee's screams turned to soft sobs, and the kicking stopped. I tried to look at her through the rearview mirror, but her face was out of my view. After we pulled into the parking lot, I craned my neck to see her. She was staring out the window, a blank, hollow expression on her face. I wasn't sure which was worse—the anger radiating from her when I picked her up, or the broken-hearted hopelessness in her eyes now.

I gripped my steering wheel and my knuckles turned white. Renee had been a happy little girl twenty-four hours ago. Now she looked haunted, defeated. The only thing that had changed was she spent time with Derrick. What caused such a reaction?

I remembered Bonnie's advice—take her home and love her. What else could I do? No matter if she responded to it or not, I would shower her with love until the hurt was washed away.

"I'm not letting her go back there." I crossed my arms.

Brian sat at his desk, across from me. His brow wrinkled, and he shifted in his seat. "I understand how you must feel, Cassie. I really do. But it's not a good idea."

"How am I supposed to let my daughter go back to that monster? He's abusing her." I threw my hands up in exasperation. Today was Friday, the first day of Derrick's weekend with Renee. After the condition Renee came home in yesterday, I couldn't let her go back. She was still not herself this morning. "Do you know what she did when I dressed her? Or I should say, *tried* to dress her this morning? She ran away, tearing her clothes off and screaming that she didn't want lice, and she wasn't going to daycare."

Brian exhaled, and shook his head. "I'm sorry. But you don't have any proof of wrongdoing on Derrick's part, other than him not getting Renee to daycare first thing in the morning yesterday. If you don't let him have her this weekend, you're denying his parenting time and judges don't look favorably on that. Since this weekend is his parenting time per the current legal plan, then he'll probably call the authorities if you don't let him take Renee. You could end up with the police at *your* door."

"Fine. I'll tell them why I kept her."

Brian's mouth twitched, a sign he was suppressing a smile. "I always knew there was a little fighter under the gentle exterior."

I crossed my arms, irritated he could find any of this funny. "There has to be more I can do than keep a journal for court." Having my mom witness the change in Renee upon her return from Derrick's had validated my fears. Mom almost had her own breakdown seeing how Renee acted, and in her granddaughter's refusal to hug or play with her.

"I know it must be frustrating." Brian's expression turned serious again. "But I have talked to a couple of friends who specialize in custody cases, and at this point you don't have enough to compel a judge to remove Renee from Derrick's care. Everything you've told me could be attributed to post-divorce trauma and normal child adjustment, depending on how you spin it."

I shook my head, hot tears stinging my eyes. "No. It's more."

Brian shrugged his shoulders. "I'm not saying there isn't, but we're playing to win the war, not the battle. If you keep Renee this weekend, even if the police don't show up at your door, you've put a chink in the armor of your case. You'll feel better for now, but it won't be worth it later."

My shoulders slumped. We kept going around this same argument. Bide my time. Keep a journal. Follow the parenting plan. Be above reproach.

"I can't win. If I do everything I'm supposed to do, I'll end up with physical custody of Renee. But if I don't do something more to help her, I'm afraid there won't be anything of my little girl left." My voice cracked, and I sucked in my breath.

"You're going to have to trust the process, as hard as it is." Brian's voice was tender, compassionate. "And remember, Cassie, you're not alone. You have friends who are here for you."

I looked in Brian's eyes. There was something in them I couldn't name, but it gave me butterflies and a warm feeling across my aching chest—a welcome relief from the pain. Lost for words, I simply nodded my head.

I watched Mom pull out of the parking lot first thing the next morning, the hood of her little white Buick covered in several layers of dirt. I waved good-bye and forced a smile, the tightening in my chest making it hard to breathe. How many times in my life had I waved good-bye when she left me with my grandparents, always with the same question lingering in my head: when will she back? Always the same fear—she won't. I couldn't blame her for leaving this time. I didn't want to stay in my apartment with its constant reminders of Renee and the helpless feeling of wondering if she was okay with Derrick. If I could escape, I would.

Today, though, I would have a small escape. I checked my cell phone for the time. 8:28 a.m. Brian would be here in half an hour to pick me up for a hike to a waterfall. I hurried back in my apartment to finish getting ready. Standing in front of the bathroom mirror, I evaluated my appearance. It would make sense to wear my hair up, but my full cheeks gave me far too much of a little girl appearance when I put my hair in a ponytail, so I left my hair down and spritzed it for the wavy, messy look. I dabbed mascara on my fair lashes and put a hint of bronzer on my cheeks. I still didn't have proper hiking clothes, so I made do with a worn-out pair of denim shorts and a faded Diamond Rio shirt. When the divorce was final, and I had my share of money from the house, the one thing I would splurge on for myself would be hiking clothes.

Grabbing my small cinch sack, I waited in the living room, leaving the drapes open so I could see the parking lot. I looked at my phone, and noticed I still had a few minutes. Should I try calling Renee? My heart ached at the vision of my daughter, remembering the look on her face when I dropped her off at daycare yesterday morning. The resignation in her eyes when I kissed her goodbye was worse than the temper tantrum I'd experienced when I picked her up on Thursday. I'd covered her face in kisses, hoping to enlist a smile, but her expression remained blank.

If I lingered on the thought, I would go crazy.

I turned my musings to the day ahead. Brian said he wanted to surprise me with his waterfall choice. When he said he would pick me up, my breath caught in my throat. It was like we were talking about a date. But that couldn't be right. I wasn't divorced yet, and neither was Brian. Why would the thought of dating even enter my mind—or his?

I saw his black Lexus pull into a spot a few spaces down from my Explorer and jumped up, eager to get out of my apartment and the pervasive sense of hopelessness engulfing me. By the time Brian had exited his car, I'd locked the front door of my apartment. He stopped in his tracks and smiled when he saw me. He was wearing sunglasses, a snug blue Nike shirt and dark grey cargo shorts. My heart did a small leap. No, this couldn't be a date. Brian looked like a movie star. A guy like that wouldn't have a romantic interest in me.

"I didn't know you were a Diamond Rio fan." Brian walked to the passenger door of his spotless car, opened it, and motioned for me to get in.

I gave a little laugh, awkward with his chivalry. "They're okay. I've had this shirt a long time." I glanced at Brian's face before scooting into the passenger seat. With the sunglasses on, I couldn't see his eyes and didn't know if he was laughing at me or approving of my taste in music.

After closing my door, Brian walked to the driver's side and eased into his seat. The inside of the car was as immaculate as the outside, with the scent of new leather and a trace of Brian's cologne.

"I don't confess this to many people, so I'm hoping you can keep it secret." Brian put the car in reverse and checked his mirrors. "But I love country music, and Diamond Rio is one of my favorites."

"Why keep it secret?" The warmth of the sun radiated in the car, and I squinted against its brightness.

Brian chuckled. "No self-respecting, highly educated man listens to country music."

I raised my eyebrows. "You're kidding, right? I'm pretty sure country singers couldn't make a living if they depended on the uneducated poor people to buy their albums."

Brian shrugged one shoulder as he turned onto the road. "If that's the case, how are Moon Pies and Cheese Whiz still around?"

"Is that what you eat, when no one's looking?" I watched Brian's reaction, enjoying the playful banter. Even with his not-so-perfect nose, he had a handsome profile.

"Of course. Everyone needs their guilty pleasures." He

glanced at me with a mischievous smile.

Warmth rushed to my cheeks, and I shifted my gaze to the passenger window. "So what fall are we going to?" Not the smoothest change of subject, but all I could muster.

"It's supposed to be a surprise, remember?"

"The suspense is killing me."

"That's the fun in surprises ... the anticipation, the guessing. Relax and enjoy the ride." Brian's voice was smooth.

My heart pitter-pattered, and I studied Brian furtively. He was focused on the road. Sunlight illuminated his dark hair, highlighting the smattering of grey in it. I noticed the faint lines on his temples, outside the rims of his sunglasses. I found those small signs of age attractive—a sign of wisdom. I exhaled through my nose, willing my pulse to slow. "I can't wait to see where we end up."

It only took a few minutes to at least know the general direction we were going—north. As we drove up the interstate, Brian talked, leading our conversation. He kept the topics light, and smattered with his witty humor. It was nice to laugh, to talk about things beyond parenting and court cases and survival. Surrealism washed over me when Brian took the same exit that led to Nannie's.

"Are you okay?" Brian tilted his head toward me.

I nodded. "Yeah, it's just that this is the way to my grandma's." I smiled, determined to keep the mood light. "You're not taking me to an old folks' home, are you?"

Brian chuckled. "I think it would be the other way around. Maybe not now, I mean, look at this amazing hair." Brian rubbed his hand over his head, and playfully admired himself in the mirror. "But thirty years from now, you're going to be saying, 'Hey Brian, let's go see a waterfall' and the next thing I know, you're kicking me out at the raisin ranch."

My eyes tingled as tears of laughter welled in the corners. "You're too funny." I smiled, bathing in the warmth of the camaraderie between us.

Road signs took the punch out of the surprise. I soon realized we were on our way to Silver Falls State Park—or, as Brian had put it—Oregon Waterfall Disneyland.

"I'm thinking this is going to be a long hike," I mused.

Brian shrugged. "I'd call it moderate. Don't despair. I've packed us a picnic lunch and tons of water."

He packed a picnic lunch? "Sounds like you've thought of everything."

"Boy Scouts are always prepared." Brian glanced at me with a small, almost mischievous smile.

"You were a Boy Scout? I didn't know they'd been around that long." I bit my cheek, pleased with my playful jibe.

"Oooh, burn. But age is simply a number. We'll see whose thighs are burning at day's end."

"You've got me there. I'm sure I'll be hurting all over if we end up doing the hike you have in mind. It's Silver Falls, right? Ten miles or so?"

"Don't worry about being sore. It's nothing a hot bath and a body massage can't fix."

I laughed, the pitch too high and betraying my nerves. Shifting in my seat, I searched for a light and far less suggestive response. "I've heard Epson salt helps."

Brian raised his eyebrows. "I think you've been spending a bit too much time in Raisin-ville, Cassie."

After what seemed like a never-ending zig-zag of a road through farmlands and forest, we arrived at a pull out labeled "North Falls."

"This is it?" I asked, surprised by the small parking area.

"This is where we begin. Because real adventurers save the best for last." Brian slipped out of the car.

I followed Brian to a trailhead labeled "Upper North Falls."

"This isn't part of the trail loop, but it's a short walk." Brian commented as he motioned to the sign.

We strolled down an easy, forested trail, lush with greenery and soft under our feet. We soon came to a short but pretty fall. I took my phone out of my pocket to take a picture. When I did, I noticed I had no signal. My heart dropped. "Great."

"Hey, I told you I was saving the best for last."

"Oh, it's not the waterfall. It's my cell signal." I held up my phone, showing Brian the screen. "No service."

"Renee will be okay." Brian's tone was soft, reassuring.

Eager to not lose the jovial atmosphere we'd been enveloped in, I nodded. "I know. I'm going to take a quick picture of this waterfall. Do you want to be in it?"

Brian shook his head. "Not this time. How about I take your picture with the waterfall? This is your quest, remember?"

I handed Brian my phone and stood at the edge of the trail, my hands behind my back, forcing a smile.

"I'm only letting you get away with that demure pose because this is a small waterfall. By the end of this hike, I want pictures of you roaring like the falls." Brian snapped a few quick pictures, then handed my phone back to me.

"We'll see."

We crossed the roadway to the beginning of another trail and were soon walking down a series of stone steps. Brian stayed beside me, stepping aside when needed to allow a few hikers coming up the steps to get by. Within moments we saw a stream of water falling off a sheer cliff. Brian looked at me with sparkling eyes, wearing that knowing smile. "Are you having fun yet?"

I could barely hear him over the increasing sound of

rushing water.

"I've been having fun since I got in your car." I smiled back.

"That, my dear, is what every man wants to hear from a beautiful woman."

I returned my focus to the steps we were descending but could feel Brian's eyes on me. The increasing cool mist as we got closer to the fall did little to dampen the heat that spread up my neck and across my face.

We came to the bottom of the stairs, and Brian motioned for me to take the lead. "I think you're going to like this."

I walked ahead on the carved path, following the curve of the rocky wall leading us directly behind the fall. I had heard about waterfalls you could walk behind, and I had seen pictures, but actually doing it was magical. Everything was wet—water dripped down the stony wall beside me, small puddles of water dotted the smooth rock path, and the guard rail to my left was covered in spray. Goose bumps erupted on my arms from the sudden decrease in temperature. I made my way to the back of the waterfall, breathing in mist. For a moment I felt tiny, over-powered, like I did whenever I stood at the ocean's edge. It wasn't a bad feeling. It was something not quite within my grasp, so full of hope it made all of life's struggles seem as harmless as the ripples in the tiny puddles at my feet.

"Are you okay, Cassie? You kind of look like you're about ready to cry." Brian leaned down, his lips only inches from my ear.

I nodded. "It's beautiful."

Brian stood beside me in the cavern, gazing at the stream of water in front of us. "When you're ready, we'll hike back up to the car and drive to the park and the South Falls trailhead. There's a hiking loop from there that will take us to the other eight falls."

I looked up at him. "I thought the entire trail system was connected?"

Brian shrugged one shoulder. "It is. This way, though, we'll see all ten falls with a bit less hiking." His dark eyes glimmered. "I don't want you to resort to Epson salt baths if I can help it."

I pursed my lips, suppressing a smile. "You've really planned this out, haven't you?"

"You learn a thing or two when you're older."

I laughed and shook my head. "Lead the way, oh wise and ancient one."

We walked up the stairs of the trail. When the falls were behind us, I stopped and got out my phone to take a picture. Brian reached toward me. "Here, I'll take your picture."

I shook my head. "No, I want one of only the waterfall this time. It's so perfect. I would only mess it up."

After a couple of hikers passed by, I positioned my phone for the picture and snapped several shots. Another group of hikers approached. It appeared to be a family—a fit looking mom, dad, and two preteen kids.

"Would you like me to take a picture of the two of you?" The mom asked, her eyes bright.

"Uhm ..." I looked at Brian hesitantly. Obviously the woman assumed we were a couple.

"We'd love that, thank you." Brian beamed at the woman. I handed her my phone with the camera ready. Brian came beside me and casually draped his arm across my shoulders. My whole body warmed from his closeness.

"Say cheese."

I smiled meekly, feeling like a fraud. The woman snapped a picture then handed my phone to me.

Brian took a step toward the woman. "I'd be more than happy to take a picture of you and your beautiful family, if you'd like." His voice was silky, and his eyes sparkled at the attractive woman. Jealousy nipped at my heart. *Don't be stupid.* What did I have to be jealous of? It wasn't like Brian and I were actually a couple, and of course I wasn't the only one he used that silky tone with. It probably wasn't even as flirtatious at it sounded. I looked at the woman's husband to gauge his reaction, but his face was stone. I noticed he was a little thick around the middle, not nearly as athletic looking as his wife.

The woman smiled and tilted her head slightly. "Oh, that would be—"

"Unnecessary," her husband finished the sentence for her. "We come here often and have quite a few family pictures. But, thank you."

The woman rolled her eyes. "Come on, children. Your dad is obviously ready to go home." The family continued on the trail, but the woman looked back over her shoulder, making eye contact with Brian, and waved.

"What a dweeb," Brian breathed.

"The husband? He did seem a little put off." Didn't Brian realize the tone he had used with the woman, the look in his eyes?

Brian laughed. "His feathers were definitely ruffled." There was a hint of amusement in his voice.

We continued on to the car. A brief drive later we pulled into a large parking lot surrounded by a grassy park that included a lodge. "South Falls is at the beginning of the trail. I think you'll be pleased. It's one of the most photographed waterfalls in Oregon." Brian found a space in the packed lot, then got out and walked to the trunk.

I grabbed my bag and followed. Brian pulled a full backpack out of the trunk and hitched it up over his shoulders.

"Looks heavy." Guilt bit at me with the realization the backpack probably contained the water Brian had mentioned.

Brian smiled. "It's not too bad. Besides, I need the extra workload to even the hiking pace." He lifted one eyebrow playfully.

We made our way to the crowded trail. Now I understood why Brian referred to it as Disneyland. The paved trail was so full of people, it was almost a deterrent. When South Falls came into view, though, I understood why people would flock here. The massive waterfall was gorgeous. A large rectangle of white water descended over a ledge, thundering down to the creek below. We descended the trail to a cavern behind the falls, similar to North Falls. This cavern wasn't as deep, so the trail and air around us was even more damp. Water penetrated my worn-out sneakers, but I didn't complain.

The crowds thinned as we left South Falls behind, but the trail was still busy with people. It was also full of beauty. Each new waterfall was like finding gold. I took many pictures.

Two hours later, my thighs burned and my stomach growled as we made our way up the stone stairs that would bring us out of the canyon and the end of our hike. When we finally arrived back at the park, I was damp with the waterfall mist, my legs were weak, and I was half out of breath.

"Let's find a picnic table in the shade, and I'll go to the car and get our lunch."

"You're not tired at all, are you?"

Brian shrugged. "Maybe a bit. But I jog every morning, lift weights four days a week." He winked.

We found a table in the shade, near the creek. I sat down and Brian handed me the backpack. "There's a few more waters in there. I'll be back in a flash." He set out at a slow jog down a paved path toward the parking lot.

I checked my phone. No signal. I sighed. I was enjoying

our hike, but being out of cell range made me nervous, even with Brian's repeated reassurances throughout the day. Forcing myself to be in the moment, I inhaled the sweet air and closed my eyes. There were sounds of other people, laughter. My stomach grumbled. We had snacked on granola bars and sliced fruit on the trail, but I wasn't used to being active. It was a good feeling, the physical fatigue, the ravenous appetite and … knowing someone cared enough to let me sit here and enjoy the shade while he ran to get our lunch. The lunch he had packed.

I shook my head, a wistful smile tugging at my lips. Had Derrick ever been that doting? My brain searched through my catalog of memories. Yes, in his own way, he had been. In the beginning. He had changed after we got married, and his temper became evident. Then he started drinking and it only got worse. I exhaled through my teeth. If I allowed myself to think about how chilling Derrick's temper had become, then I would only worry about Renee more.

I turned my gaze to the creek, and my thoughts returned to Brian. I wasn't sure what was happening between us but spending time with him was fun. He made me feel safe, protected. Plus, he made me laugh like no one else. A couple of times on the hike, he had offered me a hand up some steps. Even though I didn't really need the assistance, I accepted his hand, and when our skin touched an electrical impulse shot through my body.

Brian set a basket down on the table. I jumped. "That was fast."

There were small beads of perspiration on Brian's brow, but he smiled. "You look hungry."

"I am starving." I nodded. "But, how can you tell?"

Brian sat down across from me and began taking food out of the basket—sandwiches made from thick slices of wheat bread, a container of hummus and cut up veggies.

Healthy. "It's in the eyes," he said, handing me a sandwich and a bottle of lemonade.

"I guess I *am* an open book." I looked away, afraid of how much Brian might see.

"There's nothing wrong with that. I happen to like what I'm reading."

I hesitantly faced him, butterflies beating their wings in my abdomen, unable to hold back the smile that tugged at the sides of my mouth. "Really?"

Brian's eyes held mine, playful yet intense. "Most definitely. It's a real page-turner. Could keep me up at nights."

Heat burned my cheeks. I focused on my sandwich, carefully unwrapping the cellophane around it. "I hope it has a happy ending."

"Ahh Cassie ..." Brian shook his head. "Sometimes the best endings are bittersweet."

It was nearly sunset when Brian pulled into my apartment's parking lot. As soon as we were back in cell range I had checked for messages, but there were none. Maybe I would call Renee tonight, even if it was a hopeless venture. Brian parked in the spot nearest to my apartment and turned off the engine. I hesitated, unsure if I should invite him in. Wouldn't doing so suggest something?

"Thank you for today, Brian. I can't tell you how much it meant to me to get away like this. Everything was perfect, including lunch." I reached down between my feet for my bag. Brian's hand gently slid across my back. Sitting back up I faced him, and his arm circled my shoulder, pulling me into a gentle hug.

"It was my pleasure," he whispered. His arms lingered around me a moment before loosening their hold. Breaking away from Brian's embrace, I saw something dangerous and tempting in his eyes.

It was time to say good-night.

"I need to go." I reached for the door handle.

Brian sighed. He smoothly took my left hand in his, lifted it to his lips, and kissed the back of it with feather-like lips. His eyes flickered. "Sleep well, waterfall chaser."

The night air still held a hint of warmth, or the goodbye in the car had warmed me up so much I didn't feel the chill when I got out. Brian didn't leave the parking space until I had opened the door of my apartment and turned to wave good-bye. Once inside, I leaned against the door and dropped my backpack. What had happened? I giggled like a little girl and stared at the ceiling. Brian was incredibly attractive, smart, and charming. He was also my boss—no, my boss's boss—which was even worse. Not to mention, twelve years older than me. And still married, technically. Like I was still married. My shoulders slumped. What was I thinking? No matter how deep my loneliness, I wasn't ready to date. Guilt crept up my spine, chasing away the butterflies Brian's flirting had stirred up.

Chapter Twenty-Five

I LONGED TO HEAR MY DAUGHTER'S voice. If I called and Derrick didn't answer, I would worry. If I didn't call, I would feel guilty for not at least trying. The quietness of the apartment drained the excitement of the day away. Loneliness took its place. I dialed Derrick's number.

"She doesn't want to talk to you." Derrick's voice held its usual venom.

"I simply want to tell her goodnight, Derrick, is that too much to ask?" I couldn't hide the weariness in my voice.

"Maybe you should call earlier in the day, instead of tramping around."

Chills shot down my arms. Did Derrick know I had spent the day with Brian? And if he did know, how? "I haven't been 'tramping' around."

Derrick laughed. "You've got the queen of tramps living with you, so I'm sure you're following in your dear mama's footsteps."

My stomach clenched in anger. If only Derrick talked like this around others—work, attorneys, judges, cops—his true character would be evident. But he saved his hateful and demeaning speech for me. I needed to figure out a way to record the phone calls.

Renee. Was he talking this way in front of her ... *to* her? In my gut I knew the answer. This was why she shouldn't be there. I was still unraveling what Derrick's hateful words had done to me. I couldn't bear to think what that kind of poison did to a four-year-old mind. For now, it was best to diffuse him. "If you're not going to let me talk to her, I'll hang up."

Derrick grunted. "You better get used to not talking to

her."

"What's that supposed to mean?" I couldn't hang up now.

"It means exactly what I said. Good-night, tramp." The line went dead.

Tears brimmed my eyes. I should have known better than to think I could actually have one good day. My heart ached for my daughter. The adrenaline that seared through me made me forget my sore thighs. There was nothing I could do. If I called Brian, he would reassure me all of this would get worked out in court. But he didn't understand my mother's heart. As thoughtful as he was, he didn't understand how the hope of a better future didn't take away my fears for my daughter tonight. Missy couldn't understand because she didn't have kids. Mom was gone for the weekend, and I wasn't going to share my worry with Nannie. She didn't need this. I sank onto my bed, the weight of my distress more than I could bear.

All I could do was ...pray. But would God hear the prayers of a woman who was undeniably attracted to a married man? Would God care about the fears of a woman who didn't go to church or even read her Bible? My guess was no. But no matter what I had done, my innocent daughter didn't deserve to suffer.

Please Lord, I beg you, keep Renee safe. Bring her home to me unharmed. Make it so this court stuff moves along quickly. I know I don't deserve your love, but I plead for my daughter.

Tears streamed down my face. For a brief moment, a feeling of assurance and peace swept through me. I had to believe God was with Renee. Clinging to the remnant of hope, I drifted off to sleep.

I hid under the blanket on my bed. The tiny mobile home was cold, even though I had turned the thermostat up past

70, despite previous reprimands from my mom. It was 10:00 p.m. I should have been sleeping, but I was too scared. Hail pelted the metal roof of the trailer, the sound nearly deafening. I didn't want to be alone. Nannie had called earlier, and I clung to the memory of the love and reassurance in her voice. Her call was my only human contact on the winter-storm filled night. I couldn't make long-distance phone calls. It cost money.

We had so little money that the only food left in the trailer was two pieces of bread, three eggs, a tiny amount of milk, and some stale raisins I had found at the bottom of an empty box of Raisin Bran. I shivered under the blanket. Why didn't God answer my prayers? Nannie said God was always listening, but if that were the case, then He must not like me.

Maybe I had made Him mad. I thought over every wrong thing I had done in recent memory. Like turn the thermostat up even though Mom said we couldn't afford it. Like stick my tongue out at Maria, the teacher's pet in my third-grade class. Or wish I had parents like the ones I saw on TV shows, a mom who made dinner every night, a dad to twirl me like a princess.

I was bad, that was why God didn't hear me.

Or... He just didn't care.

Bitter tears ran down my cheeks and to the corner of my mouth. The saltiness of them reminded me I hadn't had much for dinner. My stomach didn't growl anymore. It only hurt.

I heard the front door open. Hope fluttered in my chest. Was Mom home early? Maybe she had brought some of the fried chicken from her favorite tavern. Footsteps came down the hall, but they were too heavy to be Mom's. I shivered under the blanket. Had I forgotten to lock the front door? My heart pitter-pattered in my chest. What kind of bad guy had walked in, and why was he heading straight to my room? I tried to make myself smaller under the covers and held my *breath, hoping he somehow wouldn't see me. The footsteps stopped for a moment at my door, but then continued, slowly, to my bed. I squeezed my eyes shut, willing the sound away. This was a bad dream. There was a hand on the blanket, gently pulling it out of my clenched hands.*

"Oh, Cassie." A voice full of tenderness. A voice I knew.

I opened one eye. The silhouette of a strong man stood over me. Not a scary man.

My grandpa.

I reached up my arms, and he swooped me to his chest, patting my back. "Grandpa's got you now, sweet girl. You don't need to be afraid."

I clung to Grandpa. My hero.

God couldn't save me, but Grandpa could.

I awoke from the dream covered in sweat, my throat aching. Had I been crying in my sleep? And could you call a re-lived memory a dream? I hadn't thought about that night in years. Eons. The day I was rescued and given a new life. Not by God, but by Grandpa. He was the only man I could count on. If only Grandpa was still here, maybe he could rescue me again.

Clothing littered Renee's bedroom, evidence of my several attempts to get her dressed for daycare. In the narrow space between her bed and the far wall of the room, Renee kicked at my shins and flailed against my attempts to grab her. Her face was contorted with pained but tearless eyes ringed in the darkness that comes from a lack of sleep. I managed to grab one of her hands, and she used the other to scratch my arm. Deep red welts erupted. I clutched her other hand, only for the kicking to resume.

"Renee!" I didn't mean to scream, but I was desperate for her to stop, to hear me.

Renee's face turned red, and tears welled up in her narrowed emerald eyes. "I hate you! You're a bad mommy! You don't love me!" Her words sprang out with venom, and she sputtered saliva.

My heart felt stabbed, and the pain rose up in my throat. "That's not true at all, Renee," I choked out. "Why would you say such things?"

"You're a liar!" Renee's hands turned to fists, and she plummeted them into my thighs. "You lie ...all ... the ... time!" Renee's hitting stopped, and she dropped to the floor and curled into a ball, sobs rocking her small body.

I might not have any choice but to call in sick to work. If I explained how the evening had gone, even Cynthia would understand.

Derrick hadn't brought Renee back at 5:00 Sunday evening when he was supposed to. I had called him at 5:15. When I asked him when he was bringing her back, his reply had been, "I can't bring her to your apartment because of the restraining order."

Attempting to explain his statement wasn't true was futile. "I'll come there." I'd offered.

"Nope. That would break the order too. I'm going to take her to daycare in the morning so I don't put myself at risk. Oh wait ... you still haven't switched to a safe daycare. Guess I'll keep her here until you do." He'd hung up.

I had called the police. They wouldn't do anything. The woman dispatcher said if Derrick didn't bring her back by Monday morning, I should contact my attorney. My mom hadn't returned from the coast yet. I had taken out my journal, and written down the details of Derrick's phone call, my call to the police. Looking back over my previous entries, Derrick was almost predictable in his antics. If the judge looked for a pattern of behavior, it was recorded there.

I had settled in for the evening, eager for ten o'clock to

come so I could take a Tylenol PM and hopefully lose myself to a dreamless sleep. At 8:30 there had been a light knock on my door, so small I barely heard it. I had looked out the peephole but didn't see anything. A tug in my gut told me to open the door and check outside. When I did, I saw Renee standing there, the backpack sitting on the ground beside her. Headlights flashed and caught my attention from the parking lot, and the familiar red truck pulled out of a nearby space. The windows were down, the outline of Derrick in the driver's side.

"Renee, honey." I had reached down, but Renee pulled away from my embrace. "Why didn't Daddy walk you to the door?"

Renee had looked up at me with solemn eyes. "Because of you, Mommy. He said if a bad thing happened, it was because of you."

I had been too tired to explain to her it wasn't true, and how did one explain complicated legal matters to a four-year-old? I had remained silent and brought her to bed with me.

This morning, I was again without words. Trying to get her ready for daycare had been like trying to bathe a cat. It was as if Derrick had transferred all his resentment for me into her heart, a human messenger of hate. Or was it actually born of her own hurt, of things that had happened because of me? Doubt and insecurity plagued me.

I gathered Renee in my arms. She was like dead weight now, not resistant but not embracing. Sitting on the couch, I rocked her back and forth until her tears subsided, ignoring the clock. My own tears wet her hair. If I could swallow her pain and make it my own, I would do it in a heartbeat. But I couldn't. I knew Nannie was praying for us. I had even prayed over the weekend. Yet here was my daughter—physically she was in one piece, but her spirit was broken.

Once again, God had let me down.

I finally made it to work by mid-morning. Renee was silent when I dropped her off at daycare, but at least she wasn't crying or screaming. I was ready to lose myself in the mundaneness of my job. Saturday evening, I had wondered how I would react to seeing Brian on Monday. Now I was too numb to care.

Just before noon, my purse vibrated at my feet. My cell phone was ringing. My heart kicked into high gear immediately, causing me to feel light headed when I leaned down and pulled my purse up to my desk. The caller ID showed it was Bonnie. I sucked in my breath.

"I'm sorry to bother you at work." Bonnie's voice was hesitant.

"It's fine." I glanced at the clock. "I was getting ready to take my lunch." At least that's what I should have been doing, but Cynthia had me buried in tapes. "Is everything okay?"

Bonnie exhaled. "Yes, Renee's not sick. I mean, she doesn't have a fever or anything. But she's not acting like herself."

My heart rate slowed. Renee wasn't sick, Derrick wasn't there. "What do you mean? Is she crabby? She was really tired this morning. As you know, I had a hard time getting her out the door." *To put it mildly.*

"No … she's not crabby. I don't really know what she is, because she won't talk."

"What do you mean?"

Bonnie paused a moment, as if choosing her words carefully. "She hasn't said a word since she got here. Not to me, not to the other kids. She'll nod her head yes or shake a no if I ask her a question, but no matter how hard I try to engage her, she won't speak."

Coldness rippled through my body. What had happened to Renee at Derrick's? "I think she had a rough weekend." I gave Bonnie the Reader's Digest version of Sunday night.

"Ahh." Bonnie replied. "That had to be hard on her. I'll give her some extra reassurance today and not push the talking issue. I'm sure she'll be better by tomorrow."

I blinked back tears and ended the call. My poor baby. What was going through her head? I needed professional advice, and immediately thought of Brian. I had stayed hidden in my cubicle all morning, not looking forward to the awkwardness I was apt to feel after Saturday. Plus, if our hike *had* been a date, wouldn't he be the one to seek me out this morning? I hadn't heard from him at all since Saturday. Now my need for help was greater than my pride, or the fragility of my romantic heart.

Brian was at his desk, his office door slightly ajar—his signal he wasn't too busy to be disturbed. I knocked lightly on the door casing.

He looked up, and his eyes brightened. "Cassie." He smiled warmly, immediately putting me at ease.

"Do you have a minute?"

Brian motioned to the chair on the opposite side of his desk. "For you, definitely."

My stomach fluttered, but I ignored it as I made my way to the chair, keeping my gaze on the floor. I sat down and forced myself to look in his eyes. The intensity I had seen in them on Saturday was gone, replaced by the concerned yet light-hearted look he usually had when I saw him in the office. Maybe it was best if I pretended Saturday never happened. "I had a bit of a rough weekend, and my daycare lady called because she's concerned about Renee."

Brian's eyebrow lifted, and he spoke so softly I almost didn't hear him. "Rough? I thought we had a good time."

My eyes fluttered back to the floor. I couldn't muster a playful response. "*That* part of it was good. But Sunday wasn't. Derrick wouldn't let me pick Renee up, then he dropped her off at my apartment really late. He didn't even get out of the truck, just sent her to the door alone. She's been acting weird since then and now she won't talk to anyone." The words gushed out like water from a busted faucet but releasing them only slightly lessened the knot in my stomach.

Brian's eyebrows pinched together. "Renee won't talk to anyone? Not even to you?"

I sighed. "No. She talked to me, though not much. But my daycare person called and said she won't talk to her or any of the kids. I know something bad happened when she was with Derrick." I blinked back the wetness gathering at the corner of my eyes.

"Cassie," Brian's voice was gentle. "I can't imagine what it's like to see your child go through this hell. Right now, though, there's not much you can do."

I shook my head. "You don't understand. I *know* something is not right. It's more than divorce, it's something he's doing or saying or ..." Or, what? My mind could go down a hundred dark paths if I let it, but then I would completely fall apart and be no good at all to my daughter.

Brian exhaled and stood up. His eyes on me, full of compassion, he made his way to my chair and offered me his hand. I took it, my need for human touch greater than the uneasiness that nagged at me. The next thing I knew, Brian had pulled me into an embrace. I buried my head in his chest, breathing in the warmth of his spicy cologne, feeling the strength in his broad shoulders above my head.

"Uh-hum."

I jumped. Brian broke our embrace and responded before I could turn my attention to the intruder.

"Missy, what do you need?"

Oh no. Guilt coursed through my veins, turning them cold as I made eye contact with my friend. The disapproval on her face screamed at me. I cringed.

"I'm making a run to the courthouse. I heard you might need something filed, but Ginger said she's waiting on you to sign it." Missy's voice was cold, matter-of-fact.

"Ah, yes. I have it right here." Brian whisked a brief off his desk and walked it over to Missy. "It still needs to be copied. Has Ginger left for lunch yet?"

"Yes, but I'll go ahead and copy it. I'm going to take my lunch a little late today." Missy aimed her gaze at me, her eyes hard. "Want to meet me at the Pita Palace in half an hour?"

I nodded, forcing a smile. "Sure." Missy turned and left without another word. I didn't have time to take an actual lunch break *and* talk to Brian, but somehow I would have to make it work.

Brian turned to me, hesitated a moment, then went to his chair and sat down. I sunk into my seat.

"Let me make a phone call to a friend of mine who deals with custody and divorce matters. I'll let you know if he has any suggestions." Brian shuffled papers on his desk. Was it me, or did he seem nervous? "If there's any course of action we …you … can take to protect Renee, he will know."

I waited for more. Another word of encouragement, another embrace, but Brian looked at his watch. "I need to jet. I have a lunch meeting with a colleague."

I stood, numb, confused, with the weight of a thousand bricks on my shoulders. "Okay … thanks." I walked out of Brian's office without another word. Apparently, I had a lunch meeting too, though I certainly couldn't afford a meal out. But I also couldn't afford to lose my only friend.

Pita Palace was only a five-minute walk from the office building. Missy was standing in line at the counter, surveying the red and black lettered menu. She turned at the chime of the door opening. I offered a weak smile. Missy didn't return the smile but nodded toward the menu. "Perfect timing. I'm almost ready to order. What can I get you?"

I had never eaten at the Pita Palace before and had no idea what to order. "Get me whatever you're having, and a water." I reached for my wallet to see if I had any cash.

"This one's on me. Grab us a table." Missy sounded different. Serious. Usually she was the one who made me laugh and cheered me up.

I found a tiny booth in the back and took a seat. How would I explain the embrace to Missy? Should I tell her everything, or only enough to explain what she saw in his office? Missy would see through a sugar-coated half-truth faster than my bank account ate up my paycheck. The only thing I could do was explain how I felt and hope she didn't think less of me.

Missy made her way to the table, avoiding eye contact, and plopped a plastic number six on our table. "We haven't talked in a while." She slid into the seat across from me.

I nodded. "I know. Cynthia's had me buried in work. We need to hang out again sometime."

Missy looked at me, her eyebrows raised. "I have a hunch you've been"–she put her hands up to indicate quotation marks— "*hanging out* with someone else at the office."

Heat ran up my neck. "You mean Brian."

Missy shrugged. "You two were looking awfully friendly this morning."

I glanced at the other people in the restaurant, making sure there was no one we knew there. "Well you know Brian's been helping with my case, for free."

"And I told you to watch out for him." Missy's voice was hard.

"I know. I have." I tried not to sound defensive, but my guard was going up.

"He's married."

"Actually," I leaned in, keeping my voice low. "He's separated, but he's not wanting that to be public knowledge."

Missy cocked her head. "He told you he's separated from his wife, but it's a secret. Doesn't that seem a tad suspicious to you?"

"You know how office gossip can get out of control. I mean, it's already started about him and his wife." Brian didn't want to deal with the whispering behind his back. Missy had been working at the firm long enough to know how the gossip train worked once it got started.

"You're right." Missy looked me in the eye. "It can get out of control. But I also know this—it is usually based on at least a kernel of truth, and it wouldn't be the first time a rumor has circulated about Brian and his conquests."

"What do you mean?"

Missy chewed on her lip and stared at the table. "Look...."

A young man with a nose ring set our food on the table and picked up the plastic number. "Two Chicken Souvlakis."

"Thanks," I mumbled, trying to smile.

Missy waited until he walked away. "I try not to put too much stock in what I hear at the office, especially if it comes from Lana." Missy unwrapped the top of her pita, pulled out a small piece of chicken and popped it in her mouth. "But about a year and a half ago, before Cynthia was pregnant, there was talk about her and Brian."

"What?" I almost laughed. "Cynthia and Brian? The Ice Queen and Mr. Charming? Seems a little far-fetched. Plus, Cynthia is married. Brian is … was … married." I couldn't see the two of them together, even if they were both single.

"I know. It sounds ridiculous. But Cynthia used to dress up for work, before she had a baby. She was a little more on the party-side, if you know what I mean." Missy picked up her pita and took a big bite.

I slowly unwrapped my lunch while my mind raced. Cynthia and Brian? Had I ever seen any hint of anything between them? A tad of animosity, maybe. I remembered the pointed look Brian had given Cynthia during my interview, and how Cynthia had seemed to be holding something back. But that had simply been about hiring me, the unqualified legal assistant. Or had it?

I picked at the sandwich in front of me. "All I know is Brian has been super helpful right from the get-go with this whole divorce thing. We went hiking this weekend, and met for dinner once to go over the case. That's pretty much the extent of our relationship."

Missy swallowed the food in her mouth. "So you're saying the warm hug today was a first?"

I shrugged. "Not exactly." I surveyed the room again and lowered my voice. "He hugged me after our hike on Saturday. It was kind of lingering. I had the feeling he may have wanted to kiss me, but I hurried out of his car."

"I knew it." Missy dropped her sandwich back in the basket. "Look, it's ultimately your decision, but stop and think about this a moment. He's offering to help with your divorce case, but only if no one knows. He's saying he's separated, but don't say anything, it's a secret. He was obviously a little flustered when I walked in his office this morning. Do you see a pattern here?"

The room shrunk around me. No, Missy was wrong. If she had seen the look in Brian's eyes, and heard the way he talked to me, she would understand. "When you put it like that, it sounds pretty bad. I don't think I'm explaining things very well." I fiddled with my sandwich and forced myself to take another bite.

"Maybe not." Missy countered. "Or maybe you're seeing what you want to see."

Chapter Twenty-Six

MOM SPIT A SUNFLOWER SHELL INTO the paper cup she held in her hand, then rolled down the passenger window to pour the cupful of shells out as I drove seventy miles per hour down I-5. I cringed, glancing at the rearview mirror. The last thing I needed was a ticket for littering. Thankfully, no cops were behind us.

"Nannie will be happy to hear about how things are going." Mom put another seed in her mouth. The sunflower seeds were her anti-smoking device. She normally chain smoked when in a car, but she knew that there was no way that would happen in my Explorer, especially with Renee in the backseat.

"I hope she doesn't feel like I've kept her out of the loop." I didn't say it to Mom, but I also hoped Nannie was okay. I'd called her twice during the week to let her know I'd received the notice for both the criminal and custody court dates, and was given some potentially encouraging news from Brian. Each time I called, though, she hadn't answered. The second time I had called the front desk and was told Nannie had been under the weather and was taking quite a few naps.

"Mommy, I'm hungry." Renee whined from the backseat.

I glanced at her in the rearview mirror, grateful to see the dark circles around her eyes had faded. Her Wednesday visit with Derrick had been on time and drama-free. She was quiet and tired when she returned to me Thursday, but not the complete emotional wreck I'd faced on Sunday.

"We're almost to Nannie's. Then we can have lunch." I smiled, but Renee didn't. She stared out the window, her face somber. Another loop was added to the knot in my stomach.

Brian had heard back from his friend who specialized in custody cases, and the suggestion was to take Renee to a psychologist. I'd balked at the suggestion at first, rankled by the stigma. But Brian had reassured me it was a way to not only help Renee, but also create an unbiased third-party opinion of how Renee's relationship with her father was affecting her. I had called the psychologist he suggested, but he was booked for the next two months. The divorce and custody case was in six weeks. I either needed to find another psychologist who was more available, or go to the hearing without that piece under my belt. Not to mention the psychologist office visit copay was out of my budget.

Nannie was sitting in her favorite chair when we arrived. Renee's melancholy demeanor changed upon seeing her great-grandma. "Nannie!" she squealed, running up to her.

The smile Nannie returned was small, but the sparkle of love in her eyes was as big as ever. "How's my favorite great-granddaughter?" Nannie returned Renee's hug, but looked pained with the movement.

"Are you okay, Mom? You don't look well." My mom scurried to the other side of Nannie's chair.

"I'm fine, don't worry." Nannie patted mom's hand, then looked at me. "And how are you doing?" There was both concern and love in her eyes.

I nodded. "Things are going well. Court dates are all set." I smiled at Nannie reassuringly, thankful I had good news.

"One step closer to happily ever after." Nannie smiled back. She was terribly pale, even with makeup. I needed to find out who at the retirement home I should talk to about having her see a doctor.

"That's right. The criminal court date is this Thursday. Then a few more weeks and the custody one will be done." I couldn't tell Nannie about the psychologist search with

Renee sitting there.

"Is Brian going with you to the criminal trial?" Nannie asked.

"What's criminal mean?" Renee piped in.

I hated that I had to either explain or lie to Renee, but I was thankful for the diversion. "It's grownup talk, Sugar Bug. It has to do with Mommy's work." It was a white lie, and hopefully enough to appease a four-year-old.

"Oh." Renee looked around the room. "Can I play with the box, Nannie?"

Nannie clapped her hands together and opened her eyes wide. "You know what you reminded me of? My friend down the hall brought a nice coloring book and box of crayons the other day. Would you like to color? The book has princesses and castles."

Renee jumped up, fueled by Nannie's enthusiasm. "Yes!"

Nannie directed mom to the bookcase by her bed, and within moments Renee was sitting contently at the nearby table, coloring a princess dress orange and purple.

"So," Nannie turned her attention to me again. "He is going with you, right? You shouldn't face you-know-who alone."

I sighed. If only I could divert my seventy-two-year-old grandma from the details about court as easily as she diverted Renee from the music box. "I don't really need an attorney with me, Nannie. The DA will be there. He's the one who filed the charges. If anyone needs an attorney, it's Derrick."

Nannie chewed on my words a moment, then nodded her head. "But Brian will be with you at the custody hearing, right?"

I squirmed in my seat. My conversations with Brian had been brief this week. Ever since my lunch date with Missy, I had started to doubt his intentions. Maybe Brian was having doubts too, because he had been business-like ever since Missy caught us hugging in his office. He hadn't called or texted me about going hiking, or said anything beyond what he found out from his attorney friend. As far as I knew, I would be walking into the courtroom alone when the divorce case was heard. Brian remained my unofficial help only.

"Brian's not representing me. He's giving me advice. When the hearing comes, I'll be going to court alone."

Nannie frowned, the wrinkles in her forehead deepening.

"But it's okay." I spoke quickly, not wanting to upset her "Because Derrick doesn't have an attorney now, either. We'll be on even ground." I forced a smile.

"Except he's a terrible parent, and you're not." My mom piped in.

I shot her a pointed look and nodded toward Renee.

"Oh yeah, sorry. Sometimes I can't help myself."

"Daddy says I'm going to go live with him forever, but I don't want to." Renee looked up from her coloring book with sad eyes.

The room turned quiet, the only sound the distant melody of wind chimes outside the window. Nannie closed her eyes, her mouth moving silently. Mom walked over to Renee and sat by her, picking up a crayon. "Can Grammy color with you, Sweet Pea?"

Renee's gaze dropped to the page she was coloring. Was it me, or had Renee's shoulders tightened, and had she scooted away a tad? My chest tightened, knowing the things Derrick must have said about my mom. Slowly, Renee looked up at Mom, then her soulful gaze landed on me. "Are you mad, Mommy?"

"I'm not mad at you. Not one bit."

"But you're mad at Daddy, and he's mad at you, and Grammy, and Nannie too." Renee looked at Nannie with desperation. "Daddy says you're going to die soon, because you're old." Renee's bottom lip quivered, and water gathered in her emerald eyes.

If the words had hit Nannie, she didn't show it. "Oh, my dear girl." Nannie smiled, shaking her head. "I'm not going anywhere until God says it's time."

Renee tilted her head, her brow furrowed. "But Daddy says there is no God. When people die, they go in the ground and ...the worms eat them." Renee dropped her crayon and brought her knees to her chest, shuddering as if it were cold.

I jumped up, ready to wrap her in my arms. "Renee, will you come sit on my lap for a bit?" Nannie's voice was calm, but there was a faint furrow in her brow.

Renee peeked from behind her knees, then slowly unfolded herself and went to her great-grandma. Carefully, as if she might break her, Renee climbed in Nannie's lap. There were tears on Renee's cheeks, and I couldn't hold mine back any longer. I let them fall silently, as anger burned in my chest, coursed through my veins. How could Derrick fill our daughter's head with such darkness?

Nannie stroked Renee's hair, pushing back the brown ringlets that had fallen in her eyes. "Let me tell you what I know." Nannie wrapped her arms around Renee and hugged her close. "I know there is a God, and He loves all of us so much, He sent his only son to die for us so we could always be with Him. I know that's hard to understand. So, let's look at it a different way." Nannie cupped Renee's face in her hands and looked her in the eyes. "You know Nannie loves you to the moon and back, right?"

Renee nodded, blinking more tears.

"Well God loves you, and your mommy, and your daddy, and me and Grammy, that much and more. He wants good for us, not bad. And when I *do* die, I get to go be with Him and my family that has passed on before me. See, I'm not scared about dying, Renee. And you need to know when I do, it may be sad for you for a while, but it's not a bad thing. And it's not because God is punishing me, or your mom, or you. He's simply bringing me home to be with Him." Nannie's eyes lit up like she was talking about Christmas.

There was something about the way she explained everything to Renee that comforted me and made me long for the kind of faith Nannie held onto with such ease. But it also brought a question to my mind—did Nannie know something about her health that I didn't? I looked to my mom, whose eyes were glistening. Nannie wouldn't tell Mom if there was a health issue. She would be too concerned that the worry would drive Mom back to drinking. But Nannie had no reason not to tell me … except she knew I already had too much on my plate.

Nannie looked up at me, a bright smile on her face. She didn't look as tired as she had when we first arrived, but there was still something not quite right about her. I didn't dare ask any questions about her health though, especially not in front of Renee. "You should have come tomorrow. We could have all gone to church together." Nannie spoke gently, but there was conviction in her voice.

I fidgeted in my seat. Mom had said the same thing last night, which had caught me off guard. She hadn't been to church in years, as far as I knew. I couldn't tell Nannie that unlike Derrick, I *did* believe there was a God. But unlike her, I didn't believe He truly loved me, and sitting in church only reminded me of how much I didn't measure up to His standards.

"We missed you, and I was worried after not talking to you all week. I didn't want to wait an extra day to come." That was true.

Nannie nodded, but there was knowing in her eyes. "Well then, maybe you can all go to church somewhere in Eugene tomorrow."

"Maybe." I sighed. Church would probably be good for Renee, but I couldn't bring myself to enter a church building right now. Plus, once I started going, shouldn't I go every Sunday? Now wasn't the time for starting new habits. After the custody case was done, then maybe I would find a church and start attending regularly. "I was kind of planning on taking Renee on a hike tomorrow, to a waterfall."

Renee bounced up, causing Nannie to squint in pain. "Yay! Mommy and me love waterfalls."

I shot up and pulled Renee out of Nannie's lap. "Careful honey, you'll hurt Nannie."

"I'm fine." Nannie waved her hand, but I could see the remnants of pain in her eyes.

"I think a hike will be fun." My mom, who had been unusually quiet, finally spoke. She turned to Nannie and smiled reminiscently. "Dad talked to God in the mountains."

Nannie nodded. "That's right." She sat back in her chair, studying me with wise eyes. "A Sunday hike might be exactly what you—and Renee—need."

Sunday morning I took out my list of waterfalls. The list had started with the twelve on the calendar Brian gave me, along with the waterfall from the newspaper clipping I'd found months ago. But as I heard about other waterfalls, the list grew. A few were now crossed off the list. I smiled at my small victory. If someone asked me, I couldn't put into words why it brought me a sense of satisfaction to know I'd visited those falls. Maybe it was because it was the first goal I had for myself since the divorce. Maybe it was because I felt like Grandpa was beckoning me to hit the trails. Whatever it was, the visits to those waterfalls had become a small part of who I was.

Now to find an easy one, something Renee, my mom and

I could all conquer in one day. I sipped my coffee, enjoying the quiet of the morning before Renee or even Mom woke up. The feeling of peace was increased by the fact I had not heard one word from Derrick all weekend long.

My phone rang. A quick look at the caller ID confirmed what part of me already knew. Derrick. Who else would call this early? The period of peace was over.

Don't answer it.

Fear made me push the green button, or maybe it was simply the habit of all the years of jumping through hoops to keep Derrick happy. If it didn't relate to parenting, I had every right to hang up.

"Hey, Cass." Derrick's voice was soft. Sober.

I switched to the home screen on my phone and touched the application for recording phone calls. "Renee's still in bed."

Derrick sighed, and my shoulders tightened, ready for the outburst.

"Do you have a minute to talk?"

He was asking permission? "I … guess."

"Look, this whole thing, it's gotten out of control. I know I've messed up. But you have to admit, you haven't made this easy for me. You up and left. I had no idea where you or Renee were." Derrick's voice faltered. "It doesn't have to be like this."

My mouth gaped open. This was the last thing I expected. How did I respond to an apologetic Derrick? Or was it an act? I squared my shoulders. "This isn't the way I want things to be either, Derrick, but I have to do what's best for me and Renee." The line was silent a moment. The only thing I could hear was my heart pounding in my chest, ready for the explosion.

"I get it. I'm sure we can work things out to where you and I can be friends, at least, and figure out what's best for

Renee. But a restraining order? Criminal charges? Do you have any idea what that's going to do to my reputation as a business person?" Derrick pleaded, his voice still soft but full of angst. "And think how the restraining order is going to affect Renee as she goes to school. We won't be able to attend school activities at the same time. Renee will never have both parents at her events."

Guilt twisted my stomach. He was right. I hadn't really thought that far into the future. My concern had been staying safe now, making a better life for Renee. The way Derrick behaved, a better life didn't include much, if any, contact with him. If he now realized what it was costing Renee, was he willing to change?

"I don't know what to say." I twisted the hem of my pajama shirt around my finger.

"Say you'll give me a second chance, Cass. If you and I can put this behind us and try to be friends, life will be so much better for our little girl."

Tears burned my eyes. My chest ached, revealing a longing I couldn't let myself hope for. How I wanted what he offered. Giving up on the dream of our happily-ever-after was one thing; giving up on the father of my child, the man who was once my best friend, was another. The voice I was hearing now, this was the man I had married. The man I had chosen to spend my life with.

"That would be best for her, I know, but ..." My voice shook.

"You've got to call off this criminal trial, Cass." Derrick's voice was still tender, but pleading. "I could end up in jail." He sighed, as if in resignation. "But I understand if you don't feel like you can. I shouldn't even ask."

I hesitated, struggling to put words to my emotions and the thousand questions swirling in my head. "I don't know. Trust takes time to rebuild."

"I get it. I promise I'll do my part. But you have to call off this trial. I know we can work out the custody part, just you and I. The criminal charges ...once that happens, it's on record forever. There's no way of getting around it."

He was right. If Derrick was found guilty, he'd have a criminal record. Maybe everything had to come down to this, to me standing my ground and pushing back, for him to finally see he needed to change. Maybe this was the beginning of that change.

Keep your eyes ahead of you.

I looked up. The first thing I noticed was my waterfall list, written in pen. Certain falls crossed out, but so many more to go.

"I need time to think."

Derrick didn't respond at first, and I tried to imagine what he looked like right now. Were there tears in his eyes? Or had they become hard, cold?

"I need to know by tomorrow morning if you're dropping the criminal case, Cass, because I'm not going to court without an attorney." His voice held no malice, only a touch of resignation.

My chest felt heavy as I ended the call. By tomorrow morning I needed to decide the potential fate of my soon-to-be ex-husband, my daughter, and ultimately, myself. Pushing the thought out of my head, I focused on my list. More than ever, I needed a waterfall.

Proxy Falls was labeled an easy 1.5-mile loop, family-friendly hike. It was also one of the most photographed falls in Oregon. It sounded perfect. I read the driving directions, and almost changed my mind. It wasn't far, about an hour and a half away, but it was up the McKenzie River Highway. The same road Derrick and I had usually traveled when we spent time outdoors. Was I ready to go down that road, and have those memories replay in my head, especially after his call?

I scanned the rest of the list, but when it came to the perfect combination of ease, beauty, and proximity, Proxy Falls hit the mark. Plus, it was on the old McKenzie Highway, which was a seasonal road. It was one waterfall I could only see during the summer and early fall months.

Country music blaring, Mom at my side, and Renee quiet and content in the backseat, we made our way down Main Street in Springfield. Clouds were rolling in, and the forecast called for a fifty percent chance of rain. I hoped we'd make it to the falls and back before the clouds turned dark and released their burden. At the east edge of town, the four-lane city road became a two-lane highway, immersed in trees. It wasn't long before we came upon the McKenzie Bridge, with the turn off for Deerhorn Road right before it. I swallowed the lump in my throat as I drove straight and passed the familiar turn. I couldn't count the number of times Derrick and I had taken the turnoff to find a shady fishing spot along the country road. Or how many times I had laughed and screamed as he made the tires of his 1969 Mustang spin around the curves of the road. How many years ago? Ten? No matter the number, it was a lifetime ago.

We drove over the McKenzie River, and a little bit of the weight slipped off my shoulders. The road was now a straight stretch through some farmland. Soon it would pretty much follow the river for many miles.

"You're awfully quiet." Mom set her package of red vines on the console between us. Half the package was gone, and we still had at least 45 minutes of driving time. Not to mention the ride home.

I glanced at Renee in the rearview mirror. She seemed completely engrossed in the movie that played on her tablet and had her headphones on. I hadn't said a word to Mom about Derrick's phone call. This was a decision I needed to make on my own. I shrugged my shoulders. "Derrick and I spent so much time up here when we were younger. It's like going down memory lane."

"That's hard. I've been there, in a different kind of way."

I nodded. We never talked about my dad and how young I was when he died. Like we didn't talk about how Mom spiraled out of control afterward. "It's very different actually. I mean, what you went through was harder, I'm sure."

I glanced at Mom to gauge her reaction. Her face remained emotionless, almost serene. Feeling a bit more courage, I continued. "In some ways, I think death would be easier. At least it's final. You loved someone and now that person is gone. You have your memories to carry you through. For me, it's like the man I loved died and was replaced by someone else. Same body, same vows, same memories. But this new person *hates* me. Our life together was a lie. I not only lost my husband, but also all the years we spent together and the good memories we had."

"Alcohol does terrible things to the mind, baby girl." Mom stared out the passenger window, her voice distant.

I knew too well what alcohol did to a person, but I couldn't say that to Mom. Yet, if anyone could understand what happened to Derrick, to our marriage, wouldn't it be her? "Are you saying if he wasn't drinking, he wouldn't have done the things he's done? He would be like he was when we met?"

Mom made a sound—part grunt, part laugh. "Only God knows the answer to that question." She turned to me, her eyes somber. "One thing I do know is that memory is a tricky thing. Sometimes we remember things the way we wanted them to be. Sometimes love blinds us, keeps us from seeing the truth."

The McKenzie River was to our right, wide and

glistening. Heartache rippled down my chest to my stomach. Did love keep me from seeing the truth about Derrick in the early days? My mind bounced through early memories like a rock skipping on water. What I remembered most was the butterflies I had whenever Derrick looked at me with his thick-lashed green eyes, the feel of my hand in his, the sweetness of the first gentle kiss. The feeling of coming home, finding a person who made me feel like I belonged with him. But I didn't recall conversations. I didn't remember any specific thing Derrick did or said to make me feel that way.

The words I did remember were from Nannie's warning, the one that sounded ludicrous to my twenty-one-year-old reasoning. Don't marry a non-believer, a husband and wife must be 'equally yoked.' The yoking had equaled out. My tentative faith had slipped away.

"Mom, what was your impression of him, when we first met, before we got married?" Mom hadn't been around Derrick much, but enough to at least have an impression of what kind of person he was.

"He was a charmer, a good-looking boy. At least at first." Mom grabbed a red vine and chomped down on it, her jaw working overtime.

"At first? What about second?"

Mom swallowed, shaking her head. "It was one of those things you remember in hindsight, something you kind of glance over initially, especially if someone seems nice when they talk. But … it was his hands. The way he walked around much of the time with them clenched. I watched him one time, and I could tell he caught himself with his hands in fists and straightened them out quick, acting like he was stretching his fingers."

My mind slid back through time, recalling the way Derrick walked. Mom was right. He often had his hands clenched, maybe not as tight as fists, but definitely not in a relaxed position. I always assumed it was from nerves or stress. I glanced in the rearview mirror. Renee still had on her headphones, her focus on the tablet screen. "In hindsight, what do you think the clenched fists mean?"

"I don't *think* they mean anything. I've seen enough to *know* what they mean. That man has a lot of anger inside of him. He always has. He hid it better when he was young. Add the stress of adulthood and throw in alcohol, and you have a walking time bomb."

A deep chill ran through me, giving rise to goose bumps on my arms and neck. *A walking time bomb.* I shook the feeling of dread away. It wasn't like Mom was Dr. Phil. Derrick had been quiet this entire weekend, up until his uncharacteristically nice phone call. Maybe he had learned a lesson about his anger and how he expressed it.

Once we made it to the trailhead, we reached Upper Proxy Falls in half an hour, even with Renee stopping to examine lava rocks. The falls was initially unimpressive—water coming down a rocky hill, over and under fallen, moss-covered trees. It ended in a pool of stagnant looking water. Renee squatted down and put her hands in the pond.

"Be careful," I said, though the water looked shallow. There were hikers walking up the rocks to get closer to the falls. It was a gentle flow of water that they could reach out and touch. After telling Renee to stay with Mom, I walked around the pool at the base of the falls, stepping up a natural ladder made of dirt and tree roots, and got a wider view of the falls. It was pretty, though definitely not the most impressive fall I had seen. Peering around the trees, I searched for an outlet for the water, but found none.

"Wondering where all the water goes?" A middle-aged

woman with dark hair pulled into a tight ponytail smiled at me, her make-up-free face glistening.

I managed an uneasy laugh. "It seems to disappear."

The woman smiled. "It goes underground." She pointed toward the trail. "It comes out down that way, then becomes Lower Proxy Falls."

Suddenly the nagging uneasy feeling that had plagued me all day intensified. I had assumed it was from the drive up the river. But it was more than that. It was Proxy Falls. I knew that it went underground. I had been here before, but never saw the waterfall.

The trail to Proxy Falls had been particularly crowded all those years ago, when Derrick and I had come here.

"This is dumb. Let's go back." Derrick had stopped on the trail, grabbing my hand.

"It's only a little farther. I really want to see this waterfall." I had pleaded, my face tilted up to him.

"Cass, I want to go to Scott Lake. We don't have all day." He almost whispered the words to me as other hikers stepped on lava rocks, making their way around the dusty trail we had blocked.

It had been early fall, and the highway would close in the next few weeks for the winter. We had been to Scott Lake earlier that summer, but never to Proxy Falls. We were both working full time and had recently bought a house. The weekends were never long enough.

"Actually, we do have all day, and I want to see this waterfall. We'll be done in plenty of time to see Scott Lake, and have a fun birthday dinner in Sisters." I had pulled on his hand and smiled at him playfully. "We'll get home in plenty of time for your birthday surprise."

Derrick's eyes had turned from soft green to the hard,

silvery-green they got when he was annoyed. He pulled me to the side of the trail. "It's just a dang waterfall." His teeth were clenched.

A man passing by must have picked up on something, because he stopped and looked at us with a hesitant smile. "Been to Proxy Falls before?"

"No. We haven't." I looked at Derrick, my eyebrows raised.

"Ah, well, it's a good one. Interesting too. The water from the upper falls goes underground for a way after the first fall. Then it comes back out into a creek and becomes Lower Proxy Falls. That lower fall is a beauty. Kind of magical even." The man smiled too much, his head bobbing. "You'll love it." He waved as he skirted around us and headed up the trail.

I had looked at Derrick once more with the pleading look that I rarely used.

His jaw clenched. "What's more important to you, seeing this stupid waterfall—or me?"

It was a dagger in my heart. Why did I have to choose? And why did I feel so guilty? "Of course you're more important than a waterfall, Derrick." I had looked away, not wanting him to see the tears that stung my eyes.

His hand gripping mine relaxed. "Well then, let's get back on the road." His voice held a satisfied tone. Something pricked at my insides, a spark. He sounded too satisfied, like a fat cat who sneaked on the counter when you weren't looking and ate the fish you cooked for dinner. We had gone back to the car, then to Scott Lake, and had a nice dinner in Sisters that evening. Derrick had drunk a few beers, enough to make it unwise for him to drive. I had driven the Mustang home. There had been a wedge between us that didn't dissipate when we went to bed that night. The day had ended with his loud snoring, and me wondering why my heart hurt.

"It's perplexing, isn't it?" The woman's question pulled me out of my reverie.

"What do you mean?" It was like she read my mind, knew I was trying to figure out how I had been blind to Derrick's controlling ways and drinking for so long; like she knew I needed to decide whether dropping the criminal charges was best for Renee or a dangerous mistake.

The woman smiled. "The way nature works sometimes. Looking at this pool of water," she motioned to the water at the base of the falls, "it looks dead ... stagnant. But it's actually moving, being filtered through the lava rock, to re-emerge and become something even more beautiful."

I shivered in the seventy-degree shade. "That is ... perplexing. But also very, very cool. How far—"

A splash came from behind me, followed by Mom's voice, "Renee!"

My heart jumped and I spun around to see Mom pulling Renee out of the shallow but murky water. I scrambled over the rocks. "What happened?"

Renee was soaked and muddy, her face puckered into an angry cry.

"She was reaching for a butterfly over the pond and slipped." Mom frowned and looked at me guiltily. "I was right there, but she was fast."

"That happens. I brought her a change of clothes, just in case." I reached for Renee. "Come on, honey, let's get to the car and cleaned you up, then we can finish our hike."

Water dripped on my head, my hand. The clouds had darkened. Raindrops fell silently. Renee looked at the darkening sky. "I want to go home." She shivered.

Empathy radiated from Mom's eyes. "I'm sorry, Cass. I think we need to call it a day."

The raindrops fell harder, penetrating the dry dirt around us, carrying the smell of wet earth upward. "Yeah, you're probably right." Disappointment was heavy on my chest.

Someday I would finally make it to Lower Proxy Falls. Someday.

PART THREE: THE RIVER

Your path led through the sea
your way through the mighty waters,
though your footprints were not seen.

Chapter Twenty-Seven

A ROAR, THUNDER CARVING THROUGH THE *earth. The sky is black,*
no moon or stars. I'm walking against the wind, vertical rain
pelting my face, going up my sleeves and down my collar. The
ground is mud, squishy, each step breaking suction. Water
seeps through my shoes.

The wind carries a scream, a voice I know. I run, breaking
free of the mud, my heart stabbing my ribs. The ground is
slippery, and I struggle to keep my footing as I run through
puddles, jump over rocks. The roaring is closer, the scream
louder. I lose my footing, scraping my arm against a ragged
tree branch to keep from falling face first in the mud.

The earth shifts and the clouds part, revealing the moon.
The river is ahead of me, and moonlight reflects off it in
varying shades of grey. I see her. She is clinging to a branch
stuck between moss covered rocks.

"Mommy! Help ... I can't hold on," Renee cries. She's out
of reach.

My legs are lead, but I push forward and lunge, reaching
for her.

I miss.

Her fingers lose their grip on the branch. The river whisks
her away. She sinks, resurfaces. One last time I see her tiny

head bounce above the water. Then she is gone with the roar.

"Renee!" I sat upright in bed, heart thundering. My eyes slowly adjusted to the semi-dark, and I took in my surroundings—four light blue walls, a rose-covered comforter, a battered dresser.

Mom emerged in the doorway, her eyes half closed but her forehead lined with concern. "Is everything okay?"

I nodded. But everything wasn't okay.

After going to the Falls on Sunday, I still hadn't made up my mind about dropping the charges and foregoing the trial. I needed advice, and I knew I couldn't talk to Nannie or Mom about it without them thinking I was crazy for even considering it.

I had turned to Bonnie, pulling her aside Monday morning to talk to her in private. I had felt bad for burdening her with my problems, especially after she told me her beloved dog Red was sick. But Derrick had only given me until Monday to make a decision. The tug-of-war in my heart needed an anchor.

I had told Bonnie about the phone call, about my doubts. Bonnie had looked at me with her gentle, all-knowing eyes. "Part of making things right is owning up to your actions and facing the consequences. If he's truly sorry for what he's done, he'll do the right thing now, which means going to court and facing a judge."

Her wisdom and reassurance settled the battle inside me. I had sent Derrick a simple one-line text to let him know my decision. He had not responded.

Now the criminal trial was here, and I would be facing Derrick. Alone.

"I'm sorry for waking you. I had a bad dream." More like a kill-me-now nightmare.

"Okay, baby girl. I'm going back to bed. It's only 5:30." Mom closed the door.

I laid down again, even though it was almost time to get up. Mom sleeping on the couch had me tip-toeing around in the mornings, but I didn't mind. It was better than being alone, especially now.

Renee. How had her night with Derrick gone? I hadn't spoken to Derrick since his phone call on Sunday. With the criminal trial being this morning, letting Renee go to his house for her Wednesday night visit had been tough. My only solace was Derrick had to bring her to daycare this morning in order to go to court. He wouldn't miss court—there would be a warrant issued for his arrest if he did.

The courthouse was the same as I remembered from the day I got the restraining order. Grey. Cold. Intimidating. I made my way through the metal detector like a pro, my eyes constantly scanning the area for Derrick. The District Attorney had said he would meet me outside the courtroom.

The District Attorney was a tall, thin man. His dark hair was combed to the side, a failed attempt at covering a receding hairline. He fidgeted with his thick eyeglasses before extending his hand. "Mrs. Peterson, how are you doing this morning?"

I cringed at the use of Mrs. "I'm good. A bit nervous." More like shaking-in-my-heels and ready to run. I turned through the Rolodex in my mind trying to remember the man's name. Paul? Peter?

He nodded his head, a look of practiced empathy on his face. "Understandable. But everything is going to be fine. Let's have a seat and we'll go over what to expect today."

"Paul, I have a quick question for you." Another man in a suit approached us.

"Excuse me a second." Paul stepped aside with the other man, speaking in hushed tones. I didn't know who the other guy was, but at least now I knew Paul was Paul, not Peter. My stomach flip-flopped. I sat on the closest chair, straining to hear the nearby conversation. Was it about the trial? Was it about Derrick?

It was only a few moments before Paul was sitting next to me. "Sorry. He needed to talk to me about the trial after this one."

I sighed in relief. No surprises yet.

"I want to go over this with you again, so you know what to expect. As I told you by phone after the pretrial conference, Mr. Peterson has retained an attorney, and he waived his right to a six-person jury."

My heart rate doubled. This was getting real. "Why would he waive his right to a jury trial?" Our last conversation was a blur, but I didn't recall asking what now seemed like a crucial question.

Paul tilted his head and smiled. "There are many reasons why a defendant might choose to waive a jury trial. In Mr. Peterson's case, I think it's a combination of concern of jury bias because this falls under the domestic abuse category, and also, there's less attorney's fees involved in a bench trial than in a jury trial."

"And even if he's found guilty, he probably won't go to jail since this is his first offense, right?" Guilt was trying to creep into my heart, remembering Derrick's phone call.

"It is highly unlikely." Paul pushed his glasses, which had slipped down his nose, up with his forefinger. "Don't worry, though, Judge Mitchell has been assigned to the case and he is pretty stringent. He's not a slap-on-the-wrist kind of guy."

I nodded but felt little relief.

"The police officer who responded to the 9-1-1 call will be present as a witness. We also subpoenaed your neighbors who made the call. They should be here shortly. They will all be required to sit outside of the courtroom until they are called to testify. But you are allowed in the courtroom the entire time. Whether you do so is up to you. I will have you testify after the witnesses, and before I call Mr. Peterson to the stand."

Cold sweat beaded the back of my neck. I willed myself to stay calm. "What about Derrick? Will he be sitting out here with us, waiting for the doors to open?"

"Well, yes. If he was in custody, you wouldn't see him until they brought him in through another entrance to the courtroom. But he's not in custody. He'll be in the courtroom during the entire trial."

Within moments Alex appeared, dressed in uniform. His lips pulled into a smile, his eyes warm, and he took a seat next to me and Paul. "It's going to be okay." His reassuring voice matched his compassionate gaze.

"That's what I keep telling myself, but I'm not quite sold." I tried to smile.

The neighbors showed up, the man and woman whose names I couldn't remember. I was ashamed I never sought them out to thank them for what they did that night. Now they looked almost as nervous as me. Paul stood and greeted them, pulling them aside for a conversation I couldn't hear.

"How's your daughter?" Alex asked. His light blue eyes showed genuine concern.

What did I say? She's okay, except when she goes to daycare now, she doesn't talk to anyone. She's okay, except she has sudden outbursts of anger, and fights me like I'm her enemy. She's okay, except I don't know if I'm ever doing the right thing, and how this will affect her in the long run. "She's almost five years old," I answered, willing my tears to stay at bay. "She doesn't understand what's going on."

Alex nodded. "That's tough. How are you holding up?"

"Me?" I shifted my gaze to the wood paneling that lined

the wall across from me. "I'm fine."

"Will anyone be here with you today? A support person?"

I shook my head. Bringing mom would only ignite Derrick's anger, and I knew her nerves couldn't handle this situation. In a way, I walked on eggshells again, afraid of bringing her to her tempting point, afraid she would reach for the bottle. Missy had to work, and I hadn't even asked her to come. I had hinted at Brian that I could use an attorney with me this morning, but he had assured me I didn't. Nannie, I knew, would have been here in a heartbeat if she had her health. There was no one else to ask.

Alex's posture shifted, and I looked up. Derrick was walking toward the courtroom, his attorney on his left. Derrick held his head high, jaw set. He looked directly at me and smiled smugly. That was the Derrick I had come to know, not the boy I had fallen in love with—and not the face of someone who had experienced a change of heart. My head buzzed with a sudden rush of blood through my body. Adrenaline. Fight or flight. It was time for me to fight, whether I was ready or not.

"Did the DA talk to you about being in the courtroom?" Alex's voice was barely above a whisper.

"Yes, but I don't know. It's hard to be around him. I think I'll stay out here." Derrick and his attorney had taken a seat close to the doors, and far enough away to not hear our hushed conversation. Still, having him near made it hard to breathe.

"I think you should be in there, at least while your ex is testifying. It'll be hard. Very hard. But in my experience with guys like this, having the target of their rage in the same room brings out the worst in them, and you want the judge to see that."

The next thing I knew, the doors to the courtroom opened and everyone except the witnesses began to shuffle inside. Peter asked me if I wanted to go in with him, or wait until I testified.

If Derrick didn't show his true colors to the judge, if he wasn't found guilty of any charges, there was no telling what he might do next. Alex's eyes met mine, giving me courage. "I only want to be in the courtroom when he testifies." My voice shook.

Paul nodded. "That's doable. I'll call you in when it's time for you to testify. Afterward, you can take a seat until the trial is over."

Alex made small talk while we waited. I did my best to reciprocate. By the time my pulse had slowed to a semi-normal speed, Paul's assistant peeked out the door and called Alex into the courtroom.

He stood, towering over me, and yet not one bit intimidating. "It's going to be okay." He looked at me with a combination of empathy and concern. He turned and walked into the courtroom.

Fidgeting in my seat, I fingered the cross that dangled from the delicate chain around my neck. I'd worn Nannie's necklace again, my security object. How I wished Nannie could be with me. Or Grandpa.

I'll always be with you.

I shivered at the voice in my head. Grandpa, but different. I exhaled and closed my eyes.

"Ms. Thomason." I started at the sound of Paul's assistant's voice calling my neighbor for her testimony. Alex walked out of the courtroom, his face unreadable. He sat beside me. "I want to tell you this. Don't let him intimidate you. No matter what he says or does, don't let it make you doubt yourself. Stay calm, focus on the facts, and tell *your* story." Alex's brow was creased. He definitely looked more concerned than before he went inside the courtroom.

"Thank you, for everything. I'll do my best."

Alex reached in his pocket and handed me a business card. It had his name on it, along with a phone number. "If he causes any problems, don't hesitate to call me directly. I'll do whatever I can to help."

I couldn't stop the tears from welling up this time. All my life I had been afraid of the police, and the time they came to my home when Nannie called them only reinforced the negative. Alex was different than every stereotype I had created in my mind.

"I appreciate this so much." I grasped the card in my hand—a lifeline for the future. "Thank you, again."

It wasn't long until the last witness was called. The cold sweat returned, knowing I was next to be called into the courtroom. I had put Alex's card in my wallet, behind my debit card. Hidden and safe. Was his concern because of something that happened in the courtroom, or was it the general concern of someone who has seen bad things, and was witnessing another injustice?

"Mrs. Peterson." Last call. It was time to go in.

I surveyed the courtroom. There were tables, one on the left, one on the right, each set up with seats on one side facing the judge's box. There was a microphone on each, along with a box of tissue and a pitcher of water. How many other women had sat here, watching their ex-husbands or boyfriends who were charged with a criminal act against them? There were far worse things than what Derrick had done to me. More harmful physical assaults. Unspeakable sexual attacks. So much worse. Doubt crept in again, making me want to run. Alex's words echoed in my head. *Don't let him intimidate you.*

No more running.

Exhaling slowly, I made my way to the witness stand to be sworn in. After I had solemnly sworn to tell the truth, I forced myself to look around the courtroom, my gaze falling on Derrick last. He was seated at the table with his attorney, dressed in his best navy-blue suit, with a baby-blue shirt underneath. His shoulders were relaxed, and he was leaning in toward his attorney, speaking quietly in his ear. The attorney was an older man, near retirement age, and didn't look intimidating. Paul had told me his name was Richard Webb, a well-respected but not overly zealous defense attorney. Derrick still had not retained an attorney for the custody case. Was he waiting for the outcome of this trial before hiring one? Brian said if he did hire one at the last minute, the first thing he or she would do would be to ask for the custody case to be rescheduled for a later date while they prepared. Dragging it out even longer was more than I could bear.

"Ms. Peterson, please have a seat in the witness box." The judge's voice was booming, authoritative.

I walked with shaking knees and took a seat. *Here we go.* Peter stayed seated at the long table, and I focused my gaze on him, but could feel Derrick's eyes on me. Keeping my hands in my lap, I commanded my heart to slow. It didn't listen.

Peter asked questions—my name, how I was related to Derrick. All questions I knew were coming. He had me recount the details of that night, asking me questions he already knew the answers to, but that clarified the events for anyone who wasn't there. It was easy. No surprises. Then it was the defense's turn to question me.

Turning my head slightly to make eye contact with Mr. Webb, I twisted my hands in my lap. Though I tried my best to not look at Derrick, he was in my line of vision. The slightest smirk was on his lips. He didn't look nervous at all. Here I was, terrified and alone. I reached for the necklace again. Calm washed over me.

"Ms. Peterson, you stated the defendant followed you to

your apartment, correct?" Mr. Webb smiled, showing bleached white teeth.

"Yes."

"But isn't it more likely he was simply driving to your apartment to meet you, as you previously arranged?"

I looked at Paul, whose face remained emotionless. "No." I said evenly. This was Derrick's scheme, an outright lie?

"Isn't it true, Ms. Peterson, that you and the defendant had spoken by phone the day before, and agreed to talk about future daycare plans Monday after you got off work?"

I shook my head, anger building up inside me.

"You need to respond verbally, Ms. Peterson." The judge's voice boomed at me.

I looked up at him apologetically, feeling unbelievably small. "I'm sorry. My answer is no. We spoke about daycare but we didn't make plans for him to come over."

"When you got out of your vehicle and walked to your apartment door, was your daughter upset?"

"Yes ..." I glanced at Derrick, whose smug smile had grown. What was he trying to do?

"And you asked Mr. Peterson for help, because you were tired."

"No!" My hands had become fists in my lap. Paul cleared his throat. I glanced over at him, and his warning look to me was clear. Keep your cool. I breathed deeply, waiting for the next question.

"Didn't you say to Mr. Peterson that you could not handle your daughter any longer, that you were at the end of your rope?"

I swallowed hard. The ugliness of his lie was too much. "I did not say that about my daughter. I told him to move his truck, which was blocking my vehicle, and I went into my apartment."

"Once in your apartment, you stated you were trying to

call the police, and the defendant interrupted your call. But wasn't the person who actually stopped the call your four-year-old daughter, who was having a temper-tantrum?"

This was ridiculous. I shot a glance at Derrick. How could he use his own daughter as a scapegoat? "No. That is not true."

"And when you screamed, weren't you actually yelling at your daughter, and forcing her to stay in your arms because she was reaching for her father?"

The room was spinning, and the nightmare from last night replayed in my mind. Renee. Holding onto a limb in the raging river. Holding on for dear life before the dark water took her away from me. Tears welled up in my eyes. "That's not true. It's not true at all." He was trying to make me look like a bad mom. He wasn't simply looking for a not guilty verdict, he was building a case for the custody hearing.

"I have no more questions, Your Honor."

"Prosecution rests." Paul's voice echoed in the nearly empty room.

I walked with weakened legs to the gallery and took a seat in the front. Sitting through Derrick's testimony of lies would make me sick to my stomach, but I needed to know what he was up to. Hopefully Alex was right about my appearance bringing out the worst in him. So far, he'd remained cool, with nothing more than a catlike smirk.

Derrick took the stand, and his attorney began his questioning. I braced myself. Derrick looked at me quizzically. My seat was directly in his line of sight. I forced my face to remain calm, emotionless.

"Mr. Peterson, we'd like to hear your side of the story. What exactly happened on the night in question?"

"Ms. Peterson called me from work that day. She said we needed to talk about childcare." Derrick turned to the judge as if he was a friend sitting next to him. "When she ran off with our daughter, she never told me where she and Renee were living, let alone where she went to daycare."

The judge nodded. "Please direct your answers to counsel, Mr. Peterson."

"Oh, sorry." Derrick faced his attorney again. "Anyway, she called and said I should come over when she got off work so we could talk. I was glad she was ready to be civil about the whole thing, so I agreed."

My stomach clenched. Wasn't Paul going to object to Derrick's lies?

"Okay." Mr. Webb nodded. "What happened when you got to Ms. Peterson's apartment?"

"Well, I wasn't sure where I should park, so I stopped my truck behind Cass—I mean Ms. Peterson's—Explorer and got out to ask her where I should park. But Renee was acting kind of weird, and I could tell Ms. Peterson was really upset. She asked me to help her get Renee inside, so I followed her into the apartment."

"Is it true that you closed and bolted the door behind you?"

"No. I mean, I don't remember bolting it, but sure I closed it. It was hot outside. Then Renee started crying, and for some reason Cass—I mean Ms. Peterson," Derrick turned to the Judge again, a lost schoolboy look on his face. "Sorry, it's hard to refer to my wife as Ms. Peterson." Derrick turned his eyes, now the cold silvery green I knew too well, back to his attorney. "For some reason she decides she needs to call her grandma. I guess she wanted parenting advice. She couldn't exactly get any from her own mom because, you know, she's an alcoholic. Actually, she's worse than an alcoholic. She kind of always had a revolving door of men in her life, if you know what I mean."

"Objection." Paul's tone was monotone, unfazed.

"Sustained." The judge bellowed.

"Let's focus on the events of the evening in question." Mr. Webb gave Derrick a pointed look.

"Right. Sorry. So she goes to make this call, but Renee is obviously upset, and starts reaching for me. I took a step forward to comfort my daughter, and Ms. Peterson told me to stay away. She wouldn't let Renee down, so Renee reaches out and grabs the phone and throws it. Boy. That set ... Ms. Peterson off."

My blood was on fire. The judge was listening intently, watching Derrick. Did the judge believe him?

"Okay. So what happened next?"

Derrick shook his head. "Ms. Peterson starts screaming at Renee, and squeezing her really tight, not letting her down. I was taken aback. I mean, I've seen her act kind of crazy before, but this was my kid in her arms. I reach for Renee and Ms. Peterson screams at me to get out. The next thing I knew someone was knocking on the door."

"Go on." Mr. Webb nodded encouragingly at Derrick.

Was Paul going to let the lies continue? Shouldn't he be objecting? He appeared calm, not affected by Derrick's testimony.

"Well, I didn't want to make a scene, so I told the guy at the door there was nothing to worry about. The next thing I knew, Ms. Peterson was outside, sitting on the ground. Renee was frozen in her arms like she was in shock. It was obvious things weren't going well, and I didn't know what to do ... so I left."

"You drove away?" Mr. Webb raised his eyebrows. "Were you aware one of the witnesses was calling the police."

Derrick shook his head. "No, I didn't know. If I'd known the police were coming, I would've stayed to give them my statement. Like I said, I was taken aback. I figured the best thing for me to do was get in my truck, go home, and give

Ms. Peterson a chance to calm down."

Mr. Webb asked Derrick more questions about when the police came to his house and questioned him, and Derrick continued his victimized testimony, wearing a sad and forsaken expression. Crushed under the weight of Derrick's lies, my shoulders slumped, and tears slid down my face. I couldn't do this anymore. I couldn't think like him, scheme like him.

"I have no more questions, your Honor." Mr. Webb returned to his seat, and it was Paul's turn to question Derrick. I held my breath.

Paul approached the witness box with furrowed brow, nodding his head. "Mr. Peterson, the night of June first must have been very disturbing for you."

"Yes. It was." Derrick's face was solemn.

Paul changed his line of questioning, and asked Derrick what seemed like irrelevant questions about when the police questioned him and informed him that charges were being filed. My palms were sweating, and I wiped them on my pants. What did it matter what he said or did when the police questioned him?

"Mr. Peterson, going back to what happened at the apartment, you said your daughter was very upset, and Ms. Peterson seemed ... unstable, correct?"

Derrick nodded. "That's correct."

"You weren't worried about leaving your daughter with Ms. Peterson, in her state of mind?"

Derrick's jaw tightened slightly, and he shifted in his seat. "Well, yes. But I figured since the police were on their way, she would be okay."

Paul was silent, nodding. "Mr. Peterson, didn't you say you didn't stay because you didn't know the police were being called? That if you had known, you would've remained at Ms. Peterson's apartment and given the police your statement?"

Derrick froze, and his ice hard eyes darted directly to me. He shook his head. "Well, yeah, but ... I figured *someone* would call the police, the way *she*"—Derrick pointed his finger at me— "was acting."

"You will not point at any witness in this courtroom, Mr. Peterson, unless you don't know their name and are asked to identify them in such a way." The judge's voice boomed, his brow creased. He turned to Paul. "Proceed with your questioning."

Derrick's face and neck turned red. Paul tilted his head, and though I couldn't see his face, I believed he was smiling. "Something's not quite adding up here, Mr. Peterson."

Derrick leaned forward and set clenched fists on the top of the witness stand. "I think everything adds up fine. Cass is a bad parent. She took my kid away from me and ran off so she could be like her wild, drunken mother." Derrick turned to the judge again. "Who, I might add, is now *living* with her. Now she's trying to get me pinned as some criminal so she can win custody." Derrick glared at me across the courtroom. "Not to mention, she's sleeping with a lawyer who's helping her." Derrick held up his hands, making the sign for quotation marks. "For free."

I was too stunned to speak, and my tears stopped. It looked like Alex was right. Having me here did bring out the worst in Derrick. The judge had seen a fine sampling of his true colors.

"I have no more questions, your honor." The confidence in Paul's voice was unmistakable.

The judge turned to Derrick's lawyer. "Do you wish to redirect, Mr. Webb?"

Mr. Webb shook his head. "No, Your Honor. The defense rests."

The judge dismissed Derrick from the stand. "I'm ready to make a ruling in this case. I'll allow a five-minute recess in case anyone in the waiting area would like to be present."

The judge stood up, and the bailiff commanded all to rise. I stood and watched the judge depart. Paul was by my side, leading me out to the waiting area.

Paul smiled at me. "Sometimes a man simply needs enough rope to hang himself."

"So, you think the judge is going to find him guilty?"

Paul smiled wistfully. "Between the testimony of your neighbors and the police officer, and your no-nonsense retelling—which aligns perfectly with the police report—and then"—Paul shook his head incredulously— "the defendant's testimony. If it wasn't obvious he was lying at the beginning, it became crystal clear at the end. Not to mention the hatred toward you he couldn't hide."

I shuddered. "He's been so good at hiding how he is from the rest of the world. Until now."

"Do you have an attorney for your custody hearing?"

I shook my head. "No."

Paul pressed his lips together and tapped his chin. "Can I give you some advice, off the record?"

"Of course."

Paul looked me in the eyes. "You should get an attorney."

The court clerk called us back in, and Derrick was asked to stand for the reading of the verdict.

The judge was to the point. "I find the defendant guilty on all charges." The judge's eyes bore into Derrick's. "I sentence you to twenty-four months of probation, one-hundred hours of community service, and fines in the amount of five hundred dollars." The judge turned to Derrick's attorney. "I suggest you review with your client exactly what a No Contact Order is, along with the ramifications of breaking the restraining order."

Chapter Twenty-Eight

I FOUGHT BACK TEARS AS I walked from the courthouse to work. It was only three blocks, not enough time to process what had happened, so I walked at a snail's pace, enjoying the warmth of the mid-morning sun. My chest felt lighter, like a weight had been lifted. For the first time, the world, not only my small family, saw the real Derrick. For the first time, he was paying the consequences for his actions. Yet I also sensed there were more battles to come. The cold, laser-like look in Derrick's eyes when I ventured a glance at him outside of the courtroom told me he was beyond angry. I could only hope his desire to stay out of trouble with the law was bigger than his need for revenge.

Pulling out my cell phone, I called Nannie. Mom would probably be calling me soon from the phone in the community room at the apartments, but there was no one I wanted to talk to more right now than Nannie. The one who had helped me see the light, the one who had encouraged me through this entire process.

The one who prayed for you relentlessly.

I shivered, despite the heat. Had Nannie's faith played a role in how today turned out? The phone rang only twice before Nannie answered.

"He was found guilty, Nannie. On all three charges." The tears I'd been holding in fell. Passers-by looked at me with concern, but I didn't care.

"Praise the Lord." Nannie breathed. "Is he going to jail?"

"No. No jail time." The idea of Derrick in jail gave me mixed feelings. On one hand, he couldn't bother me while he was there, but on the other, I still saw a bit of the boy I had married in him. The boy who I thought had resurfaced last weekend when he'd called. The idea of that boy behind bars was heartbreaking. So much so I had almost not gone through with today.

"What kind of sentence did he get?" Nannie's tone had turned from relief to concern.

"One-hundred hours of community service, and twenty-four months of probation, as well as a small fine."

Nannie sighed. "Well, I guess that's something. The important thing is he was found guilty."

"Yes, and as long as he's on probation, if he doesn't follow the restraining order, he's in double trouble." The legalities Paul explained to me after the hearing were more complicated than that, but double trouble was a good summary.

"And Brian's helping you with the custody hearing, right?"

I needed more than legal advice from Brian. I needed him to actually be in the courtroom. Especially if Derrick decided to get an attorney. "I'm going to talk to him about it." If he didn't represent me, I would have no choice but to represent myself.

Entering the office, all eyes seemed to be on me. I would undoubtedly repeat the story of the morning's events more than a few times before the day was over. Missy was the first to greet me.

"What's the 4-1-1?" She asked, her eyebrows lifted.

"Guilty. All three counts."

"Yes!" She held up her hand for a high-five.

Lana and a few of the legal secretaries gathered around me, and I recounted the morning as concisely as I could. The whole thing felt unreal. Brian appeared, keeping a bit of distance from the circle of women.

"Sounds like a celebration is in order," he said, smiling broadly. "Missy, how about picking up a couple dozen

Voodoo doughnuts?"

"Oh, man, I love Voodoo doughnuts," Lana crooned.

Missy looked at me, slightly rolling her eyes. "Alrighty. I'll get right to it."

Once the group of women dissipated, Brian moved closer. "Do you have a moment? I would like a more in-depth version of the court proceeding."

As Brian's eyes studied me with intensity, my heart fluttered. "Yes, I need to talk to you anyway, but what about Cynthia? I'm already getting a late start."

"Let me worry about it." He titled his head toward his office.

I followed him, breathing slowly. No matter what, I had to get up the courage to ask him to be my attorney as well as allow me to pay him when the divorce was final, and I had my share of everything.

Once in his office, Brian questioned me in his matter-of-fact, attorney way. I paced back and forth as I answered his questions, too revved up on adrenaline to sit still.

"That sentence is pretty steep for a first offense and a previously clean record," Brian said.

I nodded. "The DA suggested I retain an attorney for the custody case."

"He's right."

"But I don't have any money."

Brian sighed. "I know. Those dang attorneys, they're expensive."

Shaking my head, I couldn't help but smile. "But I need one. Like, on record."

"Cassie ..."

I stopped my pacing. "Can't you represent me, officially? I can pay you after the divorce settles." I pulled on the hem of my shirt, hating the sound of desperation in my voice.

Brian glanced at the closed door, got up, and walked

over to me. He gently took my hand and looked me in the eyes, his gaze soft and tender. "Cassie, like I've explained to you before, I could officially represent you, but I'm afraid the way things are around here, it would cause a lot of gossip." He gave me a crooked smile. "Not to mention, my hourly rate is outrageous. I'd end up with most of your divorce settlement."

I bit my lip, torn by the nausea of disappointment and the warmth of his hand in mine. "But the DA said …"

"I know. But he doesn't know you have an attorney helping you behind the scenes. My advice is this—if Derrick retains an attorney before the custody case, you get an attorney. It still can't be me, but I could make a few phone calls and probably talk someone into taking your case for a minimal retainer."

My shoulders slumped. I couldn't afford even a minimal retainer. "I don't know." I forced myself to look into Brian's eyes, hoping he could see into me for a moment, see the depth of my fear. See how much I needed him to be my hero.

Brian lifted my hand to his lips, gently kissing the back of my hand. My whole body tingled.

"Cassie, trust me. Derrick has already dug his own grave. From what you told me, he doesn't testify well. You'll be fine." Brian's eyes drank me in, and he pulled me into an embrace. I melted into his strong arms, soaking in the feeling of safety. The next thing I knew, his lips were on mine, and his hand was on my cheek, gently caressing. My heart raced as a warm, electric-like current swept through my body, chasing away my doubt and anxiety. I felt safe and no longer alone.

Brian pulled away from the kiss and glanced over his shoulder at the door, then back to me with ravenous eyes. "I'm sorry. I guess this isn't the time and place for this."

I nodded, now feeling shy, and looked away. "I should

get to my desk."

"We need to see another waterfall soon." Brian crooned, taking my hand for another tender kiss.

Waterfalls.

Mommy, help! I can't hold on.

I pulled my hand away. "Are you sure about the custody hearing, Brian? I can't take any chances with my daughter."

Brian lowered his eyes for a moment. "Nothing in life is certain." He looked up again with a hint of a smile. "But I'm fully confident you have a strong case."

There was a knock on the door. Brian bolted to his desk in three long strides. "Come in."

Brian's secretary peeked in. "Sorry to bother you. The Reinharts will be here in five minutes, and you haven't looked over the final changes to the sales agreement."

"Ah, yes." Brian motioned with his hand. "Bring it here."

I excused myself, the effects of the kiss fading, and my doubt of being able to represent myself at the custody hearing increasing with every step back to my desk. Coming around the corner into the cubicle, I almost ran into Lana.

"Oh, there you are!" Her eyes were wide, a look of urgency in them.

Cynthia was probably looking for me. "Yep, I'm ready to hit the tapes," I replied with as much enthusiasm as I could muster.

"You have a phone call. Your daycare lady is holding."

"Which line?" I rushed past Lana.

"Four." Lana followed me to my desk and lingered, close enough to catch my side of whatever the phone call entailed. I was beyond caring what she heard, or how she spread it.

"Hello?" I did my best to sound calm. It was probably nothing.

"Cassie! Thank goodness." Bonnie's voice was tense.

"Is Renee okay?"

Bonnie sighed. "Derrick showed up a little bit ago. He said it was his holiday weekend with Renee, and he was here to pick her up. I told him I needed to call you first—"

"His weekend doesn't start until tomorrow night!" I didn't mean to yell, but the panic was beyond my control. "Don't let him take her."

There was silence for a heartbeat. "I tried, Cassie. I told him I needed to call you first, and that you didn't say anything about an early holiday. He waved the parenting agreement in my face, telling me if I knew how to read I could see for myself." I imagined Bonnie shaking her head. "I told him, 'Yes, I know how to read, and I have my own copy of the parenting agreement. I'll go get it.' I walked around the corner—five seconds—only five seconds. He took Renee and left."

No. No. No.

"Red let him?" *God let him?*

"Red's still sick, Cassie. He was kenneled in the back room. I'm so sorry."

"Call the police. I'm on my way." I hung up the phone. Alex's card was in my purse, but I didn't know if he was on duty. If the police who responded to Bonnie's call weren't helpful, I would call him. Lana was still standing by my cubicle, her eyes like a hungry dog. "Lana, please let Cynthia know I have an emergency and had to go to my daughter's daycare." I grabbed my purse and walked by her, trying not to run.

"Can I tell her what kind of emergency?"

I stopped and faced her. Cynthia wouldn't understand. Lana couldn't understand. Everyone here might have heard of these things, but no one knew what it was like to be the mother of the child who may have been abducted by her unstable father.

"Derrick picked up Renee. It's outside of the court order,

and I believe after what happened this morning in court, she could be in danger. The daycare provider is calling the police, and I want to be there when they arrive."

Lana's jaw dropped slightly. "Oh, honey, you must be scared to death."

You have no idea.

A police car was parked outside Bonnie's house when I arrived. Maybe Alex was on duty, maybe he was the one who answered the call. When I walked into Bonnie's, my heart sank. There were two officers, one male and one female. Neither one was Alex.

Bonnie looked ten years older, the color gone from her cheeks and her brow creased with worry. "There's Cassie." She motioned me to join her and the officers near the sofa in the living room.

The male officer nodded at me. "Ms. Sampson said you requested she call us."

I stopped short, keeping my distance from the police. Even after the kindness shown by Alex, I was still wary of the uniformed officers. "Yes," I squeaked, emotion closing my throat. "Derrick isn't supposed to pick Renee up today. Tomorrow is his day to pick her up."

The officer nodded once and exchanged a look with his partner. "I understand. Are you sure he didn't call or make some other request to pick her up today?"

I shook my head. "No." I exhaled, trying to keep calm. "Listen, we were in court today. He was found guilty of harassment, trespassing, and interfering with filing a police report. The look in his eyes when court ended ..." How did I explain that look? "He's very angry, and now he's taken Renee. I'm ... scared ... my daughter." My shoulders shook, unable to hold back the tears.

Bonnie rushed to my side and put her arm around me. "It's going to be okay."

Even I could tell Bonnie didn't believe her own words. The officers looked at each other again. The woman had a hard look on her face I couldn't read. The male officer, though, looked at least a little sympathetic. "Okay. This is the present parenting agreement?" He held up Bonnie's copy of the parenting plan.

I nodded. Five weeks until the custody hearing. Five more weeks.

"All right. I think what Officer Branson and I are going to do right now is drive to Mr. Peterson's residence and see if he's home. If he is, we'll have a talk with him. But if he's not, there's not much we can do."

Not much they could do? "He could be taking her to Mexico right now for all I know. He's not in his right frame of mind." Not that his normal frame of mind was much better, but something told me this time was worse.

Officer Branson tilted her head slightly. "It's not unusual for an angry parent to threaten to leave the country with a child, but it rarely happens, Ms. Peterson. If we aren't able to reach him at his home, we really are at a standstill until your daughter is supposed to be returned to you on Tuesday, since the parenting plan says it's his time starting tomorrow."

Tuesday evening? I had already been dreading the long holiday weekend. Now Derrick had extended it. Or worse. They could be long gone by then. "But—"

"Ms. Peterson, I know this is extremely frustrating," The male officer interrupted me, his tone sympathetic. "But the best thing for you to do is to take this matter to a judge. He can place additional restrictions on the parenting plan, as well as order your ex-husband to pay fines. For many people, once they have to start paying out of pocket for their behavior, they change their act."

I closed my eyes, shutting out their voices. They didn't get it. To them Derrick was simply another bitter parent, not a drunken, angry, vindictive man. But I had Alex's number in my purse. If they didn't find Renee at Derrick's, I would call Alex. I opened my eyes and looked at the officers' faces. Just another day for them. I looked at Bonnie, who still looked ashen. She understood, at least a little, the amount of worry that burdened my shoulders, and she cared for Renee.

I'll always be with you.

A shiver ran down my body, carrying with it a tiny sliver of peace. I could almost feel Grandpa standing beside me. Soon enough I would know what to do next.

The police had my number, and staying at Bonnie's with all of the sights and sounds of children only hurt. I hugged Bonnie goodbye and drove down River Road, looking at parking lots of familiar places as I went. No sign of his truck at any of the convenience stores. No sign of his truck at his favorite Mexican restaurant. I circled through the U.S. Bank parking lot. Nothing. I drove further down River Road. He wasn't at Safeway. I glanced at my cell phone in my lap. No calls, no text. There was only one other place I could think of to look. I turned off River Road at the next light and drove to Emerald Park. Renee's favorite. We hadn't been back since that day when I had seen Derrick's truck. It seemed like a hundred years ago, and yet like yesterday. How naive I had been to think I could leave and live happily ever after. Or that my leaving would prompt Derrick to change. Renee's eyes were different now. Even with all the fighting she had seen, they still had a spark then, a light of innocence. Now they often looked tired and seemed wise beyond her years.

The pain in my chest was too much. Turning left, I drove slowly by the park, then through the packed parking lot. No sign of Derrick's truck. No sign of Renee. A lump with a thousand spokes grew in my throat and choked me. My phone buzzed in my lap, lit with an unfamiliar number.

Oh please, oh please God let this be the officer. Please let them have Renee.

"Hello." My voice shook.

"Ms. Peterson. This is Officer Taylor. I wanted to let you know we went to your husband's house, and we knocked on the door. There was no answer, and no sign of anyone being home." He paused. "I'm sorry I don't have better news."

Tears stung my eyes. I pulled over, finding a parking spot on the side of the road by the park. "Can you drive by later, and check again?"

Officer Taylor sighed. "We can try, but it all depends on how busy we are tonight."

I ended the call and grabbed my purse. Shuffling though it, I found Alex's phone number. I punched the number, squinting through the blur of my tear-filled eyes. He was my last hope. The phone rang and rang, then went to voicemail. My hope sank, draining all the energy out of my body. I left a voicemail, not even trying to hide the desperation in my voice.

It was shortly past lunch time, but it felt like evening. Physically and emotionally drained, I headed home. I would have lunch with mom, give her the good and bad news, then head to work. There was nothing left I could do.

"I'm going to his house myself." Mom was almost yelling, her eyes wild.

"The police were just there, Mom, there's no point." I plopped down on the couch and kicked off my shoes.

"We have to do *something*."

I rubbed my temples. If I wasn't careful, Mom's anxiety

would ignite my own, and I wouldn't be able to function. What we needed was Nannie and her reassurance and wisdom, but I wasn't ready to make that phone call. "We've done everything we can do for now. I can drive by his house later tonight and call the police if I see his truck there. I can drive by tomorrow, although at that point I don't know what good it'll do since his weekend begins at five p.m. tomorrow. Maybe he'll even take Renee to daycare in the morning and I can run over there and see her."

"You know he won't, Cassie. He's doing this to hurt you because he lost in court. It's retaliation." Mom spit out the words, her eyes welling with tears.

Nodding, I forced myself to stand. There was no winning with Derrick. At least that's what he wanted me to believe. When it came to my daughter though, I would never, ever give up. Derrick had not had a change of heart. He wanted me to lose my job, my apartment, my hope, everything. He didn't care how it affected Renee, as long as it hurt me.

"I'm heading to work."

Mom looked at me like I was insane. "How can you work?"

"Because I have to, Mom. It's the last thing Derrick would expect me to do." Not to mention I had rent to pay.

Mom sighed. "I know. You're right." She looked at me with tear-rimmed eyes. "You're tough, baby girl. Grandpa would be proud."

I hugged my mom good-bye. She awkwardly returned my hug, warming as I squeezed her tight. I smiled, tears sliding down my cheeks. Mom was kind of like a chocolate-dipped ice-cream cone from Dairy Queen. Kind of hard on the outside, but soft and sweet underneath.

After work, I drove by Derrick's. As I expected, his truck wasn't there. Mom and I spent the night watching television and avoiding conversation. I kept my phone near me, the notification sounds turned on high, waiting for a return call from Alex, or a call from Derrick. But the night ended without a call, a text, anything.

I got up an hour early in the morning so I would have enough time to do another drive-by of Derrick's house. No sign of him left me with one conclusion—he had been gone all night.

Where was my daughter?

My phone buzzed on the way to work. I answered, not bothering to pull over.

"Sorry I didn't get back to you sooner." Alex's voice was sincere, apologetic. "But I was off duty until this morning."

"I'm scared." I blurted, not bothering with the backstory.

"That's understandable. I read the report." Alex sighed. The static of a police radio buzzed in the background. "I'm on duty all weekend. I'll drive by his house whenever I can and keep a lookout for his truck. I already looked up the license number."

"I don't trust him. He's threatened to make sure I never see Renee again. I'm not exactly sure what that means, but with him losing at the trial ..."

"All three counts." Was that a hint of a smile in Alex's voice? "Look, try not to expect the worst. My gut-instinct is telling me he hasn't gone far, and he's doing this to punish you for standing up to him. Think of him as a little kid throwing a temper-tantrum. Pretty soon he's going to get tired and want to go home to his own bed."

It made sense. But what would Renee go through while with him? "Thank you, Alex. Your help means a lot."

"Take care, Cassie. I'll call you as soon as I know anything."

"Hey, Missy." Missy was at her work station, sorting through some mailing labels.

"What's up, hot mama? Any news on Woo?"

I tilted my head. "Any news on what?"

"Woo." Missy smiled her mischievous grin. "It's my new nickname for your butthead almost-ex-husband. W-O-O. As in Waste of Oxygen."

My stomach muscles spasmed with laughter. Leave it to Missy to make me laugh when I didn't think it was possible. "That's a good one. Woo." I shook my head. "No news yet. But Alex, the police officer who helped me that one night and testified at the trial, is keeping an eye out for him."

Missy lifted an eyebrow. "Oooh, Alex. So, is he a hottie? I've always been a sucker for a man in a uniform."

I laughed again. "I guess he's kind of cute. He's about your age, I think."

"Set me up, girlfriend." Missy winked. "Seriously, though, I'm glad he's helping you. I hope they find Woo and throw his rear in jail."

By midday, I still hadn't seen or heard from Brian. Shouldn't he be concerned about how I was doing? Surely, he had heard what happened yesterday. Anger boiled in my veins, and my hands started to shake. *Pull it together, Cassie, he's probably busy.*

I needed to eat. Once the clock struck noon, I grabbed my purse and headed out the door for the rare lunch break. The smells of local eateries would induce my appetite. If I could make myself eat, I would feel better. My phone buzzed as I stepped out of the air-conditioned building. I hurriedly dug it out of my purse. The number was one I didn't recognize.

"Hello?"

"Ms. Peterson? This is Gayle, from Woodlawn Retirement Home." The woman's voice was soft but edged with uncertainty.

I stopped walking. I didn't have any emotional strength left for patience or unknowns. "What's wrong?"

There was complete silence on the other end of the line for a full three seconds. "I'm sorry, there was an incident this morning. We had to call an ambulance."

I squeezed the phone, my heart in my throat. "What happened?"

"I don't know all the details, dear." Gayle's voice turned syrupy. "From what I understand, your grandma had a fainting spell, and took a fall in the reading room. She's at Salem General Hospital. Do you want the number?"

Passers-by gave me quizzical looks as I stood there, feet frozen to the ground. I could only imagine what they saw in my face. Panic. Fear. "No, I can look it up."

"I could put you through to our nurse. She could give you more detailed information."

"No. It's okay. I'll call the hospital." I hit the end button. What did I do now? I needed to eat and get back to work, especially after running out of the office yesterday. But Mom needed to know Nannie was in the hospital, and we would both need to know what had happened and if Nannie was going to be okay. I turned on my heel, the food forgotten. Cynthia would be furious, but I was going to let her know I was taking the rest of the day off for a family emergency.

"Hold on, I need a smoke." My mom stopped at the sidewalk outside the hospital and dug in her worn-out black leather purse.

The drive up to Salem Hospital had been a nearly silent one, and Mom had chewed on her fingernails instead of sunflower seeds or red vines this time. My mind went back and forth from worrying about Renee, to worrying about

Nannie. I kept my phone on my lap where I could feel it, not trusting myself to hear it over the road noise and the country music blaring through the radio.

"I'll wait for you in the lobby."

Guilt nipped at me for leaving Mom alone, but I couldn't stand the smell of cigarette smoke. I entered the hospital and paced anxiously. Mom finally found her way in and we went to the reception desk, where we were directed to the fourth floor. The smell of disinfectant and cafeteria food greeted us when we exited the elevator. My stomach turned, and my head spun for a moment. Someday I would have to stop and eat. Mom's eyes were rimmed in red. She hadn't only been smoking but crying. We walked side by side, watching the room numbers grow. The door number 434, Nannie's room, was closed. We stopped and looked at each other, unsure of what to do. I glanced over my shoulder, searching for a nurse, but didn't see any. As I was getting ready to knock, the door opened, and we were face-to-face with someone I assumed was a nurse. Her short curly hair framed a round face. Her hazel eyes held both compassion and fatigue.

"Can I help you?"

"We're here to see my grandma, Eula Bradford. Can we go in?"

"Yes, but the medication she is on has her very drowsy. She may fall asleep while you're talking to her, and she does need to get some rest soon."

Pain medication? Had she broken her hip again? "When can we talk to the doctor?"

"Doctor Patel is making his rounds. I'll let him know you're here." The nurse smiled politely and moved past us.

Nannie's room was dimly lit, the shades drawn. There was another bed in the room, but it was empty. Mom rushed ahead of me to Nannie's bedside.

"Mom," she choked out, her hand on Nannie's forehead, caressing it gently.

I walked up behind her and held back a gasp. The woman in the bed was as pale as the bed sheet she lay on and had grey roots and unkempt hair. Her eye makeup was smudged, and the rouge she usually had on her cheeks was gone, as was any trace of lipstick. My Nannie didn't have as many wrinkles as the woman I saw in front of me, and she wasn't as small and frail looking.

Be strong. You have to be strong for Nannie.

I went to the other side of the bed and took Nannie's left hand, the one where she still wore her wedding ring. Her hand was cool to the touch, but she squeezed my hand weakly. Her eyes flitted back and forth between Mom and me.

"Two of my favorite girls, right here." She smiled, but it seemed to take all of her strength.

Not knowing what had happened was eating away at me, but Nannie was not in any condition to answer questions. Hopefully she didn't ask about Renee. She didn't yet know about Derrick's latest stunt, and now wasn't the time to find out. Tears streamed from Mom's eyes, but she remained silent.

"Is there anything you need, Nannie?"

Nannie looked at the ceiling, her eyes thoughtful. "Well, yes." She turned her head to me. "Would you mind going to my room at the home, and getting my bath powder, hair brush, denture gel, and a tube of lipstick?"

Here was my grandma, looking like she had one foot in the grave, and she was asking for toiletries. I couldn't help but smile and shake my head. "Anything for you, Nannie."

Nannie turned to my mom. "And my music box, Sharon. I need it here." Nannie's eyes misted up, and her gaze at Mom intensified. "I think it's time. It's been kept locked up for too long."

Mom's forehead creased, and she closed her eyes. Her chin quivered as if she was keeping back tears. "But—"

Nannie shook her head, a sad smile on her face. "Man plans his steps, but God directs his path."

Mom's shoulders slumped, but her face relaxed and she nodded. She lifted Nannie's hand to her lips and kissed it. What was going on here? I wasn't going to drill Mom in front of Nannie.

There was a tapping on the door. A short, middle-aged man with a white coat walked in. His black hair was deeply receded, and with his beak-like nose and narrow eyes, he looked like a bird.

"Good afternoon. I'm Dr. Patel."

My mom and I offered weary greetings. Nannie remained silent and looked annoyed by the doctor's presence. Mom offered her hand. "I'm Sharon, Eula's daughter." Mom motioned to me. "And this is my daughter, Cassie."

Dr. Patel nodded in my direction. "I'm glad you are both here. Why don't we have a talk in the hallway?"

"Whatever you have to say to them, you can say in front of me." Nannie's voice was stern. "I'm not an invalid."

Boy, he must have really done something to make Nannie mad. She was usually friendly with doctors.

Dr. Patel cleared his throat. "Very well. Would you ladies care to have a seat?" He motioned toward a couple of chairs at the end of the bed.

There were only two chairs, but Mom and I sat in them. The doctor stood at the other side of the bed, looking back and forth between Nannie and us.

"Mrs. Bradford's blood pressure was quite high when she was brought to the ER earlier today, so we have begun a series of tests on her heart." The doctor looked at Mom. "I'm sure you're already aware she's hypertensive, has hypercholesterolemia, and a heart murmur."

Mom's brow furrowed. "Uhm . . . she said something once about blood pressure pills, but I didn't think it was bad."

The doctor shot a quick glance over his shoulder at Nannie, who had dozed off, then looked at mom pointedly. "I'm afraid you may have been misled."

My heart skipped a beat. "What do you mean?"

Dr. Patel inhaled deeply, looking back and forth between my mom and me, as if trying to decide which one would take bad news with the least drama.

"I'm afraid her heart has been very weakened by the combination of conditions. We are still doing more tests, but it appears she had a mild heart attack."

"No, my mom is in good health. She just has a bad hip!" Mom jumped up from the chair, looking ready for a fight.

The doctor held up his hands. "Please, I know this is not the news you want to hear, but we need to remain calm for Mrs. Bradford's sake."

Mom hesitated, then sank down into her chair. "Is she going to be okay?"

The doctor shook his head. "Like I said, we are running more tests—"

I gripped the side of my chair, my heart sinking in my stomach. "I think what my mom wants to know is, what is your best guess, as of now?"

Dr. Patel nodded, and glanced at the floor before looking at me. He avoided looking at Mom. "Based on what we are seeing so far, I think the damage to her heart is extensive."

A small cry came from my mom. She turned her face away from me and the doctor.

I squared my jaw; it was on me to be the strong one. "When will we have the other test results?"

"There's one more test we are going to run after your

grandma gets some rest. We should know more at the end of the day."

"Okay." I nodded. "We are going to go get my Nannie's things and bring them here."

I was thankful Nannie had fallen asleep during the doctor's talk and understood why she didn't like him. He didn't have any good news to deliver. I walked out of the hospital room with heaviness on my shoulders. Nannie had a heart attack. And Renee ... I pulled my cell phone out of my purse on the walk to the car. No missed calls, no messages.

We drove silently. Mom looked lost, her eyes hollow, and I searched for something to say to reassure her. I recalled when Nannie had fallen, breaking her hip. I had tried to comfort her by telling her God would not give her more than she could handle. It was trite—I had heard the phrase a thousand times, but it seemed like what she would want to hear.

Nannie had smiled and patted my hand. "That's not true, sweetie."

"What do you mean?"

"God *will* give you more than you can handle, alone. But never more than you can handle if you put your hope and trust in Him. He carries you through."

Nannie had been the most faithful, God-loving person I had ever known. She may not have been the image of the perfect church lady, she was a little too spunky for that, but a purer and more loving heart could not be found. Yet, God allowed her to suffer. I knew if I went up to her room and asked her right now, her feelings about Him would not have changed.

"What's on your mind?" Mom spoke from the passenger seat. She hadn't asked to stop for a cigarette, or anything else. She stared out the front window the whole time, in a world of her own.

"I was thinking about how unfair life is."

The veins in mom's neck seemed to stand out, and she closed her eyes again. "Yes, it sure is."

We arrived at the retirement home and explained we needed things from Nannie's room. Everyone we passed in the hallway and lobby looked at us with sympathy. An orderly unlocked the door and let us in. I found the toiletry items, and Mom retrieved the music box from the shelf. She set it on the end table next to Nannie's empty chair. I shivered.

"Let's get back to the hospital." I headed for the door.

"Cassie, stop. We need to talk." Mom eased into the spare chair.

I turned around, my heart racing. This must be about the music box. "Can't we talk in the car? I want to be there when Nannie wakes up."

Mom shook her head. "It's best if we talk now, face-to-face."

For some reason my hands started to shake. I scanned the room. I couldn't bring myself to sit in Nannie's chair, so I took a seat on the bed. "Okay, what is it? You're kind of freaking me out."

Mom looked at the ground, her shoulders slumped. "I'm sorry, Cassie. The timing really couldn't be worse. But I know this is what Mom was asking me to do." She looked up at me, her eyes filled with tears and a knowledge out of my reach.

I shook my head. "What is it? What is it about this dang music box anyway?"

Mom inhaled, seeming to gather strength, then exhaled through her teeth. "The music box was a gift to Nannie. A gift from ... my father."

I shook my head. "Nanny said it wasn't from Grandpa."

Mom looked away, and silence filled the room. "Cassie ..." She turned to me. Tears streaked her cheeks. "It wasn't Grandpa who gave her the music box."

I shook my head, irritation rising. "I'm confused. You said it was a gift from your *father*." A small chill at the base of my spine rose up, and my heart raced to keep it at bay. "You're not making sense."

The pain in Mom's eyes was immense. "Your grandpa ... he was my dad, he raised me. But he wasn't my biological father."

The chill in my spine turned red hot and spread like wildfire. The walls of the room shrunk, forcing the air out of my lungs. "No. Grandma was never married before, and she and Grandpa were young when they got married." The shrillness of my voice echoed in the tiny room. "They were childhood sweethearts since the age of twelve, a perfect love story." I restated the history I knew, fighting for its existence. For *my* existence.

Mom shook her head. "I'm so sorry, Cassie. Nannie thought you knowing the truth would hurt you, and make you turn out like me." Mom looked at the wall, a sardonic smile on her face. "But I don't think it was the truth that got me. It was genetics ... or a generational curse." Mom looked at the floor, lowering her voice. "The bottle curse. Alcoholism."

It was hard to breathe. I got up, pacing the small room. "Who was he, your *father*?" *My real grandpa. No! Not my grandpa!*

"He was ... another friend. A childhood friend of both Nannie's and Grandpa's actually." Mom drew a breath in as if she was getting ready to run a race. "My biological father, Michael, had moved away when he was fourteen. I guess he had a rough life. His dad was alcoholic, abusive. His mom died young. It's a long story, but when Grandpa went away

286

to college, he and Nannie broke up. Michael came back to town shortly after that. There was a short love affair. The music box was a gift to Nannie from him. It had belonged to his mother." Mom paused. "When Nannie told him she was pregnant, he left, and she never heard from him again. Nannie said it was ultimately a blessing, because he showed signs of becoming an alcoholic, just like his dad." Mom swallowed. "Grandpa came back home from college and married her."

"What? Grandpa didn't know?"

New tears sprung up in Mom's eyes, and they were suddenly full of light. "Oh no, Cassie. He knew. He knew everything. But he married Nannie anyway." Mom's chin quivered. "And he loved her. He loved her with everything he had."

My heart pounded in my chest. "But you weren't his daughter."

Mom shook her head. "No, I wasn't. At least not by blood."

I stopped my pacing, looking away as a thousand memories cascaded through my mind. Grandpa telling me stories of his youth. Grandpa teaching me to fish. Grandpa giving me away at my wedding because I didn't have a dad. Each moment imprinting on my heart, and on my personality. I was Grandpa's girl. He was my hero.

But it was all a lie.

The drive back to the hospital passed in a blur. I wanted to see Nannie, and yet I was afraid to, especially as the missing pieces of Mom's story took shape in my head. Nannie had a love affair and conceived Mom out of wedlock. My church-going, Bible-believing, always-praying Nannie had been someone more like ... I looked at my mom, who had found a bag of sunflower seeds in the vending machine at the retirement home and was now popping them in her mouth with machine-like consistency. Mom. Nannie had been a little more like Mom when she was younger. It didn't seem real. And Grandpa ... no, I couldn't even think about Grandpa.

When we arrived at the hospital, Nannie was awake. The doctor was leaving the room. "Sharon, may I speak with you a moment?"

She paused, looking at me. "Go ahead," I said. "I'll check on Nannie." I needed to speak to my grandma alone.

Nannie didn't look any better, but she did seem slightly more awake. Any anger or judgment I had toward her fell away. I took her hand, fighting back tears. She looked at me with love-filled, sorrowful eyes.

"Your mom told you?" Her voice was soft.

I nodded, biting my lip. Crying would only make Nannie feel worse.

Nannie closed her eyes for a moment and nodded. "Good. You needed to know, while I'm still here to answer questions."

What was that supposed to mean? I remembered the look on the doctor's face when he asked to speak to Mom, and a cold feeling spread through my gut. "You're going to be fine, Nannie," I said, conviction in my voice.

Nannie smiled. "Everything will work out for good."

There were so many questions I wanted to ask. Who was this man I didn't know? What was this bottle curse Mom spoke of? But there was one question that burned above the rest.

"Nannie. Now that I know Grandpa wasn't my real grandpa—I know this might sound silly, but ..."

"Honey, he loved you more than life itself." Nannie's eyes glistened. "You brought him more joy than you'll ever know."

I blinked away tears, nodding my head. "He was my

hero. I always believed I got some of my features from him, including my blue eyes … but I guess that's impossible." I stared at the wall, unable to look at Nannie.

"They say blood is thicker than water." Nannie's voice was strained. "But let me tell you what's thicker than blood. Love. You did get features from him, but they go beyond what the eye can see."

By the time we got home, I was more exhausted than I had ever been in my life. We had stopped at a 7-Eleven on the way so mom could buy cigarettes, and I bought a burrito and ate in the car while she smoked and paced the 7-Eleven parking lot. My stomach gurgled now, unhappy with the food I ended my fast with. I went to bed right away and plugged my phone in the charger. All I wanted was to get the day over, and I was sure Mom wanted the same, especially after the news the doctor had given us.

The heart damage was severe. It would be several days before Nannie was released, and she would need to go to a different ward of the retirement home, one with convalescent care. We were lucky, he said, that she had survived, and even luckier she was in a facility that offered different levels of care. Other people in her same situation had to switch homes upon discharge.

Chapter Twenty-Nine

SURPRISINGLY, SLEEP CAME QUICKLY. I WELCOMED the empty darkness, eager to put my problems behind me.

A loud thud, followed by a low moan, startled me awake. I jolted up, senses on high alert. My thoughts immediately went to Derrick. I listened a moment longer, again hearing a low moan.

"Mom!" I jumped out of bed, stubbing my toe on my dresser as I raced to my door. I ran into the living room, squinting, unable to see in the dark. The faint light from a security light outside shone through the bottom of the drapes. Something moved on the living room floor.

"Mom?"

"Dang it. I'm fine. I tripped on my dress." Mom's voice came from the floor.

"Your dress?" I made my way to the wall, flipping the switch for the overhead light.

"Ugh. That light is bright." Mom groaned, her arm over her eyes. She turned to her side, her eyes squinted shut. "I need to get to the bathrooooom."

What was wrong with her? I noticed the half empty bottle of Jim Beam on the end table about the same time I noticed the sweet smell of hard liquor. My blood ran cold, and I couldn't move. Where had the bottle come from? Had she snuck off to the liquor store when we got home?

"You've been drinking."

"Just a couple shots, baby girl. Take the edge off." Mom clumsily got to her feet, staggering into a standing position. Her eyes were glazed, and her chin stuck out defiantly. "Don't you dare say a word to your Nannie." Mom shook her finger at me and wavered in her steps. "She doesn't need any more bad news." Mom spoke low and slowly, but it didn't hide her slurring of consonants.

I clenched my fists. Anger welled up inside, making my head pound. "And what about me, Mom? You think I can handle much more bad news?"

Mom tilted her head. "Of course not, Cassie. But you're so strong." Mom walked toward the bathroom, each step carefully planted. I watched her warily. The last thing I needed was to take my drunken mother to the ER. She stopped and turned toward me, her brows pinched together. "You're too strong, I think." Mom shook her head slowly, and turned back to the bathroom, carefully making her way to the door. Once she was in the bathroom and the door was shut, I grabbed what was left of the liquor and poured it down the kitchen sink. I wanted to throw the bottle, break it against the wall and scream. "Thanks, Mom. When I needed you the most, you checked out."

It was the bottle curse.

I shuddered. Was my biological grandfather an alcoholic too? I didn't care. It didn't matter. It was a *choice*, not a stupid curse. I would never, ever choose to let myself be an alcoholic.

But you married one.

No. I slammed my fist on the counter. No. I breathed slowly, willing myself to calm down. Derrick wasn't an alcoholic when I married him. Sure, he drank back then, but not in excess. There was no way I could've known what he would turn into.

It was the way he clenched his hands when he walked.
Come on, Cass, we don't need to see a stupid waterfall.

I heard the bathroom door open. I rounded the corner, ready to lay into my mom, to tell her she could take her drunkenness, her "bottle curse," and get out of my apartment. That I would not have any sign of alcoholism around Renee. But I was stopped short by what I saw standing in the bathroom doorway. If regret had a face, it would be a picture of my mom. The pain in her eyes was in competition with the lines around them. The dark circles under her eyes, along with her sagging jowls, made her look older than she was. I knew there was nothing I could say that would make her feel worse than she already did. Her mom's health was deteriorating. Her granddaughter's future uncertain. Now she had blown her one shot at making things right with me.

I went back to my bed and begged sleep to come again, but it denied me. I tossed and turned and finally, right before dawn, I dozed off. I slept lightly, hearing sounds in the living room and kitchen, knowing it was Mom, probably miserable with a hangover. At 7:30 I pulled myself out of bed, my head aching and my stomach sinking into itself. The last thing I wanted to do was face my mom, but I had to use the bathroom.

Apparently, the last thing Mom wanted to do was face me, because there was no sign of her when I went into the living room. No sign at all, except a small piece of lined paper with writing on it sitting on the same table where the Jim Beam bottle had been. I laughed bitterly, knowing what it was. The infamous note. The *I'm sorry*. The *I promise this will never happen again*. The *I just need some time to work through this*. Wadding it into a ball and throwing it away was all I wanted to do, but I had to think about Nannie. What would I tell her? Maybe Mom hadn't run off and was simply on her way to see Nannie again.

Cassie-

I can't say how sorry I am. I know you don't understand, and I pray you never *do* understand, because the only way you could would be if you fought this demon yourself. I'm going back to the coast for a while. I'll keep in touch and check in on Nannie. I'm no good to anyone right now. *When Renee gets home, please give her a big hug from her Grammy and tell her I love her to the moon and back, one-hundred times. I love you, my precious daughter. Please believe.*

Xoxoxo Mom

I ripped the note into tiny pieces and threw them in the garbage. Mom had left me in the biggest mess of my life, and she expected me to believe she loved me? How stupid did she think I was?

You're too strong

Did I have a choice? The bitterness I swallowed was acid in my stomach. I would force myself to eat today. Renee would need me when she got home, and I couldn't let her down by getting sick from starvation. I put water on to boil for oatmeal and made a pot of coffee. My phone still showed no missed calls or text messages. There was no way I could get through this weekend alone. I knew Missy was with her family in central Oregon for the holiday weekend, but Brian was still in town. After forcing down breakfast and two cups of coffee, I checked the clock. It was 8:30. That was a decent hour to call someone on a Saturday, wasn't it?

My heart pitter-pattered at the sight of Brian's name in my contact list. I rolled my eyes: what was I, a teenager? The phone rang several times before it picked up.

"Hello?" A sleepy female voice answered.

I held my phone out, double checked the number. It was clearly Brian's. The voice definitely was *not*. I almost hung up, but with caller ID, it didn't make sense.

"Uhm ... is Brian there?"

"Who is this?" The woman sounded irritated.

Didn't Brian have me saved in his contacts, like I had

him saved in mine? The answer was painfully obvious.

"Sorry," I battled to keep my voice steady. "I'm Cassie. I work with Brian. I have a quick question. A work-related question." I rubbed the back of my neck, waiting for her reply.

She sighed heavily. "Brian's in the shower. I've never heard of him working with a Cassie and today is *Saturday*. Can I take a message? This is his wife."

"Uh... no. You know what, I can talk to him Tuesday. Sorry for bothering you."

I stared at my coffee table, my body and mind numb. Nausea rippled through my gut. Brian had lied to me. He wasn't separated. Missy had tried to warn me, but I'd been too foolish to listen. I had let myself believe he could save me, but sharks don't save. They simply hunt.

Knowing it would do no good, I dialed Derrick's number. All I wanted was to hear my little girl's voice, to know she was okay. *Please God, let him answer. I can't take one more thing. I need a little bit of hope.* The phone rang until it went to voicemail. Derrick's salesman voice came through the speaker. I slammed my phone down as waves of sorrow shuddered through my body.

Staying in this apartment another moment was impossible. In my bedroom, I leafed through a stack of waterfall notes and pictures on my dresser until I found what I needed. Picking it up, my heart was torn in half. Greater than the pain was the question that haunted me. I grabbed my small bag and a bottle of water. Heading out the door, I turned and looked at my apartment one last time.

I wasn't sure if I was coming back.

Chapter Thirty

WAS IT LAST WEEKEND I WAS driving down this same highway with Mom and Renee to see Proxy Falls? It seemed like a dream, a lifetime ago. The sky was overcast, with darker clouds on the horizon threatening rain. Today I would drive past the turn off for Highway 242 and keep going. The newspaper article sat beside me, with the blurred words from the water ring Derrick's beer had left on it months ago. The name of the falls was written in a caption below the picture—Koosah Falls. I had put off going there during my other waterfall adventures, waiting for the right time. Waiting, really, for this battle to save my daughter and start a new life to be over.

Everything was different now.

I drove in silence, not bothering to turn on the radio. Country music had too many depressing songs, and I wasn't in the mood for pop or rap music. The silence matched the darkness inside my chest. The darkness grew, making me numb, welcoming me into its cold nothingness. If I didn't find answers at the waterfall, there was no reason to hope things would ever get better.

After all, I was cursed.

The circular parking lot had only a few cars in it, probably due to it still being fairly early and the weather forecast calling for rain. There was a sign that showed the trail, a loop that took hikers first to Sahalie Falls, a few hundred feet from where I stood, then on to Koosah Falls. From there it went to a bridge and looped back on the other side of the river. I didn't care about the path back.

The trail was wide and paved for the short walk to Sahalie Falls. I stopped at the viewing point, willing myself to absorb the beauty. It was pretty, but nothing pressed through the numbness in my chest. I continued along the trail, following the river. The swirling rapids were steps away, crystal blue, even under the overcast light. Such beauty, but also a death trap if someone were to fall in. If I had taken Renee here, I would have been nervous about getting too close to the river.

Mommy! Help ... I can't hold on.

I shivered from the memory of the nightmare. I tried, my dear daughter. I tried so hard. But it wasn't enough. There was still no sign of Derrick. I had no idea where Renee was or even if. No. Even Derrick couldn't be that evil.

Or could he?

His cold, angry glare at the courthouse looked ready to kill. I should have run to the daycare and taken Renee, skipped work. I should have taken her to Nannie's that day, then maybe, somehow, Nannie's heart would have been better, and she wouldn't be in the hospital. Mom would not have had a reason to buy a bottle of Jim Beam. I wouldn't have learned I didn't belong to my Grandpa. I wouldn't know I had repeated a family curse that was more than alcoholism. It was a lineage of fatherless girls.

Then there was finding out the truth about Brian, the icing on the proverbial cake. The sting of his lies sucked the last bit of hope from me. Was every man who stepped foot in my life destined to betray me? Was I that unlovable?

A couple coming down the trail stepped aside as I walked past them without making eye contact. There was no one else on the trail. The aloneness was fitting. The sweet smell of trees and earth and cold rushing water would have normally lifted my spirits. Today it did nothing. I came to another lookout, rounded and made of stone, reminding me of a turret on a castle. It was the top of Koosah Falls. The view through a couple of trees showed the top of the fall. It was a true punch-type waterfall, falling down a sheer drop, with no warning at all. I pulled the newspaper clipping out of my pocket and looked at the black and white photo. This wasn't the viewpoint the picture had been taken from. I left the viewing area and continued down the dirt trail as it went slightly down hill, curving around the river.

Another viewpoint came into sight, this one also made of stone, but narrower. The entire fall was visible from this one, but it was much further away than I liked. I looked below. The hill going down to the river was steep and lined with trees, with no trail of any kind in site. Desperation gnawed at my insides. This wasn't close enough, and it wasn't the view from the picture. Looking out across the river, I didn't see where a better viewing point could be. There had been access to the river, to the top of the falls even, back at the other view point.

I returned to the trail and made my way to the other viewing area. Thankfully, there was no one there. I climbed over the low rock wall, and walked with careful, sliding steps down the soft, loamy hill on the other side of it. I stepped over tree roots and onto a large boulder, inching my way forward, holding onto a branch of the tree as I made my way to the edge of the rock.

I looked down. The water fell directly below me. Dizziness overtook me for a moment, and I held on tighter to the slender, flexible branch. My toes were at the edge of the rock. Whoever took the picture for the paper, must have had some kind of stick for their camera, and had stood here and held it over the drop, positioning the camera at the highest angle possible.

The water was serenely clear, the fall beautiful. The river fell helplessly and crashed down at the bottom of the fall in glorious splendor. The darkness inside me whispered.

Let go of the branch.

I did, balancing myself on the rock and looking down, holding my breath. One step. That's all it would take to end the torment. Maybe that's the way it was supposed to be. Perhaps the newspaper article had been the lure from the beginning, the sign of my final destination. The fall would be short, cold, but an adventure of its own, wouldn't it? How strong I was or wasn't wouldn't matter. One step would end the pain. Forever.

Except for Renee. It would only be the beginning of hers.

Renee. I had messed up her life before she was even conceived, handing down a heritage of lies. Maybe Derrick did know the truth. I had been blind to it all along. I inched forward, my heart aching in my chest.

I inhaled deeply. A cool rush of air swept over me, and I listened to the crashing of the water below. Closing my eyes, the darkness welcomed me. I was ready.

Mommy! Help ... I can't hold on.

Renee's face. Her large emerald eyes crying, terrified. No! As long as she breathed, I couldn't do anything that would add to her pain. It was my job to protect her, no matter how hard it was. With a shaking hand, I grabbed hold of the branch that had given me support. I took a step back from the edge of the rock.

What had I been thinking?

The realization of what I had almost done sent tremors through my body. I spun on my heel to head up the hill. My foot caught the tree root. I stumbled, crashing down on my stomach, knocking the air out of me. My legs were suddenly in icy water, pulled by the rushing current. Scrambling, I clawed at the soft ground, finding a hold on one of the roots. I hung on, gripping the root with all my strength, first with one hand, then the other, fighting the water that instantly numbed me from the waist down.

I couldn't hold on long.

"Help! Someone help me!" I screamed, trying to be louder than rushing water. "Help!" My throat ached with the force of my voice. The water pulled. My fingers dug deeper into the root. I closed my eyes and heard Nannie's sympathetic voice.

God will give you more than you can handle, alone. But never more than you can handle if you put your hope and trust in Him. He carries you through.

My body was weak. Too little food, too much stress. My grasp on the root was slipping. I did the only thing left to do. I prayed. "Please God, get me out of this. I don't want to die. I can't leave Renee alone, Lord. Please help me. I need you."

The icy water swept up my body, making my teeth chatter. Darkness lurked in the cold, pulling my eyes shut. In the gloom, a tiny dot of light shone and slowly grew. A figure stood in the middle of it, a man with wide shoulders, wearing a cowboy hat.

Grandpa.

He was in front of me, holding out his hand. "Hang on, Cassie, I'm right here."

"Grandpa!" Waves of love washed over me, chasing away the ice of the river.

I saw his blue eyes, his face, full of love.

I'll always be with you.

Grandpa's face changed, gently fading away. It was replaced by Nannie sitting in her favorite chair, her eyes gleaming with hope. Then her face faded, replaced by Bonnie's warm-hearted smile.

I've already given you everything you need.

I saw Missy with her spunky, mischievous grin. My hips scraped on the rock as I slid further into the river. My fingers squeezed, refusing to slip.

"Help me!" My voice echoed, impossibly loud.

I saw my mom's face, her sober one, love in her broken

eyes. As her face faded away, Brian's came to focus, but it was different. His eyes were hungry, but also sorrowful, an empty bowl that couldn't be filled. As it faded away, I saw Alex--determined, protective, driving his police car.

Remember what I taught you.

I was in Nannie's room, reading her placard with the cross on it. "How much do you love me, I asked Jesus. This much, He said. And then He spread out His arms and died."

Nannie in her hospital bed, reassuring me about Grandpa's love. "He loved you more than life itself."

More than life.

Like Jesus loved me.

And that was more than enough.

My fingers slipped, the wood of the branch scraping skin.

"Hang on!" A woman's voice shouted over the roar of the water. I opened my eyes, squinting in the sunlight breaking through the clouds. A woman's face was above me. Strong hands grabbed mine, pulling me forward. My numbed legs touched ground as I was dragged away from the river. I lay there, catching my breath, my eyes adjusting. The woman kneeled over me.

"Are you hurt? I can run up the road to get cell service and call an ambulance." Her face came into view. She was about my age, hair pulled back in a loose French braid, her face touched by perspiration.

I shook my head. "No. I think I'm okay." I moved my legs. They were prickling as the numbness from the cold slowly left them.

"What happened?" She asked, her eyes studying me.

"I was trying to get a good picture from the top of the waterfall." I swallowed, realizing how close I'd come to losing my grip on the root. "I slipped." My hand patted my shorts pocket. Miraculously, my phone was still in it. If my waterproof case lived up to its claims, it might even still work.

The woman tilted her head, a puzzled look on her face. "I'm glad I heard you, because I wouldn't have seen you at all. I wasn't even going to come down this part of the trail because I was here earlier today, but for some reason I felt like I needed to come back for one last look. I heard a scream, then I scrambled down toward the river. I saw you hanging on to the tree root."

I sat up slowly, rubbing my scraped hands on my shorts. "You saved my life."

The woman smiled. "Well I have to say that's a first for me." She held out her hand. "My name is Sandy."

I took her hand, though mine was still shaking. "I'm Cassie."

Sandy smiled, a glint of humor in her eyes. "I take it Cassie is short for Cassandra."

I nodded.

"So is Sandy." She laughed. "Here, let me walk you back to your car, so I can be sure you're actually okay.

Chapter Thirty-One

I DIDN'T HAVE CELL SERVICE UNTIL I was many miles down the highway back home. I knew I had reached reception because my phone dinged several times. Figuring I used up all my chances for grace that day, I pulled over and checked my messages.

There was one text message and one voicemail. The text was from Brian. "Hey, sorry about earlier. I can explain later. Talk to you Tuesday." I rolled my eyes. There was no explanation necessary now that my rose-tinted glasses were off.

The voicemail was from Alex. I listened to it with bated breath. "Cassie, I want you to know I've driven by Derrick's house a few times, and though he's not been home at those times, I noticed different lights were on or off. I think he's still in town. I'm keeping a watch for his truck."

Derrick was still in town? A weight lifted off my shoulders, and I almost laughed with joy at the sensation of lightness. He hadn't run off to Mexico … or whatever. Which meant he would eventually bring Renee back, once he believed I had suffered enough. I turned the radio on to find a music station before pulling back on the highway. Scanning the stations, nothing caught my ears until I came to K-Love, a Christian music station. A band with an upbeat sound and a female singer were playing.

In my heart I felt all alone
Lost and so afraid
But you were there with me, always there with me
I couldn't even see the Light
I couldn't find my way

But you were there with me, always there with me
From the mire you pulled me and held me oh so tight
You showed me that you'd never left my side

Chills ran through me, but they somehow warmed me to my core. I wasn't alone. Yes, Grandpa was with me in memory. But more importantly, God was with me, and had been all along. I was simply too stubborn and hurt to see Him. God had put people in my life to help me. When I was a little girl, He had sent Grandpa to bring me to live with him and Nannie. He'd opened the door for me to have a job—the first job I applied for—providing enough for Renee and me to live. He'd led me to Bonnie, who was so much more than a daycare provider. The job He provided brought me Missy, who had encouraged me to go to waterfalls and had been my first friend in years. A terrible event led to Alex, who was going above and beyond the call of duty looking for my daughter. Even Brian had a part to play.

I still had a battle ahead, but I wouldn't be doing it alone. I couldn't wait to get home and call Nannie.

Chapter Thirty-Two

ONCE HOME, I HAD TO DECIDE how much to tell Nannie. In her state, it wouldn't be good for her to know I had contemplated suicide, or even that I had almost fallen to my death. Then there was what had happened with Mom, and the still unknown facts with Renee. It was a big burden to carry. Too big. This time, though, I knew where to turn. I folded my hands and prayed, then dialed Nannie's number at the hospital.

"Hello?" Her voice was weak, but not as bad as the last time I talked to her.

"Hi, Nannie. How are you?" That was a stupid question.

Nannie chuckled. "Well I've seen better days. How are you, sweetie?"

I inhaled slowly. "I'm doing good. I went to a waterfall this morning."

I told her about slipping and falling but left out the part about the river almost dragging me to my death. I did tell her about the other Cassandra that came along to help me, and about the revelation I had while listening to the song on the radio. I finally told her about the recurring dream of Grandpa.

"Oh Nannie, it all makes so much sense now. God used the image of Grandpa to talk to me because Grandpa was like a dad to me. My hero." My voice stuck in my throat. Part of me wanted the dream to really be Grandpa talking to me and letting that go was like saying good-bye to him again.

Nannie was quiet for a long moment. When she finally spoke, her voice was heavy with emotion. "Cassie, that is … beautiful. I can't even tell you how much it means to me to hear this story. It's an answer to this old woman's prayer."

Nannie was quiet for a moment. "God was chasing you while you were chasing waterfalls." A hint of a smile came through the phone.

"I guess He was." My nose tingled.

"How's your mom?"

This was the tough part. "She went back to the coast for a few days—to clear her head."

"I see."

There was a long moment of silence. "God has a plan for her too, you know." Nannie's voice was resolute.

"I'm sure He does Nannie. I'm sure He does."

I spent the rest of the weekend cleaning and grocery shopping. Sunday morning, the 4th of July, arrived without fanfare from me. I had offered to visit Nannie that day, but she urged me to stay home, rest, and to see some fireworks "for her."

Fireworks didn't interest me, but the rest was needed. As was food. I ate more than I had in days, slowly gaining back my physical strength. There would be a firework show at Alton Baker Park, which wasn't far from where I lived. I determined I would go outside once it was dark, stand in the parking lot and watch them. Who knew? Maybe Renee would be watching the same show. It wouldn't be long now until Tuesday morning, when Renee was supposed to be dropped off by Derrick at Bonnie's. If she wasn't, I would take the next steps.

My phone buzzed right after 5:00 p.m. My heart leapt at the number. Alex.

"Cassie. I found him. And your daughter."

Thank you, God!

"Is Renee okay?"

Alex seemed to hesitate. I could hear commotion in the

background. "Yes, but can you come get her? We are at the corner of 5th and Blair."

He wasn't at Derrick's home? "Of course, I can come get her, but is it okay? I mean, it is technically Derrick's weekend. He'll probably try to use that against me or make a scene." Why was I even arguing Derrick's point for him? I grabbed my purse while I waited for Alex's answer.

"Cassie, if you don't come get Renee, I'll have to call social services. Derrick is going to jail."

I broke the speed limit, and only mildly followed the rules of the road when it came to right of way and road signs. There was no way my little girl was going to get hauled off to social services. What had Derrick done to get thrown in jail? Alex had to cut the call short and wasn't able to give me any more details. I prayed he would still be there when I arrived.

I saw water before I saw the police cars or fire trucks. Water shot straight up in the air with full force. I turned the corner to see three police cars and a fire truck, with a fire crew and another man who looked like a city employee working on what I supposed was the waterline leading to the fire hydrant. Behind the hydrant was Derrick's truck, the front end up on the curb. I looked around anxiously. Through one of the police car windows I saw Derrick's profile, in the backseat, but there was no sign of Renee or Alex.

"Cassie, over here." I heard Alex's voice above the commotion. He stepped out of another police car and opened the back door. Renee jumped out. She was wearing a plastic firefighter hat with a Eugene Police sticker on it. Alex leaned over and said something to her, pointing at me. Renee saw me and her face lit up. She ran at me with full force. "Mommy!"

I swooped her up in my arms and squeezed her tightly,

inhaling the scent of her skin, cherishing the feel of her little body in my arms. Tears streamed freely down my face. "Oh, how I missed you."

Renee squeezed me in return, then pulled back. "Guess what Mommy? Daddy hit the fire hydrant and broke it." Her eyes were big, and her mouth shaped in a huge "O".

"I'm so glad you weren't hurt." I squeezed her again.

"Me too. I was sleeping in the backseat." Renee frowned. "But Daddy got an owie on his head, because he got mad at the cop man."

"He did what?" My heart skipped a beat. What had happened here?

Alex finally made his way to me, a cautious smile on his face. "Is she giving you the big scoop?"

I nodded slightly. "I feel like I'm missing some pieces."

Alex looked at Renee, then me. "Those pieces will get filled in at a later, adult-only time. Suffice it to say we are looking at DUI, evading, and more."

My bottom lip dropped. "So, he really is going ..."

"Oh yes." Alex ruffled Renee's hair, and she giggled. "This little girl is quite the sidekick. I'm pretty sure she's ready to go on patrol."

"I can't thank you enough." My eyes misted over. There was no doubt whatever happened today, Renee being in my arms right now was directly the result of Alex's efforts —and more than a bit of divine intervention.

Alex shrugged. "Stuff like this," he nodded toward Renee. "This is what makes it all worth it." A police radio squawked in the background. "Get this little one home and enjoy the holiday."

Enjoy the holiday. Crazy as it sounded, that was exactly what I planned to do. As dusk approached, I dressed Renee in layers, and we drove to Alton Baker Park. I couldn't really afford the admission or the parking costs, but I would figure out the bills later. Renee bounced excitedly as we weaved through the crowds of people and found a place to sit.

"How much longer?" she asked for the tenth time.

"As soon as it's dark."

Renee cocked her head up toward the twilight sky. "It *is* dark."

I smiled. "It has to be completely dark. Like, black, outside."

"Why?"

I pulled her close and planted a kiss on her forehead. "Because that's when we can see the fireworks the best. Fireworks are brightest when the sky's the darkest."

"Neat!" Renee beamed.

"It sure is." I stared at the black sky, anticipating the light.

I showed up to work fifteen minutes early on Tuesday. I figured fifteen minutes was how much time I would use up in my day to talk to Brian, so I needed to get that much work done before my day officially started.

Missy checked in on me as soon as she arrived. "How'd the weekend go? Did you get your girl back?"

I smiled at my friend. "Let's say it went 'interestingly' and yes, I have Renee back. Oh. . . Derrick's in jail."

"Whoa!" Missy's eyes were wide. "But you and Renee are okay?"

"Couldn't be better. I'll fill you in on the details at lunch."

I listened the rest of the morning for Brian's voice. If I didn't face him from the get-go, I would lose my nerve. Derrick was in jail, but the battle wasn't over. Alex had called me Monday morning to give me more details of what happened on Independence Day. He had spotted Derrick's truck in downtown Eugene. Alex had followed him, hoping to get a glimpse of Renee. Derrick's truck had swerved unsteadily. Alex turned on his flashing lights, signaling Derrick to pull over. Derrick's response, though, had been to speed up and whip his truck around a corner. Alex had pursued and called in backup. The next corner Derrick took had been too fast, and he jumped the curb, hitting the fire hydrant. Water shot to the sky, and Alex raced to the truck, afraid Renee was hurt. At first, Derrick had not resisted arrest. Then he recognized Alex.

"You're that cop who testified against me!"

Alex had affirmed his identity. That's when Derrick threw a punch, but he was no match for the younger, armed man. After Derrick was cuffed, Alex had found Renee in the backseat of the truck, laying down, watching the water show from the fire hydrant.

"I think she was asleep until he hit the hydrant, then stayed low in the truck, looking out the window. It was like she was mesmerized by the water." Alex had said.

Like mother, like daughter.

Derrick had a long list of charges against him. Alex said Derrick may be able to get out on bail, but he was looking at serving time when all was said and done.

The custody hearing was in four weeks. Would he obtain an attorney? Would he be in jail and request that the hearing be rescheduled? I knew if he got out on bail, he would expect his parenting time with Renee. I couldn't take any chances of not being ready to face the worse.

At 9:30 a.m., I put an "on break" sticky note on my computer and walked to Brian's office. His door was open, and it looked like he was settling in for the day.

"Do you have a minute?"

Brian looked up and smiled hesitantly. "For you, of course." He motioned to the seat across from his desk.

I stepped in the office. "Do you mind if I close the door?"

Brian's eyes flickered slightly. "Go ahead. That would be best, actually."

I gently closed the door and took a seat, putting my hands in my lap. I pulled my shoulders back, chin up.

"Cassie, I can explain about Saturday. My wife wanted to talk, so she popped in ..." He shrugged one shoulder.

"That's a pretty early pop in."

"She's an early riser." Brian smiled sheepishly.

Was this the best he could come up with? "You know, I never asked you—when you guys decided to separate, who went where? Did you move out, or did she?"

Brian leaned toward me. "It's really a little more complicated than that. We have a guest cottage—"

"So you never actually left." I knew it.

"Like I said, it's complicated." Brian picked up a pencil and tapped it against his desk.

"You lied to me, Brian." I kept my hands flat in my lap. No twirling the hem of my shirt.

"Look, I—"

"I trusted your advice for my *daughter*. My *life*. You *lied* to me about your wife. You made me think ..." I trailed off, commanding myself to stay calm. "You made me think you cared." I looked him straight in the face.

"I really did want to help you. Honestly, I had only the best of intentions." Brian spread his hands in front of him.

For the first time I saw in Brian's eyes the same thing I'd seen in my vision at Koosah Falls. Emptiness. A hunger that couldn't be filled. I'd almost let myself be the one to temporarily fill that void and lose myself in the process—and possibly so much more.

"The divorce and custody hearing is in four weeks. I've been advised to retain an attorney. It's too late for me to find one now, even if I did have the money for a retainer, and I'm definitely not dragging this out by asking for it to be rescheduled."

Fear flashed across Brian's deep brown eyes "I really think you can represent yourself, with minimal advice from me. Maybe we could meet for dinner tomorrow night."

"No." I stood up, my hands on my hips. "We will not be going out for dinner. We will meet after work." I took a deep breath. "I need official representation. Something has to be filed before Derrick gets out of jail. An emergency order for supervised visitation."

Brian's eyes widened, "Derrick's in jail? What happened?"

I smiled. "I'll fill you in later. For now, I need you to agree to represent me, fully and legally. I'll pay you once the divorce assets are distributed."

"Cassie, I can't. The way things are with my wife ...which weren't helped by your phone call the other day ..."

"I imagine things might get a tad worse if she knew the whole story, don't you think?" I shrugged one shoulder. "She might kick you out of the guest house."

Brian's shoulders sunk. "Cassie, don't do this."

I tilted my head, as if contemplating my next move. "I've heard rumors about your reputation in the office. As for me," I spread my arms open, "my life is an open book. I, personally, don't have anything to hide." I dropped my arms.

Brian's gaze fell to his desk. "You win. I'll file the motion." He looked up at me and opened his mouth as if to say more, but pursed his lips shut.

"Good. Does tomorrow at 5:15 work for going over new developments and preparing for the upcoming hearing?" I asked.

Brian sighed. "I'll make it work."

I marched to the door, my head still high.

"Cassie, wait."

I stopped, my hand on the door, and kept my back to Brian. "Yes?"

"What happened to you this weekend? You're ... different."

I looked over my shoulder and smiled. "This weekend I learned the Truth, and it really did set me free."

Chapter Thirty-Three

THE MORNING OF THE HEARING, I stopped at the office before going to the courthouse. Brian and I had a few last-minute details to review. As I requested, Brian had filed for an emergency motion for supervised visitation while Derrick was still in jail. The motion was granted. Derrick was now out on bail, waiting for his trial. Brian wanted to know if Derrick had set up any visits.

"No." I told him. "He hasn't contacted me at all."

After meeting with Brian, I went to my desk. I wanted to divvy up my workload to the other secretaries before Cynthia arrived. Her attitude toward me had changed since the day I confronted Brian. She was friendlier, more patient. It made me wonder if the gossip of a previous relationship between her and Brian was true.

Missy was giving me a pep talk when Cynthia walked up to my desk. We stopped our conversation and greeted her. I felt uneasy since I was taking the day off, yet here I was engaging in small talk during my brief hour in the office.

Cynthia smiled at me. "Good luck today."

"Thank you. I need all the luck I can get."

"You don't need luck when you have courage and wisdom." Cynthia paused, as if considering her words. "You're much wiser than I was, not so long ago." Her eyes were serious but warm. "Go get 'em."

I wore my best dress to court, along with Nannie's cross necklace, and a macaroni bracelet Renee had made for me at daycare. Bonnie said Renee was starting to talk a bit again, and to interact with the other kids. The bracelet may have not gone well with the rest of my outfit, but the comfort it gave me far outweighed any fashion sense.

Brian sat beside me, looking the way I remembered him from the day we met. Tall, smart, authoritative. He had not said another word about our arrangement, or what had happened in the past, but had dutifully performed as my attorney. I knew he would represent me well if for no other reason than it was in his nature to win.

I can't say my heart didn't hurt a little when Derrick came in. He'd aged in the few weeks since his criminal trial. Lines were etched on his forehead and around his eyes. Those eyes. The soft beautiful eyes of the boy I had loved. Now they were hard, cold, full of venom toward the woman who had loved him. I touched the macaroni bracelet around my wrist.

Don't forget everything I taught you.

Maybe Derrick was never the person I thought he was. Or maybe he had simply changed and made poor choices. Whichever it was didn't matter. What mattered was keeping Renee safe, even if it meant another girl in our family grew up without her biological father. I wouldn't change the choices I had made when I was eighteen years old even if I could. Without making those choices, I wouldn't have Renee.

The judge entered the courtroom. He was younger than the judge who'd found Derrick guilty weeks ago, but had the same aura of authority. He called the court to order and began by questioning Derrick, who was unrepresented. He gave him one last chance to postpone until he had an attorney, but Derrick refused. "I've got bigger problems than this divorce case right now, thanks to her." Derrick had cocked his head toward me.

The judge looked at me sympathetically. "If you are ready to proceed, I don't see this taking long."

Brian smiled like a fat, happy cat. "We're ready."

Derrick offered his usual ludicrous allegations and a bitter defense. His lies didn't affect me anymore. When it was all said and done, the property division was fair.

The money didn't matter. What did matter was the custody determination.

"I award full custody to the Defendant." The judge looked at me. "Until such time as the court deems safe, all of Plaintiff's parenting time shall continue to be under supervision, by a third party."

"Congratulations," Brian said softly. "You won."

I had already requested the afternoon off, so I didn't return to work. I drove straight to Bonnie's and picked Renee up early.

"Mommy," she squealed, surprised by my early arrival.

I picked her up and twirled her in the air. "Mommy got off work early. How about a day at the park?"

Renee giggled happily. "And ice cream?"

"Sure." I kissed her forehead.

"I take it your appointment today went well?" Bonnie smiled at me with knowing eyes.

"Very well. The best it possibly could." I looked at Bonnie, remembering how her face was one of those I saw when I was hanging on for dear life at the river. "Thank you for everything you've done for Renee ... and for me." I wiped away a tear that escaped from the corner of my eye.

Bonnie nodded and touched my arm. "I haven't done much, honey. But I appreciate the thanks. I think God always lines things up better than we can, don't you?"

I laughed. "Yes, He sure does."

I took Renee to a park in Springfield. Once we were at

the park and Renee was happily climbing on the monkey bars, I sat on a bench and took out my phone to call Nannie. Mom had tried calling me several times over the last few weeks, but I ignored her calls. I wasn't ready to cross that bridge yet. Nannie had told me Mom had visited her twice and was back on the wagon. I couldn't imagine how much Mom failing at sobriety had hurt Nannie's heart. Nannie was doing better though and was adjusting to the convalescent section of the retirement home.

"Hi, Nannie."

"Cassie ... now don't keep me in suspense. How did it go?" Nannie's voice was fatigued.

"It went incredibly well. I have full custody, and the supervised visits will remain in effect." Someday soon I would have to explain to Renee why she wasn't seeing her dad, and that when she did it would be under very different surroundings.

"Wonderful!" Nannie's voice cracked with emotion. "Thank the Lord."

"It's over, Nannie. I'm ... free. Renee is safe." It still seemed hard to believe. I stared up at the clear blue sky, the leaves of the trees fluttering in the slight breeze.

"It's been a rough road, sweetie. I'm proud of you."

My chest warmed. "I couldn't have done it alone."

"No one can, Cassie. That's why God lets us fall sometimes, so we can find our way back to Him. He wants to lead us to where we can be truly free."

I nodded, wishing I could see Nannie's face. "Renee and I will come see you Sunday and we can all go to church."

"I'll be looking forward to it."

Maybe Nannie would be feeling well enough to tell me more about her past. A huge part of my history was missing. I hadn't burdened her with questions since she got out of the hospital. She needed time to get better, and I had to focus on legal matters.

I watched Renee play, and a bubble of joy filled my chest. Missy was coming over later to stay the night, for extra security. Derrick's criminal trial was in a few weeks, and from what I understood he would be doing time. He hadn't bothered me at all since he was arrested. Soon, I'd no longer need to worry about seeing a red truck, or being followed home, or harassing and threatening phone calls. When Renee tired, I took her to Dairy Queen and let her have ice cream even though it was only a couple of hours until dinner. Renee fell asleep on the ride home wearing a smile.

Sitting down to read and wait for Missy to arrive, I noticed I had a missed call and a voicemail. I listened to the voicemail. It was someone from the retirement home, asking me to call them right away.

My body turned to putty as I returned the phone call, afraid to hear Nannie was back in the hospital. If she was, I would have to track Mom down. I spoke to the receptionist, who put me through to the nurse on duty.

"Ms. Peterson." Her voice was formal, hesitant.

"Yes."

"I'm afraid I have some bad news about your grandma. Is anyone with you right now?"

My heart stopped. "No, I live alone. What's wrong with Nannie? Is she back in the hospital?"

There was a moment of silence. "Eula had another myocardial infarction this evening. This one was more severe." The nurse paused. "I'm sorry Ms. Peterson, your grandma didn't survive the heart attack."

I didn't remember hanging up the phone, or how I ended up on the floor. "Nannie!" I cried. "I need you. Don't leave me." Sobs convulsed my body. This wasn't fair! Why, God? Why did you take her now that life was starting to turn good?

It was her time. She saw her redemption in your victory.

The tears stopped, and for a moment peace washed over me. God had kept Nannie here long enough to know Renee would be okay.

Long enough to see me regain my faith in Him.

Find myself in Him.

Chapter Thirty-Four

NANNIE'S FUNERAL WAS A SIMPLE GRAVESIDE service. She had everything prearranged down to the last detail, sparing me the burden of putting it together myself. Mom and I had barely spoken since Nannie's passing, but she made it to the funeral. Pastor Matt had come down from Stayton to perform the service. Nannie would be buried in the plot she and Grandpa had bought long ago.

Guilt nagged at me as I watched Mom stand away from everyone else at the service. Renee sat beside me, squeezing my hand. She had taken Nannie's death hard but was being stoic today—until she saw Mom. "Grammy!" she cried. I held her back and kept her close to me. "Grammy needs to be alone right now. We'll talk to her after the service."

Pastor Matt gave a short biography of Nannie, then cited several scriptures. "One of Eula's favorite scriptures was Proverbs 31:21 in the NKJV. She is not afraid of snow for her household, for all her household is clothed with scarlet."

Pastor Matt smiled toward me. "I can honestly say this verse represents Eula well. If ever there was a woman who prayed powerful prayers for her family, it was Eula. Her main concern in life was making sure her daughter," Pastor Matt glanced at mom, "and granddaughter and great-granddaughter," he smiled at Renee "were covered by prayer." Pastor Matt shook his head. "She wasn't afraid of sickness, nor death, or being alone. What mattered to her was God, and family."

"Ashes to ashes and dust to dust."

Nannie's casket was slowly lowered into the ground. A loud moaning came from my right. Mom was on her knees, her body shaking, her head in her hands. The small gathering of people looked at each other uncomfortably. There were only a few distant relatives at the service.

"Grammy." Renee's voice cracked.

"Come on, Sugar Bug." I held my hand out to Renee, and she walked with me to Mom's side. I knelt beside Mom and wrapped an arm around her, pulling her to me as tears ran down my face. "I'm here, Momma."

The pallbearers had stopped when I got out of my seat, and now that I was kneeling next to Mom, they re-started the slow procession of the casket into the grave. My mom turned to me and took me in her arms, her tears soaking my shoulder. "I'm so sorry, Cassie. I should have been here. I shouldn't have left." She pulled back and looked at me. Her eyes were bloodshot and puffy. "I don't expect you to ever forgive me. I can't even forgive myself."

Renee inched her way in between us, becoming part of the embrace. "It's okay, Grammy. Nannie loved us all, and we get to see her in heaven someday."

My wise, wonderful girl. I smiled at her. There was a lot of Nannie in her, and some of Grandpa too, impossible as it was.

"She's right, Mom. We will see her again. And ..." I looked her in the eyes, not hiding my pain, but also withholding my judgment. "I do forgive you."

I didn't understand how Mom's mind worked, or why she did what she did. I didn't understand addiction. But what I was starting to grasp was the greatness of love, especially the love that comes from above, and gives second chances.

That's why God lets us fall sometimes, so we can find our way back to Him. He wants to lead us to where we truly can be free.

Nannie's words spoken only hours before her death. A truth for me to hold onto, to pass down to Renee. A truth stronger and fiercer than genetics or curses. A truth would pursue my daughter and lead her home if she ever lost her way.

Epilogue

AUTUMN WASN'T THE BEST TIME TO see waterfalls, but I was determined to see Lower Proxy Falls before the highway closed for the winter. It seemed right to not only take Renee, but also Mom, with me. She'd rejoined Alcoholics Anonymous after she'd moved back to the coast and had received her three-month chip acknowledging her sobriety. The hike would be our celebration.

Getting to the lower falls with Renee and Mom in tow was not easy. We were able to see the falls from a bridge, but it was a distant view, a glimpse of majesty between the parting of tall pine trees. I knew I had to get closer. The trail, though, became steep, and the dried dirt and pine needles made for easy slipping. I went first, then Renee, and Mom followed. I stepped on one rock or tree limb outcrop after the next, securing my footing so I could grab Renee's hand and help her down. It was slow going, but we eventually made it to the creek. The sound of the falls intensified. A narrow, faint trail continued up the waterway.

"It looks like we might get our feet wet." Thankfully it was warm for October.

"Yay!" Renee jumped up with exuberance. "Are we going in the water?"

Renee's excitement kindled my own, and I relished the feeling of childlike wonder. "Maybe a little bit, but just our feet." I turned my focus to Mom. "Are you okay with getting a little wet?"

Mom sighed but smiled. "Well, I've come too far to turn

back now, haven't I?" Her eyes sparkled.

We made our way down the creek side. More than once a fallen tree blocked our path along the unofficial trail, and the only way forward was over or under the log. Renee easily made it under, not minding the dirt on her knees. I chose the under route also, the logs too high for easily climbing over. Mom chose the under route without complaint until we came to the third one, with an especially narrow space between the log and the ground.

"Maybe I should stay put, baby girl. Let you and Renee go on." There was weariness in her voice, and beads of perspiration dotted her forehead.

"Grammy, we can't leave you. We love you." Renee's small voice echoed over the hum of the close falls.

Mom looked at Renee with tenderness. Mom and I had recently begun conversations about her coming back to Eugene, and the three of us renting a duplex. Renee would have a yard again, and for the first time since my youngest years, Mom would be part of my everyday family.

"Okay, Sweet Pea. Give me a second." Mom sighed, lowered herself to the ground, and scooted on her bottom as she ducked under the log.

A bit further we crossed water, hopping on rocks to keep our feet semi-dry. Then the fall came into view. The water's path widened as it got closer to the bottom of the falls, which gently cascaded over a terrace of rocks. It was so shallow and gentle that other hikers had made their way through the creek to the base of the falls to touch the water as it came down. My heart racing in anticipation, we began ascending the rocks to get closer to the falls. We were slow, three generations of women, and somehow, I was the strongest of all three—helping Renee, helping Mom, we got as close to the falls as I could safely lead them.

Waterfall mist surrounded us, tiny droplets of water

seemingly suspended in midair. The sun shone brightly on them, and reflected off the falls, making me squint. We were surrounded in water, surrounded in light. A gentle breeze brought fresh air, and I filled my lungs with its sweet fragrance. Renee's eyes were wide in joyful wonder, her smile covering her whole face. Even Mom had a wistful smile, peace reflecting from her eyes.

The woman who had spoken to me that day at Upper Proxy Falls was right. Lower Proxy Falls was more beautiful than the upper one. The first had been an ordinary waterfall. The way this fall spread out over the rocks created a gentle beauty that made my heart ache for more. The water was clear, almost crystal-like, purified by its time hidden underground, filtered by the rocks. It was the stuff of pixie-dust and dreams, of hope and refreshment. Maybe it was a bit of what heaven was like. I laughed to myself, joy bubbling out. I looked to the top of the fall, squinting through the light-infused mist. For a moment, like a leaf fluttering on the breeze, I swear I saw Grandpa and Nannie, smiling down on us.

Book Discussion Questions

1. As the story opens, Cassie feels compelled to leave Derrick and take her daughter. How does she justify her departure? With what you know at the beginning of the story, were her reasons valid? What would you counsel a woman who is being abused by her husband and may be in serious danger? Why?

2. Cassie has an enduring love for Nannie. Does Nannie's wisdom steer Cassie in the right direction? Why or why not?

3. Cassie reasoned that since she and Brian were both separated, it was okay for them to be interested in each other. What advice would you give a friend in the same situation? What does Cassie's reaction to Brian tell you about her needs as an individual?

4. What were your first impressions of Bonnie and Missy? How do these women influence Cassie's decisions as she moves forward in the story? Has God ever given you the opportunity to be like one of these women? Can you share how you were able to impact that person's life for good?

5. Cassie is surprised by Sharon's return. Was Cassie too quick to welcome Sharon back into her life? Did Cassie benefit from attempting to re-establish a relationship with her mom? What is the difference between Cassie giving her mom a second chance versus Cassie allowing Derrick to continue his treatment of her and Renee?

6. Cassie has a recurring dream of her Grandpa that seems to offer her comfort, warning, and guidance throughout the

book. After Cassie's experience at Koosah Falls, she realizes the dream is actually God speaking to her. Do you think God can talk to us through dreams? Through nature? Has God ever spoken to or comforted you in an unusual way?

7. What is the significance of Cassie making it to Lower Proxy Falls at the end of the book? How has she changed since the beginning of the story? Is it particularly meaningful that her mom and daughter are with her?

8. Have you known a woman in Cassie's circumstances? How can you help someone who is enduring this kind of abuse? What sorts of support can you offer either her or her child? Are there groups within your church or your circle of friends that offer assistance to women in less than biblical circumstances? If not, is it something you could see yourself helping to start?

To the Reader

One Woman Falling was inspired by my own story. Honestly, it was a story I didn't want to write. It was too personal and painful. Then God started bringing women into my life who were in situations similar to the one I had been in. I found myself sharing my story with them. It seemed to help, but my fumbled words of hope seemed inadequate. Still, I couldn't bring myself to write my story, even though the Holy Spirit literally would not leave me alone.

One morning I opened our local newspaper to a picture of a woman about my age with her two daughters. The resemblance between her daughters and my own when they had been younger was unnerving. As I read the story that went with the picture, my heart was torn open and tears of sorrow streaked my face. The mother had been killed by her ex-husband. The stalking order she had against him had not stopped him. Now her two precious girls were, essentially, orphans. All I could pray was, "Why God? Why?" I wish I could say He explained to me why these horrible things happened. But He didn't. Instead, through a dream, God said one thing to me: "Melanie, you have a testimony."

I finally put pen to paper (or fingers to keyboard.) The story within this novel is the result of my own experiences mixed with the stories I've heard from other women, and a fair sprinkling of imagination. My own story is different from Cassie's and much more complicated. The details of the divorce and custody battle in this book are representative of what actually happens in these cases but are by no means intended to fully convey all the complexities and timelines of the legal system.

My hope is that whoever reads this will understand a little bit more what it is like to be in the shoes of a woman like Cassie. I believe when we can understand someone's heart, fears, and struggles, we find it easier to have compassion for them. Compassion can give us eyes to see what we may not otherwise see, and to offer a helping hand when it is needed.

If you are a woman reading this and you identify with Cassie because that is your story too, I pray you know without a doubt that God is with you. He will not leave you, and the pain you're going through now is not what He wants for your life. Seek the help you need. You are worth the fight.

Resources:
The National Domestic Violence Hotline: 1-800-799-7233
www.domesticshelters.org

I'd love to hear from you if this story touched your life in any way, or if you'd like me to pray for you for any reason. You can connect with me at the following links, and you can sign up for my newsletter as well.

Website: melaniejcampbell.com. You can read my blog or sign up for my newsletter on my website.

Facebook: www.facebook.com/meljeancampbell
Twitter: @MelanieJean_27
Instagram: melaniecampbellauthor
https://abuserecovery.org/

Now, a Sneak Peek at Book Two

One Way Home

Sharon's story

Releasing September 2020

Chapter One

IT DOESN'T MATTER.

I held the vial, ready to fill it with saliva as the instructions stated. They also said not to drink, eat or smoke for thirty minutes prior to providing the sample, so last night I set the vial on my night stand, and reached for it first thing this morning. But now my mouth was dry. My skin crawled, telling me it was time for a cigarette. Something in me wanted more than a smoke, but I couldn't go there.

I put the vial down. Closed my eyes. Inhaled. One, two, three. Exhaled. It had been over six months since my last drink. Six months since my last horrible, can't-go-back-and-change-it mistake. It was getting easier and yet the strain was still there, an itch I couldn't scratch. It had also been that long since I found out the truth. My mom died only two weeks after her telephone call confessing the part of the family secret she had kept hidden from me. Now I was the matriarch of our little family.

I shook my head and laughed at the title. Some matriarch. Fifty-four-years old and the contents of my life surrounded me in the twelve-by-twelve bedroom of the duplex I shared with my daughter and granddaughter. It's a shrine of my life, pictures and memorabilia. On a shelf out of my granddaughter's reach is the music box. Who knew a simple object could hold such power? Power to unravel everything, to tint every memory of my past in a shade of gray that blurred the lines, obscuring who I thought I was—and who I've become.

It doesn't matter.

A light tapping on the door made me jump. I shuffled the vial and instructions under my pillow. The door crept open and Renee peeked in, one emerald eye visible through the small opening. I smiled and held out my arms. The saliva sample could wait. I'd spent my entire life not knowing the truth. It didn't matter, anyway. What mattered was rebuilding my life. Repairing my relationship with my daughter and granddaughter. Making the last part of my life count for something.

Renee ran into my arms. Her hair was a mess of brown ringlets, her eyes bright and ready for a new day. She climbed onto my lap. I swallowed the aching joy in my throat and held her close. Her ability to love me was still overwhelming, amazing. It had kept me going, pushed me forward. Helped me fight the scream of my nerves when I'd passed the liquor store, the convenience store, the alcohol aisle in the supermarket.

I had the day off from my maid job at the hotel. Today I'd take Renee to school and give Cassie a break from her usual hectic morning routine. That daughter of mine was like a machine, working and mothering and making a home like the whole world would fall apart if she stopped and took a breath.

"Grammy will you sing the song?" Renee looked at me with the deep green eyes I can't say no to. The eyes she inherited from her alcoholic father. If only the genetic roll of dice had been different for me—if I hadn't been born with my father's brown eyes—maybe things would have been different. Maybe the secret could have died with my parents. Who would have even suspected a thing, if my eyes had been blue or grey?

I Inhaled. One, two, three. Exhaled. I smiled down at her "You aren't tired of it yet?" I hoped she'd change her mind. I couldn't sing this morning. At least not the song she wanted to hear.

Renee shook her head enthusiastically. "It's my favorite."

I squeezed her. Looked around. My past surrounded me. For my granddaughter I'd sing the words to the song that haunted me. The song from the music box.

I can't deny my love for you
It's deeper than the bluest sea
Stronger than the mightiest tree
Darling, say you love me too
Because I can't deny my love for you

I hummed out the rest of the song as I pulled Renee close and wiped the tears from the corners of my eyes. I couldn't tell anyone why singing the song broke my heart. And who would I tell? My AA friends? Even the thought of telling them felt like I was betraying my mom, her memory. When I had it figured out—when I knew for sure—then maybe I'd tell Cassie. Mom had said it was up to me whether Cassie knew the rest of the story. Why she would leave a decision like that in the hands of someone with a history like mine, I had no idea.

It doesn't matter.

I patted Renee on the back. Like my mom used to with me. "It's time to get ready for school, Sweet Pea. We don't want to be late and get Grammy in trouble."

Renee bounced up with a smile. "Will you make pancakes for breakfast?"

"And sausage?" I already knew the answer.

"Yes!" Renee did a little jump, now wide awake.

I nodded. "Run along and get dressed. Grammy needs to make her bed."

Renee pranced out the door, humming the tune of "Undeniable Love." I reached under my pillow, found the little vial. I could do this. My mouth wasn't so dry any more. Humiliation settled on my shoulders as I filled the tube and followed the instructions. I wrote my name on the identifying insert: Sharon Gilbert. Thousands of people had done this. Millions perhaps. Whatever the number, I was among the many who had handed over seventy-nine dollars and a bottle of spit to some lab to find out what their DNA could tell them.

At least a few had done this with the hope—no, the need—to find their biological father, right?

It doesn't matter.

No. It did matter. Because until I knew his story, his reasons, how and if he ever overcame the curse that propelled my mom into blotting him out of our lives, I wouldn't know if there was any hope for me.

"I found another church to try this Sunday." Cassie spun spaghetti noodles around the prongs of her fork the same way she did when she was a kid.

I nodded, weighing my response. This would be church number three since Cassie began her quest after Mom passed away. She was a wandering sheep and I was no shepherd. I wasn't even a fence post. I worked most Sundays and heard about her experiences on Sunday evenings. My chest ached for my daughter. It looked like finding the right church for her and Renee wasn't as easy as finding waterfalls.

"They say the third time is a charm." A trite response but the most positive thing that came to mind. "Where did you hear about it?"

"One of the secretaries at work goes there." Cassie shrugged. "It's a pretty big church, which I'm not in to, but they're supposed to have a great children's program and she knows some other single moms that go there."

Single moms. I wondered if that was easier to say than divorced mom? Especially at church. "Well, let me know how it goes. If you like it, then I'll join you on my next Sunday off."

"Hmph." A small sound escaped Renee, who was seated at one side of the small dining table. Her lips curled into a frown.

"What's wrong, Sweet Pea?"

Renee threw a furtive glance my way, then focused on her mother. "Do I have to go to the kid's church?" Her voice was somewhere between a whine and a plea.

Cassie set her fork down and turned away, her focus on the dark window at the other end of the table. I studied her profile. There was so much of her dad in her. A wave of nostalgia mixed with the remnants of grief washed over me. For the millionth time I wondered what life would have been like if Steven's love of dirt tracks and car racing had been quashed by parenthood.

Cassie's eyes fluttered, and she turned back to Renee. "The first time we go, you can sit with Mommy. But if we go a second time, I want you to try the kid's church." Cassie leaned toward Renee, her eyebrows raised. "I need you to let me know if the people in charge of the children know what they're doing," she whispered covertly. I covered my mouth with my napkin, hiding my smile.

Renee's eyes widened a bit, and she nodded. "Okay," she whispered back, apparently satisfied with the role she'd been given. At least for now.

After dinner we fell into our week-night routine. Renee helped me clear off the table while Cassie ran water in the bath down the hall. I cleaned the kitchen while Cassie supervised Renee's bathing. We joined together afterward on the couch in the living room to watch a rerun of Full House on Netflix. In my opinion, it was the cheesiest show on earth, and more than a bit weird. What two single men would give up their freedom to help raise the three little girls of their friend/brother? Not many.

In my estimation, the last two good men left in this world were dead—my daddy who raised me, and my one true love, Cassie's father, who died when she was so young she doesn't remember a thing about him. But the sitcom was sweet, like any other fairy tale, and Renee loved it. Sadly, that show was the closest thing she had to a male influence in her life. But no man is better than a bad man. I could testify to that.

After enduring the sitcom, Cassie tucked Renee into bed, which always took a while. There's the double-check of the teeth brushing, the prayers, the one last drink of water, and then the reading of a bedtime story. Some nights when Cassie walked out of Renee's room, I wasn't sure if she'd make it to bed herself before she fell asleep.

I used the time to set out my uniform for the next day, get the coffee pot ready for the morning, then stepped outside for a quick cigarette. The smoke rose into the cold drizzle that was January in the Willamette Valley. The clock ticked toward 9:00 as I sat back down on the sofa and waited for Cassie to emerge from Renee's room. My mornings started early, but something was bothering that daughter of mine, and I wasn't going to bed until I found out what it was.

A door opened and closed softly down the hall and Cassie walked into the living room, looking nearly as tired as

I felt.

"You played that one well." I didn't hide my smile.

Cassie tilted her head. "Played what well?"

"The church question. The job you gave Renee of investigating how the kid's part goes. It reminds me of something your grandpa would say."

Cassie smiled wistfully and plopped down on the couch beside me. "Yeah, every once in a while, maybe I get something right."

I studied her face. It was still there. That hint of sadness and a touch of fear. "What's eating at you, baby girl?"

Cassie sighed and looked at the television, though the screen was blank. We're still working at the mother-daughter thing. It was like chipping away at an ancient artifact. If you dug too fast, you could damage it and the long-buried treasure would crumble. At the same time, with so much of it under cover, it was hard to tell what you'd find.

I patted her knee reassuringly, the way Mom would have. The clock ticked. The familiar itching, crawling feeling under my skin threatened to grow. I inhaled. One, two, three. Exhaled.

Finally, Cassie turned toward me. "I don't know. I'm afraid of messing up with Renee. She's already been through so much. I know we need to go to church, but it almost feels like child abuse or something dragging her from one church to another. I had no idea when I decided we should start going to church that finding one that fits us would be so hard. And then Renee was obviously not happy about trying another one..."

The things Cassie beat herself up about. I shook my head. "I understand your fear, but there's far worse things to subject a child to than church shopping." Even as I said it memories surfaced, the ones I had put my own daughter through. The things she'd seen, the nights when she was alone. I shuddered inside.

"I know. You're right." Cassie's eyes met mine. I still

expected them to hold resentment, but they were soft and blue and full of tenderness. "Maybe it's also that Derrick will be out of jail soon, and I don't know what will happen." Her voice cracked a bit, and despite my imaginary caution tape, I put my arm around her.

"He can't bother you anymore without going back to jail. He can't see Renee unless it's supervised by someone he has to pay. It's going to be okay." The last five months of Derrick being in jail had given Cassie a chance to feel safe. I didn't want her to lose that sense of security.

Cassie tilted her head, resting it on my shoulder. My heart swelled. I would do anything to take away the fear that still bared its ugly fangs.

"I want to believe that. And I know I need to trust God because He's brought Renee and me this far." Cassie gave me a quick hug, then stood, the familiar line of determination on her brow. "I'm going to head to bed and read my Bible for a bit before I go to sleep."

I nodded. "That's a good idea." Cassie had inherited my mom's Bible by default. Undoubtedly, the underlined passages and well-worn pages brought her as much reassurance as the scriptures themselves. I wished reading words in a book comforted me. I had tried. But the words usually blurred before I got much out of them. I'm glad my daughter was more like her grandma than she was like me.

"I love you, Mom. I hope you sleep well."

I smiled, forced myself up off the sofa. "I love you too." Then Cassie was gone, and it was time to turn out the lights and head to my own room. The silence felt like death. I had an old CD player on my dresser. Music had always been my solace. I switched the radio on and found an oldies station. The reception wasn't the best so there was static, but the bee-bop happy tune of a Beach Boys song took the edge off the silent night.

I pulled my calendar from the wall and counted out the weeks. According to what the pamphlet with the DNA test said, it could be three months before I received my results.

That meant early April. Ironically, I would have answers in time for Mom's birthday. I was pretty sure my DNA decoding was not what she would have asked for if she were still alive. I took my pen and drew a heart on April 12th. The first birthday since Mom passed. That would be a hard day.

I placed the calendar back up and took my journal out of my dresser. It was really only a spiral bound notebook from the Dollar Tree, but it worked. I wrote down my accomplishments for the day. The last one was "Got Cassie to open up to me a bit, even got a hug."

Night time was the worst, and I wondered if Cassie's bid to me to sleep well was because she'd heard me wandering around the house at night, searching for distraction. Sometimes I'd have a bowl of cereal or an ice cream bar at midnight. Sometimes I went outside for a cigarette. Another habit I needed to quit. I hated the way Renee's nose scrunched up in disgust when I got too close to her after having a smoke. Before turning off the radio and my lamp, I wrote myself a note and set it on my nightstand. Tomorrow I would call the doctor's office about getting nicotine gum or patches.

"Baby steps are better than no steps at all, right, Mom?" I talked to the ceiling. The crazy thing was some part of me heard an answer. "Yes, sweetheart. Keep your chin up." Water clouded my vision. I blinked it away and set the alarm on my phone.

No matter how old you are, you never stop needing your mom to reassure you, even if it's only the echo of her voice in your subconscious.

Coming September 1, 2020

AUG 2019

CPSIA information can be obtained
at www.ICGtesting.com
Printed in the USA
LVHW080753070819
626725LV00011BA/523/P